Dancing with Dasein

Dancing with Dasein

and Other Stories

Mark Morganstern

Inga and Roger,

Like that good Cajun music
You two are straight up,
Two step righteous folks
There's no pretense or
Excessive packaging about you
You are just what you
Seem to be, a lucky find
In this world of imitations
May you always dance to
That vibrant fiddle, that speaking
Squeeze box—that music that
Exemplifies your lives and
Shines on the rest of us.

Mark

February 2016

Burrito Books
Rosendale, NY

Printed in the United States of America

ISBN: 978-0692495759
Library of Congress Control Number: 2015949355

Burrito Books
PO Box 279
Rosendale, NY 12472
markmorganstern@gmail.com

Cover illustration by Staats Fasoldt
Cover design and author photo by Brent Robison

Acknowledgment of previous publication:

"Zen Master of the Hudson Valley" – *Prima Materia*
"Tomorrow's Special" – *Chronogram*
"Electric City Blues" – *Tribute to Orpheus II*
"Story for a Cold Night" – *Expresso Tilt*
"The Maestro" – *Piedmont Literary Review*

To Susan, Luke, Lily, and Harry

Dasein, noun, German: "being there" or "presence," often translated in English as "existence;" a fundamental concept in Martin Heidegger's philosophy, referring to the coherence of "being-in-the-world."

Contents

Dancing with Dasein   1

Zen Master of the Hudson Valley   24

Electric City Blues   37

Adrian Comes Calling   52

The Maestro   83

Tomorrow's Special   98

Glenna's View   108

Story for a Cold Night   135

The House of Morgan   142

The Dear Departed Horseman of Worcester   156

Fireball Fitness   191

The Future of France   204

I-287 Investigations   223

Three Baskets   244

About the Author   283

Dancing with Dasein

I followed the guy into the Stewart's Shop trying to recall where I'd met him. He looked familiar but ravaged: a stained plaid trench coat, sporadic hair, camouflage of dirt spread over his forehead and cheeks. His fogged gold-rimmed glasses reflected the fluorescent freezer lights. He ambled over to the pet food shelf and pawed about three dozen cans into a shredded Earth Day bag, which he dragged to the counter, his right side somewhat disabled, hauled it up, and then began digging for change. His billfold was deep inside the layers. The woman behind him took a step back, widening her nostrils. He slapped a crisp fifty on the chocolate egg display next to a toy duck in a tiny pink t-shirt that read "Happy Easter!"

I trailed him outside to his shopping cart wondering why I found him so interesting. Perhaps it was that I had very little else to do at the time, having been recently dealt a round kick to the groin by Cynthia, now retuned to Idaho to reunite with her ex-boyfriend. He dropped the bag into the bent frame; the tires were worn down to the metal. If he could run, sparks would fly. "Professor Marsh?" I was surprised that one year could have done this much damage to him, or he to himself. He stared at me, then nodded, giving an exhausted exhalation. "Polhemus?" It sounded like he hadn't spoken in a long time; his voice was a dry rasp. "Polhemus, you owe me a paper." He remembered me. "I thought I'd say hello, Professor," watching his encrusted nails twitch on the rubber handle. He continued staring at me. "Do you need a ride somewhere?" I asked.

"Schopenhauer, right? You only had to turn it in. I'd stopped reading by then anyway," he said.

This was a painful revelation because I had been slowly closing in on a Master's Degree and could have used the credit. "I have it on my flash drive," I offered. I don't think he heard me; he was on to something else. "I passed everyone except you and that crazy bitch from the Brudherhof, Kat something?"

I remembered a woman named Katina Mound who insisted that Professor Marsh teach some Thomas Aquinas along with all the atheists he shoved down our throats. She was a pale, slight woman with a grayish grim jaw. He answered her by pouring coffee laced with cognac (his usual seminar beverage) over the Bible, the Old Testament. He kept one on the far corner of his desk referring to it during his lectures as, "The Ultimate Handbook of Torture." He followed this baptism with an incomprehensible rant about the administration, comparing them to mindless brutes, coming after him with primitive weapons in a landscape of devastation ruled by nihilists. He then evoked Heidegger's *Being and Time*, which was ironic because none of our professors were ever on time even if they slept in the lecture hall. Katina swung a rosary over her head chattering in German. It struck a chair and the burnished beads flew, popping necks and faces, pinging off ear buds, then raining to the floor. The small wooden crucifix bounced off the overhead, leaving a shadow cross on the white board, and then disappeared. The class sat motionless waiting for The Rapture or at least an early dismissal. This was typical fare; professors acted weird, launched into tirades, and took sabbaticals to write perplexing books that no one wanted to read except other competitive academics so they could discredit them. Marsh compared them to disgruntled little boys picking up their marbles and going home. And we students supported this with our tuition money.

He was staring at me with unhealthy faded eyes as if a dim paste had been infused into them. "I also failed the foreign language exam," I added, to top off my conviction record.

"Of course," he said. It seemed to confirm something for him. "But you weren't stupid like some of them…provincial racists and spoiled brats from Westchester." He wiped his nose across his sleeve and considered the thin gleaming line it made. "All language is foreign as it's interpreted." I accepted this enigmatic pearl and again offered him a ride. He didn't seem like he had the gas to make it to the curb.

"Do you live nearby?" I asked, wrangling his cart toward my battered Corolla. The inspection sticker was out of date, time being relative to the next ticket I got for it. I resisted registering or reregistering things. That was the result of an anarchistic streak from childhood, refusing to sign my notebooks and papers or register for courses on time, which led to failing grades. My recalcitrance was a defense mechanism against an abusive father, the only safe form of rebellion I could practice for many years until I walked away from him in the hospital. The last thing he saw was my back. Unfortunately, there was no hospice muse posted in the hall to tell me that I would regret it. I have.

I followed him in a slow crawl to the second floor of a huge apartment situated just outside of campus. It overlooked a busy street of contiguous bars, a thoroughfare dedicated to collegiate lust and alcoholism—and all, at one time or another, having benefitted generously from my debit card. I still frequented one of them in particular, Shenanigans, because of its selection: fifty-two tap handles of some of the finest liquid courage ever brewed. It was impossible to take the world tour, though a few freshman had tried and been hospitalized.

As he nudged the door open a hoard of unruly cats massaged his pant legs mewing and hissing warnings at each other. They pounced and bobbed up and down knocking their heads against the cans they knew were in the bag. We were engulfed in a pervasive cloud of cat urine that took my breath away. Somehow he made his way to the kitchen with a ring of starving cats precariously circling his shuffling feet. The electric can opener complained continuously as he handed me cans, instructing me to dump one into each of the twelve bowls lining the wall. It was tricky work as there was some snarling and clawing going on. I was also getting nauseous from the smell of minced liver, turkey with giblets, and mariner's enchantment. One of them, an immense gray fellow swaggered toward his chow, the others prudently giving way. "That's Diego," he said, with a sputtering laugh or cough. After that chore he withdrew into the bathroom to clean up a little, which would be a daunting task.

I decided to tour the apartment. The bedroom shades were drawn; a dank, foul odor pestered the air, pushing me away. But I managed to switch on the light. I peaked at the bed, a twisted quilt, a sleeping bag, and something that resembled burlap or brown wrapping paper. I saw a pair of definitively female furry slippers and assumed the old boy had a friend or maybe he'd found them in a trash can. A large parchment floated off the wall. It seemed to be in Sanskrit, the Upanishads with notes scribbled in the margins. There was a thick magnifying glass hanging from a string. Could he actually read Sanskrit? A clear plastic coffee cup sat on the nightstand, half full of a dull bronze liquid that I didn't bother to smell. He'd gotten to the point where he sipped his booze through a straw, the poor bastard.

The hallway back to the living room was littered with cat toys, soft, squishy, unwholesome things. I suddenly remembered the paper I hadn't turned in to him. It was called In Defense of Women, in which I raised a tepid argument against Schopenhauer's essay Of

Women, 1851. I tried to refute his opinion that women are childish, frivolous, and short-sighted with examples like Madam Curie, Clara Schumann, Ruth Bader Ginsburg, and Joan Jett, a woman of vast talent and gravity. Even that misogynist Schopenhauer would have had a hard time not singing along to I Love Rock and Roll. He also claimed that women lacked a sense of justice. Sadly, I agreed with him on that one. Cynthia... my rural Idaho beauty, who'd come east to study Environmental Studies, a woman whose pastoral charm condensed my emotions into a radioactive knot. A woman who made love like she was weeding a thorn patch, rough, direct, and thorough. Not a stick left standing. I had hoped to remain a stinging nettle in her garden for many seasons. She was a singular prize and my loss was devastating. She'd moved home to become a forest ranger, the same as her ex, Gabe. I'd seen a picture of him in her bedroom and feared someday he would fell a tree on me. A strapping mountain kid with an ax handle to reckon with, I assumed. My grief and disorientation gave way to irrational anxiety to the point that I could no longer eat an Idaho potato if my life depended on it. Torment and loneliness were my mistresses, hence my presence in Professor Marsh's rooms. And so what? Marsh wouldn't have read the paper anyway. Knowing now that all I had to have done was turn it in, I resisted an urge to fling myself on the floor and cry. I might have my Masters now instead of taking my courses online and working in a sporting goods store, in the camping equipment department no less; I hated camping. The scent of pine made me sick.

I followed a train of milk crates through the dining room, packed and spilling over with books. Maybe he planned to move or was giving them to the Sojourner Truth Library. Though I'd heard he'd been banned from the building for tampering with reference books, the only professor to hold this distinction. He'd cut out passages he disagreed with and taped his own opinions on the page.

To my left there was a monolithic round oak table laden with unanswered mail and professional journals: Bioethics, Isis, Heidegger Studies, interspersed with empty liquor bottles, Chinese food containers, and a fishbowl filled almost to the top with pennies, just pennies. Two large ornately framed photographs hung on the adjacent wall. One of a much younger and more dapper Marsh, his arm around a woman whose face exuded light and a stirring soulfulness. She was of the old world, quite beautiful, and I kept looking at her with an aching sensation. The other was of a young man with a square jaw, and a direct, determined gaze, a coiled rope around his shoulder, his hair glistening with snow. His outfit suggested he'd been mountaineering or was about to. There was a slight resemblance to Marsh, whose expression suggested that he had his arm around everything he knew to be good in his world. I assumed I was meeting the family, but where were they?

The living room was even larger, with a row of front windows that reminded me of a control tower. A Bose Acoustic Wave Music System sat on a marble pedestal. It was black and looked brand new and could easily fill an airplane hangar with sound. There was music playing softly, the faint sound of strings. It was Verdi's Requiem, a devastating work, the sweet and sour hell of a Catholic funeral mass. It made Madame Butterfly seem like a walk in the park. I had enjoyed both pieces at the Met, eschewing the critics' warnings. Critics, like my father, represented authority figures, but are just the myopic Seeing Eye Dogs of art. The Prof must have had a backup left from his retirement package. I had priced one of these units and given up on it. I wouldn't have filled out the warranty card anyway. Across the room from this outsized concert hall was a psychedelic burnt-orange La-Z-Boy, the leather pockmarked as if it had been brushed with a corrosive. He'd probably slept in it, as there was a knotted up blanket stuffed to the side. There was one other item on the far wall, a grotesque painting in the style of Brueghel. A peasant driving a tractor with a demonic smile, his head turned out to the viewer as if it were bobbing on a spring. A field of grazing cows in the background. The guy looked like he'd ingested multiple tabs of California Sunshine. There were words written under it on the wall: *Heidegger returns to the farm.* I had a vague recollection about Heidegger being criticized by his detractors for an agrarian sentimentality at the end of his career. And why would they give a crap? Marsh was supposed to be an authority on the guy, brilliant but crazy was rumored throughout the philosophy department. He destroyed the remainder of his dwindling credibility with a blog called HerrHeideggerSpeilDaDa, in which he accused the "duplicitous Nazi" of being hot for Jewish girls. He asked the question, did Heidegger consider his dick an actual being. And if so, was he himself there, present in time, when he nailed Hannah Arendt. Who was the screwing being done for? Did he know he was getting laid or was it a question? And who cares? This one almost got him canned, but the American Association of University Professors protected his right to Freedom of Speech. He was bringing forward challenging ideas to enhance the discussion and stretch the boundaries. That same year a professor in Florida was dismissed for demonstrating to a shocked lab class how he'd trained a female chimpanzee to give him oral sex (without biting). The entire Florida Christian Conference and the ASPCA made short work of it.

If I lived in Marsh's place I would have spent most of my time looking out the windows. They were thrown wide open without screens and the fading April light was slicing at angels through the just-budding trees. There was a fragrance of new grass, barbeque, and beer wafting up, a welcome relief from the alkaline cat perfume. The neon lights were glowing softly to attract the thirsty moths fluttering down from the dorms. Revelers hooted and laughed their way into the bars, one dressed in a full rabbit costume hopping inanely in place—Saturday night in a college town. A barefoot kid sat on a bench strumming a guitar. A line of bikers gunned their engines in front of Buster's. The girls paraded by in their spring uniforms: sandals, shorts, or form-fitting jeans, thongs peaking out, halter tops, tattooed shoulders and lower backs, their voices light, musical, husky, lifting against the buildings like a chorus to the equinox. Confident, convinced of their sensuality, they were immune to the cool air moving in from the mountains, soon to be followed by a caravan of hearty day climbers heading for Main Street to increase the gene pool in the biosphere. I rested my head against the window jamb watching their faces, their flouncing or short-cropped hair, upturned breasts, their thighs lifting into their surging asses. A hammering ache pounded my body. The rejection by Cynthia, the abrupt and harsh lack of female companionship, access, conversation, the uncertainty of a viable future, even friendship—I could not stand another round of Frisbee and drinks with my guy friends. I am, I said to the darkening scene outside, utterly, pathetically vulnerable. This is not self-pity, but an existential ice pick through the solar plexus that can only wait for the remedy of time. And time, I'd read somewhere, has a way of going by too slowly until you run out of it. Maybe that's why I was following an old, vagrant college professor around. I had also heard that he ate out of dumpsters as a practice, something to do with the Korean Son Line of Zen. But why? He seemed to have the means to satisfy himself and the cats as well.

A shrill female voice called out, "We're over here." Tomorrow would be Easter Sunday. This was a night to partake heavily and arise from the tomb late in the day with a redemptive hangover and eat Eggs Benedict. This likely scenario of the evening hours to come sank the remains of the miserable boat I struggled to reach shore in.

I must have jumped straight up, raising my arms with such force that both wrists smashed under the window sill, sending a shock wave up to my armpits. Such was the sudden deafening power of the Dies Irae with full orchestra, double chorus, an auxiliary brass section, and a percussion unit that rivaled Mardi Gras. Verdi's Requiem was considered to be some of the loudest unamplified music ever written. But this was delivered to me through proprietary Waveguide speakers, flooded through Folded Waveguides, enhanced by Direct/Reflecting Speaker Technology at an extreme decibel level, rendering me a Bose casualty. I thought I was having a heart attack, finding myself in the dining room, where I had involuntarily fled, leaning over a chair, trying to breathe.

And there was Marsh, ensconced in the La-Z-Boy, dressed in a black silk-looking bathrobe, eyes closed, his head nodding to the various orchestra sections, conducting until the final angelic strains of the Requiem finished, leaving a sound like a dial tone in my ear. He appeared to have cleaned up a bit; his face conveyed an aspect of dignity. He'd combed his hair back. It felt like I'd stumbled into the parlor of a nineteenth-century gentleman. But the sparseness of the room, the large chair, the reclining white-haired man seemed more like they belonged on a stage, a single prop in a play exploring alienation. The piece was over; he bowed his head in recognition of the consequential significance of the work rather than the composer, then clicked off the remote as the host began asking for contributions. He looked at me as if I were another being he was too weary to consider. "Polhemus, you look flustered."

"I wasn't expecting…that sound."

"I have to make it loud to hear. I have to hear it," he said with some urgency. Suddenly, I didn't want to witness him anymore, frail, resolved, eminently peculiar as if he were being borne away to a tormented afterlife. I began to improvise an appropriate departing phrase. Then it dropped on me like a safe snapped off a rope; he looked an awful lot like my father. A jolt of anxiety and rage shot through my chest combining with the cocktail of emotions I was already nursing. A realization raced by, a banner headline: *That's why you're attending him. You're waiting for your father to acknowledge you, to give back some of what he took...* which was mainly my full sense of security in the world, which he usurped by his dominance. I'd spent several years on this in therapy and here it was again. Marsh had allowed me to tag along. He'd been civil; there were no insults. But he had nothing to lose either. Haltingly, I opened the door. I asked if I could get him anything, water, arsenic, something? "Check on the food." I stood there, mute like an inept footman. "The food," he motioned toward the kitchen. "Go check."

I was at a loss, my autonomy having been consumed by a black hole, so I obeyed (like I had obeyed my father), finding myself in the kitchen filled with the smell of meat, potatoes, a vegetable, maybe corn. The microwave was beeping officiously, and two Hungry Man Dinners were bubbling out the sides. Salisbury steak, mashed potatoes (I checked the wrapper to see if they were from Idaho) and gravy, mixed vegetables, and a square of apple confection with a dab of something that aspired to be whipped cream. I found a tray and some utensils and made my way back through the squishy mine field in the hallway. Apparently, I was invited to dinner, the guest to the feast or some such arcane summons. Two lonely men eating Hungry Man Dinners that would not satisfy the core hunger that clawed at them. One old, one younger, both with no better place to hide before the resurrection. And neither expecting to be saved any time soon.

He had managed to clear just enough space for us and I set the tray on the table. The mail and journals had been thrown on top of the milk crates, the empty bottles piled on the floor. One of the cats, a scrawny Siamese, had climbed into the tank and positioned herself on top of the pennies. Maybe she liked the coolness. Marsh was seated waiting to be served. "Polhemus, over there." He nodded toward a little Italian Ornate cabinet mounted on the wall. I opened it. Inside, the words "Irish Whiskey" were engraved on a brass plaque. There were soapstone shot glasses. My hand shook as I poured out the drinks. Both wrists ached from the collision with the window, the left one completely bruised yellowish brown. I steadied the glass with both hands and waited. There was no toast to our health or the future. He drank his down and slid the glass over. I filled it. He drank half and snorted, examining his meal. We sat in silence except for a Vivaldi concerto, his dining selection, filling in the afflicted space that hovered around us.

I had never tasted such fine whiskey. Jagermeister was the standard in most of the bars, usually followed by a short beer. The amber heat spread slowly through my chest, and stomach, and then to my head where it sang to me along with the oboe and violins. Marsh slid his glass over a third time and I filled it. I felt a deep, sun-rich glow, the day's travails pushed slightly to the side, toned down for a precious moment. I wanted to remain in that state until I was over Cynthia, but that wasn't going to happen for a long time.

Professor Marsh ate tentatively, cutting his food, poking at the mashed potatoes. It seemed that he was hungry, that he'd intended to eat, but was restrained by something inward. Something choked off his appetite. I watched him, expecting maybe some effort at dinner conversation. But what could he have to say to me, a failed student, sitting there drinking his whiskey? I looked at him closely again and it occurred to me that something had violently drained the vitality out of him, destroyed him. He wasn't crazy. He hadn't planned to become this person. Intuitively, I stared at the photographs. It seemed that the woman gazed down on us, a figure of mercy. He may have noticed me looking, or was perhaps done eating, and set his fork down.

"Your wife?" I asked, barely audible.

His hand shook, his face contorted. "Yes."

"And son?" He nodded.

"Where are they?"

He swirled the whisky at the bottom of the glass and set it down noiselessly. "Dead." He shoved his chair back and stood placing his hands on the table for support. He repeated quietly, almost instructively, "They are both dead." He hobbled to the La-Z-Boy and collapsed in it, dragging the blanket across his lap.

One of the cats sat on my foot, nuzzling my leg. I slid the remains of my tray under the table, igniting a skirmish. I thought they were going to rip my shoe off. When that subsided, the adagio, resolute and present, the strings vibrating, a series of breaths, filled the rooms of the apartment. I slumped down listening. I was partial to Vivaldi's slow movements. He threw everything he had at you. There is a device called the Cycle of Fifths. All the composers used it. It's a compelling deception, but with strong emotional impact. The sequence of chords used in this manner, is to me an aural representation of life's brevity and inevitable loss. It said to me: Here is life and here is beauty, take them; but you will lose everything you love and cherish when it's done. That, I understood, was the psychic depot Marsh was stranded in. I felt ashamed that I almost unloaded my heartbreak on him, that I was about to whine to him about Cynthia, my puerile whimpering before the stone of his tragedy. This small insight signaled me that I was going to have to relocate the steel in my backbone, fall into mortal formation, and march forward even if I didn't know where.

I finished my shot, collected the dinner things, and cleaned up a bit, then stood by his chair waiting to be dismissed. He seemed to have sunk into himself. The agitation in his eyes revealed that there was no peaceful place for him to go. I winced at his naked pain as it occurred to me that this broken man who looked like my father was receiving from me the deep concern and sympathy I had denied my father. I squinted the tears to the side. "Sorry, I'm very sorry." He asked me to pass him the bottle.

Exhausted, I fell on my sofa. It seemed like some essential element or previous condition had been drained out of my rooms. The missing ingredient that had made my life tolerable, even without Cynthia, was gone, leaving me appallingly alone, desolate, and sad. Was this what they called rock bottom? I posed the question: Am I desperate, suicidal, or just horny, which would be the preferable state to endure at this point. In less than ten minutes, my being was seated on a bar stool at Shenanigan's (and I was certain of it), telling myself that I was going to revise and lengthen my paper on Schopenhauer and present it to my advisor at the Philosophy Department. I would make generous and copious use of the Internet and paraphrase like a grease monkey, a skill I possessed in abundance. I'd tell them that I'd just rediscovered the flash drive behind the radiator and Marsh had agreed to accept it. Though how much weight would that carry? The steel I intended to insert in my backbone was a limp, synthetic material. I could not bear to categorize the class of ethics I squirmed in at the moment. Direct sunlight would have killed me. Sometimes you just have to survive and do better the next day. Most of the brave individuals who laugh in the face of adversity are in the movies. The background music that accompanies my actions on life's stage is the pounding of my heart against my breast bone.

There was an unadvertised Easter special on tap, an IPA with a splash of tomato juice to replicate the blood of the Lamb. They called it Joyce's Choice, as ever the Irish in secure possession of hyper-irony. I anointed my liver with a few of them, struggling to downplay my utter collapse of moral principle. How could I be that person? I crawled along this line of thinking until the inevitable question of the female and the ephemeral female body took up its usual forward position in my mind. And there were multitudes swirling around me, in ritual gaiety, the tribe that guarded the gates of exaltation, the retro-fitted dancing goddesses, inexplicably but deliberately opposite the male prototype, which is: a bowl, a mug, meat and bread, and a piece of fur to sleep on. Odds like these could only have been penned in the Devil's Play Book.

Somehow this self-induced excoriation lifted my spirit to the point where I became aware of and returned the smile of a smile seated next to me. It was Dale, the gun-nut conservative from the sporting goods outlet I languished in. She'd invited me on several occasions to accompany her to the rifle range, an activity I considered one notch above clubbing baby seals. She'd intimated in a forbidding but coy manner that we could maybe roll around in the spent cartridges afterward. I beheld her person, in a full-length beige plus-size dress with a round neckline, asking the question, was this the person I was to care for tonight in order to avoid caring for myself? In comparison to Cynthia the word comparison was a misnomer. Dale was as plain and businesslike as the weapon cases she sold. And as forward-thinking as an asteroid in retrograde, but I was not anticipating a union of the minds. She was a viable female with arms and legs and hopefully some skewed desire on the inside. Facing my apartment alone this night was a grim prospect. I, the entity void of all moral protein, now too drunk to care, bought her a Lava Flow and ordered a shot of Jameson's for myself, my private toast to my father, both of them. Our official toast was to smaller government. She squealed approval and leaned into my shoulder, clumsy and girlish, her torso a solid block. I could get injured if we made it to bed. The pressure I sensed on my thigh as I reached down was the bear claw of her hand. The alcohol had obliterated my ability to calculate units of weight and measure.

I was adrift. I think she was nuzzling my neck. How odd if I were cannibalized on Easter, I thought. I heard her say, "Let's go."

I awoke from the pain, a car accident type of pain. My first thought was that I'd fallen down the stairs. I felt around and everything was sore, bruised; there were multiple bruises on my chest, arms, and legs. Both wrists throbbed from banging against Marsh's window. My lower back felt like it had been kicked and my jaw felt rearranged. I crawled out of bed and confirmed my injuries in the mirror. I looked like I'd been thrown from the top of the science tower. I swallowed the remaining three Advil and sat down to wait. I was too weak to make coffee. There was a note on the coffee table, "You couldn't perform, so I did." This induced unwelcome chills that caused my muscles to flex in rippling waves of pain. The bitch, I thought, crumbling the note. There was more on the back: "You need to learn respect for women." I vaguely recalled that as I slid into my blackout last night the landscape presented surreal and threatening symbols. I think she did a routine of nude muscle flexing and poses for me, something I would have enjoyed a few hours earlier. At least she had the courtesy to wait until I was unconscious to practice her Bok Fu strikes on my body, I think.

I could not attempt the stairs until about 5:30 PM and used a Lacrosse racket for support. The street was relatively empty, the students down with massive hangovers or having succumbed to mandatory dinner with the folks. There were smashed eggshells scattered around in a range of pastels. I groped two tickets off the windshield and rolled them into my pocket. Getting in the driver's seat was an exercise in physical therapy. I went through the Rite Aid drive-through and got a bottle of Aleve, a few Ace Bandages and a Gatorade. When I arrived, the mall was closed, as expected, darkened for the holiday. I passed the entrance to All Sports and Camping,

Ltd., certain in my resolve to never return again, though I would seek unemployment benefits. After all, I'd been injured by one of their employees. I knew this was faulty reasoning, but screw it. Briefly, I considered pressing charges against Dale, but the specter of public humility would be overwhelming. I remembered one day when we were short handed and I saw her in the fitness station display area, assembling units. She picked up seventy-five-pound wheels of steel like they were doughnuts. I could only hope her hand gun would discharge while she was cleaning it.

About a quarter mile further down the parking lot past every established edifice of mercantile endeavor, which is our state religion, was a massive building constructed to resemble a Disney-type mosque, a friendly mosque that wouldn't scare patriots. It shimmered with high tech lights and synthetic gems implanted in the walls, which were interspersed with all-knowing rolling eyeballs for the hell of it. This was Hamid Ziegler's Pet Culture Coterie. Hamid was a famous local character who'd fled Kabul for the crime of being half Jewish and half Muslim. He'd been sentenced to death without the encumbrance of a trial, but landed safe on our shores, via Quebec, to our college town to pursue his acknowledged calling in life, the service of innocent animals. He'd little patience for humans, but would sit up for nights with a rescued parrot teaching it to swear in Yiddish and Pashto. He'd also trained a raccoon (Reyna the Raccoon) to lie perfectly still on the counter. He'd hand customers their change and say, "Say thank you, Reyna." She would swish her tail in response. They'd buy more dog toys or whatever to see her swish her tail again. Hamid considered animals to be sacred and at the same time denounced all religions and religious holidays. He liked to say, sometimes over the store intercom: "Be careful my friends, others' beliefs can kill you." Hence, the Pet Culture Coterie was open 24/7 like the Greek diner on Route 299. And, he expressed in his credo that since animals have no special holiday, neither should men. This and other dictums were prominently displayed at the entrance to his store, ironically similar in their appearance to the tablets of Moses. A few disgruntled citizens wrote letters to the editor demanding that he be shut down, the perversity of a mosque, even a contrived one, in proximity to the elementary school, etc. Pet lovers worshipped the products and exotic specimens in his aisles. He'd strut around with a friendly viper twirled around his neck handing out candy to the children. People on long RV trips stopped there on their way to Vegas. He made more income per week than the SUNY chancellor did annually.

After a long tutorial on pet nutrition, which included a brief history of the significance of cats in Egypt, a treatise against organized religion, and something like serious davening, Hamid's youngest son, Gordon (he was born in the States), wheeled the carton out to my car and dropped it cheerfully in the trunk. "Allah be with you," he whispered, "Don't tell my father; he will beat me." I struggled to pull a few bucks out for the kid. There seemed to be fresh new areas of pain to endure. It was time for more medication or something richer. *The bitch*, I thought. I could slash her tires, but that was not the mission I was on tonight. He observed me for a moment in the harsh LED glare. "Dude, you look fucked up."

"Yeah, I'm getting a new mountain bike, steel and aluminum frame."

"Cool."

I parked directly in front of the house and rested my head on the steering wheel waiting for the new dose of painkiller to arrive at its destination, which was everywhere in my body. There was a set of cement steps up to a walkway, which led to a steep wooden staircase up to the porch. I couldn't think about the other stairs leading up to the apartment until I made it inside the front door, if I did. I popped the trunk open and studied the packaging. Hamid had talked me into the very best, the paramount, the Oscar of cat foods: grain free, gravy free, zero carb, enlightened Tiki Cat. Premium Wild Caught, highest quality, Human Grade Seafood. I'd bought the variety packs of Ahi Tuna with Crab in Tuna Consommé, Sardine Cutlets, Wild Salmon & Chicken in Consommé, etc. They averaged about $1.03 per can and I'd gotten 12 cartons, which is 144 cans, approximately 27 pounds of product.

I stared at the box wondering how I could get it out of the trunk. It hurt to bend over. I looked up at the bank of windows. The lights were off, but Berg's opera Lulu was blasting its atonal racket through the neighborhood, the Berlin Philharmonic, I guessed. At the moment, Lulu, the soprano, was agonizing over her choices for committing suicide. Perfect. But that would be accomplished in the third act thanks to Jack the Ripper. It occurred to me that Lulu and Dale might have been good friends. Finally, I wedged the Lacrosse racket underneath the box and pried it up, got it over the trunk frame and let it slide down my legs to rest on my feet. My first attempt failed and the box slid out of my arms. I was determined not to dent the cans after dropping about $140 on them. I lifted, actually heaved it up and tried to steady the end on my belt buckle. I fell forward and off the first stair onto the lawn. I lay there, my eyes watering with pain as I looked up at the two women, tribal priestesses in full regalia. "Are you drunk?" one asked.

"No, I was injured in a soccer match and I'm having trouble walking."

"Do you need help?" I noticed the buttermilk of her breasts as she bent over and lifted the carton. The other one offered me a hand, then two hands, and I got to my feet. The first one set the box on the porch and came back to help get me to the door. The combined aroma of creams, deodorant, and perfumes was intoxicating. I slumped down next to my package. They offered to help get me upstairs…wrong stairs, wrong night, wrong existence perhaps. "No, my sister's coming from work any minute. Thank you so much."

They seemed reluctant to just leave me there. The other one with pubis-high shorts said, "You should go to the emergency room. We can drive you."

"That's kind, but my sister's a doctor. She's just leaving her shift at Emergency One." They nodded disbelievingly and slowly receded into the paradisiacal spring night. If I'd only been myself…. Now all I could do was try to catch my breath, locate some gumption, and wait for my penis, the source of my misfortune, Herr Goll, to achieve status quo. "I'm a fucking idiot," I said out loud. When addressing oneself, I wondered, should one say, "You're a fucking idiot," which raises the question of who is asking whom the question. "Fuck that," I said to both I and me.

I only thought that the door might be locked as I turned the knob. It opened. This was going to be something akin to building the pyramids, but turned out to be more like the Myth of Sisyphus. I determined that I would have to tilt, lift minimally, and raise the box up on to each separate step, hoist my butt up on to the next and so on. I could not carry it. I would not chance standing and catapulting down the stairs to my death or into permanent disability. I sat on the first step for a few minutes calculating the absurdity, but utter necessity of this endeavor. Fifteen agonizing minutes later, I'd made it up three quarters of the first stair case, panting like a hound, my shirt soaked through. I accomplished this and started up the second flight with less strength but more purpose than the first. My mind swirled with disparate thoughts and clichés, like no-pain-no-gain. The strains of Lulu's death agony followed by Countess Geschwitz, as Jack carved her up, made a perfect score for my task. Jack might have given Lulu a break seeing as she serviced him for free.

I encountered a crazed and threatening feline half way up the second flight. She snarled and hissed at me with her entire cat soul. I sat still as she was convincing and made Diego, for all his machismo, seem like a pussy. I guessed that she'd been inadvertently closed out of the apartment. She let out a vicious yowl. I thought she might pounce on my head, claws first. Maybe she was hungry. It would at least be a distraction. I began to work my nails into the cardboard seam and pull at it. It was impenetrable, the strongest cardboard I'd ever encountered. Perhaps it had been developed at NASA. I slid my belt off and began stabbing at the box with the metal stem as the Countess professed her dying devotion to Lulu. Jack and I were amigos. Finally, I got enough of a hole to peel it back and tear it open. My index fingernails were bleeding. I managed to squeeze a can through the opening, Molokai Luau Tuna on Rice with Calamari. I popped it open and set it on the stair beneath me. She was on it like a shot, a scrawny white shot.

I continued my pilgrimage up to the landing, sliding the box ahead of me toward the professor's door, now crawling behind it. I placed it next to the door jamb out of harm's way and rested my head on top. I could have slept right there, but refused any additional theatrics. He didn't need to find me there in the morning, the Tinker Bell of pet food delivery, or whatever the hell I was. Holding the banister spindles, I took each descending stair on my butt until it was so sticky from the filth I could hardly slide off. Again, I faced the scrawny white terror, now purring mindlessly, and wanting to be friends. She hopped in my lap and got cozy, which caused a series of aches throughout my trapezius. She did not have my complete trust, and was too disgusting to pick up, so I continued my butt-drop descent with her in my lap, adding weight to my sore haunches. The porch steps were steep and weather worn, and moistened now by a light drizzle. Finally, I made it to the cement steps. My butt cheeks were aching from the workout. I could not stand to grind them further down the cement stairs. We are not meant to walk on our ass. I checked my cell. "Holy shit." I'd been at this for almost forty minutes. Something rustled under the porch and the cat took off to investigate, digging her claw into my thigh for traction. I sat there overcome by a wave, exhausted and confused. What the fuck was I actually doing here? What was I trying to prove? Yes, I was facile and dishonest, even opportunistic, but there was a small medallion of decency attached to my astral body. There fucking had to be.

"You're still here." I looked into her curious face. There was something askew: her features were slightly misplaced as if a child had applied them on a Ms. Potato Head toy, but the overall effect was friendly. It spoke of Western New York State farm girl, maybe Herkimer. She was one the two tribeswomen, the one in high-rise shorts, having appeared out of the dark, weighted down with shopping bags. "Didn't you say your sister was coming?"

"She...got called back...an emergency."

"So, what are you doing?"

"Going home." Usually, my verbal skills were sharp, but not sitting there like an evicted client from a group home. "My car is there." What a simple sentence, I thought.

"How far?"

"Four blocks, Hasbrouck."

"OK, you're not a perpetrator, or anything?"

I convulsed with laughter that exasperated my physical discomfort. I couldn't think of a word to say. I wanted so much to be clever, even appealing in my dilapidated state. She loaded her groceries into the back seat, and then helped me into the passenger's side. The proximity of her flesh was intoxicating. "I'm driving to my apartment and getting out. Can you drive yourself home?"

"Yes, I drove here."

She got in and adjusted the seat and mirror, then grabbed a tube of lipstick from her purse. Nice touch, I thought, she wants to look good for the ride.

"See this?" She pulled the top off. I wondered if the color matched her shorts. There was a little push button instead of lip stick. "This is pepper spray, so nothing weird, OK?"

"Nothing weird," I assured her. Nothing weirder than the last eighteen hours had been. She was a cautious driver. "I got it from WomenOnGuard.com," she explained. "Comes in five colors."

"Nice," I complimented. "Have you ever used it?"

"Once, on a hog. I fell in a pen and it cornered me."

"It worked?"

"Yeah, but he ate it."

"Hogs," I blurted with an exasperated tone.

"You're funny. You know that?"

"Yeah, I'm funny."

As soon as she parked she backed out of the seat with the vial aimed at my face. She hustled the bags up to the porch glancing back at me. I observed her bending over the bags to shove them inside the door. Her butt seemed a muscular tiny star fallen to earth. I let out an extended, lamenting sigh and struggled into the driver's seat.

I tried to lie perfectly still as I waited for the last dose of painkillers and beer to engage. There was Marsh's tormented face. What would he think when he saw the carton of cat food? He'd know that I left it. My gesture would probably be an insignificant bleep on the screen of his day. He wouldn't have to buy cat food, so what? Maybe he'd see that it was organic and eat some himself. I wondered what he was listening to now. Was he asleep? Dead? I thought about our strange meal together. He'd been kind to me, deferential, fatherly in a way. He made me food, shared his booze. He'd even complimented me, sort of. *And what does all of this mean?* my cynic asked. *It means,* I explained, *that this is what took place between us.* I thought about hog girl. I wondered if she slept in the nude. Did she realize that I knew where she lived? I decided to order her a wallet size Stun Master. I'd seen one in Ms Magazine. It had 2.7 million volts, bright LED light, red flashing lights, alarm, and it came with a wrist strap. I'd leave it on her porch with a nice card. She'd see that I was proactive about her safety and maybe we'd have sushi. Or I'd invite her to the Ulster County Fair to see award-winning animals.

My father looked much younger than I remembered. He was seated in an open car on a miniature train like the ones in amusement parks. There were no other passengers. He was seated upright, his hands folded in his lap, where they would no longer be used as weapons. He was quiet, not quite serene, and there was a formal pall over the scene suggesting that a ritual was being enacted. I could not see the engine or the engineer, if there was one. We were in a cavernous underground station with paved walls and dim yellow lights which lent an eerie glow to the tracks. It was a terminal area that allowed for the train to enter and switch back around. He was about to make his departure down a long, dark tunnel. Somehow we acknowledged each other without a parting word, nod, or gesture, both aware that this was a twofold journey. We'd come to a junction where we would separate, agreeably, ceremonially, where one soldier surrenders his weapon to the other and neither takes satisfaction in the submission. The wheels jerked silently into motion. I watched him until the train was swallowed up in the dark, apprehensive, anticipating the moment when I would make such a journey. A great aching cry that sounded like the word "sorry" echoed throughout the passageway.

Zen Master of the Hudson Valley

$H$is name was Co. He shook my hand firmly, then bowed. His face was lined and seemed waxed; perhaps electrolysis accounted for the look, Pacific Rim. I confirmed later that he was Italian-American, Co DeNunzio. Co, maybe for Columbus, probably for Co-dependent. He had a crucifix and a signed picture of Elvis in the living room. Gus, Co's disciple, lover, houseboy, I couldn't tell which, reminded Co that I was there to ask questions for a book. A book about prominent Zen figures in the valley, to be authored by my editor, Brian Falcone, for the Wittenberg-Zenith Press in Woodstock. Not far from Mt. Tremper, where the heavy Zen-heads roam.

The whole project smelled of patchouli oil, and there was gossip that this was a tourism ploy by the Woodstock Town Council to get bodies on the Village Green during the slow season, keep the legend going as it were. I didn't live in Woodstock, couldn't afford it. I had seen Woodstock go from peace and love to, "Hey man, can you spare $175 so I can detail my Hybrid?" I only go when summoned by Brian for meetings. He also publishes the local Deals on Wheels rag that markets everything from electric guitars to vintage VW Euro Vans. Me, I make my home in Port Ewen, a lesser burb with a substantial pizzeria, but still overlooking this glorious river. My theory is that we—those of us who dwell up here—are vitalized by the river; it carries us along. As one bumper sticker says, "Henry Hudson Hung Out Here." Stupid, I know.

I found myself in Rhinebeck that autumnal day following Co around his back yard, pleasantly situated above the river, the commuter trains bellowing below like wounded quadrupeds. Until something better came along, this was my bread and almond butter.

"I don't give interviews," he told me. His accent was from a town further down river, the Bronx. "If people come for tea and ask questions, I share my insight. They relate to my experience as Zen."

Five minutes there and I already had an extreme dislike for the guy. "What's with the sign 'Zen Counseling'," I asked. It was hanging off his mailbox.

"What I do." He raised a thin eyebrow as if he found the query distasteful. He glanced at Gus. I reminded myself not to become too unpleasant. Gus was a huge piece of manly man, shaped like a Porta-San. "It's counseling," he said, with a condescending tone, "that employs the concepts of Buddhism."

I nodded and followed him to the edge of the property. We watched a tugboat push a barge up river toward Albany, gulls trailing in the wake. The air was invigorating, the day crystal. Finally, he said, "Perhaps, Gus, Mr. Kauffman would like some tea." So, he was going to talk to me after all.

Gus lumbered off toward the house. His long hair hung in a gray, frizzy braid, and his feet looked like logs in tennis shoes. In a high pitched voice that I didn't expect, he said, "The water's boiling. It's always boiling." I assumed that was some Zen precept. Was he a Jewish Sumo wrestler, or what? Sports, definitely, had been in his past.

Now that I was getting an interview, and would therefore get paid, I quickly scrolled down the list of questions I'd composed in the car, regretting the last one Brian always insisted on. I began: "I suppose you've taught at Omega Institute?"

He'd never heard of Omega, something I found questionable. Fifteen minutes down the road from one of the foremost, venerable New Age body shops in the country, Esalen east. Further research would reveal that Co was one of two all-time practitioners asked to leave Omega. His crime: feeling up abundantly soy-fed breasts on yoga mats, and doing more when possible.

I rolled a cigarette, asking if he minded. He didn't. I drew in the beautiful air and smoke and began to see the backyard. A cheap set of swings, a plastic turtle sandbox, some blow-up toys, all pink, and a propane grill on wheels. He must have ascribed to the chuck wagon variety of Zen. "You got kids?" I asked.

"We all have children," he said. Hmm, more Zen.

I found the garden and pushed open the gate. It was loaded with stunning heads of cabbage, marbled lime, white icy-looking heads of cabbage, bathed in river light, an awful lot of cabbage. Maybe he grew them for one of the ashrams in the valley. "You like cabbage?"

He tilted his head in reply. "Gus cooks. He makes a nice brisket." He began circling an apple tree. I stood by, scratching his sayings into a notepad.

There wasn't anything unusual about the apple tree, but Co observed it as if he'd discovered the Burning Bush. I continued: "Do you think people should meditate?"

"Why go to the trouble? It makes the culpable more culpable, like mice sneaking kernels of corn."

"Isn't that the mouse's destiny, to steal corn?" I liked my reply. He didn't.

"You're an asshole, Mr. Kauffman." He put this out as a matter of fact, deliberately, without malice. "You're here for money. The book mention will bring me more business. Let's be symbiotic."

"OK," I said, slowly. He circled the tree and began to squeak. He did a good imitation of a squeaking mouse, speeding up for effect. He eyed me and squeaked. I missed the meaning in this, unless he was mocking me.

"Are you culpable?" I asked.

"Of course," and he sighed. His shoulders curved under the black sweatshirt. He gathered a handful of small, ravaged apples. "Goddam worms. I should've listened to Gus and sprayed."

"Eating the apple is meditation for the worm," I offered. Since we understood each other, I thought I could be a little frivolous.

Co actually looked hurt. "I like apples." Then I noticed the gold cobra link chain glinting around his neck. I was going to ask him if he was a Barry White fan, but checked myself. He caught me judging his chain and gazed at me the way you burn a hole through a leaf with a magnifying glass. The glance had some power to it, which gave me pause. I pressed on. "Where'd you get your training?"

"One man, Kombu. I lived in a community of monks for about five years. Kombu was the master. He was it."

"Tea time. Get it while it's hot," Gus cheered.

I trailed Co up the steps to a newly constructed deck, the red factory stamps visible on the pressure-treated wood. It still smelled wet, and I made a note to try and not breathe. "Kombu?" I said. "What was he like?"

"Like nothing you've ever seen."

Co arranged himself at one end of a patio sofa decorated with daisies. Gus poured from a ceramic teapot. The tea bags were from Pathmark, a discount grocery chain, more evidence. Gus blocked the lowering sun as he filled my cup. I was grateful for the sugar cubes, but thought better of it. Gus smelled of baby oil. Maybe he had a rash. Big guy in the summer, chafing was a possibility.

I tried to focus. "Five years? Not very long. I've heard that attainment can take up to twenty years."

Co blew on his cup. "It shouldn't take any longer than it does to become a dentist." He didn't smile after this, so I assume this was truth for his world.

"Well, what'd you learn from Kombu? Did you have a spiritual awakening?"

Co snickered, then erupted into a belly laugh. "A spiritual awakening?" His mouth split wide with laughter—bad teeth. "My given name was Shrimp Squat."

"Shrimp Squat," Gus echoed appreciatively, "to attest to his inconsequential nature." The big guy settled himself on the other end of the sofa, slightly elevating Co.

Co studied the curls of steam above his cup. "To attest to my inconsequential nature." Now he looked directly at my third eye. He seemed...serious. "I am going to tell you my story. Maybe it'll help one of your readers cut through some shit."

I doubted it, but Brian said he had a grant and I'd get $15.00 per hour to do his legwork. I flipped a page in my note pad and indicated that I was ready to receive wisdom.

"First of all, I am an alcoholic."

Gus immediately chorused: "I am an alcoholic."

"I'm not an alcoholic," I said.

Co waved me off and continued. "I was a colossal drunk on a suicide mission. When I felt like I was about to end it, I pulled a last stunt. I borrowed money from friends who didn't want to be my friends anymore, flew to Japan, enjoying cocktails on the way, then straight up to the monastery in the mountains."

Gus stuffed a ladyfinger in his mouth and slurped tea. He cocked his head toward the kitchen window, listening. Co reached for a ladyfinger. I declined.

Co went on: "I burst in on the old man just before dawn. I smelled like a bar at closing time. I told him who I was, that I had a bit of a drinking problem, and could use a quick fix. I didn't have time to sweep floors or study bamboo patterns." Co laughed uproariously, Gus followed. "Shrimp Squat, that was a compliment."

Gus rolled back pumping his tennis shoes, straining the aluminum tubes that framed the sofa. "Shrimp Squat." I was beginning to feel like I was at a Moose Lodge meeting where the code words were "Shrimp Squat," followed by the secret handshake. I stared at the mass of fat, muscle, and braid. Who was this guy? "You work construction?" I asked.

"No, but I've spent time around concrete and steel. Want more tea?" I lifted my cup and took a hit. Gus' mug had a rainbow on it and the words Super Dad. He poured some for Co. We got quiet for a few moments. We watched the river. Above us, a hawk circled confidently, waiting for its supper to scurry out of the brush. Gus twirled his teabag and let it fly toward the compost heap near the cabbage patch. In the fading light, in even rows, the cabbages reminded me of monks' heads, bowed in evening meditation.

I was getting hungry and thinking where I might stop on the way home. I picked up the story. "So, you tested yourself against Kombu as soon as you arrived," I said.

"Tested myself, that's a good one. Kombu followed the Rinzai Line. That means when you asked him a question, or answered one, he'd give a Katsu, a shout. Then he'd chop you in the neck or balls, whatever was handy." Co chopped the sofa. "That first morning, when I dropped in on him, it ruffled his aura. He motioned me to come forward. I did. He was smiling like a shark. Then he punched me out, one punch, out like a light."

"Sounds like a rigorous school of Zen," I observed.

"Kombu's love tap was the end of the booze train for me. He could have hacked me up with ceremonial swords for all I cared. You see, the man gave me what I asked for. Of course, I do AA, keeps my nose clean."

"He cured you?" I said. "Just like that."

Co nodded. "He initiated a process."

"Did you get chopped much after the first meeting?"

"Like a rare steak, but it accelerated the learning. Kombu demanded that you understand in the moment, not later, after you'd thought about it. Some of us, Mr. Kauffman," he eyed me craftily, "need a hit in the head once in a while, wouldn't you say?" I didn't answer. And I was definitely not up for a physical contest, if that's where he was going.

I made my voice sound unaffected. "So you did five years of apprenticeship. Did you part on good terms?"

"Let's put it this way, it's the smartest five years I ever did. But I couldn't live the life. I still missed my mother's marinara sauce." Gus leaned over and clapped Co on the thigh. They laughed uproariously. Whatever they were, I realized that they could have a good laugh together. There was something tender about the exchange. Maybe they were lovers, or a couple of oddballs who'd found sanctuary with one another. That seemed all right to me.

"So what's next," Co started.

Gus helped: "It was a very cold day."

"Yeah, a bitter cold day. We kept the village surgeon busy cutting dead skin off our hands. There was this steep path leading down from the monastery. I was on my way to gather wood for the evening meal—one of my jobs."

Gus chimed in excitedly. "Tell him about the Bengal tiger."

"It doesn't have anything to do with the story," Co said, gently.

"Tell him." Gus was insistent, like a child.

"Well, my predecessor in gathering wood was a monk named

Osho. One morning we found his sandals in the snow. We assumed he'd been taken by a Bengal tiger."

"How do you know? What'd Kombu say?" I asked.

"Nothing, he put his hands in the sandals and clapped them together and sang. He sang about joy."

Gus looked very appreciative, almost reverential. "Joy," he said, softly.

"What happened?" I was more interested than before.

"I was going to get wood. I slipped on the path and landed, appropriately, at Kombu's feet. He was on his way in from the woods, where he spent afternoons. So, I drag my sorry ass out of the snow and stand before him."

"Did he hit you?" I was hoping so.

"No, he bowed to me. I told him I was going home. That I was going to use what I learned to start a practice, Zen Therapy. I told him I couldn't deal with the life." Gus edged over to Co like a friendly St. Bernard. This must have been his favorite part of the story. Co put out his hand. I thought he was going to scratch his ear. "Kombu stared at me, a trace of a smile. That flat old face, pale tumbled gray eyes taking me in, tossing me out." Co finished his tea and looked out at the gathering dusk. He lowered his voice and spoke deliberately. "Kombu said, 'Pardon me, Mister, but do you have a match?'"

I waited to make sense of this. Co fell silent. "He needed a match?" I asked.

Co went on, "When Kombu asked me for a match, he spoke in the voice, the exact persona of Jimmy Stewart. I reached into my pocket for a match, but there were no pockets in the robes we wore. I was looking directly at Kombu and I saw Jimmy Stewart's face. Then I saw a collage of faces, the face of everyone I'd fucked over in my life. I saw my mother's face." He stopped for a moment and swallowed hard. "Then I saw a faceless face, or something with no face, and it scared the hell out of me. I think maybe it was a reflection of the face of my actions, my rap sheet, as it were."

"A faceless face," Gus repeated earnestly.

I had no idea what to say. "Do you mean Jimmy Stewart the actor, like in *It's a Wonderful Life?*"

Co looked at me with deep sadness, moving his head in a gesture of loss. "I don't think you will ever ride the tiger, much less grab its tail."

"Hopefully not the one that Osho rode," I said. We glared at each other for a moment.

Gus gave me an unfriendly look. "You ought to listen," he said.

The moment passed and Co continued. "Kombu took me by surprise. He suspended, or evoked for me a clip of reality to look at. It gave me a chance to glimpse something most people never see. That's what the little match trick was about. You look skeptical, Mr. Kauffman."

"Well, that's quite a story," I said.

"I experienced a small awakening, Mr. Kauffman. Kombu poured a little into my bowl from his."

"And you're a therapist based on this?" I said.

"A small insight is better than none." He gave me one of his looks. I was starting to feel like an empty container.

Gus was up again and into the house. I heard him talking to someone. He emerged smiling ear to ear, carrying a sleepy child pressed snugly against him. She had golden curls. "Stinky girl," he sang. I watched as he emptied his pockets on the coffee table: a wad of napkins, the rest of the pack of ladyfingers, a jar of pureed sweet potatoes, more teabags, and a disposable diaper. Gus lay the child on the sofa and changed her. Co blew her a kiss. "Oh, nasty rash." Gus bolted into the house. Co lifted her into his arms and kissed her forehead. She was awake and looking at me in wonder. Most babies are beautiful; this one glowed. Gus returned, applied the cream, and got her diapered. He opened the baby food and pulled a spoon from his shirt pocket. The girl grabbed a ladyfinger.

"Who's this?" I asked.

"This is Shay," Gus said, looking adoringly at her. She yelled something and mashed the cake against her little mouth. "Long nap," Gus commented.

"Hello Shay," I said, then back to Co, "Anything else I should know? Can I refer to you as a half-realized Zen Master?"

Co said, tilting his chin toward the tree, "Those worms are making a living from my apples. Your problem is that you identify with the worm more than the man."

"I didn't come here for therapy," I said, setting my cup down harder than I intended. "How old is Shay?" I asked, to get out of the spotlight.

Gus answered for her. "Tell him, I'm two and a half. Big girl." He nuzzled her chin. Her laughter was like silver chimes.

"Is she yours?"

Co took this one: "We're babysitting Shay. Her mom's one of my clients. She's in rehab." We fell silent again, until Co spoke. "You don't approve of us, Mr. Kauffman."

"It's not my job to approve or disapprove," I lied. "I came to get your story, and I think I have it."

"Rinzai had a saying," Co went on, 'When hungry, I eat my food; when sleepy, I shut my eyes. Fools laugh at me; the wise understand."

I was exhausted from the repartee. I just wanted to head for a diner and score an open-faced turkey sandwich with gravy, mashed potatoes, and cranberry sauce. I could see it like a painting, still wet with oils. "Well," I offered, "everyone in this country is on a special diet." As an afterthought, I asked, "Where'd you guys meet?"

Shay thought this was a funny question and laughed wildly. Then she began grabbing the flesh under Gus' neck and pulling it like Play Dough. He nibbled her little white hands and she howled gleefully. "We met at the meetings," Gus said, between nibbles.

"AA and NA," Co told me. "We weren't partial about our addictions. We were also both on parole. So, lots in common."

Gus chuckled. "I got coked up and put a cop through a windshield…stupid. Got banned from the NFA, did time, got straight, got happy."

"You were a football player," I said. That made sense.

Co held his palm out and introduced. "This is Gus Genovese, the Foot, the Field Goal Maven."

I searched my football files. "Yes, Gus Genovese." I'd grown up near Syracuse, so the Buffalo Bills were part of the local culture. "Wow," I added.

Gus patted his tummy. "I could kick. I could kill," he added as an after thought. I watched how gently he cradled Shay's back. "Uncle Gus was mean," he told her in a cartoon bear's voice. She slapped at his face.

"Oh," I winced, glancing at my pad, the standard question I was instructed to ask at the end of each interview. "What would you do if you met the Buddha on the road?"

Co responded quickly, "I did. Kombu contained Buddha essence. In a generous moment, he imparted a seed of it to me. He returned my life to me, as you would toss a nut to a squirrel. It can only be done without effort." He added to this, and I felt persuaded, "I may not be a good man, but I have never hurt anyone since that day."

I must have been staring by now, just looking at Co. In the black shirt, gold chain, and styled hair, he could have been headlining at the Holiday Inn, singing Feelings. Yet, there was something about him.

Co got up and went to the steps. He stopped next to me. "Action, Mr. Kauffman, not thought. Kombu could perform because he could act, and there was nothing he disliked." He put his hand on my shoulder in a fatherly manner, and said, "There's nothing the man dislikes, Mr. Kauffman."

"I think we dislike each other," I replied, apologetically. Co smiled and said, "No." Gus was scooping Shay up into his arms, and we filed down the steps into the darkening yard, the sun just about even with the river.

I was wondering how I could exit on a good note. Co took Shay from Gus and hoisted her up on his shoulders. She palmed his head like a drum. "The cabbages, Gus. Would you mind showing Mr. Kauffman your style?"

"Sure." Gus made for the gate; we followed.

Gus stretched down, untied his sneakers, and slipped his socks off. The toe on his right foot was dark and swollen, perhaps a souvenir of his football days. Gus seemed to have removed himself from us. He stepped over the vegetables looking intently at them. He poked and prodded a few, then stopped before one. I thought he murmured something. He plucked it with one wide hand, and broke off the remaining stem. He began turning it in his hands, very slowly, rotating it, his concentration complete, best I could tell. He said, very softly, "You have to catch it exactly on the right spot or it explodes."

Cradling the cabbage under his arm, he moved gracefully to the end of the garden, a few feet before the fence. He stood there, motionless. All that was left of the sun was a blood red cap spreading into the Catskills. He leaned forward into the earth, his weight pulling him forward, though gravity didn't seem to be the controlling force. He stepped forward, picking up momentum, and dropped the cabbage, which seemed to fall in slow motion. There were two faster steps, I think, then he caught the object with his toe, his leg rising to span his forehead. We watched the cabbage rise over the fence into the air above the valley in a graceful arc, spinning so it reflected some of the crimson light. It climbed like a miniature moon, up and up. I could hear Gus breathing. Shay, who had tracked the ascending cabbage from the moment it lifted from the garden, threw her arms open to the sky and squealed. She squealed and shrieked, joyously, incomprehensibly.

Electric City Blues

I coveted that violin, but it was too late. It had been painted white, streaked with silver, and hung in an oval frame backed by maroon velvet. It floated over the angular turquoise sofa. The violin was my sister's. She'd hung up her bow in the sixth grade, which was also mounted in the frame. Painted instruments and turquoise sofas were fashionable in the early Sixties. My father had an eye for color and my mom loved to decorate. The customized violin was her work. She also loved paint-by-number kits with Oriental courting themes. My parents had removed the manufacturer's plastic from the sofa, unlike my Aunt Rae and Uncle Jack who kept their furniture sealed up to the time of death. My cousin Walt used to secretly slice at the plastic underneath with a pineapple knife. He felt like his lungs were coated in plastic and he couldn't breathe.

Next was the accordion. At seventeen, I'd sneak into sleazy bars and listen to Sal Bento—Salvatore Rosa Bentonomo, my inspiration and mentor. What cinched it was a memorable night at the Quality Inn where Sal played "How High the Moon" to a cadre of vodka-breathing businessmen. They stuffed singles and fives into his tip jar. Sal had mastery; he supported the melody and then the solo with a juicy bass line, at an impressive tempo as well. His small hands contained a great gift. More surprising was that the accordion was Sal's second instrument. He was a killer guitar player having spent years on the road with the Paul Whiteman Orchestra and he was still tight with Bunny Berigan. Hearing Sal that night was my first experience of the exhilaration and openness that animates jazz. It was, I didn't know then, the sound of freedom—what I longed for. I lived under the shadow of an authoritarian father and a subdued mother whose dream of becoming a nurse had been crushed by her father. When I got up the nerve to ask about lessons, my mother said, "Jewish boys don't play instruments they have to squeeze." Resistance on my part would have incurred my father's wrath. I let it go.

After school I haunted the music stores looking for what might become my instrument. The trombone was daunting and expensive; the bongos I knew would not be tolerated, as they were the weapons of Bohemian poets. I loved the smooth, cool sound of the vibraphone (ala Milt Jackson), but it wouldn't have fit into our cramped apartment. I kept tuned in at night to jazz stations, my transistor radio hidden under the covers. I wondered how these guys played like this. It seemed like they were flying.

In eleventh grade Mr. Sullivan needed a bass player for the orchestra—or at least a kid who could hold it up in the back row next to the drummers. He explained that the bass was a versatile instrument. You could pluck it or bow it. You could play Mozart or Brubeck. There were only four strings, less trouble than a mandolin. "You don't need a lot of chops," he said. This last statement didn't quite bear out in the professional world. Leaning in close, with a breath full of tuna fish dreamboat, our usual Wednesday lunch, he whispered: "Marty, you can play club dates until you drop." I signed on. It was the sound I'd dreamed of, rich and deep. The bass player was the foundation upon which the others constructed their solos. He let me take the school bass home to practice. It was welcomed like a ham and cheese hoagie at a Lubavitcher picnic.

My cousin Walt was way into the drums; he had a poster of Art Blakey hidden on the inside of his closet door. Walt was ecstatic. He sprayed his inhaler into his throat and kept saying, "It's a gas, man, a gas—bass and drums!" With a piano player we'd have a rhythm section, assuming that I excelled quickly. Mr. Sullivan could only teach me "The Merry Widow Waltz" played with a German bow. I needed to walk and growl. I found a book of bass lines for the blues in every key and slept with it. All we needed was a horn man, somebody like Dexter Gordon, preferably Dexter himself. As it turned out, I got to play with some very fine horn men later on, but not Dexter. He was celestial by then. Walt and I practiced intensely, mostly in private because jazz music was not acceptable to Jack and Rae. They had determined that Walt would become a lawyer. My mother listened to The Klezmer Show on Sundays. Those guys knew how to swing. When the radio went off, the house sunk back into accusing silence.

As aspiring young jazz musicians, Walt and I needed a designated greasy spoon to hang out in. The criteria were that there be grease, hyper-brewed coffee, and a jukebox. Quickie's was our spoon, our caffeine temple where we meditated on the future. Walt, who had consumed all of Kerouac, could wax fairly poetic. He said, while snapping his fingers, that the fat black flies that landed in our Navy Bean soup were angels come to announce our greatness. The blinking jukebox of wisdom would someday spin the very cool sounds of our music. The names of the tunes were just inside the mouth of the goddess, as sweet and moist as her kiss.

Our host, Quickie, was more than supportive. He'd seen some of the greatest jazz men come through town, playing the Proctor's Theatre, and then taking a late night breakfast and a smooth joint at his place. He knew Illinois Jacquet. Quickie was walleyed, pigeon gray with yellow specks. It was like looking into a fish head. When he spoke he raked change in his pocket. He spent a lot of time in the phone booth taking numbers and bets. The Saratoga Race Track was located just up the road.

Quickie's other interest, perhaps because of the proximity to the GE plant, was electricity and its folklore. Professor Kogan, habitually perched on a counter stool, had been, according to Quickie, one of Steinmetz' boys in the day, a "young master of light." It was hard to believe, watching the Professor fumble with his butane lighter. He chain-smoked Pall-Malls in a jade cigarette holder, eating bowls of Cream of Wheat with pads of butter and sides of maple syrup. He packed them into his ninety-eight pound frame. Quickie slid into our booth one time and gave us the dope on the Prof. "Fifteen, twenty years ago he'd come in here talking electric theory. I mean what electric is, protons, wontons, the whole pasta fagioli. He was Steinmetz' boy. But he knew too much and the little hunchback sold him out." At this point Quickie lowered his voice. "The Prof knew the secret of light. Then the big boys took him into to the lab and juiced his brain—permanent. Poor bastard." We'd look back at Professor Kogan spooning down Cream of Wheat, smoke hovering over his head. Quickie concluded with a pronouncement: "You're looking at the GE, boys. It's him." Walt reminded Quickie that the dilapidated building next door was called the Edison School after the inventor of the incandescent light. Quickie waved his hand in a gesture of dismissal. "Yeah, he played with it, radios, phonographs. But the Prof here, he had electric shooting out his asshole." I'd study the little man with renewed interest to see if any sparks were flying off his spoon. There were none.

Our parents kept telling us not to hang out at Quickie's. And we were to stay away from people like Professor Kogan. Aunt Mona said he lived in a halfway house. I had also been banned from sneaking off to the Quality Inn or following Sal around town. Musicians were not fit company, not our kind. But in my private, cultural soul, something hadn't incubated right. I wasn't our kind. The dominant characteristic of my family, besides silence, was a penchant to view other people, no matter how useful or beautiful, with disdain and distrust. My parents were the opposite of alchemists. We were a tribe, stoic and mute, lacking in nourishment like the wax fruit on the dining room table. We gathered Friday evenings for a cheerless meal, lit with Sabbath candles that caste no light into my life.

At the Salvation Army, Walt and I shopped for gig suits: oversized, double-breasted jackets, spacious trousers, key chains, wide silk ties featuring flamingoes and palm trees, and shiny cordovans. We bought discarded ensembles the Black folks didn't want any more. Our parents had saved our Bar Mitzvah suits, wrapping them in plastic. Christians like to collect bone and hair from their saints. Jews like plastic and are buried naked. Christians were buried dressed as if for a Sunday buffet. Walt and I needed outfits that spoke of the Thirties and Forties when the big bands held forth, and Bird invented something akin to a musical atom bomb.

I recognized my attachment for everything that was Black. When I walked through the neighborhoods the music calmed me, the deep living blues and driving bebop worked like a healing salve. These people laughed, joked; they talked loud. They said, "We are here. This is our music." In my house, my father did the talking, often with the back of his hand. We kids listened, shrinking away like serfs bound to the manor, and nobody dared to squeeze anything.

But at Quickie's we were unhampered, enraptured by the jukebox: "Take the A Train." The soft hair under our chins, gathered into goatees, brushed over fried eggs and past-life home fries as we planned our escape. We evoked the names of the saints, working through them like a rosary: Bird and Dizzy, Art Tatum, Billie Holiday, Max

Roach, Miles Davis, Ella Fitzgerald, Dexter Gordon, hmm, Dexter. But the prayer would evaporate each time Walt cast a furtive glance across the street. The long, gray, squat building with gas pumps erupting above the cement islands—Uncle Jack's City Service station. Most days after school, Walt pumped gas, changed tires, checked oil, and wiped windshields. Inside, in a pale yellow office with flickering fluorescent lights, Aunt Rae typed out the invoices, did the books, and said less than Uncle Jack, which was an accomplishment. Walt would petition Rae to allow him to apply to the Berklee College of Music, a jazz school. Rae would not answer him, or she'd scribble on a desk pad, *No*. She wasn't just tight-lipped; she was secretive about ordinary things. If I called to talk to Walt, she'd say, "Not here." If I pressed it and asked when he'd be home, she'd say, "Can't."

Attached to a steel pole rotating high above the gas station was a flying horse, a muscular, red stallion. It reared back, wings spread, white hooves rampant as it trampled the exhaust fumes that rose above Broadway. The horse's neck was taut as a heavyweight's, its ears erect, mane blown straight back, its expression one of immaculate self-confidence, its eye casting a smart, penetrating look at the motorists and pedestrians below. The horse was an invention of the artists and copywriters at Mobilgas in 1951. They had borrowed it from mythology. The ad copy on the station windows said: "Give your car a Flying Horsepower Lift!" Everyone on Broadway looked up at the flying horse, floodlit at night; it was impossible not to.

From its great height, the flying horse had a panoramic view of the valley, our houses, where Hispanics, Whites, and Blacks fitfully shared the neighborhood. There was Mt. Pleasant Hill, circuitous and steep, cars wafting down sideways in the winter. The Mohawk River trailing off toward Amsterdam. The Pulaski Bridge, known as Suicide Bridge, the last stop for some of our neighbors after decades in the turbine plant and bars, the endless bouts of Northeast depression, long winter nights. After the snow has crusted up and yellowed, it can work a grave mood on a person.

There were the railroad yards with endless lines of screeching and moaning freight trains, shadowed over by the stadium-sized General Electric turbine plant with its monstrous neon eye fading in and out, in and out. The fifth parental eye of my childhood. It was said, in very few words and hand gestures, that as a toddler I'd stand in my crib staring out the window at the sign, the light pulsing out of the darkness, sizzling into script letters, G.E., G.E. Then it would fade back to nothing. During the holidays, the letters were red and green, a festive touch. I have only the vaguest memory of this, but years later a Jungian therapist speculated that my psyche had been "branded," as it were, by the big neon sign. That an archetypal impression had been stamped in my forming consciousness, creating an opposite of sorts, the bright light translating into darkness; hence, a penchant for depression.

This was supposed to explain my recurring dream. I am walking down the center of Erie Boulevard, a historic wide road that leads to the entrance of the plant. I am in my gig suit but barefoot. I am walking toward the light, now the size of a small planet about to implode. I notice that my clothes are smoking from the heat. But I can't stop; I just keep walking toward the colossal light, G.E., G.E. And I think it's strange that there is no sound track, no music. And if there were, it would be Stan Getz playing his hallowed tenor, "Fly Me to The Moon," about a man who wants to play among the stars and see what spring is like on Jupiter and Mars—a love song.

On Saturdays Walt and I skipped Shabbos and headed down to the Accordion Center to hang out with Sal. Between students, we got to jam with him. I used the plywood bass I'd borrowed from school. There was a full drum kit there for Walt. He was sounding pretty good, having logged many hours playing with LPs of Max Roach. I was beginning to sound like something and could manage a credible walking bass line, but had difficulty memorizing chord changes. I stumbled through solos, but got lucky sometimes. One time Sal said, "Nice lick, Marty," and I beamed.

At five o'clock, the last student gone, the dented trumpets, French horns, accordions, all shoved into felt lined cases, the room stale with effort, valve oil, and sweat, the wine would come out. Not the thick over-sweetened syrup we got after services, but a sharp, dry Chianti that warmed our stomachs and solidified our membership in the club. "Europe," Sal would say, "that's the place for musicians." He'd drink and squint at the fading light in the gold tinted window. "This place makes dog shit out of you."

Sal would lock up and we'd reconvene at his apartment. I'd carry his guitar case, Walt on the other side, and we'd amble down State Street, past Crescent Park where a fountain of colored lights splashed erratically like pissing drunks. Sal lived in the old part of town, the Stockade area, once burned by the Iroquois and rebuilt by the settlers who hadn't been scalped. Behind Sal's apartment the Mohawk River stretched out in muddy gloom like a bruise. Sal would quip, "It ain't the Seine, man." We'd play records, some featuring Sal Bento, allow ourselves to laugh, and drink more wine. He'd talk about the clubs, the architecture, how vibrant and cool Paris was. He recounted the exploits of the guys in the Whiteman Band. The guys he'd jammed with, the time he'd backed up Dakota Staton at The Five Spot after her guitar player overdosed. My favorite one was about Django Reinhardt, the Gypsy guitarist. Sal had met him in Paris, traded choruses with him, got drunk and woke up in the same whore's bed in Pigalle. "Hippest night I ever had, man."

The fact that Sal, our Salvator Rosa Bentonomo, Sal Bento, professionally, had been tight with Django, played with him, was simply huge. Sal had been to the mountain, and we attending him were at least in the foothills, dreaming of very cool peaks with beautiful women abounding. And every time Sal told the story, even though I had heard all of Django's records, I had to ask him: "How did he sound live?" Sal would cradle his guitar, his stomach protruding out the side. We'd listen to the clock tick for a few seconds. "The cat's missing a couple fingers, you know." There would be another anticipatory pause, "He's a fucking monster." At this pronouncement, Walt and I would fall into a reverential silence. One day, maybe we too, through arduous practice and devotion to all that was down and out, would be elevated, transformed actually, into fucking monsters—the only desirable state worth attaining. Eventually, Sal would nod out. We'd cover him with an afghan and tiptoe out of the house.

Another Station of the Cross was the train depot, a holy shrine, the sacred place of departure. You could leave from there and hopefully never come back. Of great interest to us was the man who mopped the valley of marble floor and cleaned the bathrooms, Mr. Roy Jackson, semi-retired piano man, and long-time associate of Zoot Simms. After thirty-three years on the road and enough recordings to build a high dive, he had come back to settle in his wife's hometown. "Sneck-a-dee," he called it. Schenectady, to the rest of us, the Electric City, home of the GE. The tax base, the main employer, supplier of turbines and toasters to the world, and a century of PCBs in the Hudson River.

Roy played every weekend at the Eljoy Club, the Black club on Broadway. He did weddings and Bar Mitzvahs as well. Anyone of substance coming through town would call Roy in on piano. In our senior year we hung out in Roy's garage absorbing everything we could, including the cloud of marijuana that hung over his bobbing head. He'd lay down a tempo and use every chord and substitution that entered his mind. We were either there or not there, mostly not.

"It's how you learn the craft," he liked to say. After several months of this he admitted that we were sufficient accompanists, but not quite ready to gig. If we could manage some woodshed time, raise the bar a little bit, he might consider using us on one of his projects. Walt was still ahead of me, playing very good time, filling in tastefully. He taught me how to trade fours. I wrote out all the changes to the tunes Roy might call and flipped through them frantically, trying to commit them to memory. I was not a retentive learner. I couldn't memorize formulas and literary passages. My highest grade was a C, Business Math. This was before learning disabilities were discovered.

We finally got to smoke some of Roy's homegrown weed. It was a February evening, just after dark. Roy was closing up the train station and we helped. By this time the Professor had joined us in our pilgrimage around the city, a willing companion. He was studying acoustics and had formulated a theory. Quickie predicted that the Prof would bring to the science of sound what he had done for electricity. We still didn't know what he'd done for electricity. Walt observed that maybe lightning had struck the Prof when he was a kid. He was a deliciously Bohemian little guy in his plaid trench coat, ball cap, high-top sneakers, and ferret-like movements. The high, vaulted ceiling of the train station was good for bouncing tones. He'd brought a toy xylophone, which he held at arm's length, striking the plates with a little mallet. He'd wait for the sound to return. "You see, you see," he kept saying. "It comes back." It did.

The New York and Buffalo trains had been canceled that day because of the blizzard. The snow hurtled down on us as we huddled on the southbound track, watching Roy Jackson pounding an invisible keyboard, scat-singing "Stormy Weather." Plump snowflakes covered his thick black hands. We achieved our first official musician's high. It was an epiphany; we were released suddenly from the numbness of our managed lives. Transported into a world of swirling snow, we glimpsed the future, our knighthood on the road, alive inside the music, the recording sessions, the adulation of elegant, multi-national females, the chicken á la king and coffee and pie to go. And the inevitable ordination: monsterhood; we would become fucking monsters. We were jubilant. An unannounced freight train overtook us on the northbound track, its horn blaring, the engine's dull Cyclops eye enlarging as it approached, overshooting its mark, and sliding treacherously ahead on the buried tracks into drifts of snow. Walt got scared and began to cry. It was pretty strong stuff we'd smoked. And of course it triggered his asthma. I had made a habit of keeping an extra inhaler on me at all times. We took him downstairs to the vending machines and calmed him with potato chips and candy bars. Roy had some coffee left in his thermos. Gradually, Walt recovered and we slunk home.

The gig came together unexpectedly. Fortunately, most of the good local players were on the road. Roy thought we could handle it. A few blocks east of Quickie's a new club had opened, The Fro, named for the teased out Black hairstyle. They had instituted a Sunday Evening Concert series featuring the best of the local cats and those who were touring. Roy got the call to bring in a house band. On a cold Sunday in March, sporadic snow flurries zipping in a sharp wind, we made our debut. Roy's nephew, Jerome, was up from Baltimore, a highly accomplished tenor man and a devout Moslem, already with four years on the road with Nancy Wilson. Sal Bento was in the guitar seat. Walt Gordon on drums and Marty Hoffman on bass. I was nervous and sweating through my freshly ironed shirt. I couldn't disappoint Roy or the others. The MC introduced the "inimitable Roy Jackson on piano and vocals," then the rest of us. I shuddered when he called my name over the mic. Roy kicked off the first set with "Night Train," a crowd-pleaser. Immediately, people were up and out of their seats, dancing, hitting the bar, yelling approval up at the stage.

Appropriately, Roy took the first solo, digging into a battered Steinway upright. The cigarette burns on it looked like hieroglyphs. His combination of stride and barrelhouse got everybody up and moving. It is not hyperbole to say that the joint was jumping. I could actually feel it through the soles of my shoes. Jerome cradled his tenor sax, rocking back and forth, both meditative and appreciating his uncle. He would not reveal obvious pleasure in the music because his offering was directed to an audience of one, Allah. The applause was deafening after Roy finished. Then Sal took it, looking happier than I'd ever seen him, his beautiful Umbrian face aglow with a torrent of improvisation passing through him. I understood then what better days would have awaited him if only he'd gotten out of this town. When Jerome took it over, the room seemed to lift. His horn, the ancient horn that called the tribes together, the horn that calls us to life and death, the horn he played sounded like the mouthpiece was in his soul. Walt and I gave each other a quick look of recognition. It was clear that Jerome had a certain date with monsterhood. He played chorus after chorus, each one elevating the dialogue, further igniting the crowd, some of whom were standing on chairs and waving their arms. Others set drinks on the bandstand. But Jerome wouldn't have any of that. Roy reached down and grabbed a beer. When it was my turn, I managed a credible solo without sacrificing any time, after which I opened my eyes and saw Roy's smiling face, an awesome African mask, smoke pouring from his wide nostrils, sparse lower teeth, nodding at me. My chest tightened and tears came to my eyes. I had never felt so loved before. Walt's drum solo was great. He played without restriction or self-consciousness. Jerome, who had at first resisted playing with a "white" rhythm section, momentarily raised the bell of his horn to Walt when he finished. My happiness for Walt was unbounded. I wished I could inhabit this moment forever and do this for the rest of my life.

Walt and I showed ourselves to be worthy of the more seasoned men we were playing with. We were a unit, a fury of sound that had taken on its own life, a dominant but graceful steamroller. The camaraderie was potent; the room was hot, the bar windows fogged and splashed with neon. A woman in a purple cocktail dress and glittering tiara called out, "Hey, bass man, make it talk." I went down into myself and offered a solo to "All the Things You Are." The goodness of these people gave me a sense of buoyancy and confidence I had craved. These people, whom my family would have preferred I did not congregate with, were the ones who made me feel valued. The ones who spoke to me. The ones who allowed me to have a voice.

It was magic, but suddenly we were at the end of the last set. We had just finished "Night in Tunisia" and my hands were throbbing. Roy liked to begin and end with the blues, so he called out "K.C. Blues," by none other than Charles Yardbird Parker. Jerome naturally took the lead on this one and again the room elevated another notch. It was like Bird himself was playing. I looked out at our audience and smiled.

Then, at a small table I saw my dad and Uncle Jack sitting motionless before untouched glasses of ginger ale. A shard of fear knifed through me and my arms cramped. I redoubled my effort to keep the tune moving. I glanced at Walt to see if he'd noticed them. I guessed he had because his head was hanging down almost to the snare drum. I managed to control myself, to lay down the bass line like I was spreading flower petals before a great procession. I looked at them again, hoping for something. I searched my father's eyes with tears in mine. I wanted him to know that my part in all of this was what I had to give him. If he wanted it. My father and Uncle Jack effectively withstood the gaiety, the propulsion of the music, and the evidence of the crowd. They were like petrified trees in a hurricane, unbending.

I couldn't look anymore and continue to play. I threw my attention on Jerome who was now walking across the stage and wailing like he was in some supercharged waiting room. It was all there: the hope, the heartbreak, the degradation of the martyred, the centuries of longing. Walt gave me one last smile, engraving his sweaty face in my mind forever. I had this thought: *We are of the greatest tribe on earth.* I looked back at my father. The table was empty, the ginger ale bubbling slowly, exhausting its carbonation on the little white napkins.

Outside it was blustery and dark. A chill whipped through our damp, smoky, clothes. There was no hint of spring hiding in the dull green buds. A street lamp caught some pale snowflakes in its light. We could see our breath as we carried the cases across the lot. Both cars were facing the street, parking lights on, engines running. Uncle Jack's trunk was already open. My father sat reading the newspaper in his car. I helped Walt stow the drum cases in the trunk, closing it with a dull thud. "You can really play, man," I said.

Carefully, I slid the bass in the passenger door over the seat, making sure the bridge did not hit the interior light. I sunk in next to my father. Walt was already gone. We drove down the length of Broadway, past the gas station. The horse was turning away from us, reflecting its muscular red butt in the windshield. In between Quickie's and the Edison School I could see the GE sign dilating up to full power, a sizable disk, an emblem of despair, a branding iron.

Years later I came back through town on a Billie Holiday Tribute tour. I had distinguished myself, but had not reached the heights of the musicians I'd worshipped. And soon I'd be following another career, that of a booking agent. At least I knew who to call. After the gig that night I had a couple hours to kill before the bus to Syracuse. I walked through the old neighborhood. I noticed that Quickie's had burned down. The gas station was boarded up. But the horse was still there, no longer revolving, but committed and resolved. A pink crime light illuminated it. A part of its wing had broken off. I heard someone sobbing; it was me. "You saw all that," I said to the horse. "You saw it and you never flew away."

Adrian Comes Calling

Chloe banged the pitcher on the service counter window. "Water!" she yelled, then stared ahead at something to my right, wiggling her nose ring, pulling her lip to the side, to widen her right nostril. This relieved whatever was bothering her about the new piercing. It was also her stock expression—blank pony. She continued to manipulate the wire hoop against the blond hairs of her upper lip. The nose wrinkling suggested that something smelled bad—not an attractive message in a café setting. I had been trying to get her to stop wriggling her nose ring and to speak in an indoor voice. Chloe was completing her degree in Women's Studies and had been encouraged by her mentor to articulate her thoughts and opinions in a direct, if not trigger-happy manner, no matter who she was speaking to, even her boss, in this case. "There's a man here to see you." *Loud blank pony.*

"What's he want, Chloe?" I asked quietly, modeling my voice for her, and coddling my irritation. "Tell him I'm not buying ads."

"He says he knows you from college." College was a long time ago. I got up on my toes and leaned into the window, nudging a pile of chopped onions on to the floor. I peeked…holy shit! It was Adrian, Adrian Bruck Currier, my sparring partner and nemesis from the Brooklyn College writing workshop, fourteen years ago. Of all the tofu joints in the world, he'd walked into mine. He was chatting on his cell, announcing his arrival to some fascinated party as if the Eagle had just landed. "I found it. Yes, it's…quaint." He threw his head back and laughed with abandon, "Decidedly Sixties." My stomach soured as I spied him from the window. He looked a bit older; his face was pallid as if he'd recently been ill. He had never been a beautiful man, but was quite capable of physical charm and a myriad of facial expressions crafted to fit the circumstances. Disapproval and disgust it had usually been in my case. He was smooth, articulate, and thoroughly dismissive of other writers. His voice sounded the same; it bubbled up sweet and sinister as if from a hexed well in a fairytale. I noticed that he still preferred black, expensive cotton, a perfectly tailored jacket with a thin gold pen clipped smartly in the pocket—he was frequently approached for autographs. I was frequently approached by the produce man to write checks. And he still sported the serious Skecher street shoes, ego crushers, I use to call them. The memories flooded in. I hadn't forgotten anything, much less forgiven anything. I despised him. He had haunted me over the years—his interviews on NPR to which I half-listened, his book displays at Barnes and Noble, from which I fled. Once I picked up a tabloid with him on the front, descending into St. Mark's Bookshop with an unidentified friend. The caption read: *Author Adrian Bruck Currier Arrives on Time and in Style for Book Signing.*

It all came back suddenly and viciously, the degree of his success, and how he'd outdistanced me. A successful novelist, a darling of the New York literati, more so when he was younger, and one lucky son-of-a-bitch. And at this particular moment in my world, on this seriously muggy evening in late June, with the air conditioner faltering, reeking in chef's livery, devoid of glamor, without a decent shave, not quite on either side of paradise, I was not up to chitchatting with him.

I wiped my hands in dismal resignation and turned to meet the baleful, aggrieved eyes of my longtime kitchen associate, Raneisha Washington. Revered and feared by the entire wait staff, she was known as Raneisha Washington, Dishing Queen of the Mount—there was a mountain behind the café. She blocked the doorway, a stout, cheerless phantom. Ceremoniously, she raised the slotted spoon she used as a talking stick and said, "The grease trap is angry." I didn't like the way she personified the grease trap, an honor it did not deserve. Her reverence for it was like that of an islander toward a fuming volcano. Any allusion to the grease trap was not good news. It meant that soon, foretold by a certain odor recognizable to the initiated, it would convulse and back up, coating the tiled floor with a stinking sludge. A foaming noxious stream of decomposed rice, beans, shards of peppers, altered peelings of eggplant and carrot, rotting skins of apples, tomatoes, and pears would spread around our shoes, sending me on the run for the Shop-Vac. The actual procedure of evacuating the grease trap could not be performed while humans were dining. Grease trap work is akin to pumping out a septic tank, or bagging ripened surgical waste. I assured Raneisha that it wasn't going tonight; I had cleaned it out just three weeks ago. She gestured solemnly with the long spoon at the corroded metal box under the sink. "It will blow tonight," she prophesied.

I wriggled past her, adjusted to my full height, assumed a commanding presence, swallowed hard, and presented myself before Adrian like a supplicant. "I heard you owned a café—it's so sweet!" His tone knob was set on bright. He was chipper as hell and obviously pleased that I recognized him in his victorious literary vestments. "I found you on the alumni web site," he chortled. "Tried Poets and Writers..." The first shot over the bow, *prick.*

"Yeah," I mumbled, "my subscription lapsed."

"I see." His face was animated, but somehow altered as if from a medical procedure. Awkward moments ticked by, me nodding like a bobble-head. *Say something, asshole.* I was in the habit of hurling insults at myself and others as I monitored my actions and ongoing dialogue. My therapist suggested that I should let the "umpire within" go, that self-deprecating dialogue was a hangover from my childhood, and was, in fact, the voice of my father's disapproval. My father couldn't forgive me for wanting to be a writer instead of a podiatrist. "Everybody has feet," he said. He'd never read *The Killing Fields.*

Adrian beamed beneficently at me as if something about my presence pleased him thoroughly, that I was his favorite person at the moment—that there was no one else he'd rather be with. I was not a good sport about failure, and Adrian's curious, unannounced visit focused a harsh light on my defeat. "I'm reading at the college tonight." This exploded from his thin mouth, sending a small shockwave through the room. He made a flourish with his well-formed hand in support of the announcement, lest anyone doubt its authenticity. *Fucking town crier.* The folks down at D-1, the big front table, looked up from their garlic bread and salads. They were a group of irritable poets and fiction writers, a couple of them retired academics who met weekly to share their work and discuss the business of publishing, by which they were mainly ignored. I'd given up observing them vaguely disparage one another's work, and never mentioned my own. One of them was a Dickens enthusiast who fancied himself a scholar. He tipped like Mr. Bumble from *Oliver Twist.* Their heads perked up at Adrian's pronouncement. He smiled coyly; he could spot a competitive literary enclave like a vulture circling a scribe's carcass. I had been primarily a fiction writer, infrequently published in some mildly prominent magazines, now and then a runner-up in this or that, with a novel that bounced around various houses for two years before finally being rejected (with positive comments), and I had always allowed myself a veil of superiority over the group. But that now disappeared as I stood next to Adrian, breathing in his Chaps or some Macy's fragrance he preferred. Finally, I responded with muted enthusiasm, "That's nice."

"You should come. You'll be my guest." It was like he'd just thought of it, such generosity. *Perfect closure, ultimate humiliation.* He could pick me out in the audience as an old friend, a writer of "reaching emotion, craft-competent, but not quite prime-time, as yet," as he had once let slip.

I squirmed and tilted my unshaven jaw toward the kitchen, "Can't," I mumbled.

"Oh, of course, how silly. You have a business to run. He feigned a slightly dejected smile, relieved.

Yeah, a business to run. "Sorry," I said, and scanned the room. The kids were up to their usual antics, checking their messages, texting, forgetting to bring napkins and flatware to the tables. Some guy was looking around for something, hoping to contact a server somewhere out there, maybe send up a flare.

Chloe was at the service window, barking, "Order up! Order up!"

"Karl, there's an order up." Here was Nelson, tall and lanky Nelson, towering over my chair. "Karl?"

"Yes, Nelson, I heard Chloe," I answered in a measured tone. Nelson was another of my revolving cadre of art, philosophy, and undeclared-major students / wait staff. Nelson created concept art. That meant he'd make nothing, name the pieces, create stickers for them and a price sheet, all priced at $0 because he believed that money for art was corporate manipulation. I'd been to one of his openings. The pieces had names like Scope 4, When Benjamin Died, Short Take, etc., but the wall space was empty. He refused to "instruct the viewer" about what to see in the work. Whatever they took away from it was fine with him, which was no image at all. I asked him what he did if someone bought a piece. He said he'd peel the tag off the wall and give it to them. He accused me of artistic timidity because I refused to let him display his work in the café. *What work?*

"Have dinner with me." I felt vacant; I couldn't think of anything I'd enjoy less than having dinner with Adrian Bruck Currier. *Eating crow with the foe like a submissive ho.* He sensed my hesitation, if not my revulsion. "Have a glass of wine, at least. You have time for that."

I bowed slightly in irresolute agreement, saying, "I'll just get this order out first," then added, hopefully, "Are you sure you have time?"

He gave me a winner-takes-all smile. "I'll wait for you." *Fucking why?*

I fluttered into the kitchen like a shy farm girl and assembled the meals, trying to ignore Raneisha's alarming presence—she had taken a squat and was speaking to the grease trap, an incantation of sorts, an effort to appease it. I would be obligated to mention this to her caseworker, Myra. Myra would get flustered and frustrated and offer to find Raneisha another job in a warehouse, The Peoples' Place, "or some other dungeon." As usual, I'd withdraw my concern about her behavior, which was actually pretty standard at the moment. After all she had showed up every single day and worked through stupefying piles of dishes, pots, and pans for the past eleven years. She was the senior employee, and commanded respect, which is why she was referred to by her full name, Raneisha Washington. She had not been in a stable situation when she started all those years ago, and I'd decided to help her. She liked paper products and used to steal them from the basement. She'd amble across the parking lot dragging a contractor's garbage bag to the dumpster, but looking more fully realized than usual as she'd stuffed the products into her sweat pants and shirt. She'd dump them into her car. I'd go out and look in her car window to demonstrate that her work hadn't gone undetected, but I didn't mention it. She'd watch me, irritated, as if I were intruding—being inappropriate somehow. Eventually, she came to me and said, "Stealing shit is wrong—sorry."

I said, "OK, I appreciate that." It never happened again. In fact, she started bringing things to me, like a miracle vegetable slicer that could dice a whole potato in one whack, but broke into pieces the first time. The incredible "No Hot Pot" pot holder that adhered to a skillet, out-gassed something toxic, and then set off the smoke detector. All of the items were purchased from late night TV offers, and she got two for the price of one—all in the trash.

I prepared the orders carefully, but I was nervous, agitated, completely off my game. I kept an eye on the floor as the bell jingled incessantly and a steady stream of folks entered the room, regulars and others; some, I knew, to get a quick bite before the movie, others for a leisurely dinner. Normally, I'd be thankful for the influx of business, but I cursed it now. I'd have to throw Nelson into the kitchen and see how well I'd trained him to put out food. I was taking a chance; he was quirky—that's why we called him Half Nelson, because he was mentally there half of the time.

I couldn't leave Chloe alone on the floor. As assertive as she was expressing her opinions and upholding feminist doctrine, she became meek when she waited table. She stood about three feet away from her party, twisting up her order pad, and squishing her nose ring. Sometimes people didn't know exactly why she was there. I made the perilous decision to call in Sarah Beth. Though hugely incompetent she would be available as no one else would hire her for more than a week. Once she arrived at a table, people actually liked her. She had a mild, peculiar disposition; she was calm in a comatose kind of way. Hence her pet name, Sarah Death. Her serving style, I had been advised by a local food reviewer who wrote us up, was "congenial, but lifeless, almost nonexistent. You can't tell if she's actually taken your order." And like the Tin Man, she occasionally froze in place, some hybrid form of epilepsy. Service was our Achilles' Heel. No matter how many good food reviews I garnered, they always rated our service a half star—very, very poor. Some of my regulars claimed to enjoy the sideshow and brought friends in to see how it would go on a given evening, viewing their dining experience as a bit of theater. One time I found a guy stirring his coffee with a Swiss Army Knife. He couldn't get anyone's attention to ask for a spoon. None of my workers possessed the acuity one needed to be a server, a fact verified widely in print and by word-of-mouth.

But for tonight I'd be goddamned if I would further demean myself before Adrian, let him see what a nut house I ran. I told Sarah Beth it was urgent, to come immediately, not to make extravagant preparations. "Don't meditate. Don't take remedies or apply essential oil. Just come now!" I ordered Nelson into the kitchen. "Just put out the food the way I showed you—nothing creative, just do what I showed you." I'd have a glass of wine with Adrian, maybe an appetizer, find a painless way to acknowledge his success and excuse myself to slink off and lick my wounds. I checked the floor. Adrian was ensconced at C-5, a carafe of wine before him with two glasses; he was chatting animatedly on his cell. He glanced back at the kitchen and threw his head back and cackled like a circus geek, a high shrill laugh. *The motherfucker is laughing at me. He's sitting there laughing at me.*

Adrian poured us each a glass of wine, though I would have preferred a beer. "You look frazzled." He was solicitous. I was squirming in my chair, feeling out of control. He lifted his glass and paused to consider what, I'm sure, he'd already scripted to say: "Here's to Arts, Letters, and home cookin'." He winked. *I'm going to retch.* Then he clinked my glass, which had the impact of a minor collision. I smiled inanely and drank. His cell phone belched out a few measures of rap, enough for one fuck, one bitch, and the usual n-word. He studied it. "My agent," he mouthed. I busied myself with the wine, keeping an eye on the room, but my ears were glued to his voice, never having been called by an agent before. *And you probably never will, loser.* Adrian smiled and mooed contentedly. "Marshall, you're too good. Tomorrow, mwah," he blew a kiss into the phone.

"I'm being translated into Bahasa Indonesi, even my poems." I didn't know he'd also published a collection of poetry, but why not, *and a cookbook as well.* I could imagine the title: *Song of Me, Myself, I'm Adrian.* I raised my glass limply, and we toasted his oeuvres. He insisted that we exchange cell phone numbers so we could keep in touch. *Why? I'll never call you.* But we did it anyway.

I entered his number and checked to see if Shea had texted. She'd probably be in Corfu by now with her über-horny friend, Iris. It was driving me nuts. My beautiful, *faithful* Shea, traveling through Europe on a wine and art tour with "yours for the asking," frisky and risky, Iris. Shea was excited; she liked to experiment with combinations and flavors and she prided herself in picking the perfect wine with each dish. I didn't believe in pairing wines; it pissed me off. I thought of wine as something tasty and satisfying to have with your meal as it had been done for thousands of years—something to wash down good food with if there wasn't any beer around. I served two good wines, red and white, but that would change when Shea got back. So when the wine and art tour (and man tour for Iris) opportunity came up, she announced she was going. She would return with new recipes, fresh ideas, and her "battery would be recharged."

I hoped it would be just her battery recharged, and not her undercarriage. Iris was a travel agent, so it was a great deal. I acted thrilled for her good fortune as I constructed an internal levee against the crushing wave of grief that was sure to follow. This happens when you date a woman a decade younger than yourself.

I hired Shea after she'd graduated from the Culinary Institute of America. Unlike some of their celebrity chefs, she was sensible; she didn't feel compelled to turn basic dishes into unrecognizable servings that required either a straw or tweezers to eat. They reminded me of squared-off marshmallows dyed in autumnal colors with sauce oozing out the bottom like abdominal waste. I don't believe in piling food like dominoes or miniature log jams to give *discerning people* a thrill. I don't cook hipster; I cook food. She was a vegetarian so it was a perfect fit. She spruced up the menu and invented a signature dish, a seitan, spiced pinto bean, and sautéed cabbage burrito with a touch of smoked Monterey Jack, and pineapple salsa; it got rave reviews. I hired her strictly on merit. I was, like most restaurant grunts, burnt out after five years—not on the food, but the *clients.* She wasn't overly demanding about salary; she just wanted a laboratory where she could invent and perfect her entrées and desserts, and eventually open her own place. I figured she'd probably go out to New Mexico where she had family. One of her deep-pocketed real estate cousins had offered to front a bistro for her. Meanwhile, she was good for business and I got some time off to figure out what I might do next with the other novel in retrograde progress.

We'd hooked up after a catering job; she was too exhausted to drive home. We had some Chinese food, watched the Duke girls continue to rule the universe, and turned in. Unexpectedly, miraculously really, she came into my room from the sofa, said she'd had a bad dream, probably the General Toa Eggplant with walnuts. I wasn't trolling for her. It was like a call from the Pulitzer Committee, but more satisfying, a bit of heaven randomly dropped in my lap. Or as Kirby, one of our "customers" from Melrose Hall, a goat-bearded young man who'd hitchhiked here from South Carolina and stayed because the "possum huntin' was good," liked to say, often: "Sometimes, even a blind frog gits an occasional fly." Shea, my occasional fly, after we'd established intimacy and been together for about a year, was prone to outbursts and ranted frequently about my thoughtlessness, real and imagined. I think that women are eager to establish a relationship so they can get down to the real business of reconfiguring their man's personality into their own image. When she felt pleased with me I was a happy frog, but still worried that one day she'd pack her Conestoga Wagon and head west.

Kirby, who was known as Kirby of Melrose Hall, claimed he had ties to such a place of the same name in the Lake Region of England. "I come from gentle folks," he liked to say. The Melrose Hall I knew, all too well, was located down a side street behind the movie theater, managed by the Ulster County Mental Health Department, a group home for those who required supervision and others who were transitioning into the community. Kirby liked to give me advice. He had Shea all figured out. He said that women were like chainsaws. Once you got them started they'd rip your arms and legs off. He also claimed to have eight wives back in South Carolina and to have fathered about twenty-six children—his "legacy." I asked him why he hadn't stayed with his families. He said because he got the call to come north to freedom, then he gave an unintelligible explanation about being just another lonely rider on the Underground Railroad, which didn't add up because that would have been well over a hundred years ago, and he was as white as baking powder. I enjoyed Kirby's folksy company. He was a character I'd like to have invented. But the other two from the hall were a different story. Brenda and Rudolph frequented, haunted actually, the café on an endless trick or treat / scavenger hunt basis, which was also why I welcomed Shea's stewardship over the business whenever she was in the mood.

Brenda was a wily, toothless crone, with a croaking voice like the Dunk the Chump guy who taunted you at the fair. Her specialty was recycling cardboard. She piled it neatly, tied it with string, and deposited it in the cardboard container. For this daily service, one or twenty boxes, she extorted sliced tomatoes with mayonnaise, ice cream scoops of coleslaw, and coffee. Everyone at Melrose Hall drank prodigious amounts of coffee—the fuel of artists and crazy people, one and the same. Even when Brenda had pocket change for coffee she depleted the profit margin as she required preternatural amounts of sweetener and cream.

Brenda's counterpart, Rudolph, had emigrated from Russia as a child. He'd been raised in Brighton Beach by a distant uncle and at some point found his way up the Hudson River Valley to our town. Rudolph was a short, stocky guy with shiny black hair like a ventriloquist's doll. He had a wide, shark-like mouth and a Third Reich mustache. His chief pursuits were: game boxes, close friendships, and romantic liaisons. Sometimes Brenda and Rudolph would tag team and clean us out of coffee, sugar, coleslaw, tomatoes, pasta, and butter. One time I entered the kitchen to find Rudolph with his arms wrapped around Shea's waist. He was pleading with her to marry him and referred to a plan he'd previously outlined on how he'd "take care" of me. I slammed the pot rack to get his attention and told him to get out. Shea gave me a look of death and waved me back. Rudolph trembled, his back to me; Shea spooned out a soup bowl of garlic mashed potatoes with a thick slice of butter. He took it by me on tip toes. When he was gone she took out her wallet and showed me a picture of a young man in uniform. "That's Chris, my brother. He came back from Iraq fucked up. He couldn't sleep inside and wouldn't accept free food. We finally found him in Zuni

Pueblo, dead. I don't care," she was crying, "if we feed them or let them hang out here. Don't you ever…" she stopped. I went and sat with Rudolph and watched him inhale his food. "Is good, Karl, very good."

Adrian smacked his lips then shot his tongue out and caught a stray drop off the side of the glass. *Like a friggin' frog.* Unusual behavior for a guy who ate at some of the most peerless eateries in the city. I'd read about some of his favorite haunts and chefs in New York Magazine. I couldn't imagine that he licked his wineglass at Le Cirque.

"I got your Shepherd's Pie. Was that a good choice?" He was asking me like a confidant or someone on a dinner date. Automatically, *mindlessly,* I began listing the ingredients, concluding that it was a good choice and that I hoped he'd ordered the Spicy Oriental salad dressing for his salad. He hadn't so I motioned to Chloe to come over, but she hollered from across the room, "Yeah?"

I motioned for her to come close so I could stab her with my fork. "Please bring a side of Oriental dressing." I glared at her. She glared back in her frayed tights and café tea shirt she'd modified into a garment of ridicule. Her nose ring glistened; I wanted to rip it out with needle-nosed pliers. She wrinkled her nose up, as I knew she would. I made a note to mention it at our next staff meeting. Not that anything would come of it. In the meantime Sarah Beth floated across the room like an apparition. Chloe yelled to her to get the dressing. She stirred slightly, but stood there dazed like a bomb victim. *Get the friggin' dressing.*

Adrian shoved bread into his mouth. I noticed that he'd buttered it on both sides. "I'm sure you do well here? Just the bar alone probably."

"It's…a business. It goes up and down."

"I see," he sympathized. "Looks like it's going well." Then he dropped the bomb. "Do you still have time to write?"

I commanded myself to be calm, took a sip of wine, and said, "I write a few stories, do a food column, got a stalled novel going, nothing much."

"You're a restaurant reviewer?" He said this hopefully as though he were tossing me a gourmet barbequed chicken wing.

"Not exactly." I wrote a seasonal folksy food column for the Mountain Ledger. Recently, I did a piece on root vegetables and soups. I offered tips on steaming, the proper rendering of vegetables, stuff like that. I wasn't going to mention that my last publication was entitled *Let's Buddy up with Winter Potatoes.* Sarah Beth arrived with Adrian's dinner. I was relieved to see the steam curling off the plate and that Nelson had thought about the presentation, which meant that he had stuck sprigs of parley into the mashed potatoes in the shape of an X. He'd also found time to fashion a peace sign made from peppercorns glued with egg whites. *More art I don't need,* I thought, *even if I can see it.*

Adrian reached into his backpack and grabbed an EZY Dose AM/ PM Travel Pill Reminder. It contained pills of all shapes and sizes; he downed them quickly with his wine. It seemed like a lot of pills. He tilted his head and said frivolously, "Pills." I figured he had a personal nutritionist and trainer. I didn't care much for exercise machinery, but walked whenever I could. I was struggling to lose a few pounds before Shea got back, so I'd give the appearance of something I'd once been—hopefully keep her interested. She liked the way my stomach roll tickled her when we made love, the slightly older guy thing. If, that is, despite Iris' urgings and suggestions, she did come back (visions of hot slender Greeks bearing gifts that get hard in the night, and hot slender Italians, and French guys with their wine and cigarettes and little erect *Francophiles* seeking American ladies like heat-detecting missiles). Shea was a woman men noticed. I could only hope that Iris didn't louse things up for me.

I noticed a shadow looming over the table. Sarah Beth had docked there after serving Adrian. Maybe she was waiting for her battery to recharge. "Please get me a beer," I said. My jaw was tense. She observed me without recognition, like a laboratory mouse she was about to drop into a centrifuge. "Now, please," I added. Slowly she drifted away from the table, a planet realigning itself to its usual orbit. I drank the wine while I waited.

Adrian nodded, "Nice girl, she seems meditative." He ate ravenously. "This salad dressing is phenomenal." He placed an airy accent on the first two consonants. And he thought the multi-grain bread was a bonus, whatever the hell that meant. He buzzed on about his book tour and the movie options. "Matt Damon, can you imagine?" He licked his lips as I retreated into a dark cave of despair. Then he dove into his backpack again and slid a copy across the table. "For you." The dust cover looked expensive, the kind of investment publishers sink into a potentially successful property. There was a dramatic silhouette of Adrian on the back. He stood atop a tall building, dressed something like an Eighteenth Century Lord, looking out over the great city. His gaze suggested that he was about to single-handedly relieve the metropolitan area and the greater world of its collective boredom and general ennui.

Adrian's characters were complicated professionals, each famous in their own right, playing out their dramas in the great city—all-powerful, sometimes sadistic, and cloaked in intrigue, even if they were picking up their dry cleaning. And there was always a hint of underworld activity, some danger that might threaten the unstoppable fulfillment of his characters. It was a smart formula; he gave you one with everything on it. One reviewer had dubbed him the "High-Rise Honcho of Romance and Intrigue." The characters dined in trendy bistros, like Adrian, sometimes disguised to fend off unwanted media attention. Everybody was so fucking famous they couldn't jog through the park without being snagged. And everything his characters did, even taking a crap, seemed to have great significance attached to it. People ate this stuff up.

In contrast, my narratives were blue collar. I came from an industrial town, a dreary upstate backwater. My characters lacked glamor, but I tried to make them real. They worked at the transfer station; they ate in diners, creamed chicken on points of toast, lime Jell-O with Dream Whip, if they felt like it. They proposed in bowling alleys, screwed in pickup trucks, lost fingers on the assembly line, and were occasionally abducted, but always returned.

Lately, I'd been writing tirades in the café log, a battered marbled notebook that lived between the cash register and the two-pot Bunnomatic. We communicated in it between shifts. After each disastrous night I wrote scathing criticisms and threats to the staff, mordacious notes and brief treatises like: *The food industry is a service industry. Please be willing to serve or go elsewhere.* The kids mainly doodled, created cartoon panels or wrote love notes to each other. One particularly bad night—they'd celebrated a new low in table service—I threw the notebook on the floor and cornered them in the wait station. I was livid, shaking, and irrational. I said to them in a threatening voice, "Don't ever ask for a recommendation when you apply for your next job." Then I told them the Mustard Parable: "There is always some guy out there who might want the mustard. Your job is to get him the mustard." They listened, their heads cocked like goofy dogs. Nelson said, "What if we're out of mustard?" I should have had him drug tested on the spot.

Adrian seemed to gather himself in, and got serious, almost morose, his eyes steely and narrowed like when he used to take my measure at the workshop table. "Karl, I want to ask you something." He sighed, picked at a crumb on the table. "Are you happy for me?"

No, I thought, *I'm not happy for you. You're a famous writer reading at the college tonight. I'm the proprietor of a graceless café overseeing a flock of wayward kids who can't get a basket of bread to a table or a candle lit unless I tell them to. And why the hell would you care if I were happy for you, which I am not.* Then I looked at him, earnest and deceitful, "I am happy for you. You've earned it." He sighed, wiped his mouth, and leaned back in his chair as if he'd been released from some debt. He seemed to have reached some equanimity. I got up abruptly and took his empty breadbasket. I noticed he hadn't finished his salad. I also took his empty glass. I kicked open the kitchen door. They contorted like a nest of slugs suddenly exposed to sunlight. "Who is he?" Chloe squealed. I growled and she scurried out to the floor. Nelson cowered and yanked open the oven to check on the apple crisp he'd forgotten to put in. Raneisha Washington, the slotted spoon tucked in her apron, stared steadily at me. Sarah Beth watched us from the service window, a picture of restaurant chaos, a study in culinary dysfunction, not quite Gourmet Magazine. "Move," I snapped at her. Her eyes widened as she retreated slowly. The iron hand of anxiety squeezed my torso, reminding me of when I'd suffered a bout of agoraphobia in the city. This was a defining moment. I could fire them all now, explode into the dining room and rip the meals off the tables. *Get the fuck out. I'm closing. This fucking place is closed.* I leaned on the three-bay sink, inhaling mouthfuls of commercial detergent fumes. The yawning pots and burnt pans closed in on me. I could hear a high-frequency blender though none was in use. Raneisha Washington gestured toward the grease trap. "I know," I whispered harshly, smiling like a friendly demon. "Don't worry. Don't worry," I told her, backing away. "Tonight,"

she prophesied, stoic in her foreknowledge. I fled the kitchen, grabbing a wine and a beer, which I drank half of before reaching the
table. I was out of breath, dropping into the chair. Momentarily I
hung my head between my legs and inhaled deeply, telling myself to
be calm, that I would find a way out of this place, away from *them*.
Adrian was smacking his lips over the Shepherd's Pie. He certified
the food to be some of the very best he'd had anywhere, including
some illustrious rooms in Manhattan. "Really, this is how I'm eating
these days, so much healthier." Exhausted, I responded, "It's just simple food."

His face, somewhat puffy and stretched, softened; his eyes looked
moist—probably the Spicy Asian dressing—and he reached across the
table and placed his elegant hand on top of mine. His fingers were
long, like a concert pianist's, and quite dry. I noticed that he still
wore the pinky ring with the onyx crescent. He used to push it into
his chin when he was vexed by one of us inferior scribes. *His hand is
on top of mine,* I told myself. *I know,* I thought. *OK, so now what?*

"It is good," he said, looking steadily into my eyes. "Your food is
delicious and it's made from the heart. I can taste it and I can see it."
I looked down at his hand, confirming again that in fact it was resting
on top of mine. I scanned the room, then shrugged as if this were a
typical moment in my day. I sipped my beer with the other hand.
Move your hand away, I commanded myself. But I couldn't move my
hand. His hand might have weighed two hundred pounds. I tried,
but my hand wouldn't budge. I felt my face begin to blush. *Don't
do that,* I advised myself. *He's gay,* I thought. *So what? I don't care.
But I didn't know he was gay.* I wracked my brain to remember if he'd
had a girlfriend when we were in Brooklyn. There were women, but
mainly watchdog types. *Maybe he's just touchy-feely. Sure. I don't care
if he's gay.* Perhaps Adrian was coming out to me as a gesture of rec-

onciliation, as a lesser wolf offers its throat to the pack leader. But I just didn't remember him being gay. Could I have blocked that out, and why? He continued to gaze at me with kindness and warmth, which was not altogether unpleasant. Then, quite unexpectedly, surprisingly, something shifted or rather softened inside of me. It felt like a material change. I realized that I could not move my hand away because I was attempting to move the noxious weight of fourteen years of resentment and self-pity. What needed to be moved or removed was the ugly thing that had grown inside of me. I also realized that I would still like to be accepted by Adrian, that I did appreciate his kindness, even if it was, in part, mercy for the defeated one. I could accept this act of friendship from him, if that's what it was. Why not heal the fictional scar, let the red ink dry on the palm or whatever? Why not be friendly. We didn't have to climb into bed together.

I noticed Sarah Beth at the cash register, her face brimming with pride and delight, as if she were witnessing a defining moment in my life. I knew what she was thinking, that I had experienced a sudden shift in my sexual orientation. Her current boyfriend, Owl—he called himself Owl, like in Winnie the Pooh—we assumed was gay. Neither of them seemed to know it yet.

When I did speak, I managed to only utter one word hoarsely, "Adrian." This added to the scenario of lovers running toward each other, arms outstretched, on a sunset beach.

Finally, deliberately, after a brief ice age, he withdrew his hand from mine, saying, "I was unkind to you." Immediately, the sanguine feelings melted away and I thought, *No shit, Sherlock.* I recalled Adrian's cruelty. I remembered him in the workshop glancing across the table, a fine disgust trimming the corners of his mouth, thin as an Eight O'Clock Mint.

I remembered something with all the intensity of chewing on it for fourteen years. "You called one of my stories roughage." He shifted uncomfortably, mussing his salad with his fork. "Roughage, good for the colon, but not the brain." I still felt the icy slap of the words as if he'd just said them.

Momentarily, he looked pained; he seemed about to offer a conciliatory statement, but I cut him off. "And Gwen agreed with you. She couldn't help smiling at what you said, you clever son of a bitch." We stared at each other through an icy pane of glass streaked with harsh memories. Gwen was Gwendolyn O' Dwyer, the visiting writer that semester, a once sought-after Irish beauty who'd retained her brogue and marketed it like a precious commodity in the States. She was elegant and impeccably dressed in tweed skirts and snug silk blouses, and she wore the kinkiest black-heeled tie up shoes I'd ever seen—a vixen/schoolmarm look. Her new book had been trashed by the Times, reducing her to a Gaelic Blanche DuBois. More than once she broke down in the workshop when we discussed the business of writing. She referred to the book critic as a Dullahan who tore out the heart of honest writers. She listened to our fictions and doused us with writers' advice, then excused herself to the ladies room where, it was rumored, she uncapped sampler bottles of Jameson. She hugged each of us "precious wordsmiths" good bye after the last session with a sweet breath of whiskey. Gwen and Adrian bonded from the onset, she acknowledging his likely future, he pandering for the blurb she'd later supply for his first book.

Adrian answered in a harsh whisper, "And I didn't like the comment you made." The comment he referred to had become well known throughout the writing program. In confidence, I had mistakenly said to Jill, one of Adrian's admirers, that Adrian had his tongue up Gwen's ass so far, we'd need the Jaws-of-Life to extricate it. Jill nodded appreciatively then went directly to Adrian to report. She was, it turned out, one of his "girls." There were several of them he'd charmed into his camp. They did his bidding. If anyone criticized Adrian's work they lashed out like Brides of Chucky, slashing the perpetrator, until he lay wordless on the floor. So much for open literary criticism.

"It was a fair observation," I said. "And it hasn't affected your career." We eyed each other for a few seconds wondering where this would go now that civility had been retired from the field.

"Look Karl," he spoke in a tone of resignation. "You befriend whoever is there. We all wanted to be the one. I knew what I was doing. "

"You didn't have to piss on me to do it," I said. The alcohol arrived C.O.D. in my brain all at once, so I decided to go for it. "You treated me like a fucking serf. A serf with rotten teeth. You did everything but hold a scented hanky up to your aristocratic nose." *Cut. Cut. Enough already.* Adrian looked shocked; disbelief contorted his face. He pushed away from the table as if he was going to storm out of the room. He snorted a sharp breath of indignation. We glared at each other. Then a faint, wry smile spread across his mouth. It grew wider until he burst out explosively and laughed. He slapped the table, tumbling the bread basket on to the floor. I stared into his dental work, which looked extravagant, and for some reason I started to laugh. I didn't know why, but suddenly, for nothing, we were laughing uproariously, without restraint, laughing as if we'd been restricted from laughing for years. We laughed hard and loud until everyone in the room was staring at us. Adrian caught his breath and said, "Tell the servant girl to bring more wine." And we laughed again until we slid down in our seats. *We're laughing like equals,* I thought. I don't remember when I had laughed like this. He looked much healthier in the throes of laughter. We could barely catch our breaths, then we laughed some more. I signaled to Chloe to come over. She was prodding Sarah Beth, who stood frozen with a tray of orders in her hands. Chloe was trying to push her toward a table of eight who did not seem satisfied with their service experience. Sarah Beth had morphed into her dreaded persona of Sarah Death, Our Lady of No Service. *I'm definitely selling this fucking place.*

Nelson came over to tell me that some woman complained that she'd found a hair in her Gazpacho and wanted her meal for free. He handed me the hair; it was long and silver. I scanned the room, "Her?" He nodded, whispering, "Bitch." It was the yoga teacher who came in once a week and always asked if the sour cream was actually a dairy product. Her long silver hair was tied back with a bandana. "Give it to her, and get us a wine and a beer."

"That's bogus—the bitch pulls this shit every week."

"I don't care...I'm feeling..." I almost said gay, "lighthearted. Put her bowl on the floor and tell her to eat it in Downward Dog."

This started Adrian again. And we laughed until a two-top walked out annoyed. "Wicked," he hissed. "Perfect." We watched Nelson deliver the message. She smiled coyly and dove back into her Gazpacho. "I'm gonna fire them, close the friggin' place," I confided.

"Don't, it's precious. This whole thing," he surveyed the room "is charming...perfect. People love it." I wasn't getting that impression. I eyed him closely, but didn't detect any irony. He raised his glass and we toasted. This time to friendship and humor, little cafés and Shepherd's Pie. *And loser writers.*

The Audubon clock struck seven-thirty; a congested wren cawed the hour. All of the birdcalls were muffled because the clock had slid into a crock-pot of Southwestern Chowder—one of our specialties. I made it thick and sprinkled in bits of Facon Bacon. People loved it; even those who considered nightshades the Black Death gobbled up the mashed cherry tomatoes in it.

Adrian checked his watch. "Merde, I have to be at the college in twenty minutes." He fell back and began laughing again. It got me started, and we laughed as if we'd dispelled a bad memory, and honored the present. We fell silent, exhausted, checking one another like weary wrestlers. What moves were left? Adrian stretched mechanically. "You know, Karl," he said gently, "it was a place to make connections, not to learn how to write. We knew how to write, both of us." He laid his hand on his book as if he were testifying, then pushed himself up, a bit unsteady, and hoisted his jacket from the chair. "Is that the bathroom?" I nodded.

I studied his picture on the dust jacket. He never would have complimented me back then. None of us would have deferred to the other, only as much as the murky rules dictated. We were all in the mix, trying to cozy up with the famous workshop leader, hoping to convince each other and ourselves of our talent. Each of us busy decorating our Fabergé Eggs. It happened for him, Adrian Bruck Currier, and not me, Karl Hirsch. Was it about the name, the Anglo Saxon versus the son of a salesman who dreamed for his son to be a podiatrist, not a writer? I ground my sneakers against the floor until my toes ached. I felt empty, despairing, and curiously hopeful. One could always begin writing again just as one doesn't forget how to ride a bicycle. But one had better write with a bit more skill than one rides a bicycle, which reminded me that my bike had a flat. His pronouncement that we both knew how to write was surprising, perhaps manipulative, but a piece of flattery I was willing to wrap myself in. Whoever I was, cooking food, slopping floors, hauling trash, there was still a writer sitting inside, impatient to tell a story. I exhaled heavily. Suddenly a pair of arms wrapped tightly around my shoulders. He kissed me on the back of my neck. His lips were wet. *Jesus Christ.* "Bye, Love." He said this in a breezy English accent. I sat there. Finally, the bell jingled; peripherally, I saw Adrian pass by the window down the ramp and into the parking lot. He was gone.

I grabbed the book, bolted for the office, picking up another beer.

"Close up, don't bother me," I snarled at Nelson. "Tell them to clean up like their lives depended on it. Help Raneisha with the trash. Don't forget to pay her." I locked myself in and began flipping through the pages, reading a few lines here and there. I could hear them talking through the intercom on my desk—they never remembered. It was another tool to keep track of the mayhem in the dining room. My office was a cramped, windowless room adjacent to the kitchen, a sanctuary where I did paperwork and hid from the staff and the customers. They were crafting their own story about me, a ridiculous tale about how I was Adrian's lover as a young writer in the city. Chloe said, "He was probably OK looking then." *Fuck you.* Nelson cautioned them to hurry. "He's pissed at us. Let's clean up and get out." *I'll fire you little twits tomorrow.*

I went back to Adrian's book. Five hundred and seventy-six pages—not short. I skimmed another paragraph toward the middle where a stunning mulatto dwarf was having water play with a corpulent banker dressed in a chiffon teddy, "...his puckered face half-submerged in the swirling aqua pura. A final gleam over his popped eyes flashed like stark roadkill through the marbled room in the candlelight. He declined a sip of Dom Perignon, as she'd fastened a silk tie snug around his rippled neck earlier in the evening. She tossed it down and took up the blade, dove perfunctorily for his member as the perfumed water chanted a hygienic chorus, jetting over their entwined limbs. She surfaced with the prize and tossed it into a waiting marinade of spices and brandy. Only then did she caste her eyes at the opened attaché case resting on the bidet with its crisp packets of fifties and hundreds."

I yawned, my eyelids weighted with fifties and hundreds. *Why is this good? Because he's the High-Rise Honcho of Romance and Intrigue. And I'm the slumlord chef of Cirque du Café and the bumbling ringmaster to incompetent clowns.* I leaned forward, exhausted from the evening's jousting, closed my fading eyes, and rested my forehead on the page—for just a minute. I needed a scant pinch of reality. The water from the penthouse Jacuzzi flowed over my body, numbing my mind. The mulatto dwarf beckoned to me, her beautiful breasts the color of sweet beignets. She held up her champagne glass. I felt my eyes widen and my groin ache, immediately protecting it with my hands. I awoke with a loud snort, startling myself. I must have been asleep for over an hour; the desk clock said 9:45 PM.

I could still hear the soft water sluicing off the page where I'd stopped. The sound of water flowing, gurgling. I pushed myself up from the desk. My sneakers squished. A steady stream of grayish water was pouring over the threshold into my office. I leapt up and ran through the kitchen, almost going down, and got the Shop-Vac. The puddle was already half an inch deep. The familiar smell of *eau-de-cologne*-of-rat-trapped-in-wall engulfed me. "Fuck this," I took up as a mantra. "Fuck this. I mean really, fuck this." At least we were closed; they were all gone. Raneisha Washington was not there to shake her head solemnly. I vacuumed up the surface water then grabbed the milk crate and slid it in under the sink. I pried the iron lid off the box with a flat-edged screwdriver, hoisted it up and kicked open the back door, then leaned it against the porch railing. I shoved the Shop-Vac nozzle into the crap. The top level was gray and foamy, like sautéed brain. Whatever this shit was, the mixture of hot water and rotted vegetables was perfect to grow in. The machine slowly but efficiently lowered the level in the box.

The chunks and bits swirled into the nozzle. Some of them resembled words and images, the strands whipping around like cursive letters spelling out the words *loser, fuckup*. Then I felt the suction die down and knew it was time to empty the canister. This part was harder because one person couldn't lift it. I had to take the top off and scoop pails of it out, maneuver the greasy back stairs into the garden and dump it along the bushes and plants. It made them grow like crazy. From previous deliveries over the months the ferns, Clematis, and groundcover had attained prehistoric growth proportions. The combination of rotted black beans, brown rice, carrots, butter, tofu, and sour cream had created a super fertilizer. I potted some tomatoes with the stuff and grew Big Boys larger than softballs.

I dipped in a large plastic tofu bucket filling it to the top. Then I filled a second. I negotiated the slippery steps carefully but my foot caught under the mop handle Raneisha had neglected to hang up and I went headlong on to the lawn, dumping one of the buckets over myself from my waist to my sneakers. The other had spilled so that the contents flowed over my back, shoulders and head. I lay there noticing the full moon as the putrid liquid soaked my clothes. I thought of Adrian, smartly dressed and confident before his audience, quipping cleverly between questions. I said to Mars, that faint, distant tomato, *What is the difference between Adrian and me? He's being lauded at the college and paid an honorarium and I'm on my back drenched in garbage.* When I got to my feet I was limping. I must have banged my knee on the ground. Carefully I stripped off my clothes and threw them aside. I snatched a tablecloth from the patio area, tied it on like a cape and another around my middle, but it slipped off. My head was beginning to throb and I wasn't thinking clearly. I removed the tablecloths, got down on all fours and crawled to the nozzle, and began spraying myself off. The coolness felt good on the hot June night. Something slimy fell out of my hair.

My cell phone rang. I crawled over to my pants and pulled out my phone, which slipped out of my hand. I crawled after it, an eel escaping my grasp. I checked the time, almost eleven.

"It's me," the voice joyfully proclaimed.

"Adrian? Where are you?"

"On the train heading back to the city. They paid for it," he tittered.

"What is it?" I didn't want to hear his voice. I just wanted to forget the entire night, which at this point seemed to have a thundering lack of meaning. Then I snapped, "Adrian, I don't care if you're gay. I don't care about stuff like that."

"I'm not gay." He sounded hurt. "I'm bisexual." I didn't answer. Then he said, "I'm sick, Karl."

"Jesus, Adrian, I made the Shepherd's pie today. The salad was fresh. The bread comes…" I stopped myself. "What kind of sick?"

"I have the party disease," he said quietly. "I'm not dying," he added quickly. "Don't get your hopes up." He wasn't being sarcastic. "I have to be careful, take my medicine." I remembered his box of colored pills, a cocktail of medicine. "And I may go completely vegetarian to keep you in the loop," he chuckled.

I exhaled into the phone, "I didn't know."

"Well, I didn't tell you. I am now." Why? I wondered. A long pause, listening to the space between us. I felt something crawling on my butt.

"I've been seeing this therapist. She said that it's important to connect to people who mean something to me in my life."

I was stunned. Surely Adrian had an adoring coterie surrounding him, people who'd supported his work, who would be more current than me. "But why me," I asked. "Our only connection was the workshop. And that wasn't so nice."

"I don't know why. You're a quirky Jew, Karl—you're cuddly. And your writing…" I could feel him struggling. "I told Gwen that I thought you had the most potential in the group, besides me, of course." *Of course, asshole.*

I did not want to ask. I tightened my shoulders and neck and tried to wait a moment longer. Finally, with absurd nonchalance I said. "Really, what did she say?"

"She said she thought you should open a restaurant." Then he started in with his crazy laugh again. I tried to resist, but couldn't help it. I howled in the moonlight like a stinking dog. As if offended, the moon skirted behind a cloud, then emerged just above the power lines, perfectly served up like a ball of clotted cream. My abdomen still ached from laughing so hard before, but I couldn't stop.

"You fucker," I blurted when I could talk again. We were quiet for a few moments.

"I owe you a dinner. I forgot to pay."

"They forgot to give you a check. They do that."

"Come to the city. There's a new Indonesian place on 3rd Avenue. We'll eat like kings."

Kings and serfs? I thought, how strange this is. Why is Adrian back in my waking life? By this point my head was spinning and I was about to vomit. Would I actually go visit with Adrian in the city, meet his friends maybe? A bizarre thought crept in: Sex would be out of the question even if I were gay. It's funny how you think when you're naked in the moonlight, your skin slick with vegetable rot.

"Why?" I asked, thinking, *Do you want him to beg you to come?*

He said, "Karl, you probably want to." His arrogance was disarming. I did want to. "And I know a gaggle of agents and publishers," he tossed off. *The bastard's chumming.*

"OK, I'll call you next week," I heard myself answer.

"Cheers," he said.

"Good night," I replied, sitting down on the patio. The new molded plastic chair was quite comfortable. I could see the empty street from here consumed in darkness, the sky with its stunning moon, and vaguely, the hills that rose toward the mountains. And in this surreal moment, sitting naked as I was born, fairy dust seemed to rain over the café building and transform it into a bigger version of the witch's cottage in the forest, where Hansel and Gretel learned about overeating and time management. For some reason I thought about the last thing I'd written—maybe because I'd soon be in Adrian's company again. It was also for the Mountain Ledger. I'd entitled it: "The Taming of the Kale: How to tenderize and flavor one tough leaf." It occurred to me that I could fictionalize my food column a little more, make the pieces a bit longer. Tell about the time I'd wrestled the Killer Kale that ate Kalamazoo. I could add snippets about the café. No, that would be bad for business. I had to go back to the novel, the Cadillac of art forms. The scratch-off card that might be a winner, usually a clinker.

As usual, the staff had forgotten to bus the patio. There was a heel of multi-grain bread and a glass of wine on the table, an offering. I took them as a sacrament and the simple taste of bread and wine was wonderful, especially eating *al fresco* in the nude. I rubbed the soles of my feet on the gravel; it felt good.

I jumped, not expecting a call. "Karl, I'm on my way home. Do you still want me?"

"Shea, yes, Shea. I definitely want you. Right now."

"I'm at the airport in Athens."

"Where's Iris? Is she coming with you?

"I left her in a stable. She was screwing three of them." *Nice manger scene.*

"Greeks?"

"That's what's here, Karl. Lots of them."

"And you?"

"What?" she snapped.

"Greeks, are you stabilizing Greeks?"

"Fuck you, Karl." This was good, she was direct as usual. She softened a bit. "I want my fat old man." It was a mixed compliment, but

I'd learned to like it; usually good things followed. I didn't want to risk telling her I loved her. It might bring bad luck.

"Did you get some new recipes?" I asked, to make conversation.

Her answer was blunt: "I had diarrhea for five days." I set down my wine. "What are you doing? Where are you?"

"I'm working; well actually I had dinner with a friend." Immediately, I added, "A guy from college."

This raised her hackles, which were many and easily raised. I like feisty women. "Who? You don't have dinner with people. Who'd have dinner with you?"

"A guy from the writing program, Adrian; he's a writer. Adrian Bruck Currier."

Shea gasped into the phone. "Oh my god. I'm looking at his picture; he's on the cover of Esquire. He's designed a line of casual evening wear, "for the cad in you," she read.

Suddenly I wished I had some Rolaids Extra Strength or something. "Really," I managed. *No shit. Oops, no diarrhea .*

"Does he really look like that?" she asked, forgetting I wasn't with her.

"Probably worse," I said.

"You know him?"

"Well, yeah. We kind of got back in touch."

"He's famous!"

"I know, I'm going to see him next week. You can come. We're going to a *fabulous* Indonesian restaurant." *No friggin' Greek.*

"Really? Karl, that's cool." I wasn't above using my close friendship with Adrian to help tuck Shea back safely into bed. We got quiet for a few seconds listening to the calming music of the international airport, designed to take your mind off the guy in the Fateh cloak.

I waited a moment longer and said the word, "Baby."

She said, "I know, Karl."

"Fly home."

I breathed in the shimmering night air, the coolness encircling my bare, hungry body, and raised my glass to the pulsating, clotted moon. This time, my own toast: "To you, you mysterious son of a bitch who makes us crazy in the night. To my lovely, hot, faithful Shea. And to my best friend…confidant and colleague, Adrian Bruck Currier."

The Maestro

Tony nicknamed Frank Bozonski the Maestro because he orchestrated disaster in the shop. All goofiness and carelessness, Frank destroyed a 55 Ton Edwards Ironworker with an overload. He'd been tossed out of the marina for welding a manhole cover on the stern of a cabin cruiser. Since he arrived, our shops safety record had dropped an astounding forty-one percent. There was no union at the marina to protect him, not like our District 15 IAM, which he joined before anyone could challenge him, locking Steve, our shop owner, into an untenable position. Luckily, no one had been killed or maimed, but Frank was working on it; he had a talent for disaster. He couldn't seem to remember to turn off the lathe. He left files and ratchets inside machinery, near careening belts that might hurl metal through a man's skull. He spilled grease and toxic solvents and was responsible for numerous back sprains and twisted ankles. I was not surprised when he broke the band saw, almost ripping his hands off. He used it to cut a pair of handcuffs that Al Cornetta had slapped on him.

The guys were at lunch and I was checking on the shop. I'd been promoted to foreman, so I took pains to make sure everything was secure during downtime. I found Frank hunkered over the band saw, being slowly drawn in, his wrists dangerously close to the teeth. I dove at the safety switch and stopped it with my shoulder. If I'd had more time to think, I would have tapped it with my boot and saved a bruised muscle. The chain that joined the cuffs was jammed in the saw chamber. Instead of cutting through the metal, the action trapped Frank, almost sacrificing his hands.

My shoulder throbbed and I was pretty upset. "Asshole," was all I could say.

"Don't tell Steve, would ya?" As usual, Frank was more concerned with covering his butt than safety or equipment worth thousands of dollars.

"The blade's shot," I said, and slammed my clipboard against the machine. "I've got to tell him. And I've got to fill out an accident report."

I cut the chain with a bolt cutter, and noticed that heat had singed the flesh on the inside of his wrists, two nasty blistered wounds. He didn't seem to mind. "Don't tell him. C'mon Ray, I just got engaged." Frank rubbed his wrists with nervous jerks. He flashed a venal grin, his usual expression. His black hair receded into a V on his forehead and the stubble of his beard crawled down his neck inside his shirt collar. "C'mon, Ray, it was a joke. I bet Cornetta I could break out of the cuffs."

I tossed Frank the mangled handcuffs. "Who's the lucky lady?" I asked, disinterested, but he took off.

Frank knew I couldn't fire him. Even Steve couldn't fire him easily, and Steve owned the shop. You could screw up in any number of ways, but as long as you paid your dues, and voted correctly, the union took care of you. I liked that idea, but a guy like Frank Bozonski shouldn't have been allowed to operate a waffle maker.

I unplugged the unit, examined it for damage, changed the blade, recalibrated, and went out to the loading dock. The guys sat around eating from their lunch boxes, taking in the afternoon sun. Frank stood over Al Cornetta smiling idiotically. He dangled the cuffs then dropped them on Al's egg salad. Al slid a hammer from his tool belt and smashed the steel toe of Frank's boot, denting it. The guys looked at the twisted cuffs, at Frank, and then at me. Tony paused, a perfect apple skin spiral dangling from his deer knife. "The Maestro strikes again."

On Friday, Frank wedged a steel bar through the housing of a chopping machine. He pretended to walk a tight rope down the center aisle of the shop using the bar as a balance. On his way, he toppled a container of 380 Black Max that later required a sander to get up off the floor. The chopping machine shot a plume of smoke and sparks up to the exhaust fans. Dime-sized metal fragments sprayed the room as men dove under workbenches and shielded their faces. Cutler flipped out, having recently returned from the Persian Gulf, his patience for ordinance very low. He started for Frank with a Gator Edge Digger. Cutler was our everyday reminder of what a useless war brought home, a broken man. There was not one of us who wouldn't carry him as long as we could.

Steve ran in and caught a shard in his thumb. He jumped up and down, and recited a Sicilian curse. We managed to steer Cutler into the finishing room. Steve seethed with anger. "Get the fuck out!" He ordered Frank, who retreated timidly over the war zone, and stepped in the Black Max, which instantly adhered his heels to the floor. He shrugged with a look of helpless embarrassment.

I drove Steve to St. Vincent's where they pulled the shard out with something like a needle nose pliers. He refused painkillers, and took five stitches in his thumb and a lot of Iodine, and a Tetanus booster. It was already 6:45 PM by the time we got out, too late to go back to the shop, so we went to Shea's.

Steve had a shot with his good hand. The thick bandage made it difficult to grasp the glass, and interfered with his opposable thumb. It looked like he was giving a constant thumbs up. "Friggin' asshole." He drained the shot and knuckled the bar for another. "Friggin' Pollack asshole." He was not the kind of guy who would benefit from sensitivity training. He was straightforward with us guys, plainspoken, honest, and his heart was as big as a wheel of provolone. When Cutler first returned, deep into PTSD, Steve assigned him the least stressful jobs, away from the machinery, and let him leave early for meetings, with full pay. He took care of Cutler; that was Steve.

"We might have enough for an incompetency hearing," I said.

"Fuck, we got enough for attempted murder," Steve snorted, the whisky starting to ease the throbbing pain. "But he'd be in good company." He was referring to our union president, Jerry Barcoff, aka Jerry Knock-off, who'd recently been acquitted for dropping something that appeared to be a body in the Gowanus Canal. The culprit turned out to be a guy who resembled him. Now Jerry was being tried for tax evasion after paying off a condo in Jersey City, probably with Union cash. Despite his legal entanglements he fought like hell for us.

"He'll show up Monday, I guess."

"Sure as shit he will." Steve pumped his bulbous, gauzy thumb in the air. Esperanza came over with the bottle and poured Steve another. "I'm in pain," he told her to justify the shots.

"Another Coke, Ray?" Esperanza's hair was so thick and black, it gleamed in the neon lights, outlining her sculpted nose and lips and stunning Spanish eyes—a living El Greco.

"Nah, I'm good." I'd been trying to cut down. For a while there my relationship with beer was getting too intimate; it was like a troublesome family member who moved in and wouldn't move out. Cutler insisted that the way to get off beer was to try heroin, but I was afraid of that. Besides the PTSD he was dealing with, he'd also had to kick heroin when he got back to the States.

Steve was slurring a little and I figured I'd better get him home. "Don't let him touch nothing that's got power. The asshole can count bits."

"I promise." I watched Esperanza move down the bar, brightening the worn faces of the men who moved heavy objects through space, built and rebuilt machines, maintained the infrastructure, kept the wheels rolling, men who were grateful for the work and anxious about when it might not be there. She had to have a boyfriend, probably kids. I left her a good tip, feeling like a kid staring in the window of a toy store.

Steve was slightly tipsy so I gave him a hand out to the car. "Or maybe we throw the shithead into the consolidator." I laughed a vapor cloud into the cold air.

We sat in front of his house and watched snowflakes melt on the windshield. I was kind of waiting for him to go in so I could be alone with my thoughts about Esperanza. Maybe I'd go back to Shea's, have just one beer, and ask her out. He started in on Clara again, how I ought to give her a call. I had two dates with Steve's sister, and that was enough. He made it excessively clear that he hoped it would lead to something permanent, like marriage. He wanted to think of us as a family. I understood, but I just wasn't there. Clara was sweet, kind, had a great sense of humor, and was plagued with an eating disorder since childhood, growing up on their mother's pastas, meatballs and sausages, eggplant parmesan, escarole, canolli, and everything else that crowns a traditional Italian table, and in a time when portion control was not a consideration. She was a binge eater without periods of remission, no bulimia or meals skipped. The girl could eat like Road Runner could run. The last time I'd seen her was at Thanksgiving, wedged in a captain's chair, tears in her eyes, eating stuffing from a Pyrex bowl. I remember crying in the car afterward because she said to me, "Ray, do you think someday my prince will come?"

She was a gifted cook and fed her brother like a king. Steve could put away a pound and a half of Ziti with mushrooms and peppers, a half bottle of Chianti, and not gain an ounce, but not poor Clara. I felt really bad, but I just couldn't do it, couldn't imagine a lifetime of handling such a large woman. I didn't want to be like that, but I couldn't help it. I sunk down staring at the steering wheel. I'm a shithead, I thought. And it wasn't like women were seeking me out. If only Esperanza…

"She lost fifty pounds," Steve said, an obvious lie.

"That's great." I didn't sound enthusiastic.

"You should take another look at her."

I swallowed, "Uh ha." Jesus, I thought, it's not like buying a car.

Steve thumped me on the side of the head, affectionately. "Ray, it's not 'cause of Clara I gave you foreman. You're conscientious, that's why. Just keep an eye on the asshole." He slammed the door. "Monday," he yelled at the window. I slunk home and watched girls' volleyball until my eyes closed.

Early Sunday morning, Steve called in a panic. "It's the evil eye. It's the fucking evil eye, Ray." He was breathing heavy, his voice rasping.

"Are you OK? Is it Clara?"

"It's Clara, all right. She's going to marry the asshole."

"What?"

"Bozonski, she knows Bozonski."

"How?"

"Chemistry frickin' dot com. They matched up on two of them. Lava Life or some bullshit. She's been seeing him for two months."

"Does she know Frank works for you?"

"No, and she's not gonna know. She said he told her he works in a shop, that's all."

"She'll find out. He'll tell her," I said.

"Maybe he'll forget. Ray, what the hell am I going to do?"

"Maybe it's OK, Steve. It might be good. A family, she'll have kids. You want that, don't you?" I was more relieved than I should have been.

"You want that shithead giving it to your sister?" There was no answer for that one. "You've got to talk to her, Ray, please. Talk to her."

"What can I say? I can't tell her I know Frank."

Steve's voice dropped down to a conspiratorial tone, his old neighborhood voice, "I'll pay him to leave town and if he don't I'll call in a favor."

"Steve, that's not really an option. Besides, she wants to marry him."

"Don't say that," he growled. "Call her. Talk her out of it." This was a command, not a request. And he was my boss. "Tell her she's too young to commit. She ought to play the field first." I couldn't imagine what field that would be.

"Steve, she's thirty-four."

"You gonna do this or not?"

I waited until noon figuring how to accomplish my mission without getting sucked in. At first she didn't want to get on the phone, but Steve coaxed her. I could hear him whisper something about how the worm turns.

"Hello, is this Mr. Hard-to-Get?"

"Clara, how have you been?" My palms were wet. What if she thought this was an overture. She warmed up quickly. "Ray, I have wonderful news." I suggested she tell me over a guilt dinner to buy my freedom and some job security. I didn't want to talk her out of marrying Frank. "I'm hungry now," she said firmly.

"OK, 6:30." I tore a coupon out of the paper. It was for Genghis Kahn, a new Mongolian buffet, located in a box store where they'd set up a giant yurt with fake torches, composite bows, halberds, spears and lances—not quite dining for pacifists. There were fierce wooden horse heads set up around the perimeter that looked like they'd been appropriated from a merry-go-round, but decorated in colorful scarves. The food was served with small metal shovels on to brass platters. Guys in deels and head gear banged each other around in mock combat.

After we'd worked through a pile of dumplings, sweet biscuits, and yogurt, we watched women dancers perform as they berated us in guttural tones. Clara reached across the table and took my hands in hers. "Ray he's wonderful, looks a little like Bill Murray, shorter. You know, the hair thin in front. And what a sense of humor."

Humor wasn't what I thought of when I thought of Frank. Danger, yes, humor no. "You really like him?" I encouraged.

She looked at me earnestly, quite attractive in her pink blouse with white frills. "Ray, I'm going to be the mother of his children," she confided. "And he wants a house full." The excitement in her eyes shown, and then darkened. "But Steve is so negative about this. He's suspicious. It's as if he doesn't want me to be happy."

I squeezed her hand. "He's just protecting you. You're his baby sister."

"No, Ray, it's something else. He got weird the first time I told him about Frank. He flew into a rage."

"Well," I stumbled, "it's just been you and Steve for a long time. He needs to adjust. He'll miss you."

"He won't have to miss me. Frank said he could renovate the attic, including a big nursery. He'd see me every day." I could imagine

Steve's satisfaction with that plan. "Steve can't boil an egg. I'd take care of both of them." I pictured them around the table, Steve hands around Frank's throat.

Clara released my hands and swiped a remnant of sweet biscuit through the gravy, which she ate with innocent verve and desire. She asked if I would mind getting her a little more. At that moment she looked as attractive as any woman I've seen. It's a cliché, I thought, but it's true. Clara's beauty flowed from the inside of her; there was loveliness about her bright as a Roman Candle. She would be a good wife to him and a loving mother if Frank didn't back the van up over their children.

She gave me a shy, sweet smile, a bead of gravy in the corner of her mouth. "It could have been you, Ray. You know that."

I looked into my coffee cup, Mud of Mongolia, delicious. "I know."

"It's because I'm overweight, isn't it?"

"God, Clara, it isn't that at all. I'm just a career bachelor," I lied.

Her face brightened again. She looked angelic, like a fountain cherub. "Frank likes a woman with a little meat on her bones," she said. "Says there's more to love."

I smiled at the hyperbole and looked directly into her eyes, "I think you're a beautiful woman, Clara. And whoever this Frank guy is, he's a very lucky man."

She basked in the compliment and added, "You know I've lost twenty pounds. Can't you tell?" I couldn't tell, but it was thirty less than Steve had fabricated, not that it mattered. There'd be more for Frank to love. We shared a block of Mongolian Fudge with heavy cream sauce, and I took her home. Steve was rattling around the windows, peaking at the street, no doubt hoping that Clara and I had somehow rerouted the course of love. She gave me a sweet fudge kiss. "You're not sad, are you?"

"No, I'm happy for you." I almost said, "and the Maestro's a great guy," but caught myself. I drove home ashamed. I'd let Steve down, and I didn't feel the relief I'd anticipated. There is no more bitter an entrée than self-loathing.

Monday morning Frank showed up with a large box of coffee, bagels, doughnuts, and Danish for all. He even remembered the cream and napkins. The spring in his step was unsettling. Maybe he was planning the Big Kahuna today, take us all out with a miscalculated setting on welding tanks. Cautiously, the guys approached the box, checking for battery acid or iron filings. He went around the shop apologizing to each of us. "Al, forgive me. From now on, it's safety first." Cornetta just stared at him. "Cutler, I'm sorry." Cutler ducked stealthily and went for him with a precision angle block. Tony stepped between them. Frank started toward Steve's office, but stopped short and gave a furtive wave. Steve held up his bandaged thumb up and bared his teeth.

We worked tenuously. Despite Frank's promises a cloud hung over the shop. For all the whining and humming of the tools and machines, it seemed quiet. We were nervous that Frank's new leaf would wither, and he'd kill us all in a terrific mishap. But he was good to his word that day and every day after. He counted fixtures, cleaned and reorganized the socket holder, sorted through an unmanageable pile of bearings. He did everything I asked him to do immediately and skillfully, no more screwing around. He tried hard to convince Cutler he was a friend, but to no avail.

After a couple of weeks, I let Frank use the drill press to make some speakers for his car. Within a month, Steve begrudgingly put him back on the lathe where he turned out superior work, remembering to shut down each time. He even signed up for a course in machine shop repair, which would make him even more indispensable. I began to wonder if he was looking to get my job now that he was taking on a wife. Slowly, the guys came around. After he finished a dozen perfect tractor brace rods in record time, Al Cornett said, "All right, Maestro." This time it was a compliment.

Steve hung back. He wouldn't talk to him, or me either, which made me nervous. On payday, he'd leave Frank's check stapled by the door, with grease smudges on it. He treated Frank like he was invisible because he wanted him to disappear out of Clara's life without understanding the harm it would cause her. He never told Clara that Frank worked for him. Somehow, it would all go away. Maybe the evil eye would take Frank out of the picture. I didn't believe that Steve would actually "call in a favor," though there were guys who hung around the union hall who didn't have day jobs.

It could have been malice, but most of the guys agreed that it was an accident, when a few weeks later, Steve sheared off three quarters of Frank's pinky, as he demonstrated the new, state of the art, ten-inch radial saw. The machine had just been installed, and there was a Factory Rep from Toledo on hand to show us the fine points. We stood around admiring the thing. It had a Kromedge blade with a twenty-six inch rip capacity, and it was quiet, a real bonus. Frank was standing next to Steve. "Hold the end of this," Steve snapped at him. They guided a two-by-four into the housing and the blade turned red. Like most mishaps, no one reacted for a few moments. Then everybody started running. Frank squeezed the injured finger, tight in his other hand. He let out a loud exhalation, but no scream, no swearing.

A steady pulse of blood squirted between his fingers. What stands out in my mind was the way Frank dealt it. He let Al wrap a handkerchief around the wound, then walked out of the shop, his arm above his head, dignified and self-possessed. He stood by his car and waited for someone to drive to the emergency room. Tony jumped in and they took off. About five minutes later, Cutler scooped up the piece of Frank's pinky out of the sawdust and rushed it to the hospital. Cutler had suddenly broken through. A comrade was down and he reacted. We'd almost forgotten about the severed pinky. Automatically, the guys followed him. I stayed with the Rep and shut everything down. The Rep made a stupid selling point about how you could do surgery with a Kromedge blade. I told him to fuck off.

Later on, Al observed that just as Steve had gotten his bandage off, Frank was about to get one on. Steve wound up with a squiggly scar that ran down his thumb and ached before snow storms, of which there was no deficit that winter. I wondered if Frank would be as lucky. It seemed too, that the letting of each other's blood joined them together in some way, a perfect seal for a marriage contract, though they would probably never be blood brothers.

Clara was waiting in the emergency room and we moved cautiously around her. They'd already rushed Frank to the operating room for surgery. The guys looked down at the tiled floor. She stared icily at Steve, who cowered against the soda machine blubbering like a puppy.

"How did you think I wouldn't know? You goddam bastard." This was not typical language for Clara and we all sat up straight in our chairs. "I love him, and you did that. How could you do that, Steve? Your sister?"

"I'm sorry. So sorry, Clara. Whatever you want. All I care 'bout's your happiness."

"Bullshit," she thundered.

"And you," she stood over me. "Friends, right Ray? What a friend."

"Sorry." That was the operative word at the moment, useless and empty. I wished she would just swing her bag at me, but that wasn't Clara. She sat down and sobbed.

"Bastards, all of you."

A nurse approached us. "Are you Frank's family?"

"I'm his fiancée."

"The doctor says it's good you got his finger here quickly. It was a perfect cut. It's been sterilized and they're attaching the tendons and veins now." She hesitated a moment. "There was some shock, which is common, but he's stabilized at this point."

"But he's all right? He'll be able to use his finger?" Clara asked anxiously.

The nurse smiled. "Your fiancée is lucky. Dr. Cabrera is supervising the team. He's an expert in this type of surgery." She chuckled, "We call him Dr. Digit around here."

"Can I see him?" Clara grabbed her handbag.

"It'll be a few more hours. I can call as soon as he's in recovery. He'll need to sleep."

"I'll wait."

I put my hand on her shoulder. "Let me take you home. We'll come back when she calls." Clara shrugged my hand off, staring hate at Steve, who retreated to the exit.

The nurse returned a couple hours later. She was smiling again. "It went well. He's in ICU."

"His finger?" Clare asked. The nurse held up two crossed fingers. "Cabrera says it looks good. Best thing is to let him rest."

Al convinced Clara, and we all went to Steve's house and ate leftovers. Steve wasn't there and I figured he was at Shea's washing down his guilt. I hung out with Clara until she fell asleep on the sofa. I promised to be there first thing in the morning, or whenever she called. I drove home past the hospital about five AM. Steve's car was still there.

The wedding took place in the beginning of February. A Nor'easter courteously held off and we congregated at the Sons of Italy Hall for the ceremony and reception. Father Gregory, who'd confirmed Steve and Clara as teenagers, did the honors. The night before, we'd taken Frank to the Dimpled Kitten for his bachelor party. It was pretty tame, even with the dimpled kittens prancing around in fur thongs, and teased whiskers, but the pitchers of beer crowded two tables and I surrendered. We got feeling generous and booked five nights for them in Atlantic City, plus two hundred dollars in chips. Al had been there so many times he had an app on his phone for reservations.

When I got home from the party there was a message from Esperanza. Apparently, Steve had invited her to the wedding and told her that I didn't have anyone to go with. I was going anyway, but this was a shock. He was turning into a mob-like Santa Claus. I listened to the message repeatedly. She didn't promise anything; just that it would be nice to be there. That is if I wanted her to go with me. Duh?

She wore a yellow dress with yellow shoes, springy for winter, but I wouldn't have cared if she wore a bag. Her hair splayed over her shoulders like a black silk fan. I told her, regretting it immediately, that I was proud to be with her. She nodded, "I'm married, you know."

Clara was grace and beauty as Steve walked her to the front of the room. She stepped on my toe as they went by and I blew her a kiss. Steve rustled in his tux, straining his neck against the tie. We all quieted down for the prayer. Al Cornetta sniffled during the exchange of vows. Cutler had the honor to stand by Frank's side. The two had been close since the accident. I saw Frank's pinky wiggle as Clara slipped the ring on his finger. Thank God, I thought.

After the ceremony, which took up most of a box of Kleenex, Father Gregory told us each to take a glass of champagne. Steve took a scrap of paper from his pocket for the toast. He stammered, but stayed on track. "To my beautiful sister Clara…God bless her on her wedding day. My baby sister." He swiped a tear with his jacket cuff.

"And my new brother-in-law, and...friend." It took a while to get that out. "Frank Bozonski, Frank and Clara Bozonski." He seemed amazed as he heard himself say the name. "Long life. Many children. And...God bless." We tossed down the bubbly.

"Go Maestro," Tony called out. "To the Maestro!" The band covered every Dean Martin hit ever recorded, more Steve's choice than Clara's. She was a devout Carpenters fan, a hopeful romantic. Taking a rare vacation, a decade earlier, Steve had flown to Vegas and caught Dean's entire engagement at the Sands, including a surprise drop in, another Frank—Sinatra. He said it was one of the high points of his life.

After Clara and Frank had the first dance to "Everybody Loves Somebody Sometime" I danced with Esperanza. It was like holding an earthen treasure in my arms.

"Your husband?" I stuttered.

"He's a dick."

"That's good," I blurted. "I mean, I'm sorry."

She leaned back, breathing life into my face. "I'm not ready for anything."

"Of course not," and my heart beat like a tin drum monkey.

At some point, after the feast, the wine, shots, and cigars, Frank and Steve found themselves at opposite sides of the hall. Frank scuffed his shoe against the floor, snorted and bobbed his head. He hunched his shoulders and roared. Steve made similar gestures and animal noises, and tossed off his tux jacket. They both snorted and bobbed like bulls, eyeing each other threateningly. Frank whooped and charged Steve full on. He covered the length of the hall in a moment. Steve threw his arms open. The impact carried them over the dessert table. The flower arrangements went airborne and the two guys, arms locked around each another, crashed into a stack of folding chairs. The band struck up a tarantella, and I asked Mrs. Bozonski to dance.

Tomorrow's Special

From his perch at the counter stool, Kenneth watched Helen sweep the tiled floor. He pointed out bits of straw wrapper and matches with powdery black heads—and the occasional lucky penny. By all rights he should have been sweeping, being the hired man, but Helen preferred to sweep, though she missed a lot of crumbs by refusing to wear her new prescription. She worked along the cigarette machine where he called her attention to a piece of piecrust poking out from under. "If I don't see it, it ain't dirt." This was her standard reply and though they both hailed from the Tar Heel State, he loved her Boone accent. People agreed that you sounded like you were from North Carolina if you were. But people from Boone spoke Boone. It just sounded different, softer, a bit of mountain music. He swiveled thoughtfully, pinching a speck of tobacco from his tongue, and sighed as Helen bent over, angling the broom under a peach-colored booth, vinyl glowing in the twilight. The Formica table tops sported peach-colored flakes and ivory trim. In fact, all the furnishings in the restaurant were colored peach. And it was called The Sweet Peach Café.

Over the years, Helen had added a few touches: peach napkins, award-winning peach cobbler, and a peach-colored jukebox. Atop the roof was a huge peach, created by a neon artist from the college in the mid-sixties. The sign dwarfed the squat building and had been designed to look as though a big bite had been taken out of it. A local acid tripper claimed that a giant mouth had roared out of space one night and bit it. For many in the town, especially the college kids, the glowing peach was more inviting than the smooth chrome cross in front of the Baptist church.

Smoke streamed like a vaporizer from Kenneth's nostrils, slow and warm. This added pleasure to Helen's haphazard end-of-the-day cleanup. Five years he'd watched her do this. Five years ago he'd responded to her ad for a dishwasher/cook—No Alcoholics Apply. He had been hired on the spot by the distinction of being the only applicant for the job. He didn't actually want a job at the time. He was recovering from a colossal career setback. He had just been dismissed from the Carolina Culinary for poisoning most of the school's board at the Easter dinner, including the President's wife, a corpulent, unkind woman. It was not his fault; the tainted pheasant was bad luck, a result of unsanitary farm practices. But he was the student chef in charge and responsible for all aspects of the meal. There was a saying at Carolina Culinary: "The chef goes down with the gravy boat." He went down.

At the dismissal hearing he became sarcastic and said that many board members looked like they'd eaten too much already. Purging might have added years to their lives. This did not bode well. Later, he received a certified letter saying his chef's certification would be withheld in perpetuity. He considered moving to Virginia where there was no reciprocal food service agreement. But he took the job with Helen. He could flip burgers, make Caesar salads, salmon stew, puddings in his sleep, and a whole lot more if he wanted to. But he had sworn off pheasant. That was his cover reason anyway for taking the job. He liked Helen's voice and her facial expressions. Whatever she thought seemed to be right there in her eyes and mouth.

She told him that it was time for her to get out from behind the grill and broaden her horizons, take a look at the world. Mainly this amounted to her becoming the hostess/waitress in her own cafe. She did get to sleep later and see more movies. One day in the summer, she left Kenneth in charge and took a trip up to Manteo to see The Lost Colony play. It was performed outdoors and featured folks like Sir Walter Raleigh, Miles Standish, and Virginia Dare, come to life on the stage. There was a weekend trip to Elizabeth City where, Kenneth gathered, she went to say goodbye to her old boyfriend, a carpenter who drank too much and had tried to rough her up. Helen said, proudly, that she had thrown him into a wall of sheet rock. Kenneth hoped that it had not been a fond good bye, though she came back home crying. The main thing with Helen was that he had to keep on his toes, find some middle ground. Her emotions ran hot, cold, and boiling over with temper, all of which he found attractive.

The Bunnomatic spit fresh, hot coffee into the carafe. Kenneth sniffed appreciatively as he set up two mugs, spoons, peeled the tops from three creamers and set them by hers. "Doughnut?" he called out, clicking the tongs rhythmically. "Cinnamon's good." She was two stools away jabbing at the debris. When she got to him, he raised his long spider legs, thinking it made him look silly. She swept vigorously around his martyred Nikes, almost impatiently. "Frosted," she said, accenting the second syllable, a bit irritated. "It's always been frosted." He took in her aroma, faint bleach from the apron, K.T.'s Firebird Chili, some salesman's cigar. Maybe something faint like Lily of the Valley. He wished she wore perfume. Somehow that might make things easier; she might be more receptive. After five years and several anxious days, he had decided to declare himself to her. Tell her how he felt. Dread cramped his stomach. Perfume or not she was plenty feminine enough. Finally, at the far end of the counter she bent over and swept the dirt into a dustpan, her peach skirt lifting above her legs. A well pronounced calf. Soft, fleshy skin behind the knees. Her butt was wide, but nicely shaped. His face was suddenly warm.

She plopped down one stool away from his and began pouring out the creamers. "More on the floor than gets in their mouths," she quipped. Kenneth deliberately stubbed out his cigarette and stirred coffee. He was feeling a bit listless now, tired. Maybe all this could wait. Speaking up had never done him much good before. And, if it didn't go well, he'd most likely be packing up tomorrow. He could just let it go on this, a cozy, discontented life. Keep an eye on Helen from a distance. One night, about a year ago, they were talking about the menu. Helen had selected a few tunes on the jukebox; she was a big Patti Page fan. Kenneth had stood up suddenly and planted his hands on the counter. He uttered a word that she couldn't understand. "Dance." He wanted to say, "Helen, dance with me?" but he froze. His hands stuck to the counter as if they'd been super-glued. He stared straight ahead into the refrigerated dessert case. He felt Helen next to him, breathing, waiting. He couldn't speak; he couldn't look at her. Finally she left, slamming the door with a decisive bang, upsetting a bowl of plastic peaches from the shelf above. He thought he'd tell her he'd had a spell of some kind, but neither of them mentioned it the next day or after that. There was something in both of them, a shy carefulness, some undercurrent, a silent agreement that things would take their course when it was time. Now Kenneth, though frightened, felt that he had to move on it. What if some carpenter or plumber came along that was really nice to her?

He took a gulp of coffee, got up and went to the front window, unhooked the blackboard from its chain and wiped it clean with his bandana. He made a note that the Kale and Ginger soup was probably too fancy for Peaches. He set the board between them. A bit of doughnut fell from Helen's lips as she said, "What's it gonna be?" This signaled the start of their daily meeting to decide on the next day's specials. Kenneth always knew what the special was going to be, but he enjoyed the process.

"Hmm," he feigned some uncertainty. "Let's see…I'm going to take those meatballs out of the sauce and use 'em for a taco salad."

"Why?" Helen demanded.

"Because that sauce is tired."

Helen pressed on: "How do you know the meatballs are good?"

"Sauce kept 'em good, juicy. Now the sauce is tired." She looked at him skeptically. "And," he went on, "I'm going to take all those farm eggs you got from Mr. Clarence and make a Julienne Wrap out of 'em."

Helen set her mug down, abruptly. "I don't trust wraps. I've told you that."

"Everyone's making 'em now. It's the new sandwich. A little strip of ham, egg, mesclun, hint of relish. They'll get eaten up."

"I'm not a wrap type," she announced. Her edge was starting to show.

"They're simple, Helen, like salad, but rolled up."

"Huh." She looked back toward the kitchen, then examined the ceiling. "God damn place needs painting."

"Yeah," he drew the word out.

She went behind the counter and took the carafe, splashing coffee into her mug. He looked at her hands. The cuticles were stained with red-eye gravy, a variety of food smudges over her fingers. He glanced at her waist. She had been trying to diet, lately, eating a lot of tuna and lettuce, though she liked to sop up the salad dressing with heels of Italian bread. She hit the no sale button and extracted a coin envelope and slid it across the counter.

"What's this?"

"It's Friday," she said, "Pay."

"Oh yeah, forgot." The envelope was thick with stuffed bills, thicker than usual. She didn't like to write checks. She believed that a business should pay as it goes, avoid building up debt.

"It feels thick," he said.

She always smiled when she paid him. He thought she might have read in some management book that you're supposed to smile when you pay the help. She flipped her guest pad and recited: "Nineteen grilled cheese steaks, eleven shrimp baskets, five Roman Omelets, and seven bowls of Firebird Chili, Kenneth, just seven. Your chili did not achieve celebrity status."

"It's real chili with handpicked Mexican habaneros," he defended.

"It's too damn hot," she pronounced.

He felt a little hurt. "I'll fix it, make a foot-long sauce that'll make love in your mouth."

They locked eyes. Helen swallowed the last of her doughnut, then licked the sugar from between her thumb and forefinger.

"Well...you know what I mean," he trailed off.

She moved down the counter, poured some water and drank it, then turned to look at him. "No, I don't know what you mean. Exactly what do you mean, Kenneth Tucker?" He knew it was trouble when she called him by his full name.

"I don't mean nothing," be blurted quickly, struggling to say what was on his mind.

"What I know is you been acting weird for days, sneaking around here like a guilty rabbit."

"That's not true," he snapped, nervously shaking a cigarette out of the pack.

Helen slammed the chalk down on the counter, smashing it into shards and dust. "God damn it, if you've got something to say, say it, because I know what it is anyway, Kenneth Tucker."

"Don't call me that."

"It's your name, isn't it?"

They looked toward the door, where Moses, the lumpy Boxer, was whining and scratching to get in. He licked the glass, cocking his head to one side. Helen went and unlocked the door. Moses made his way toward the back, checking under each booth for scraps. Helen had done a good job this time and he whined some more. Looking sorrowful, he dropped down in a heap in front of the jukebox. He knew if he bided his time and wasn't too much of a bother, dinner would be forthcoming. Kenneth eyed Moses resentfully. She has more regard for him than me, he thought.

Helen retreated to the kitchen and was banging things around. "I know what's going on," she yelled out the service window.

He splashed coffee into his mug and drew on the cigarette. What the hell's goin' on, he asked himself. Then he thought, this is taking a bad turn.

"I heard 'bout it," Helen yelled.

"What, what'd you hear?"

"That you'd been down to King St. looking at the storefront where the barbecue place closed. I know what's up." He had looked at the storefront. He did have ideas about someday opening his own place, a place the two of them could have, use some of that expensive training, but under a different name. Maybe do a higher level menu, but nothing too fancy. Something people would like. They could make a decent living, together, maybe. But he wasn't going to mention that until he'd worked things out with her.

"You're gonna open a little gourmet paradise, aren't you? Poison some more good folks. Isn't that your plan?"

He stood up angry, "I told you that in private, Helen. For you to bring that up is just...ugly."

"There's an extra week's pay in your envelope," she shouted. "Take it and get out." He felt the lump in his pocket. That explained the stuffed envelope. He was completely flustered. He looked at Moses threateningly. This was not part of his plan. Should he just walk out? Slowly he took a guest check, touched the pencil to his tongue and wrote on it, then slid it cautiously through the service window. She snatched it up. A moment later it sounded like she hammered the stove with a cast-iron frying pan. Moses jumped up and whimpered. The banging seemed to strike Kenneth's chest. The coffee suddenly turned his stomach sour and he retreated to the head.

He took care of his business and then stood looking into the mirror. He was surprised to see himself crying. "I'm crying," he said to himself in the mirror. "This is just great, I'm a mess. Army Corp of Engineers ought to come clean me up like a hazardous spill." He snuffed, wiped his nose, and whispered hoarsely, "This wasn't supposed to happen." He opened the window and leaned out. "Am I going to run away now? Is that it?" he asked himself. "J-e-e-sus!" He looked out across the stubble of an empty lot at the Woolworth's. Above, the sky was purple and thrumming with stars. It was still, too early for the college kids to be carousing the streets. A vine of Honey Suckle grew up the drainpipe. He grabbed some and held it up to his nose. Such sweetness, such bitterness, he thought.

He resolved to go out and face her, and cracked the door open cautiously and peered out. Moses was sitting there looking at him, a line of clear drool falling off his jowl. She wasn't there. He went toward the kitchen and looked in the window. She was standing over the grill, a look of demonic satisfaction on her face. There were two large steaks sizzling and a wad of golden onions slithering on the side like transparent worms. A small side of chili bubbled in a blackened pot.

She flipped the steaks violently, banged two platters down, shoveled them in with the onions, some slaw, and a spoon of chili, then set them down in the window. "Table two," she barked.

"Helen," he began.

"Table two," she commanded. Kenneth picked up the plates, peering in at her, slightly comforted by her crazy expression. "You're a touch odd, Helen."

"I ain't no Normal Nancy if that's where your taste runs."

Moses followed him to the table, his wrinkled snout angled at the dishes. Helen kneed open the door, carrying two 16-ounce cans of Pabst Blue Ribbon, and a plastic bowl she held with her teeth. She set the beers on the table and the bowl under it, where Moses jarred Kenneth's knee diving in. She extracted some quarters from her apron pocket, "A-7 and B-5, C-1, and," she paused, "whatever…"

He considered this request, then went and entered the selections. He sauntered to the table and popped the beer and took a big swallow. It tasted good and cold and right. He followed it down with some more. Helen sawed a piece off her steak, heaped some onions on top, and began chewing. "God, this is good."

He sat down across from her. Thought about picking up his fork, took another gulp of beer. "Helen, I said something to you back there."

She stopped chewing, her eyes wide, surveying him. She spoke even-toned. "You didn't say nothing to me. You wrote something."

"That's true," he said, squirming in his seat. She kept looking at him, waiting. He said, "For some time now."

"For some time now, what?"

"Well," he was sweating, "The note, I mean what I wrote on the check, plus for some time now." He swallowed hard.

She pointed the tip of her steak knife a few inches away from his throat. "Don't play with me, Kenneth."

"I'm not playing...I... thought you knew," he said pitifully.

She leaned back, closed her eyes for a moment, exhaled a deep sigh, like resignation. The milkshake-smooth voice of Patti Page spilled over them. *You're sure to fall in love with Old Cape Cod*, she sang. "That's where I want to go. I've never been further north than Maryland. I want to see the ocean in Cape Cod. I like lobster stew."

"How about some swan's eggs with artichoke hearts in champagne sauce? I could make that for you, Helen."

She cocked a suspicious eye at him. "How's that, Kenneth?"

"Or maybe shrimp with ginger and leeks, angel food cake for dessert. I'd love to make that for you." He was looking squarely down in his lap.

They sat quiet for a while. A man looking in his lap. A woman with her head back against the booth, Patti Page singing with strings, *Remind you of the town where you were born.* Moses slobbering under the table. When Kenneth finally looked up he saw how soft Helen's face looked in the light. She seemed to be luxuriating, spreading out like a calm lake. He felt something push against his thigh. Annoyed, he reached under to push Moses' begging muzzle away. But it wasn't Moses. It was a foot, her foot, and he took hold of it. Tight at first, then he relaxed his grasp and began massaging it, running his index finger between each toe. He brought his hand up to his mouth, kissed his hand and touched it to her foot. Her eyes opened up to him and they looked at each other till the next song began. He was holding her ankle now with both hands, his fingertips at the bottom of her calf. "How long's it take to cook a swan's egg?" she asked.

Glenna's View

Glenna always fretted, but slyly anticipated her appointments with Dr. Burns. There were other doctors in her plan, but she needed Burns' brand of medicine, which was mainly an unorthodox approach to healing the entire woman. Dr. Rhea Burns' passion for her work was commendable, and her belief in women's power—absolute. At each visit Glenna tried to soak up some of Burns' fire, which all but sparked from her flailing silver hair, but it seemed to drain from Glenna's tired limbs as soon as she left the office. Glenna's fibroids had reached a critical mass and Burns wanted them out, "harvested," as she put it. She vigorously recommended, campaigned actually, that Glenna have a hysterectomy and alleviate the problem in one definitive procedure—to "liberate" herself.

"I know, but Roy wants another child?" she said reluctantly.

Burn's left eyebrow arched toward her hairline. "Roy? What's Roy have to do with it?"

"It's just that he's—"

"He doesn't live in your uterus," Burns snapped. She fastened her muscular surgeon's hand around Glenna's ankle, squeezed tightly and gave a firm tug, causing Glenna to spasm on the table. She usually did this at least once per visit to impart some force into Glenna's flaccid resolve. "How much more of this do you want?" She lifted her right hand; the exam glove gleamed with blood clots. "There's enough iron here for a tank." Glenna was shocked at the sight, but it was true, she couldn't stand the endless periods, the frequent urination, and the dull, sometimes shooting pain, as if a clamp were attached to her uterus.

"I know, it's just that—"

"Why would you want another child sucking your breast and a man on the other one?" Burns said, and stomped the heel of her loafer for emphasis.

Glenna was awed at her authority. She answered, her voice like thin soup without stock, "He's my husband…"

"Have you ever heard of Aisha bint Ahmad?"

"No." Glenna searched Burns' face; her sharp features, piercing hazel eyes, curved nose, all protruded into the antiseptic air without apology, yet emitted a quality of concern or love Glenna didn't have a word for. And here I am, naked under a sheet, her hand just inside of me, and now a story. Why not? Burns made it a point to tell her about courageous women who put men in their place.

"This was around 975 BC. Some snotty poet asked her to marry him. Do you know what she said?" Glenna asked if she might start getting dressed. Burns nodded and stepped behind the instrument tray, and placed her hands as she might on a lectern, forgetting to remove the soiled gloves. Usually, she'd leave Glenna to dress and wait in her office, but her concentration was focused on an earlier century, recalling the tale. "I am a lioness / and will never allow my body / to be anyone's resting place. But if I did, / I wouldn't yield to a dog – / and O! the lions I've turned away." She pounded her palms on the tray in a tribal call to arms. "You see?" Glenna strapped her shoe in place and nodded meekly.

"Think about it—freedom! I want to see you in a month, no

longer." Glenna paused to scan the latest collection of revolving photographs on her desk. There were a series of pictures of Dr. Burns with a woman, both dressed as Kaisers in full Dunkelblau, swords at their sides. Another of the two completely covered in mud at what appeared to be a concert. Yet another of them standing atop an elephant in skimpy acrobat outfits, giggling like coeds. If fact, all of the photos were of the two women. "That's Miranda," Burns pointed out, barely containing her pride. "She's named after Miranda Stuart, Chief Surgeon of the British Navy. They didn't find out she was a woman until after her death." Rhea escorted Glenna through the waiting room to the elevator. Her patients, a smart looking group of women of mixed generations and ethnicities, nodded or smiled appreciatively. Before exiting the room, she spun Glenna around. "Take a look." Glenna squinted at an indecipherable charcoal sketch of a fierce African mask. "Read it," Burns said, and nudged her closer. *Gudit Isat (Judith the Fire) who overthrew the Axumite Empire in 10th century Ethiopia.* Glenna wondered, does she expect me to subdue Manhattan and the boroughs under a flag of feminine authority by dinner time? The elevator yawned open, and Rhea took Glenna's hand firmly in both of hers, captured her eyes, and hissed, "We are women at our own commandment."

Outside Glenna shielded her face from the intruding late-June sun spotlighting her between the apartment buildings. She fished through her bag for glasses and checked for the bottle of tablets that would relieve the vice grip in her stomach, at least for a few hours at a time. The traffic sped past and maneuvered aggressively in both directions on Amsterdam Avenue. A steroid truck's horn startled her. Slightly anxious, bewildered at how Burns' elixir drained so quickly from her supplicant's cup, she realized she could not tolerate riding the train downtown to the gallery. The percussive screeching of the wheels,

110

the sweaty bodies heaving back and forth, the perusing glances—it would be too much.

Panic shot through her as she slid into the cab. She was late and the chief curator, to whom she owed indelible allegiance and the economic security for her family, would be furious, or worse, disappointed—a particular trait of his, a miserable affect he presented, that brought her to her knees. She'd promised to be there as early as possible, nine at the latest—it was now ten-thirteen.

It was to be a momentous day for The Shatz-Gabor Gallery, and the greater New York art scene as well. She swallowed three tablets with available saliva, as she'd forgotten her water bottle on the morning train, choked pathetically, and then finally got them down leaving a chalky trail down her throat. The driver pumped the Muslim Brotherhood Song through the speakers at a nerve shattering level. He stared at her suspiciously as she was certain he stared at innocent women in his village thousands of miles away. He pointed at the pulsating speakers and yelled, "Mohamed Kilany! Mohamed Kilany!" informing her of the song's composer. She wished she could tell him to fuck off, to let her out and she wouldn't pay him, to mind his own man's business. She chose not to tell him there was cream cheese in his beard from his bagel—that would have to pass for revenge. She cowered, prematurely fatigued, in the seat and allowed herself to be helplessly transported to work. *I can't even command a fucking pill to go down my throat.*

Frasch Kunslicher and her diminutive assistant had arrived, or rather, burst upon the Shatz-Gabor Gallery and made their presence excruciatingly obvious to the staff and chief curator who'd welcomed them lavishly. Frasch was the featured artist in the current issue of Art Review, described as *the* young emerging German artist of the last five years. She took umbrage with the word "emerging," and cut up and slashed all the copies of Art Review in the gallery. Glenna slipped through the towering metal doors to witness Frasch and her assistant, seated on the floor, surrounded by strips of colorful print, scissors and pocket knives. They'd cut out figures of dolls, planets, and animals. Frasch completed the exercise by stabbing her pocket knife into a pyramid of subservient fruits including a welcoming pineapple. She'd attempted to topple the hospitality table, but it was bolted to the floor. The German artist was in New York for her inaugural installation, which was to remain for six months then travel to the MOCA in Los Angeles. The Shatz-Gabor Gallery was considered to be the leading institution, other than the Museum of Modern Art, for presenting prominent young cutting-edge artists.

In preparation, Glenna had met with the chief curator to design strategies and protocols for handling the Frau Kunslicher experience. Glenna's assignment was to shadow her and her sidekick around the massive facility and warehouse and keep her out of trouble. Frasch was notorious for making scenes in galleries throughout Europe; most recently, at The White Cube in London, where she'd dumped a decanter, purportedly of goat's urine, in reaction to the YBAs, The Young British Artists, whose work she deemed derivative and factory-like. The chief curator was explicit: "Jolly them up. Take them sight-seeing if they want it. There's booze and champagne in the kitchen. Just don't let the bitch kill anyone."

This would be a difficult and ultimately defining task, which Glenna didn't quite feel up to. She'd become stressed the previous week negotiating with customs at JFK. The crate containing Frasch's sculpture had been detained by Homeland Security. Based on imaging of the contents there were concerns. The piece incorporated stainless blades, carving and hunting knifes, meat cleavers, Bic Razors, remnants of a cannon from the Austrian Empire, rifle sights, wads of piano wire, pigs' knuckles, and timing devices, placed and dried in HazMat-orange-dyed, six-foot cement columns. It was entitled Homage to Walter, in memory of Frasch's father, and required a forklift to move around. She considered the Americans' suspicious behavior to be disrespectful, an insult to the good people of Cologne, and unforgivably, to herself.

Frasch's dad, Walter, up until his death, was one of Cologne's singing butchers, a stout, red tenor who sang in the only remaining butchers' choir, a relic of the guilds, going back a hundred and ten years. The qualifications to sing were that one eat meat and sausage and that he bought it from a butcher. Walter qualified on both counts. Frasch's sculpture was in honor of her father and the sturdy men who provided animal flesh, chops, loins, organ meats, hooves, and a variety of products to the carnivores of the Cologne. One East Village critic, a grumpy vegan, found the work inimical to sustainable living, and wrote: "Kunstlicher, a proponent of Death Amphetamine, celebrates the centuries old great Teutonic picnic once again. And who cares?"

The crate finally arrived at Shatz-Gabor with a police escort. The chief curator, upon assessing the additional cost of liability insurance, determined that it would have to be enclosed in an acrylic case. Frasch reacted violently against the fact that her work would be displayed in this protective manner, muting its effect and power, as if it were something obscene, a peep show. She ranted in German and broken English and stomped through the gallery flicking lit cigarette butts on the floor. No sooner did she toss one, then her assistant, Ding Drie, placed another in her mouth and lit it with a Zippo lighter, emblazoned with Mazzi Winter Wolves. Frasch unleashed a venomous torrent upon the chief curator, who'd taken refuge in his office. She kicked his locked office door, scuffing it up with her Diba Battle Boots. He texted Glenna from the closet: "Tell her I've gone to a meeting."

Ding was fluent in English, French, and of course German. Glenna hoped to encourage Ding to mitigate Frasch's rage, to defuse the situation. "I am Frasch's everything," Ding pronounced. "Do you understand? She would kill for me." Ding whispered operatically, as if raising her voice might unleash Frasch's fury upon Glenna. Glenna nodded that she understood, taking in this petite woman, just over five feet tall in platform heels. In her one-piece, black, skintight bodysuit and spiked orange hair with waxed tips she looked like something from a Munchkin whore house. Glenna admired her superb strangeness. She was toy-like, a curious collectible, something you'd take home and cherish. Dr. Burns would have lavished approval on Ding, celebrated her as a goddess of the underworld, Persephone's ally, assisting her escape from the male dominated underworld up into the Olympian mountains to a clan of free, like-minded women. *Not timid like me.* Glenna marveled at the juxtaposition of body types—Frasch was a hulk.

Ding's demeanor, her charming peculiarity drew Glenna in; she thought that they could be friends, if that were possible given the situation. Her instinct about the quixotic realm of the art world—there were any number of aspirants in close proximity who'd be thrilled to step into her place—told her it was best to keep it professional. She dare not disappoint the chief curator again. She had friends in other galleries, assistants, handlers, consultants and resources. Latitude for those who bungled assignments shrunk rapidly. They found themselves on a one-foot diving board.

The artists themselves, unless they'd secured massive reputations, and commanded aggressive representation that held sway over gallery owners, were freelancers, many sentenced, after poor reviews, to obscurity in one season.

While a student in the School of Visual Arts, Glenna's encaustic work received praise; she was one of the youngest artists invited to participate in a prestigious show at the New York City Gallery of Encaustic Art, adding a booster rocket to her yet to be established career. The close personal interest of some of her instructors got her the name "the girl with the hot heat gun," which was an unfair characterization. She was expecting Tory and hiding under a smock. That she would be a mother in six months, likely derailing her progress, threw her into a panic. Roy was encouraging and supportive, but exacting of her time and body in the clear spring light of their relationship. That and completing six new pieces, pushing limits before the show opened, nearly resulted in a breakdown. In the company of fellow students and professors, even those interested in acquiring her work, she felt like prey—at any moment a winged adversary would snatch her to its nest and devour her orange and magenta intestines. The chief curator met Glenna at the opening and commissioned a piece. Later, he offered her a position at the Shatz-Gabor Gallery. After an anxious weekend debating the pros and cons with Roy, taking into consideration the advent of Tory, the mortgage, and health insurance, she accepted, avoiding what she sensed would be an emotional disaster if she continued to play the cutthroat New York art game at the level she was entering. She could not forgive herself the decision, but felt it was the only one she could make at that moment in their lives—it was for all of them. She would toil in the art world, work at home, which she did once or twice over the years, and support her family. There had to be some nobility in that.

Undeterred, Frasch continued to maraud through the gallery mocking the installations, inventing poses to portray her disgust, feigning hostile gestures like a WWE wrestler parading around the ring before a match. "You see that?" Ding said. Frasch had picked up a crowbar and made straight for a vast rotating globe that had offended her stylistic sensibility. "That is the face of Modern Art." She smiled like a mother regarding her prodigy.

"Oh my God." Glenna threw herself in front of the delicate globe and raised her arms in protection. It was the work of an Argentinean artist renowned for his intricate glass spheres, constructed of thousands of pieces, garnered from churches, dumps, shot out windshields, precisely assembled, adhered, then coated with a tinted transparent agent. The piece was valued at twenty-eight thousand dollars. Frasch swung the crowbar over her head threateningly, her eyes warrior crimson. Ding approached her casually, whispered something in her ear, then ran her tongue along the inside. Frasch relented, her gorilla-like torso deflating into her wool tunic. She glared at Glenna. Ding placed another cigarette in her mouth and lit it. Frasch spit on the cement floor. "Piñata." She swerved by Glenna and palmed the globe, setting it into a precarious orbit around the room. Glenna tried frantically to catch hold, but had to wait until it slowed down. "Piñata," Frasch ejected. At its apogee, it veered dangerously close to the spokes of an exposed sprinkler system. Finally, Glenna managed to receive it gently in her arms and bring it to rest. She was sweating, horrified, exhausted, and her fibroids had organized into a garage band.

Shaking, her mouth dry from anxious exertion, she plucked a mutilated pear from the hospitality table. They were gone. She found them in a preparation room where two technicians were backing cautiously out a side exit, carefully supporting a huge painting they'd been restoring. They glanced nervously at Glenna and she waved them off. But Frasch seemed to be neutralized for the moment. Ding had her stretched out on a divan and was massaging her feet and singing to her, a German lullaby. Glenna leaned against the door frame mesmerized, taking in the soothing melody. Frasch had huge, thin feet like turnips, knurled and misshapen. Ding cupped her hand and poured out pink lotion and continued to massage Frasch's feet. The big woman grunted and groaned with pleasure. Ding ended the song and began another. Frasch hummed along, her warrior's face dropped away for that of a contented but slightly frightened child. Glenna became uneasy, embarrassed to be witnessing something so personal, *so utterly human*, she thought. She felt that she had never seen someone as beautiful as Ding; her dedication, her singular devotion to Frasch was inspiring. Tears filled her eyes; she ached for something like this in her life, though she knew that Roy would, if need be, sacrifice himself for her and Tory. Why couldn't she reenter his gravitational pull? Where else could she go? A momentary insight suggested that it had something do with the schizophrenic pieces of her abandoned career as an artist, the high-pressure stakes of the gallery, and her barely manageable role as a suburban wife and mother. This thought provided her with several breaths without her chest tightening.

Frasch was fast asleep; from her gaping mouth issued a combative snoring that reflected off the cavernous ceiling of the prep room. Ding retreated, tiptoeing out. Glenna offered some espresso and biscotti. Ding smiled graciously—something had softened in her—and followed Glenna up twenty-two wrought iron steps with ten-foot balusters, which brought them to the mezzanine. They sat catty-corner on huge interactive lounge chairs that intermittently emitted mild electrical current through the cushions, to remind the viewer that they were sitting on art. The vast tinted rectangular windows tilted open, allowing the soft wind from the river to caress the women. Several barges, a tug boat, and the Circle Line ferry churned south toward the lower Manhattan seaport.

Ding looked tiny in the oversized lounge, like a kewpie doll waiting to be snatched off a shelf at a fair. Glenna could hardly take her eyes off her. She watched her gaze at her cell phone, then smile. "Oh, that's the place."

"What place?" Glenna asked.

"Golden Ladies on Little West 12th. Frasch wants to check it out later."

"Oh, of course. I think it's actually not far from your hotel."

Ding looked at her earnestly, kindly. "You should come—it's just women." There was a devious tone to the invitation.

Glenna was shocked to hear this after having gone several rounds with Frasch. "I don't think Frasch would—"

"Frasch thinks you're very good—professional. The curator is a pussy—she said that." Ding leaned forward. "Really, she said that." A warm IV of gratification flowed into Glenna's limbs, emboldening her. After all, she had dealt with Frasch, as much as one could deal with Frasch. She'd have a merit badge to show Dr. Burns next time.

"So come. We can see what Golden Ladies is about."

Glenna knew what it was about. "Oh, I've got a toddler at home—"

"You're married, of course!"

"Yes, eight years." Glenna felt that she was melting into the chair. What extraordinary power or magnetism was it that Ding asserted over her? Ding reminded her of something she'd known about or believed in long ago. Without explanation or cause, Glenna felt there was something truly "magical" about this miniature woman. "But you two will have fun," she offered, after the fact.

Ding's response was introspective. She said a long, thoughtful, "Yeeees. Frasch likes to dance…but sometimes…."

"What?" Glenna pushed herself up; she was sinking into the chair. "Well, she gets a bit… Darwinian at times, you know?" Glenna stared blankly. "But only if she's challenged," Ding added quickly. The women sipped their espresso, balanced in the golden moment, enjoying each others company.

"Do you mind if I ask you…."

"Yes," she laughed, "ask me."

"Your name, Ding—"

"Ding Drie," she cackled. Frasch gave me that. Your American, Dr. Seuss—The Cat in the Hat. He wrote about Thing One and Thing Two, those bad things. Well," she winked, "I am Thing Three." Glenna tilted her head, toward meaning. "Because there is nothing like me. Things One and Two," she said with appetizing wickedness, "are nothing like me." Her smile pierced Glenna's chest like a sugared arrow head.

Before she checked herself, Glenna said, with full adoration, "No, there is nothing else like you." They shared another private moment, holding each other with their eyes.

"But why is she so angry? There are thousands who'd love to be in her place." *I'd have loved it*, Glenna thought.

Ding winced, and looked off at the river.

"I'm so sorry. I shouldn't—"

"Her mother," Ding pronounced corrosively. "Irena was too good to be married to a butcher; she despised both of them."

"Both?"

"Yes, Frasch as well. She hated him for who he was, a tradesman, just a butcher. And Frasch…she saw what Frasch would become and hated her for that."

"But why? Wouldn't she be proud of her, an internationally celebrated artist?"

"Because she was nothing, schist! Irena was arrogant; her life one conceit after another. Her talent was hating. Frasch was challenging—she was making things when she was four. Irena…beat her."

"I didn't know," Glenna replied, hollow and aching for this woman who'd intimidated her.

"No one knew—Walter didn't know. But…"

"But what?"

"Scars," she repeated softly, "scars, there are scars."

"Diiiing!" The scream caused the women to evacuate the lounges as if the art chairs had short-circuited under them. "Diiiing!" Frasch staggered below in the lobby, panicked. She swung blindly into a decorative marble gazelle suspended from an elevator cable. "Ding!"

"She needs me." Ding was down the stairs in a moment. Glenna stood by the railing and watched as Ding spoke softly, soothingly, to her, reaching up to touch her face, which appeared to have suffered a gash from the gazelle's horn. Frasch cried, "Ding, Ding." She coaxed her back into the anteroom, singing the lullaby she'd calmed her with earlier. Glenna lingered above the scene. Ding shot her a glance before they disappeared into the room, her playful elfin face turned ashen with care.

As usual, Glenna was running late, panting like a sled dog. Fortunately, the Mount Kisco train was also late and crowded. She only then remembered the fundraiser as she boarded and collapsed into her seat replaying the astonishing events of the day. She observed the other women in the car. *Are any of you as desperate as me?* Sensing the error it would be to not show up at the fundraiser, she dutifully resolved to go. Her cell hummed with a new text: *Remember, you are a woman at your own commandment. R. Burns.* She smiled at the screen. *If only I were.* The unpleasant tinge in her uterus caught her off guard but tipped the scale. *You fibroid bastards are going.*

Roy had gotten there earlier and was wedged tight in a half circle with baby Tory on his lap. The child clutched a heel of multi-grain bread and rubbed it over her cheeks making a crumby mess. Glenna stood in the vestibule eyeing the group warily, so markedly different from those she spent her days with: artists, agents, reviewers, the brilliant and the bizarre who toured through the gallery studying the art like ancient manuscripts. And of course the chief curator, whose neurotic expertise put the Shatz-Gabor on the map, and whose expanded ego rivaled the Hindenburg. Here were her neighbors, the committee, intent on the next fundraiser, the new room at the birthing center, the wooden play park. It didn't matter which one anymore. It was the same tired effort, the artificial enthusiasm, the spinning brass cog of community service irritating her skin until it felt like her flesh would burst open and stain the sacred fabric of her community. She could feel bile rising in her esophagus. Why hadn't she skipped this one? She could have taken a cab home from the station instead of going to the restaurant, drawn a hot bath and poured a glass of wine, which she'd recently begun drinking from tumblers, a dry California white with a splash of seltzer and a lemon wedge.

Baby Tory spotted her and raised her arms to Mommy. Roy handed her clumsily over the dishes and carafes. Tory was a plump toddler and Glenna strained not to drop her in the guacamole platter as she sank into a chair. Tory latched on to Glenna and pushed her face into her chest, leaving a wheat stain over her nipple on the fine silk blouse Roy had given her for her birthday. A waitress set down a glass of wine. Distributing Tory's weight across her abdomen, Glenna drained half of it at once and hoped no one noticed how much she wanted a drink. Tory continued to work her over, grabbing at her tit, which was progressing toward misery. None of the others noticed the struggle, as they were so earnest in their planning. She swallowed bitter emotion with wine. Tory persisted, her strawberry ringlets flailing as Glenna reminded her that big girls didn't nurse anymore, at least not in public in front of vampires.

Roy offered a furtive wave from across the table, resigned and apologetic like a drowning man. Aware of the eyes around the table, she let her mouth form a tight smile. How she had come to detest him? In eight short years she'd progressed from mad love to loathing. To: *we live in this house together. We share this child.* The trouble began with Tory's birth. Roy seemed distracted, not a hundred percent present. What followed was a nightmarish month of postpartum depression that triggered something dark in her, that gave her a glimpse into an abyss she'd rather not have seen. And Roy had become the Minotaur roaming around the labyrinth, hungry for her flesh, ever so needy. His demands for sex, even before the stitches fully healed, and Tory's relentless nursing brought her close to a breakdown. She thought at the time: *they are cannibalizing me. Soon there will be nothing left.* She glanced at Roy; he greedily ate tortilla chips—a thin line of salsa coursed down his chin. *My blood.*

"Easy on that wine, girl." Warm hands massaged her shoulders. The dreadful Felecia had appeared from behind. Glenna felt the woman's oppressive body heat engulfing her as she leaned into the chair, pressing her bulbous stomach against Glenna's back. Felecia must have been in the bathroom. She caressed Baby Tory's ringlets. *Don't touch my child, you bitch.*

"She was crying for you before, poor thing," Felicia reported, sliding in next to Glenna, so close she could feel her breath. "Poor thing," she repeated, widening her eyes. The widened eyes, Glenna knew, were for emphasis and mainly disapproval. Glenna's hatred of Felicia was thorough and undiluted. *You fucking bitch.*

Felecia made fundraising, and all aspects of social life, a competitive event. She could ice cupcakes like a machine, fill out agendas, and organize committees simultaneously. "You're probably too fried for this," she suggested coyly, tilting her head toward the group. "I've been on this for a month—I'll cover you." Felicia took every opportunity to let Glenna know that she wasn't up to the task at hand, and that she wasn't the mother she should be. Felicia continued to caress Tory's ringlets.

Glenna shifted Tory to the side. "She's fine, thank you." Tory seemed content for the moment to lay with her head back and watch the activity in the room upside down. She felt wet. Glenna instinctively sniffed her hand, then leaned down and took in the sweet, earthy smell mixed with bread and rosemary diaper cream. She studied the little face, the red mouth, the plump cheeks. The familiar wall of love, so distant of late, crashed over her, a protective wave that swept her and Tory in a glassy sea to a place without contention and hardship, a place where committees didn't exist.

The second glass of wine lessened the grip in her stomach and she allowed herself to float calmly just an inch above the table and avid chatter. Felicia was in the throes of a succinct statement, chopping the air in front of her with blunt fingers. Glenna didn't listen, but watched her chin and massive breasts heave with effort. Her soft white body striving for dominance. Glenna remembered a moment at the end of a Tequila party, Felecia sprawled drunk on a sofa. She had begged Glenna to sit by her. There was something provocative and helpless about the request, Felecia's dress hiked above her thighs, which widened like past-dated mushrooms, a purposeful vulnerability. Glenna pretended she didn't hear and collected glasses and plates.

Roy drove through the village, sullen and depressed. The small shops that had given them so much pleasure, riding Tory on the bike seat, shopping basket bouncing on the handle bars. The colorful striped beach chairs and umbrellas in front of the hardware store promising a bright season of bracing waves and Tory's sparkling laughter. But as he thought about their timeshare on the Cape it seemed to be so far in the past as to be irretrievable. He eyed Glenna, silhouetted by the street lights, the unusually warm late-June air steaming in on their domestic anarchy. He checked Tory in the rear view mirror. She'd howled since they'd left the restaurant against the constraint of her child's seat, her ringlets collapsed, limp on her forehead. Her mouth a small circle of complaint that couldn't articulate or resolve her parents struggle. She could only cry. He loved her so, but didn't know if he could ultimately carry her safely over the treacherous, uncharted territory their marriage had become. His wife was evolving into someone else that didn't require his participation, in fact, forbade it, which made him hate her and desire her more than ever.

Roy turned at the railroad crossing and headed up circuitous Swan's Hill above the commuter town, then west into open country. The last half-mile of plowed fields, blacker than the sky, pulsated with swarms of fireflies, undulating curtains of them, circling, spiraling like a circus midway. The smell of rich, freshly-plowed soil streamed into the windows, reminding them that soon there would be produce—organic fruits and vegetables for Tory, ponies and rabbits for her to pet.

A solid stand of welcoming pines guarded their driveway. The mailbox, which their carrier preferred to leave open, appeared to be inhabited with bills, art magazines, and catalogues. As there was no rain forecast, and a subtle, unarticulated tension in the car told him that they should get into the house, Roy decided it could wait until morning. The farm house, a renovated prize, circa 1890, the repository of their dreams, rose up before them.

He noticed Glenna, as always, peering at the second story where her special light glowed, a soft expanding orb in their bedroom window that seemed to change aspects of hue and intensity as one observed it. Roy always left it burning, so she'd see it first thing when she arrived home, an eternal light of hope for what had once been so beach-noon-bright between them.

Glenna's light was the final touch to one of Roy's stay-at-home-dad projects—undertaken, as usual, for her. It was a Crystal Burst Possini Mini Pendant light he'd found in the city. It was mounted to the crown molding in the window. The dimmer switch was calibrated to deliver luminance ranging from a pale yellow night-light to a brilliant ballroom chandelier. The house featured deep-set windows, with ample room to construct a generous thick foam rubber seat upholstered in silk fuchsia material he'd found in Chinatown. Both sides of the window casing were upholstered with the same material running up seven feet to the top, creating a virtual habitat in a window, soft and luxurious.

Roy would awaken at odd hours and see Glenna there, curled up reading, sipping wine, or texting someone. Mostly, she stared out at the sloping stubble field that dropped and spread itself into the woods, above which, on most nights, a mob of stars raised torches. Seated, leaning back—Roy had upholstered the sides as well—her book open, sometimes just as a prop, her glass of wine glinting, she allowed herself to inhabit this artifice of comfort. He had created a place of refuge for her, but he wasn't allowed inside. The receding moments of their passion, like fireflies, had burst through the air, left a faint brief trail, then died in the impersonal darkness that divides each of us from our sacred dreams.

Exhausted from her fussing, Tory was asleep in his arms as Roy carried her upstairs and put her in her bed. Her room adjoined theirs so there was no need for an intercom—they could hear her slightest stir. Roy knew that Glenna had recently been fighting a resistant strain of insomnia and was monitoring Tory above her usual pointed mothering skills. Without a word, she lay down beside her child as if to sleep the rest of the night there. The house was unnaturally quiet; the overhead fan wobbled obediently, but seemed to have gone mute. Roy shifted his weight against the dresser, studying his family. "Glenna…"

"What?" Her reply was wrapped in aluminum foil, metallic, and dismissive.

"We need to talk." He moved closer.

"Tomorrow."

"You'll be at the gallery."

"That's what pays for…this…"

"This what? This house? The pool? This what, Glenna?" He caught himself with fists clenched against his thighs. "This fine life we have?"

"I don't know what." She was crying now, quietly so as not to wake Tory.

He stood scanning her form under the sheet, once so accessible to him. He wanted to drag her from the room, pin her against the wall, and force her to speak, to tell him about the unreported collapsed bridge between them. Where were the sirens and flashing lights to attend the disaster—there were no rescue vehicles in sight, and worse, no acknowledgement, no forthcoming investigation to determine the cause of the structure's failure. It had simply crashed between them, without comment or concern on her part.

His voice came in a harsh whisper: "Where are you? Where the fuck are you, Glenna?" He waited as his options like defeated ghosts fled from the room. She continued to sob. "Who the fuck are you crying for?"

Finally, he retreated, slunk out to the patio, rolled a cigarette, and inhaled deeply as if solace might be one of the ingredients in the vaporous smoke exhaled from his mouth. A half moon hoisted itself hesitantly over the pines lining the road. The beginnings of pinkish clouds tangled in the East, and the Western sky spread a black canvas for starlight to prick holes in to telegraph the earth. The pool filter hummed agreeably, then sputtered ominously for a few seconds, prompting Roy to investigate what had been, since designed and installed by The Very Cool Pool Guys, a sinking repository of cash. The cost of chemicals and maintenance alone, though Roy had become a decent technician, were steep. But Tory spent joyous hours on her Little Mermaid floater with Daddy—he wouldn't deny her that. Not for as long as he could hold on to this, whatever this was.

Glenna's cell startled her awake, disoriented, gasping, sickened by a grotesque visage that refused to recede from her mind's eye. They were on their honeymoon eight years ago in Hawaii. Roy had convinced her that they should spend two nights on Niihau Island, arid with rugged cliffs, also known as The Forbidden Isle. He'd gone to great lengths to get permission through a college friend who'd gotten a grant from the State Seabird Sanctuary to study the Hawaiian lobelioids, an endangered species. It was the last night of their honeymoon and they were treated to a luau. The islanders prepared the feast; the guests in colorful leis enjoyed fruit cocktails. In the dream, she and Roy walked along a path of carved shells and paper lanterns. As they got closer, Glenna realized that the guests were the same folks who'd been at the fundraiser earlier in the evening, including Felicia, stuffed in a flowered muumuu, and drooling from her painted mouth. Unsettled, she continued with Roy toward the fire pit where the islanders had prepared a massive kalua pig, which was to be the main course served with poi, other vegetable and fruits. The native chef attending the roast stabbed a long wooden fork into it and offered Glenna the first morsel. She looked into the pit and saw that the pig's face and body were hers, horribly disfigured, the snout opened in a tormented scream, hair burnt to the scalp, body blistered and crackling. She screamed, "Roy," but he'd joined the guests moving toward the smoke and seared flesh to consume his share of the feast.

Glenna was on her hands and knees now, turned away from Tory so the baby wouldn't hear her gasps. After a series of yoga breaths and several cat and dog asanas, she finally began to recover. Steadying herself on Tory's Wizard of Oz wardrobe she stood, waited some moments, then pulled a bottle from the pile of shoes in the closet and poured wine into the toothbrush glass from the bathroom. She gulped it like she did water after her Willpower and Grace class. Calmed, she leaned over and brushed Tory's hair with her lips. She remembered the call and tried to decipher the unfamiliar number. She dialed.

"Frasch has been arrested."

"Ding? What happened?"

"They've arrested her," she said frantically. "We are in the police station. They are very rude, these American policemen."

"My god, what happened?" There was muffled yelling in the background. She heard some of Frasch's broken English, "Bastard fascist....bastard...."

"They've handcuffed her like an animal." Glenna remembered Ding's comment that sometimes Frasch went "Darwinian."

"Ding, what happened?"

Ding was screaming, "Stop, stop, you bastard! They have a Taser."

"Let me talk. Ding, let me talk to them."

"They're saying to shut the fuck up."

"Ding, tell her to be quiet—sing to her. You know what to do."

"They won't let me near her."

"Who is this?" It was a man's voice, an unfriendly voice.

"I'm Glenna Reardon of the Shatz-Gabor Gallery. The woman you are abusing is an important international artist. The German Consulate is on notice and responding. Do you hear me?"

"She's under arrest, charged with assault and resisting arrest. She also injured two of my officers."

"Who the hell is this?" She was surprised by the sudden authority in her voice. "I said, who is this?"

"This is Lt. Frank Silver. Who the hell are you?"

She lowered her tone, shifting into a snake voice, and spoke quietly. "Listen to me, Frank, Representative Beckenbauer is on the board of the Shatz-Gabor. He lives about three blocks from the precinct." It struck her now that the endless openings, fundraisers, and cocktail parties were paying off.

"I've met Beckenbauer, so what?"

"And now you've met his niece. She's in your cell." She turned away from the phone and palmed her forehead. Where am I getting this from? She felt giddy, but pumped up in a way she wasn't used to.

"Yeah?" but with less conviction.

She took a shot in the dark. "Frank, aren't you approaching retirement age?" She bit her lip, hoping. There was a long pause.

"Are you threatening me?"

She almost laughed into the phone. "I have a call coming in from the German Consulate; stay on the line," she commanded. She signed off, suddenly remembering that she did know someone at the German Consulate, Hans. He'd been helpful and over-friendly trying to get Frasch's sculpture released from JFK customs. She'd have him put in a call to Lt. Silver when she was done with him. "Silver, are you there?" This time no title.

"This woman here, this little one—she's put her to sleep."

Glenna's mind was a magnet, picking up every useful shard spinning in the air around her. "She will need medical attention within an hour." She waited, nothing.   "Silver, do yourself a favor. I have a call in to Beckenbauer about his niece. She's fragile; he knows her condition." She waited, then added deliberately, "He's very much a family man."

She hung up and pressed her hand against her mouth. She could probably be arrested for this. She's never done anything like it before, put herself so forward. It was too late to call Burns and crow a bit; she'd only get her service. She decided to make an appointment right away.

Glenna's risky playacting may have helped, but didn't ultimately turn the key for Frasch. The woman she'd injured at the Golden Ladies showed up at the precinct and dropped the charges. Despite her bruises—Frasch had body-slammed her on the dance floor—they were after all sisters. The charges dropped, and a subtle but pervasive fog of homophobia leaching out of the crowd of blue uniforms, Ding and Frasch walked out into the Manhattan night.

She'd get the rest of the story from Ding the following morning. A terribly aggressive woman broke in between them to dance with Frasch. She danced with her once, but at the end of the night the woman demanded that Frasch dump Ding and come home with her. Frasch had been drinking American beer, which annoyed her from the beginning of the evening. The woman persisted that Frasch go home with her instead of "that fucking little elf over there." The rest was post Darwinian Theory, followed by a house call from New York's finest.

Exhausted, she dropped her clothes and threw Roy's shirt around her bare shoulders. She climbed into her window seat and stared at the cascade of fireflies—she'd never seen so many. She'd watched them swarming the last few nights, and now she was remembering her grandmother's story. She was only two years older than Tory, running through the backyard, catching the insects on her arms and legs. Grandma told her that June was the month of magic, when the fireflies were out. It was the time to make wishes. The fireflies carried your wishes in their flickering lanterns to a special place where they would be granted by a fairy princess. Glenna dabbed at her eyes, forming the incantation with just her lips: *June is the month of magic.* The incandescent light of the clumsy insects crushed her with nostalgia; but she wanted to feel them again on her skin. She stood on the cushion, felt the shirt slide off, and pushed open the window, extending a hand on either side of the frame to keep balance. The first one bumped against her cheek, the another at her shoulder. Soon they landed on her breasts, stomach, and legs. The bobbing and crawling tickled her flesh. She glanced around to see the room populated, blinking, and glowing like a fairy land. *Now if I could just fly….*

Roy stumbled over the garden hose, caught himself, then paused to urinate in the Butterfly Bush. He'd planted it when Tory was born. He wiped his forehead with his t-shirt sleeve against the stifling humidity, a preview of a steamy July that was almost upon them. The air was thick with fireflies; one bounced off his eye and maneuvered into his hair. He blew one off his lower lip. As he approached the pool he heard the frogs sluicing about and croaking plaintively at their predicament: trapped and trying to escape before exhaustion and chlorine finished them off. The pool's electronics hummed a bass accompaniment under their croaking. A bloated band of them had managed to board Tory's Little Mermaid Floater, bulgy-eyed explorers peering out in search of a more hospitable land. The FrogLog had detached from the side of the pool, stranding the victims without an exit. He coaxed it over with the aluminum pole and reattached it. The explorers abandoned their raft, dove in and went to it. They hopped up the FrogLog clumsily, then onto the warm flagstone, making for the safety of the ferns. Once there, they made their way through fence links, and headed toward the fresh water creek below the treeline, to final safety. Roy wondered what enticed them to the pool in the first place. One landed on his foot and sat there several moments. Dazed, it slid off and disappeared with others in to the ferns. "Go on, you lucky bastard. Get out of here."

He felt mildly virtuous about the frog rescue but, still depressed, made his way up the extensive sloping lawn, reminded of how efficiently humidity coaxed grass up from the soil. He stopped to scan his surroundings. The Nasturtiums and Geraniums waved pompoms at him from the sidelines as if he were a victorious quarterback. *But I am not victorious*, he thought. *In this house I am just a water boy*. It seemed that all the fireflies on the Eastern seaboard had converged on his property for some unannounced convocation. Beetles really, he remembered, but named for the light organs under their abdomens that take in oxygen and combine it with…*what was it*—he'd just read the article in National Geographic.

He had time to catch up on reading at the library on Thursdays during story hour, Tory favorite time. She and her little contemporaries got to scope each other out, have a few laughs, learn about sharing, and practice for their eventual adult roles of dominance and submission. With any luck, she'd be raised by two parents who'd set her on a course to accept what grace and beauty there was to be had in this world. And if they were very lucky she'd learn to create her own.

The air was thick with them now, glossing over trees and grasses like polished stone. Luciferin—that was the word. Oxygen mixes with luciferin and produces light with almost no heat. Light with almost no heat…what passed for relationship between him and Glenna. He decided to roll another cigarette and witness more of the spectacle—when would this happen again? Soon enough he'd scrutinize Glenna's sleeping body, a nightly vigil, then he'd lie down on the cot next to Tory's bed. He liked to see her eyes open on the new day. It would be morning soon and she was a dependable little rooster.

When he reached the patio, out of habit, he raised his eyes and saw Glenna as if she were floating in the open window. A searing jolt switched his lungs into high capacity. She wasn't about to jump, was she? Standing on the seat, she commanded about three-quarters of the window's height. She leaned forward into the frame like a ship's figurehead, her slender arms stretched outward, her cascading autumn hair fallen over her shoulders, and her full nursing breasts thrust forward, challenging the night. A multitude of fireflies illuminated her naked body, casting a resplendent glow upon her flesh. Her torso, stomach, hips, and the indecipherable patch between her legs scintillated. Roy thought she was looking up at the moon, but her eyes were closed.

The Crystal Burst Possini added to the composition of color, mixing in the pulsing hue of the fireflies. The various hues and a dim offering of moonlight resulted in a subtle display of shadow and light over her body. It was as if dabs of paint, Charvin fine oils, Cezanne's preference, had been applied to her by a master's brush—as if she'd been recreated and suspended in the frame, an ephemeral exhibition.

Transfixed, he stared at this strange apparition, his wife, Tory's mother, overwhelmed and captivated by her beauty—a paralyzing image. It had happened before, with less intensity, when he'd stumbled upon a work in an obscure alcove in a museum. If there is genius in the production, there is always a subtle exchange between the viewer and the object—appreciation and devastation exact fair coin from the observer.

It was several minutes before Glenna cast her eyes downward, her head tilted toward her shoulder. Again, Roy's breath froze in his throat; his heart sped like a treadmill. She stood expressionless, somehow conclusive within herself, a martyred voluptuous saint, but vibrant as anything the universe could offer. They watched each other for long moments, without expression or gesture. Each firefly, Roy recalled from the article, had a blinking signal that helped it find a potential mate with gifts of nectar and pollen. He recalled as well that the blinking was a warning to predators that this morsel would have a sickening taste—protection. Which was it? Now she was slowly sliding her hands along the frame, kneeling, then backing away, withdrawing from view. Rigid, a sentinel on extreme watch, he waited, his t-shirt soaked, his vision slightly blurred. Presently, the light switched off and she returned to the window, this time regarding him below, arms at her sides, another sentinel on watch. Time, and then more time, and what seemed like all of time, present and past, each continued to view the other through a rising veil of fire-flies, precious green and white pearls tumbling in the air between them.

Story for a Cold Night

Ron says to Harry, "This guy inherits an island from some benign son-of-a-bitch."

Harry presses his palms on the cement, adjusting his butt against a piece of insulation, his daybed. He watches forms passing in the street, the dusky light slanting. "Must be six by now."

Ron hikes his sleeve. He wears the watch just under his elbow. "5:22." He checks the temperature, 41 degrees, quartz accuracy.

Harry says, "I need a bottle."

"The island has fruit trees, lots of them. Good fishing, a fresh-water spring. And birds, birds of all colors like oil paints. Heh, maybe they drip when they fly. The man should have been a bird," Ron adds.

"Gonna freeze tonight." Harry studies the pre-rush hour traffic.

Ron gropes in his parka. "I had a cigarette." He finds it, most of the tobacco slipped from the paper, no matches.

"I'll get Fred; he owes me." Harry's face is gray; the stubble on his neck is white. He looks as though he's been submerged for a while. "Fred'll be around."

Ron pinches the end of the cigarette to preserve the remaining tobacco. He runs his tongue along his teeth. It pleases him that his teeth are still well rooted in his mouth. Even the caps are holding up.

Most of his colleagues have lost their teeth by now. They say that the dentine breaks down in about six years on a wine diet. Not true for him. "So, there's a condition. The guy can't take anybody with him. And once he's there, he stays. No visits home, no nothing."

Harry gets to his knees, palms the wall for support, fiberglass and fluff stuck to his coat. He waits for dizziness to pass. "Go to the lot. We can't have no fire here."

Ron considers this and says, "So what do you think the guy does? He gives up his life, as he knows it. Kids, wife, spa, a sweet little Mercedes. He tosses everything and inherits an island where he has to live alone. Now, why would he do that?"

Harry starts down the alley, swaying, "You stay, you die."

Ron observes Harry's unsteady retreat. The sudden sweet smell of roasting chestnuts wafts through the air. He remembers himself jogging across a park, a younger man, the smell of chestnuts, then heading down for the train home. Suddenly it's snowing. He looks up at the network of fire escapes. The head of a shaggy dust mop stabs the air. "It's not snow," he says. He picks a dust mote from his beard.

Ron takes a piece of Harry's insulation and wedges it between his back and a Dumpster he's leaning on. He slides his legs up under the parka. A pigeon rests unsteadily on a discarded box, bloated, one eye whited out. "You want to hear?" The pigeon doesn't answer. "Perversity. The man is perverse, the famous death wish. Accepting a life of isolation accelerates the process. Just the ticket for the man who has everything. I don't envy this guy."

Button announces his entrance shaking a cookie tin, filled with buttons. His army coat displays the patches and medals from several campaigns in Nam. It's tied off with a thin gold chain. Hanging from the chain is a cup, spoon, and some high-up sneakers. "If a billy goat cross your lawn, that your billy goat."

Ron scans Button's pockets for a bottle. "If a billy goat *don't* cross your lawn…" Button's eyes widen, mouth turns down, then up in a smile.

"Button, where ya been?" Ron asks. "You hear about the guy who inherited an island? Thing is, he has to stay there alone the rest of his life. Sound good?"

Button sits next to Ron, crosses his legs. Ron notices two pink combs in his kinky hair, new items. "Drinkie?"

"Drink would be very good, Button." Button produces a large half-gallon from his backpack. Ron swallows fast. "Hmm, strawberry, sign of life." He takes another swallow. "You know, there's strawberries on the island, all kinds a fruit. The guy builds himself a raft, paddles out to a coral reef for some spear fishing. Never taught his kid how to fish. At night, he's got a fire, an occasional iguana cutlet. Soon he's looking for ways to kill himself permanent."

Button takes a sip of the wine, offers it again. "You are a very generous man, Button." Button pulls some cigarillos and a lighter from his sock. Ron leans forward. The cigarette paper burns to ash leaving a red glow of tobacco, enough for several deep drags. Ron leans back, eyes closed. The wine moves through him, the warm smoke in his chest. He exhales, satisfied. Smoke pours from Button's wide nostrils like a Chinese demon.

"One night, after a day of depression about his family, the guy swims way out until he's exhausted. He lets go, starts to sink, panics, thrashes back to shore. He lies there, terrified self-pity. The stars offer no solace. The moonlight is disinterested in his dilemma. So, what's he do? He asks God to kill him. God's not around. But the whore is, hope. He starts to hope. Tomorrow he will build a big fire, send smoke signals. He'll write in the sand: H-E-L-P. A trawler, an airplane will spot him."

Button lights another cigarillo, drags on it, hands it to Ron. "Billy goat talkin' shit tonight." They smoke quietly for a few moments.

Ron regards Button's PFC stripe. He traces the long scar from Button's ear to his collarbone.

"There's more," Ron says.

Button says, "Man gets hisself a mermaid, take care a him."

"A bird," Ron tells Button. "He falls in love with a Great Blue Heron."

"Shit," Button looks disgusted.

"Not that kind of love, friendship. The heron befriends the man, hangs out with him in the lagoon. Tosses him some fish. Of course, the man doesn't know anything about friendship. He has plans for the heron. But he gets used to it. When the bird flies in from the ocean, it circles the man, majestically, saluting him with its powerful wings. The bird flies low along the shore. He can touch its wings as it passes. It looks like it was painted by Van Gogh, flying art. But he doesn't know what it is." Ron leans forward and extends his hand for the bottle.

Button cautions, "Freezin' tonight." He relinquishes the bottle, and adds, "Goin' to the lot?"

Ron nods, shakes off a chill. "You see, Button, that's the problem. The man doesn't know what the bird is. The problem is knowing what things are."

"Wanna get me a mermaid girl."

"You will," Ron assures. "Well, after a while the man forgets some of his troubles. He's not so lonely. One night, he comes in from the ocean, naked as God made him, trim and tan from healthy living. Throws himself down on the sand. He's talking to the bird, looking at the moon, thinking how it seems to get brighter each night. The next thing he knows, it's lights out. Two quick jabs of that sharp beak, the bird skewers his eyes out."

"Fuck that. They s'posed to be friends?"

The bell tolls from the Episcopal Church, where the evening star takes residence in a clear sky. A blast of cold air sweeps through the alley. Ron pulls another piece of Harry's insulation over his legs and chest. "They are friends. The bird just accelerated the man's process. He rendered the man physically what he already was mentally. So he runs off terrified, banging into trees, stumbling over rocks. He can't fish now or find food. You know what's on his mind? Revenge. He wants to kill that bird, break its long feathery neck. The irony is the man is dead, stumbling dead, but he wants his revenge."

"The man's blind. He ain't doin' no ironin'."

They drink. Ron coughs some back up. The cold has entered his bones. "It's a different kind of ironing."

Button is up, dancing foot to foot. He pries open the cookie tin and stirs with a long, black finger. He tosses Ron a button, red with speckles, maybe from a woman's blouse. "Your luck," Button says, as usual. The wind carries it off target. Ron gropes for it, squeezes it in his palm.

Button starts off. "Don't you want to hear the rest?" Ron asks.

"See a man 'bout a piece a steak. Get yourself to the lot."

Ron looks around. Windows are lit up now, warm blocks of light thrust out into the dark, the smell of cooking, urine, and rotting trash. A chilling gust of wind lifts newspapers up the vertical shaft of the alley like clumsy angels with newsprint wings. He checks his watch, 6:38, and then the temperature, 35° F. "Shit." The pigeon is still where it was, the faded eye closed now. It trembles, claws the cardboard.

"I don't know what I can do for you," Ron tells the pigeon, "and vice versa." He pulls at the insulation but it comes part. "So, the guy gets hungry. He scrounges for food and water. Fortunately, he knew the island somewhat when he was sighted."

Ron sighs, leans back, and closes his eyes. The story goes on in his head; a word or two escapes his mouth as if he's chanting. *He gets good at catching crabs, crawls along the beach tapping the sand until he finds a hole, digs them out. Whatever falls from the trees, his. Each day he makes a bang-up pilgrimage to the spring, tripping on roots, his flesh welted from thorns and branches. He gets better at blind man skills, sounds and smells. At night he sleeps badly in his hut, listening for wings in case it comes back to finish the job.*

Ron leans forward and pinches his toes, numb. His legs, getting numb. He doesn't think he can get up. The pigeon looks frozen in place. *He spends his days sitting on the beach, waiting, listening, the sun browning him; his eye sockets baked dry. He listens, ships' horn, helicopter blades, no luck. Just the pounding of the waves and the sun, hotter each day as if the island has drifted below the equator.*

The pigeon stirs. "I've decided to call you Gray Bird Dying," he tells it. "I'm not feeling too well myself. So one day, the heron returns. Hovers over him, beating its wings. At first, he runs from it, covering his head with his arms. The bird follows him. Finally, he stops, reaches out, and feels the familiar softness. He rests his hand on the bird's back, strokes it a few times, slides his arm around its side, stroking, working his way up to its neck. The bird stays perfectly still. He takes it in both hands, lifts it off the ground, and strangles it. His arms stretched out, he squeezes its neck as hard as he can. The bird doesn't fight; it goes limp. The man releases his grip, is suddenly overcome with grief and a hundred other things he doesn't know anything about. He buries his face in the bird's feathers, listens for a heartbeat. Nothing. He stands it up in shallow water, hoping instinct will return to its limbs. Its spindly legs collapse in the waves. He douses water over its head, but its head hangs, feathers matted to its breast. Now the man has had his revenge."

The pigeon stirs, fanning a bent wing. Its claws are bloodless pieces of notched wire, a white paste formed on its beak. Gradually, it's rolling off the horizon. Ron wonders, should he, if he can, hold it in his arms, or give it a stomp, save it the misery. Ron hasn't moved since last night, and he can't now. He thinks he'll try to crawl out to the sidewalk.

"OK," Ron says, "We're about there. This time the man plays with his old fishing spear, wedges it in a tree, runs up against it, not hard enough. He positions it at his heart, but he can't force himself into it. He prays for courage, but can't do that either. Then he stops, listens, and pricks his ears like a dog. He hears it, nothing, no surf, no wind, no nothing; sound has ended. He drops on the sand; its soft coarseness pulls something from his body. He feels adrift. There's a studying you do before you die, a kind of quick calculation. He sits there on the beach, no more sun, no wings flapping. He sits there waiting for that benign son-of-a-bitch who endowed him."

Harry comes cursing through the debris in the alley. Fred is in tow, drunk and reluctant, clutching his pea jacket together. "Fuckin' asshole." Ron doesn't hear Harry, but smiles at the feeling of being lifted up. "He's fuckin' freezing. Get his arm. Fred, get his fuckin' arm."

Fred complains, "He ain't walkin.'"

"Drag him," Harry commands. They manage to get Ron's arms over their shoulders and theirs around his waist. They drag him into the pinkish streetlight, people sidestep them, give them lots of room. Harry lets go, slaps Ron's face as hard as he can. "Snap to, goddamn it."

Ron feels a grinding, crippling ache. But he also feels Harry's blow like the stroke of a feather, soft against his cheek. They drag him toward the lot, Ron's feet starting to find the pavement, but he keeps his eyes closed to prolong the sensation of rising up, rising up.

The House of Morgan

I don't know if Dad read *Romeo and Juliet*; I don't think he knew about the House of Capulet or Montague. He'd only got up to the sixth grade, and then worked for his dad traveling around the South selling something. My mom said that whatever they were selling, they had to be out of town before dinner time. He and his dad were constantly on the move. His mom, when she was there, stayed in St. Petersburg. Near the end of his working life, Dad sold furniture and did interior design for The House of Montague, a high-end furniture store in upstate New York. But he always wanted his own business and had a few of them over the years, mainly swap shops, which was used furniture and anything else that could turn a buck. Maybe that's why he called his The House of Morgan, to add a bit of luster to the family name.

But our house was not medieval style with stone arches and balconies. It was a white, undistinguished, two-story wood-frame structure, situated in the Woodlawn section of Schenectady, on Route 5. And the only servants were us kids.

Dad had a sign made. It was an artist's palette with a paint brush jabbed through the thumb hole. It had dabs of color: green, orange, yellow, blood red, and it advertised the name of the business in antique gold: The House of Morgan. Actually, it was two businesses. Downstairs, formerly someone's living room, was my mother's dress shop. She sold dresses, hats, belts, pocketbooks, shoes, and costume jewelry. There was a screen, with a painted peacock; women stood behind it to try on dresses. Mom was skilled at picking out accessories to go along with the dresses the ladies bought. I used to like to coil the sparkling necklaces and chains and hold the earrings in my hand. It was a small treasure I could have for a little while. Mom had decorated the walls of her shop with paint-by-number pieces she'd done, all with Oriental themes. Mainly, they were of young women posed in gardens, fanning themselves or observing vibrant flowers. Suitors serenaded them with stringed instruments. Mom collected jade and ivory carvings of animals and joyous Buddhas, their arms thrust above their heads. But joy had no place in our daily lives.

There was a set of sliding doors behind the dress shop. That was Dad's showroom, where he put the best pieces of furniture and antiques, and conversation pieces, like a dented trombone I had polished to a fine luster, and carefully hammered out the dents. He'd hung it from the ceiling, so it revolved and caught the light. It was twenty-nine dollars. The showroom was previously a dining room, so you had to pass the kitchen entrance to get to it. Sometimes Dad would lead customers into the room as we sat eating in the kitchen. We had an inhospitable dachshund at the time. We'd named him after a character in a popular TV show, Paladin. He growled at anyone who walked past the kitchen, and bit us infrequently. My sister and I did not like the fact that our home was a retail outlet and that strangers passed through at all times of the day. In the summer, the shop was open until nine PM on Fridays. At least no one ever went upstairs. That's where we lived, four bedrooms and a bathroom. My parents slept on a pull-out sofa in the big room facing Route 5. Pink and white were the predominate colors in my sister's room. She had a white canopy bed my dad got from The House of Montague—it was on discount. My dad called her Princess. My brother Phil and I were called less affectionate names like Junior, Ignatz, and Nuttsy Fagan. And Skunk. I guess that was a Southern thing, to call someone a skunk. My brother always called me Alexander and pronounced each syllable precisely, in reaction to the names Dad called us.

Dad had mistreated Phil for many years, beat him up pretty badly. The day Phil left for the Army, Dad wouldn't give him a ride to the bus. Phil had already failed out of his first year at Buffalo University. He'd spent his first semester hanging out at a fraternity house drinking a lot. Then he was back home for a while, writing ads for the local newspaper, the Daily Gazette. He was already broken the day he left; the beatings, physical and mental, had taken a toll. I ran after him crying, down to Union Street where he could get a bus that would connect him to the station downtown. I was crying hard, maybe because I thought Dad would be more unpredictable with Phil leaving. He told me it was the best thing for him to do. It would be all right. But it wasn't.

Dad kept an appointment book and on weekends we'd make calls. The apartments and houses all had their own distinct smells, some rotten with decomposing walls, piled-up trash, thousands of meals cooked and eaten in desperation. We'd go into attics, garages, and basements; Dad would inspect dining room and bedroom sets, roll-top desks, lamps, vases, silverware, even rugs. He'd always ask if they had any old jewelry they wanted to get rid of for cash. He knew his gold and gemstones pretty well, and the advantage it would bring if he got them cheap. He also bought refrigerators and stoves, which I had to move with him. I did not like trying to fit them in the back of the station wagon. Carrying a refrigerator down several flights of stairs was hard work. He usually took the lower end, where the motor was, and backed down step by step. I had to hold back the weight as best as I could on my end, so I wore rubber gloves for traction. At least one time I thought of letting it go. We tied the mattresses and box springs on top of the roof. Nothing seemed designed for convenience—we should have had a pickup truck.

When it came time to make the deal, Dad would splay his wallet, flashing twenties and fifties, explaining that he wouldn't be able to get much for their stuff, what with it being used and all. But he was willing to take it off their hands, do them a favor. Cash was a big incentive for people who sold us parts of their lives. Their kids would always hang around and stare at us, strangers with money. They all seemed subdued, or perhaps mistreated, nothing to suggest that there was hope in their lives.

We'd take the appliances over to the county dump and get more than what he'd paid for them, and sell the TVs, which we got for five dollars, to a guy there who fixed them up. He sold them for thirty-five, color TVs for more. On the ride home, Dad would chain-smoke another Camel cigarette and muse about how well we'd done and how much we could expect to sell the various pieces for. I knew he wanted me to admire him, to acknowledge how shrewd he was, his ability to buy valuable items for almost nothing. I would nod, and look at him in my peripheral vision. He was the same man who beat the hell out of Phil and me. The same man who said I didn't have a mind for school. I wasn't motivated to glorify him.

He'd smoked since he was a teenager—cigarettes were inexpensive in Florida. He'd come north at seventeen, on a train he'd hopped. He'd lived off of apples and cigarettes for two weeks. That was the story Mom told me. His dad had, after his "sales" career failed, taken up boxing and earned the title of Lightweight Champ of Florida, Kid Morgan. Maybe that's why Dad was so quick with his hands. His palms were calloused and hard. One time he slammed me across the face so hard that I saw stars. I thought that was something that only happened in cartoons, like Sylvester and Tweety. But Dad's parents weren't that interested in him, which was maybe why he was the way he was with us kids. I burned to ask Mom why she'd never stood up for us. I think she wanted to. She told me one time he'd raised his hand to hit her. She told him she'd walk out and never come back. He never tried it again. I wish I had stood up to him. I did later in my dreams, smashing him in the face until he went down. But there is only so much satisfaction in beating a dead man.

My Aunt Rose and Uncle Sol had offered to take him in. They raised him until he was twenty and opened his first swap shop. That was in 1939, the year Phil was born. Over the years the cigarettes destroyed his arteries. About fourteen years later, after The House of Morgan was demolished to make way for a restaurant called The Red Barn, he switched to filtered cigarettes, but it was too late. The doctor said that his arteries were in shreds. He died on Memorial Day. We were going to have a family picnic at my sister's house. Later on, I asked Mom about his death; she didn't want to tell me, but I kept at her. Dad wanted sex that morning. She didn't want to, but decided to give in to him, which was the usual way things went. He died in bed wanting to make love; he didn't get to. It was hard to think about that, my dad wanting love when he'd given so little to us.

Returning home after our stop at the dump, we'd unload the remaining junk in the backyard. Drawers were opened to air out in the sun. Occasionally, there were cockroaches skittering around through the dust, shreds of paper, and bobby pins. We'd lean the box springs and mattresses against the back porch. Sometimes they were stained and I sprayed them with a cleaning solvent that lifted or hid the stain. Rugs had to be unrolled and hung from the clothes line, then beaten with a rug beater. Dad had a cabinet full of polishes, stains, waxes, wood putty, steel brushes, and a variety of cleaning products and rags. I'd go over each item, cleaning, polishing, reaching into crevices and vents with a toothbrush. I replaced handles, tightened existing ones, glued and clamped chair legs. I fixed the floor and desk lamps as well, having learned to do it at BOCES. I was in my junior year of high school and had done so poorly that my guidance counselor suggested that I learn a trade. I learned how to rewire lamps, toasters, blenders, and clock radios. This pleased Dad, and gave me a mild sense of pride. I had this bit of skill, but really wanted nothing to do with it.

Eventually, everything would have to go down to the cellar. During the winter months we didn't have the luxury of airing things out in the backyard. I didn't like wrestling the mattresses down the stairs. The smell of cigarettes, the exhaustion of labor, sour poverty, and what I thought might be the smell of sex rubbed up against my face. I wondered how many children had been conceived on those beds, how much fucking had taken place. I very much wished to join the society of adults who enjoyed sex, but that was a ways off for me. The mattresses and box springs had to be wrapped in plastic to prevent mildew. This tedious process seemed like a waste of time. Nobody wanted to buy used mattresses. Anything of obvious value, china, a sterling silver tea service, a mission oak table, and antiques, went upstairs to Dad's showroom. I spent a lot of time in the basement fixing and cleaning up his inventory. Another reason I spent time there was because of the cello. He'd picked up a battered cello on one of his calls. It had a long crack on the table and was missing the lowest string. It made a rasping sound when I drew the bow across it, like an old man's last breath. I got a beginner's cello book and tried to play it. I couldn't get it to stay in tune or sound good, but I kept trying. Finally, when I got it to a repair shop I learned that the sound post had fallen out. The guy said it was like trying to start a car without gas. With a new sound post, the crack glued, new strings and tuners, it sounded like something.

I decided to get some lessons and joined the community chamber orchestra that rehearsed in the high school auditorium. My teacher, Mr. Roth, was a camp survivor. He lived in the Stockade section of town, a pre-Revolutionary neighborhood abutting the Mohawk River and the Western Gateway Bridge, which was later deemed deficient by the NYSDOT. The Stockade was burnt down and many inhabitants killed during the French and Indian War. The Schenectady Massacre always seemed like a potent reference to me. Mr. Roth only took one or two students at a time because it made him nervous to have more. At each lesson he would demonstrate for me how to hold the bow correctly, play a phrase or make a proper trill. He would play several bars of a sonata and then stare off as if he'd seen something move. His hands would tremble. I asked him one time what he was looking at. He leaned the cello back as he sank in his chair, the bow dropping to his side in surrender. "Bodies… blood in snow."

Phil came home from the Army in less than a year, his discharge circumstances unclear. Something had happened and he'd gotten into trouble. I heard my mother mention "outstanding debt." Dad reluctantly wired him money to get home, but treated him badly. Dad said that the Army couldn't make a man out of his son. He had a way of making us think we deserved very little, and we pretty much believed it. Of the three of us, I was the only one to get a college degree.

At night, Phil and I set up camp in Dad's showroom and listened to music on a Phillips stereo Dad had bought for ten dollars. Phil had a good collection of LPs, jazz and folk music. He also liked Edith Piaf and Marlene Dietrich. He'd been stationed in Germany, but said he heard Edith sing in Paris. Listening to Marlene Dietrich sing "Lily Marlene" touched something in me; it made me think that I'd have to get away from our house as soon as possible. That if there was something of value in me, it would never grow in this place. The flowers in the gardens Mom painted and hung in her shop were so bright compared to the colorless mood in our home. My life had to be about something else, anything else.

Phil had brought home some Gauloises from France. They were very strong and made me cough at first, but I kept trying, thinking that somehow it granted me an honorary citizenship in European culture. Maybe I could go there some day. The strong, wafting smoke of the Gauloises intermingled with the gray cloud from Dad's Camels floating downstairs.

It wasn't long before Dad drove Phil away, for the last time. Phil had a friend in New York he stayed with, and quickly got a copy-writing job with an ad agency. I didn't find out until much later that he'd lied about his college background, telling them he'd attended an Ivy League school in Massachusetts. And that his parents owned a chain of jewelry stores in the tri-state area. This was before background checks were mandatory. But he'd gotten the job and even managed to rent an apartment in Brooklyn. From that moment on my path was decided; I had to get to New York as soon as possible. Whatever my life was going to be about, whatever light there would be, whatever Edith Piaf was singing about, I wasn't going to hear it where I was. Not in my town, repairing furniture in a basement.

Phil would call me ofttimes when he thought Dad might be out. He'd hang up if Dad answered. We made a plan. There was a community college near Prospect Park. Basically, you could enroll and take classes. I wouldn't have to show a failing high school transcript to get in, or impress Admissions by rewiring a toaster. He also described the park, with its great lawns, botanical gardens, paths, and sculptures. Beautiful women sunbathed there on Sundays. He sent me a postcard with a picture of Grand Army Plaza. He didn't sign it. I told him I would come; I would get there somehow. I was going to Paris. I would enroll in college, read in the park on Sundays, and master all the stops on the F train. Maybe I could find a job fixing electronic appliances, make a little money, and help Phil out with the rent. In that case, I would love being a repair man, a noble occupation.

That fall, my sister left for Buffalo University as my brother had before her. She was going to get a teaching degree and then apply for a job in Connecticut where the pay scale was higher. The night before she left I gave her a desk lamp she could use for studying. It was brass and had a Tiffany green and blue glass shade. It looked like junk when he'd bought it, and I hoped that Dad wouldn't miss it. I'd rewired the lamp and polished the brass until it glowed, and put a soft light bulb in it, one hundred watts, bright but easy on the eyes. Then I took it apart so it would fit in three pieces in her suitcase. She said that she was afraid to leave home, afraid of being alone in a dorm room without friends. But she'd be back for Thanksgiving. She said she was sorry to leave me there. I told her that I was moving to New York soon and not to worry about me. She thought I was just talking. "Alexander…" she hesitated, "I hate him."

I had four hundred and seventy-two dollars saved. Dad paid me twenty a week for hauling, cleaning, and repairing, as well as electrical work. The bus to New York, one way, was thirty-nine dollars. I had more than enough money to get there and enough left over to take care of myself for a while, including the community college which was about as cheap as a YMCA membership. And I would get a job. I didn't want Phil to pay for everything. I was excited; I felt that I would be able to make out all right. I got a book on Brooklyn and studied every section of it. Out of the money I earned from Dad, as well as yard work for neighbors, I also paid for my cello lessons with Mr. Roth. It was ten dollars an hour, but he never paid attention to the time. I didn't mind paying him because, when he was in the right mood, he'd tell me about the town he'd grown up in, his family, the mountains, the Ukrainian National Orchestra where he'd played in the cello section. Until he and all the other Jews were fired. I listened carefully and was always respectful with my questions. Even with his shattered life displayed in front of me, he was a link to another world. I wanted him to know that I was leaving for New York. That I would hear lots of great music and write him about it.

I found out there was trouble with my sister when I heard Dad yelling at her on the phone. He'd only slapped her once that I knew of. She had disagreed with him about something, talked back to him, and he slapped her. She ran up to her room and wouldn't come out for a full day. He never apologized. She was extremely sensitive, and later on, after she'd married, she controlled every aspect of her household. Her home was sacred. She wouldn't allow her husband to leave anything that had to do with his business around the house. His basement office was stuffed with paper work, from the floor to the ceiling.

I found out from Mom that Elaine had met a boy, and she was spending time with him. I wondered why that was a problem, wasn't she happy? The boy was Spanish. So what, I told Mom. But Mom said that it was wrong. She should be with her own kind. In this case, Mom agreed completely with Dad. They put so much pressure on her, threatening to withhold tuition payments, that she was home by Halloween. She suffered from migraines and began smoking. She spent a lot of time in her room reading, waiting for what was next. I remember going down to the basement that day. I was furious. I kicked over a coat rack that needed repairing anyway. I was standing next to an ornate French provincial mirror, punching the air. Tears were sliding down my face. What kind of people are we? I looked in the mirror and watched my mouth: *Not my kind.*

When I finally got a chance to see Mr. Roth, there was a Hassidic rabbi standing on his porch. He looked around as if he were keeping guard. When I got close enough, he eyed me warily. "And you are?" he asked.

"I'm Alexander, Mr. Roth's student."

"Oh yeah, so you play the cello?" He lightened up a bit.

"Is he home?" I asked.

He let out a long sigh and looked out over the dark river that flowed west at the end of the block. "He has died," he said, in a matter of fact way.

I stood there listening. Horns and sirens were sounding at intervals. There must have been an accident on Erie Boulevard. "Is he still here?" I asked. Not that I thought he'd let me go in and look at Mr. Roth's corpse, but I needed something more than to just walk away like I'd gotten the wrong address. The rabbi swayed as if he were reciting or praying for Mr. Roth. Finally, I turned to go.

"Alexander, there will be a service at Temple Sinai tomorrow morning." I nodded and kept walking. I would be at the bus station in fifteen minutes. I'd already stowed my backpack there and bought my ticket. I was afraid that Dad would find out and show up at the station. He would try to stop me. Would I finally be able to defend myself? I preferred to imagine watching his face disappear, the aggressive stance of his wiry body, as the bus gained speed moving toward the Thruway. I thought, maybe he would smile, glad to finally be rid of me.

"Alexander, go in," the rabbi commanded. "Mrs. Shonfeld is packing up."

The curtains were drawn, the lights out, and a single candle flickered on the kitchen table. I looked around waiting for my eyes to adjust to the dark. A woman with long white hair sat on a folding chair piling sheet music and exercise books into a milk crate. In the corner stood his cello case, the burnished finish glowing in the candle light, about four feet tall—a sullen figure, suspended in the shadow.

She looked up and saw me looking at the cello case. "That, we sell. Pay the burial plot, the stone—he had nothing." She spit the words out with distaste. I understood that I didn't need to say that I was sorry he'd died. "Which one are you? There's Ronald and Alexander. Which one?"

"I'm Alexander."

"Good, there on the bed, take." She had stripped the sheets and quilt; the mattress had pink stripes on it like a circus tent. I picked up his bow case and opened it. He'd let me use it once before. It was a beautiful, hand carved, cherry-wood bow, with mother of pearl inlay, perfectly balanced and made by a violin maker from his village. At least fifty years old. I held it in both hands, letting it rest gently in my palms, then put it back and latched the case and waited. It was as if I were waiting for Mr. Roth to tell me what to do next. I started for the door.

"Take," she said. "It's for you. He wrote it down." She was up now at the closet, throwing his suits and shoes in a duffle bag as if they were trash. Outside, the rabbi was gone. I sucked in the chilled October air as if I'd forgotten to breathe inside the apartment. Then I sat on the stone step with the bow case across my knees, my hands protecting it. A barge sounded its warning horn as it shoved its way under the bridge toward Amsterdam. The great blaring horn, commanding and singular, sounded twice for a good twenty seconds each, blowing everything before and after it out of its way.

Two and a half years later, I stood in the bright spring light near the student center at Kingsborough Community College in Brooklyn. I was one of a hundred and seventy students in line, waiting to have my hand shaken and to receive an Associate's Degree. The guest speaker was a Brooklyn politician who'd attended KCC and was giving us an uninspired commencement speech about bright futures and the great storehouse of knowledge we had entered and would surely continue to receive nourishment from for the rest of our lives. Like most untalented orators he was repetitive. He repeated the phrase storehouse of knowledge over and over until it became a mantra. I was feeling depressed, completely unsure of my bold entrance into the future. And was a bit hung over from the previous night's celebration with some friends.

Again, he invoked the storehouse of knowledge. And our house came back to me, sudden and vivid, as if it were sitting on the quad. There was the sign, the artist's palette glinting in the sun, the modest white house, faded and shrunken with time. I knew that it had already been demolished a few years back, unceremoniously, for another entrepreneurial endeavor, The Red Barn, purveyor of specialty burgers, chicken salad, corn on the cob, and sweet iced tea. The House of Morgan was gone; perhaps some vestiges were left in the ground: varnish, steel wool, a rhinestone earring. And gone too, was the less-than-noble family who suffered and eventually fled that house. Not in a procession through the ancient streets of Verona, celebrated with horns and drums. But like ghosts, one at a time, carrying their anguish in paper bags. Phil was in a VA hospital being treated for an alcoholic overdose. Elaine was happily married for the moment in Albany, adopting her first child. The patriarch, who'd ruled his family with an iron hand, was dead. Mom was living at The King's Arms, an assisted living community, which I visited every two weeks my entire time at Kingsborough, despite the difficulty of travel and a tight student's budget.

I let the house on the quad break silently in two, without thunder or a flash of light, and sink into the new soft grass. I could no longer focus on the man's speech, as my present accomplishment dwindled compared to what was stirring in me. And I realized that I'd already departed. The future he espoused, the world that was graciously opening up to me because of my time at KCC, began across the campus, beyond the neighborhoods where Oriental Boulevard stretched either way through the borough, to the basin and the river. And the house that I hoped to belong to, my true home, if there were such a place for me, was somewhere out there.

The Dear Departed Horseman of Worcester

At four PM there was a foot of wet snow choking I-290, with five more inches predicted. The highway department employed every unit in its arsenal, but could hardly keep up. Even their new weapon, the Falls Heavy Duty Snow Wing, was struggling to fulfill its reputation and perform "maximum casting ability." But it still outperformed the older rigs. A few lucky motorists, who hadn't skidded off into the thick white banks and were stranded, followed the plows all the way into Leominster, if that was their destination.

As they passed the Polar Beverage Plant in Worcester they could just make out Orson, the inflatable polar bear. He smiled and waved from atop the roof; the guy wires strained and groaned against the continuous blast of Arctic air, resonating low, dull notes. Orson, in his form-fitting green t-shirt, was in his element and waved and flashed his anchor-shaped smile at the struggling motorists—a friendly, buff polar bear that looked like he'd spent time at the gym.

A few miles east in Shrewsbury, Millie the Shire mare was not so happy. She thrashed against the heavy-duty, horse-rated fence, bruising her muscular chest as the posts began to splinter. She neighed

156

fiercely, sending a sharp chill through Catherine, who refused to open the gate so Millie could take refuge in the stable. If she had broken out now, instead of later as she actually did, she might have trampled Catherine, who was trudging through drifts around the property to see where Paul had got to. Paul had disappeared, and Catherine didn't realize that this was the evening her life would change.

Their farm overlooked Lake Quinsigamond, where the Northeast college crews competed. Paul and Catherine enjoyed an elevated view of the regattas. In happier times, on a summer's day, sitting in their Adirondack Chairs, sipping wine, sharing the binoculars, it was invigorating to watch the young people strive for ribbons and cups to bring back to their campuses. Catherine always rooted for the Clark women's crew as they were underdogs and lost most of their competitions. They were hefty, strong girls, but they couldn't seem to outrow their opponents. Paul was a diehard Holy Cross fan, as he was chair of the English Department.

Their property was well-situated for maximum sun exposure, and the sturdy three-story, Federal brick house was historically handsome. The house, their "dream home," was the vision of a retired sea captain who'd escaped with his life and two belts of gold coins, hauling a cargo of molasses that ran aground in Narragansett Bay. A good captain, faithful to his charter, he was the last to leave the ship. In part, it was because he didn't want his men to see him strap the belts around his shoulders. Fortunately, he was a strong swimmer. After he crawled upon the shore, almost drowned by the weight of the gold coins, he looked back at the churning waves, crossed himself and spit. He got a room in the Atlantic House, ordered fresh clothes, ate an entire roast, got boisterously drunk, and vexed the bar maid until he passed out. The next morning he set out west; intending to remove himself from the sea, as far inland as possible. When he arrived in Shrewsbury, he made a close inspection of Lake Quinsigamond and dismissed it as a mere pond compared to the open sea, unworthy of his attention. He set about to build his house: The Captain Owen Baines Bunting House, 1785, listed on the National Register of Historic Homes.

Paul was finishing up his last semester as chairman of the English Department at Holy Cross, looking toward retirement with a mixture of dread and relief. His job satisfied and irritated him depending on the day, committee meetings being his nemesis. They were endless and tedious: discussions of policy, appointments to be made, criteria and procedures to be manufactured, and always the vying with long-winded, opinionated colleagues. Some were divorced or recently widowed and had little social life, so the meetings were a kind of support group. One knowledgeable person could make a sound decision and put it in place. Paul often did that, resulting in ridicule behind his back, though never any about his academic prowess or teaching skills. He often compared college administrations to slaughterhouses, except slaughterhouses were straightforward in their purpose.

Paul's passion, the real connection in his life, was Millie, a gift from his younger brother, Ron. They'd bought the property together after Paul received tenure. Their parcels were large and productive; they were populated with healthy sycamores, elms, sugar maples, and quaking aspen. Ron had his veterinary office and home built in the woods several hundred yards above Paul's property, which was separated by a masterful stone wall that ran three, four, and five feet in some places, a link in that great necklace that winds through the New England countryside. There was a breathtaking view of the lake and ample roaming space for all the animals he rehabilitated. There were pigs, pheasants, turtles, cats and dogs, and of course, horses. The SPCA brought them to Ron after rescuing them from abusive owners. Some were starved; some had been beaten, or left in their stalls for inordinate amounts of time. Ron always found room for another one.

The horse was unusual—she just appeared one afternoon in Ron's garden. He could see her from the window, so immediately he checked his web contacts for all the local horse farms. No missing horses were reported.

Apparently she had managed to jump five-and-a-half feet with no damage to the fence. She was making a meal of his peas, beans, and alfalfa, and looked slightly starved. But she had well-defined muscles and was quite poised for a stray. Her legs were supple and remarkably long. She was definitely a jumper, which was curious for her size; she was a big horse. As he approached he noticed the determined cast of her eyes and a compelling authority in the way she stood. She was a self-contained animal and, it seemed to Ron, remarkably *conscious*.

Paul, who'd come over to return Ron's log splitter, was getting out of his truck as Ron stepped closer to the horse. She reared on her back legs to give warning and snorted threateningly. Ron tried repeated approaches without success, which piqued him, as he had a way with horses. Paul observed the animal closely. Ron retreated and latched the garden gate, "I may have to sedate her to check her out—make sure she's got all twenty-four teeth."

"Don't bother doing that." Paul strode through the gate and stood directly in front of her—immediately she settled down. He reached up; she drew her head back, swayed to see through the blind spot before her eyes. Then she placed her muzzle gently in his palm. He began to walk and she followed him, out of the trampled garden and into the adjacent corral, which they circled for the next ten minutes. Astonished, Ron stared at them. Paul coaxed her to the fence, placed his foot on the railing, and mounted her bareback. Ron panicked and started for the gate. What if she got spooked and threw him? She didn't; they stood there, motionless like a bronze figure, horse and rider, connected in perfect understanding. With a soft pat on her neck from Paul, holding her head high, she carried him around the ring without malevolence or complaint.

"Wow," Ron said. "It looks like she's your horse."

"Really?"

"Well, I'll definitely hear about it if she's escaped from anywhere around here. Until then, she's yours."

"I'm naming her Millie," Paul shot back. Ron thought that was strange, naming the horse after their mother, Mildred, who'd passed a decade earlier. A peculiar idea entered his mind. Did Paul think that the horse was some form of reincarnation of the spirit of their mother? He dismissed the thought out of hand; though as a veterinarian, Ron had witnessed many unusual, seemingly spiritual transferences between animals and humans, especially at the time of death—cats standing in doorways, dogs howling under beds, a lama crashing through a window to be with her beloved mistress. The connection, the depth of love some people shared with their animals, was almost surreal. That was what had drawn him in to his profession in the beginning. He was as interested in helping animals as he was in studying the psychology between them and their owners.

In a short period of time Millie gained weight and more solid muscle tone, and she was inseparable from Paul. He trained her to perform simple and then complex tricks, which was unusual for a thirteen hundred pound Shire horse. She learned to back, bow, paw, and Spanish Walk. She was a natural jumper with extraordinary power. She easily cleared four- and five-foot stone walls. When harnessed, she could pull a four hundred pound boulder across a field without strain. Paul liked to demonstrate how gentle she was by lying on the stable floor. With a prompt of his hand, Millie would rest her hoof, which was the size of two adult heads, on his chest; he barely could feel it. They seemed to have a unique perception of each other—she lived to please him. When he spoke to her, she'd rest her muzzle on his shoulder and tilt her ear toward his mouth. And she responded obediently to each quiet command he gave, as if she'd anticipated his instructions.

Catherine's horse days had not gone so well. She'd participated in equine sports in college, as an elective, but had taken a bad fall attempting to jump a Swedish oxer, which resulted in a transverse fracture of the greater trochanter on her left hip. She required crutches for two months, a regimen of Motrin, and then three months of physical therapy, but was left with a slight limp, favoring her left side. After the accident she refused to go back to competition and developed an intense distrust and fear of horses. Paul's relationship with Millie was an ongoing insult and irritation to their relationship, especially now that their only child, Wesley, was off to study law at Columbia University.

At a time in their lives when they might have enjoyed a renewed interest in one another, there was a widening gulf between them. Catherine had begun to keep a score card of sorts to track Paul's transgressions, big and small. If he forgot to bring in the milk and it froze, it was duly noted. If he neglected to lower the toilet seat, that too was recorded. If he'd had too much wine at dinner with friends and said something Catherine found off-color, that too was inscribed, with a spiky lecture on the way home. Mainly, his friendship with Millie was the greatest cause of consternation. He said to Millie, "At some point in your life you just want to be accepted for who you are, whoever that is." Millie swung her massive head gently to the side and lifted her lips in agreement.

The question of just who Paul *was* had troubled him most of his life, and it intensified in his early sixties despite the fact Paul had, and still enjoyed, a successful professional career. He was a well-liked literature professor—students eagerly signed up for his courses.

His reputation for dry humor and a less than devotional approach to the masterpieces of English Literature was appreciated. He skillfully combined the writers' books with their characters, personalities, and flaws, making them more human and accessible to the students. He also welcomed student input. He respected their opinions and insight. "Everyone has something to contribute," he liked to say. Some professors thought that sentiment overly precious. His seminars were considered inclusive literary parties, not dry presentations with copious note-taking.

He'd been less popular with his own son. He'd tried to be a nurturing father to Wesley, but it was a difficult relationship. Wesley had been an angry child who suffered bad immunization reactions. After a measles inoculation he ran a 105-degree temperature for almost a week. It frightened Catherine to the point where Paul obtained a letter from Wesley's Sudbury School, whose parents declined vaccinations en masse. Paul was not a fan of the Sudbury approach, which he considered to be education in negative numbers. A student was permitted to wander the grounds all day or just play video games, or whatever, and for a steep tuition. No instruction was offered unless a specific request was made. If a student decided he wanted to be an astronaut, the administration would scurry to find a rocket scientist. Privately, Paul referred to it as the Dingle Berry School and he resented the money they'd thrown at it.

Even when in good health, Wesley resisted any authority or correction. He carried the anger into his young adult years, causing many scenes which resulted in crying bouts for Catherine. The household atmosphere was constantly filled with tension and anguish. By the time he was sixteen he'd totaled two cars and a truck, driving while intoxicated. His sense of entitlement never wavered as he insisted on the best of everything, especially Italian suits for college. And his ability to argue and refute any suggestion or position was limitless. There seemed to be nothing, no advice, no expression of love or encouragement Wesley could accept from his parents. Paul was secretly relieved when the boy left for school. He'd make a good lawyer with his take-no-prisoners mind set, but he'd suffer a contentious life.

The sudden onset of Catherine's menopause seemed timed to Wesley's departure. Her symptoms were overwhelming and severe. She skipped perimenopause and dove in full-tilt. She paced about the bedroom most nights enduring insomnia and hot flashes. Her libido dropped shockingly fast; it sank like a ten-ounce Pike sinker. Up to this time they had enjoyed occasional sex when the scorecard was put away long enough and Paul wasn't preoccupied with department issues or Millie. Their couplings were polite, designed to satisfy both participants; it was a gentle combining of their bodies to honor the years and accomplishments of the life they shared, but had already started to diminish incrementally. The dryness made it too painful for Catherine to tolerate penetration even with a lubricant. Initially, Paul was caught off guard, his masculinity thrown in along with the kitchen scraps. He made some harsh remarks, which he later regretted. He wasn't ready for this part of his life to be over and almost without notice. There were some bruising verbal battles, and at least one hand-painted Chinese mug, a Khaki Senseo, was smashed on the butcher block table.

Soon, without more discussion, sex and intimacy receded like the landscape observed from the back car of a train. Intermittently, Paul felt its loss as an object of sadness and hurt pride he carried around, something unwieldy that he couldn't quite put down. He secretly blamed her for this. He wasn't aware that his Leydig cells had decreased, spinning him into an andropause phase of life. Men are usually the last to know. As Catherine's reproaches increased in virulence he withdrew from her. He read Millie an entry from his journal, "And like Rip / I retreated deeper into the tavern / against the shrill cry of her voice." Without a friendship with Wesley—there were only infrequent, unsatisfactory, obligatory holiday visits—he turned to Millie for companionship, and she responded with all of her twelve-and-a-half pound heart. He loved her for her purity of emotion, something animals are capable of—but humans struggle with.

Paul's colleagues invited him to lunches and readings, but it didn't interest him. He felt, and it would have been difficult for him to explain, that those activities took away the time he needed to *realize* himself, whatever that meant. He no longer defined himself as a husband, though he would do his duty, take care of Catherine, and do whatever was necessary should she become ill. He cared less about his longevity, but feared that Catherine would have Millie put down after his demise. He consulted a lawyer; a terse paragraph was inserted in his will to put aside a portion of his estate to care for the horse. They would continue to share the house, take some meals together, listen to an occasional opera, but for all practical purposes there wasn't much left for them to do together. Paul had a fleeting interest to travel out west through horse country, but Catherine wasn't a traveler. She preferred her gardening and quilting to new locales. And he carried some residual resentment; he wasn't going to travel with a woman he wasn't sleeping with. And with the average run of menopause, eight to ten years, he figured he wouldn't be around to partake of her gifts even if she rediscovered her sex drive under a tomato plant some afternoon. He mentioned to Millie, "Menopause is not the pause that refreshes." Millie scuffed her hoof in agreement, secure in her intuition that mares didn't get menopause symptoms.

When Catherine finally found Paul in the stable that snowy afternoon she stared at him for a long time, as if she'd come upon an antiquity, something extremely curious. Her overall feeling was that he was out of place; he should be in his study or starting the tractor to clear the driveway. What was he doing lying on the floor, his glazed eyes staring at the wall of hanging reins and harnesses. Not fully cognizant that she was entering shock, she became irritated. "Paul, get up and act like an adult. For God—." She shrieked and bolted from the stable, then retuned and felt his chest, pressed her ear to his mouth and sobbed, "Paul, Paul, what are you doing to me?" She sank down on a hay bale and watched him closely; she realized that she must watch him in death as we are all destined and helpless to watch our loved ones who will never move or speak to us again. The unanimated human body is the greatest mystery to the one left behind. It breaks us, but we are compelled to move on if we are to survive. The words caught in her throat, "Paul...I loved you...love you." She rested her head in her hands and cried.

She didn't know that he could hear her.

When she wandered outside it was dark and the snow continued to fall as if it had been shot straight down from the sky with cannons. She stood and waited...for something. Shouldn't something momentous happen following Paul's death? How could nature ignore this loss? She knew the absurdity of that thought, but at that moment a solid sheet of ice and snow let loose from the roof, ripping the metal snow guard off with it. It landed about ten feet in front of the house, the sharp claws of the guard shining eerily. Had she been standing closer it might have killed her. She nodded approvingly. She looked up and felt the thick flakes like dull stings settle on her face. She resisted an urge to lay down in its softness and try to sleep. The strange thought occurred: "It's just me and the snow now." She glanced at the corral, "and you." She scowled but couldn't see Millie, who'd already trampled over the gate and trotted into the edge of the woods waiting for Catherine to return to the house. For no reason she began to sweep the porch, thinking it was somehow useful. She noticed that patterns of snow snaked up like soft white veins from the foundation of the house to just under the eaves of the third floor, prominent against the background of dull red brick. Not until after she'd made a cup of tea and smoked a joint did she think to call Ron and tell him. Ron was incapacitated with grief; it overtook him instantaneously as if it had been pumped through his body with an IV. He felt as if there were a hand pressing on his shoulder, pushing him to his knees as he accepted an oath of duty—to honor his brother, Paul, who'd always looked out for him. And he resolved to care for his widow. Catherine heard Ron's wife, Trisha, in the background quizzing him about the call. "Don't bring her with you," Catherine whispered.

Ron paused, "I have to. The power is out and…I can't leave her alone." He waited, and added, "You know…." Trisha had just been released from a program that specialized in bipolar disorder and was, as usual, tentative and edgy. She was under strict orders not to miss one dose of medication. Over the years Trisha had clashed with Catherine and caused Ron much hardship and disruption, though Paul had stood with his brother and treated Trisha with respect and deference. She'd gone as far as emailing nude pictures of herself to Paul, which Catherine discovered while mail-ordering asparagus seeds. She accused Paul of something that was quite beyond his range of behavior; and it added to the tipping load of their marital conflict.

"All too well, I know," she muttered.

"Where is he, I mean now?" Ron asked.

"The stable."

"You're sure…?"

"What?"

"That he's…dead."

"Dead, he's dead," she answered.

"Did you...cover him?" Catherine hadn't thought to do that. "I'm coming now," Ron said, suppressing a sob that clenched his throat.

Neither Catherine nor Ron could have guessed, much less imagined, that Paul had been experimenting with Datura Stramonium in his quest to find his true identity, and to discover his totem, which was nibbling some winter berries at the edge of the field. He'd taken just a scant bit too much of the Jimson weed, causing an intense trauma to his nervous system. His body responded to the imminent threat by violently entering into a state of tonic immobility, or death-feigning. He was trapped in this episode, apparently not breathing, which convinced Catherine he had passed. But Paul's mind was a vivid paroxysm of images and flashing lights. He raced through high peaks atop Millie, jumping huge crevices and boulders, dodged ledges of ice spears, skirted stands of towering pines, and clouds of snow swirling around them like figures in a Christmas display under glass. He was, at the moment, more alive than he'd ever been, but he couldn't move; he couldn't share his wonderful discovery with Catherine. He'd found his element, his psyche lit up like a Jersey Jack pinball machine; he was on sensory overload. Now he'd be lucky to survive it.

Catherine wandered back out to the stable, numb with disbelief. She checked the thermometer, which read +3 Celsius—about 37 degrees Fahrenheit. She knew from watching Six Feet Under that that was the correct temperature for storing a corpse in a morgue cooler. She went to the closet and dragged out a heavy, worn Oriental carpet. Carefully, she unrolled it until it was a flat surface of nine by twelve feet. She hoisted his legs and then arms on to the edge of the rug, surprised that he was still warm. She assumed that the body cools slowly after death. But yet it seemed strange. Should she try giving him mouth to mouth resuscitation? Was it really too late? How could this actually be happening? It happened to friends and acquaintances, not them. His expression was so distorted, so ironic and frozen as if the last thing he'd seen had been utterly preposterous. Resolved, her tears dropping on the fabric, she rolled him slowly into a tight cylinder, which required all of her strength, causing her to break into a sweat despite the chilled air. He was completely enclosed in the carpet. The result almost seemed comical, a giant, scratchy, multicolored cigarette.

She rested on her knees and patted the fabric. It had once been brilliant with peacocks and parrots, as everything in her mother's home had been about birds, domestic and exotic: water colors, books, and numerous species in cages, parrots careening through the rooms, mounted specimens, feeders and baths in the backyard. A roost for homing pigeons on the roof. Her mailbox was a huge, beaded turquoise Pelican's mouth. Catherine felt that she'd grown up in a rain forest.

For the last fifteen years of her life, after retiring from her job as a medical stenographer at UMass Memorial Hospital, Catherine's mother, Gwen, had been the secretary of the local Audubon Society at Broad Meadow Brook Conservation Center in Worcester. It had the distinction of being the largest urban sanctuary in New England—four hundred acres plus. Her passion for birds extended into literature. In her retirement, she wrote bird stories and insisted, through Catherine's agency, that Paul edit them for her so she could submit them to the Autobahn newsletter and various publications. In a fifteen-year period, she'd been politely rejected each time. The stories featured talking birds and were conceived to interest children in the diverse bird population of the northeast. Paul dreaded these tales, page after page of such lines as, "Woodpecker paused drilling into the White Pine and observed the Black-billed Wood Dove with disdain. 'Buck up little dove. You must show some spunk if you'd have a good meal.' But the dove was content to peck at the tender young grass and seeds before her. 'To each his own,' cooed the dove. 'Watch out you don't crack that bill of yours—drilling and drumming, drilling and drumming the whole day through. I should think you'd have a headache.'" Paul would wince and groan and suppress the urge to retch, then insert a few commas, delete a few others, recast the most skewed sentences, which were most of them, and then return it ASAP, hoping he'd never find another in his mailbox again. He refused, as Gwen hinted, that she be allowed to add Paul's name as the editor; he wouldn't submit himself and the Holy Cross English Department to such a disgrace.

In the last year of her life, Gwen became obsessed with ravens in particular, as well as crows and grackles, in anticipation of the statue of Edgar Allan Poe to be unveiled in Boston in October of 2014. The statue depicts Poe hiking purposely home to his birth place, two blocks south of Poe Square at Boylston and Charles Streets. His expression is determined, a bit mad, of course, and slightly disgusted as he is returning to the city of the "Frogpondian" literary establishment for which he held small regard. He was not returning to share bunk beds with Longfellow. A psychotic wild raven is rampant at his side, lest anyone impede his progress home. It is inevitable that there always exists a group of well-meaning folks who conspire to rearrange history for good intentions and commercial gain. Poe probably had no more interest in revisiting Boston than the orangutan did in shopping in the Rue Morgue. Poe created the genre, built the artifice, then went on to build the next one. But by golly, Poe was returning to Boston, leaving his grave and birthday gifts behind in Baltimore, a more southern clime to his liking.

The dementia worked a cruel trick on Gwen; suddenly her stories were cast as Sam Spade type mysteries with talking birds. The language was high flung and was supposed to "resemble" Poe's narrative, which it did not. Paul cringed at dialogue like: "'You're one little hopped up birdie, ain't you Sparrow. Well I got a cure for that,' Blackcoat said, as he extracted the luger from his downy vest.'" An un-Poe-like prose that Paul referred to as Poe-lish. There was little he could do with the pieces except to return them with a variety of emoticon faces, which Gwen interpreted as approval. This incensed Catherine and resulted in numerous strikes against him on the score card, and prompted her to say, in her own manner, that she would never do it with him again even in the afterlife. And then Gwen died, and as is usually the case, family and friends circled their mortal wagons around her coffin to say good things about her—how she was well loved. Paul was saddened, but secretly relieved—another burden lifted from his shoulders.

More interesting to Paul, as he'd taught Hardy, Hawthorne, and of course, *The Crucible*, over the years, was the harsh treatment the European settlers visited on these intelligent feathered creatures. They were considered to be ill omens and they exterminated them to best of their ability, even to the point of clear-cutting forests. By the 1800's there was hardly a raven left to say "Nevermore." They hated crows as well and hunted them to death. The grackles were considered pests and targeted too, but grackles were skilled in inhabiting settled areas. What was it about these early New Englanders? Paul's theory, which he shared with some colleagues—ruffling a few feathers—was that European settlers disliked anything that was black: black people, black magic, and ravens. Black was evil. Hanging white witches was of course God's will.

Paul was considered to be a scholar of the New England school of writers, but took great pride in the Ancient Greek program as well. He was fairly proficient. Holy Cross was one of the only colleges with the expectation that their students would learn the language. Paul participated in editing the Homer multi-text project which included analysis and electronic presentation of Homer's epic poetry. To gain advanced proficiency he delved into each of the three dialects: Dorian, Aeolian, and Ionian. He was most attracted to the Dorian dialect because of its connection to Asia Minor and the Pella Curse tablet from the first half of the Fourth Century BC. The "mixed curse" lead scroll, which was a plea for love and for rivals to be vanquished, contained the word EPHMA, which he made use of in a letter to the editor on the shabby job FEMA had done for the folks in New Orleans. If you rearranged the Greek letters into PHEMA, meaning *abandoned*, that was pretty much what FEMA had done in the aftermath of Hurricane Katrina. He delighted in making connections with words and phrases, and more so in igniting his students' imaginations with them.

He liked to introduce *The Odyssey* to his classes by quoting a line from the flyleaf of a J.P. Donleavy novel, *The Ginger Man*: "There was a man who built a boat to sail away, but it sank." He did this in part because it was how he felt. Somehow he was meant to get away, but his boat had sunk some time ago. He didn't realize that ultimately his vehicle of escape would be a noble white horse.

Ron knew and was on good terms with Police Chief Montecalvo. He'd spent days with him working on a horrendous murder and barn burning that had shocked Worcester several years earlier. Ron had the sad task of euthanizing some of the horses that survived the fire. They agreed that they'd send the van for Paul in the morning as the roads were impassable—he wasn't going anywhere. Ron checked the gas and oil in the snowmobile then followed Trisha around the house with a flashlight as she gathered her things. She packed as if she were traveling several hundred miles instead of three hundred yards over three feet of snow. Her makeup alone, including tanning oil, took up a small backpack. She insisted on packing a bulbous blue snow suit, a sequined cocktail dress, and Grady, her outsized, cuddly Koala bear Ron had brought back from an animal rights conference in Auckland. Grady was the product of the Steiff Company, a German toy maker, and had set him back five hundred dollars; such was their love connection at the time. She refused to travel without Grady and had recently begun having long, private conversations with him. When she and Ron fought, which had become more frequent, she'd storm into the guest room with the bear and lock the door. From the bits of conversation and cooing, Ron guessed that Grady enjoyed the attention he was denied.

It took about thirty minutes to maneuver the snowmobile around the tree stumps and bushes which looked like overstuffed lounge chairs. There were a few sinking patches of snow that might have caused the machine to flip over, and somewhere there was an old pump handle to avoid. Momentarily blinded by the storm, Ron paused trying to decipher a safe path. He could not see ahead three feet at the moment, but was aware that something told him which way to go. Trisha, riding close behind, her arms around his waist, knocked her knees into his thighs. "Come on, Ron, it's freezing. My hair is frozen." She'd insisted on washing her hair before they'd left the house, including a rinse that kept her graying tresses blond. When they arrived, Paul's house looked like a Currier and Ives drawing of winter hospitality, awaiting guests for a celebration, except for Catherine, who paced madly at the far end of the porch, a vapor of cigarette smoke expanding from her nostrils. Her silver hair tossed in the wind; usually she wore it up in a neat bun at the back of her head.

Trisha dismounted and trudged petulantly up the steps with her belongings. Her knee-high white fur boots disappeared in the snow. She entered through the wide oak door, which was flung open. Soft light from the fireplace rippled off the wide planks of the floor. Ron secured a tarp over the snowmobile, took up his vet bag, a habit he could not break, and went up the stairs to Catherine. She pressed her full weight into him for support. He felt the double edged grief of a brother and a brother-in-law. "What will I do without him?" Ron wondered the same thing. She felt like a broken thing in his arms and he gave her what strength and comfort he could, and allowed some to return to himself. Suddenly, the door slammed with a resounding crash. "I asked you not to bring her.

"She can't be left alone."

"I'm alone now," Catherine said, looking closely at his face. Her voice sounded as if it came from a great distance.

"I won't leave you alone, Cat."

She looked at him coldly. "He loved you more than me."

"I know he loved you; he told me." Ron reached a bit here, as Paul had told him how he'd *once* loved her. "He really did."

"That's what you talk about."

"What?"

"When someone dies. You talk about love," she said. "Why is that?"

"Because it's all you have...when you can have it."

"But aren't there other things?" Her question confused him. A sudden movement caught them off guard. A large form sprinted out from the stable area in the distance, playfully kicking snow into the air. It turned swiftly and was gone into the great gray shadows over the field.

"That's what he really loved, that fucking horse."

"How'd she get out of the stable?"

"She wasn't in it."

He was reluctant to reprimand her under the circumstances. "You really shouldn't do that," he said gently. "She couldn't get to her food."

"Fuck her. And her too," she said, looking toward the door. Ron winced at her sudden flair of hostility, but said nothing.

Inside, they found Trisha on the divan, her legs tucked pertly beneath her. She wore a gold Hoodie-Footie, and held a glass of scotch in her hand. She never forgot where the bar was in a house no matter how far off she went.

"Oh, it's the snowbirds," she said, sarcastically.

"I'll get some sandwiches and coffee," Catherine said, glaring at Trisha.

Ron patted his veterinarian bag and set it by the end table. He carried in it, among other necessary items, a Dan-Inject dart gun for dogs. But it contained a small vial of tranquilizer that Trisha's doctor had approved if it became necessary to sedate her for her own safety. Her strength doubled during an episode. She had one time swung wildly and ripped Ron's lower lip open with her diamond mounting.

"Trish," he said quietly. "Let's go easy."

"Let's go easy," she mocked. "You want to go easy on her, don't you?"

"You have to respect her loss," he said, carefully taking the glass from her hand, his shaking a bit, and surprised that she let him. He wanted to swallow it down straight, but set it on the table.

"What about me," she sobbed. "Who gives a fuck about me?"

He sat next to her, "I do. You'll be all right."

"You'll lock me up when you can."

"You know it's voluntary. They can't unless you agree," he reminded her.

She stiffened suddenly, "I hear something...out there." She looked toward the front door.

Ron listened. "It's the wind."

"No, something is clomping around, running. I can feel the vibration through the cushion." She grabbed his hand and pressed, "Do you feel it?"

He lowered his head and sighed, "No, I don't"

Catherine returned with a tray of sandwiches. She'd made grilled cheese and chicken noodle soup for some reason. And a pot of steaming coffee. She set it on the table and Trisha snatched up a sandwich and ate ravenously. "I haven't had dinner." Ron poured out the coffee. Trisha took five spoons of sugar. They were quiet for a few moments, sipping the coffee, trying desperately, each in their own way, to find their place in this small, human grouping, bound loosely by loss and the tumultuous history of one another. Catherine took a joint from her flannel shirt pocket. "Do you mind?"

"Of course not," Ron said.

"I want some," Trish said plaintively. "You have to share."

Catherine slowly took her measure, leveling her eyes on the gold Footies that she'd set on the table. "Do I really?"

"I have to go out there," Ron interjected. "I need you to…"

"Play nice?" Trisha guessed.

"Yes," he said with an exhausted exhalation. "Just be…"

"Civilized," Catherine completed. Both women laughed an eerie unnerving laugh.

"Please…just do this." He took up his bag and started toward the door.

Suddenly, Trisha spilled her coffee on her chest and didn't react to the heat. "He's there. He's alive—I feel it."

"You fucking…" Catherine began, and then listened.

"Paul's alive, I can feel him," Trisha said, almost smug, as if she'd just won a spelling bee.

Catherine rushed to the picture window. "The stable door's open. The light is on. But I probably did that. I must have. How else…?"

"No," Ron said, alarmed. "It wasn't when we were just on the porch."

"No, it wasn't," she gasped.

"I brought him back," Trisha whispered. "They couldn't have him." She pronounced this like an incantation.

Catherine swept a vase off the mantle, and smashed it on the hearthstone. "Shut up you fucking…"

"Fucking whore? Is that what you were going to say?"

"Quiet!" Ron yelled. They stopped. He was usually soft spoken. "Listen to me. I'm going out there. Stay here. Keep the door—"

"What, locked? Why?" Trisha said.

"Keep it closed, that's all." He gave them each a stern look to confirm their cooperation.

The snow was knee deep but the storm had begun to let up and he could make out a dull three quarter moon. In the West there was fat white dot, rather a pinwheel-shaped star or planet. He watched the sky begin to open its black case, taking on its jewels, and placing them as if in a crown. Had this been a normal night he would have delighted in the spectacle. But there was the grim task; he had to see Paul, to see for himself. He carried his vet bag along. If he couldn't do anything for his brother at least he'd check on the horse Paul had loved so much.

When he entered he saw horseshoe tracks of fresh snow. The rug Catherine had described was unraveled, lying askew. He pulled it flat on the floor—nothing. He felt as if he'd been struck in the back with a shovel. The realization that Catherine had lied, or worse. The idea that Catherine might have done something to Paul was horrifying. He knew about her score card and fits of anger. She wasn't capable of that, he told himself. But what had happened to his brother? He turned to leave and stepped on something. He lifted the rug and found Paul's wallet containing various credit cards, some cash and a business card from Niko's Greek 'n' Eat. There was a phone number written on the back. Stunned, he slipped it into his pocket. Paul had been there. He considered the rug again and left.

The sky was clear now, brimming with stars and planets. The Milky Way appeared as a glowing, diaphanous scarf fluttering leisurely in the sky. He paused a moment; he thought he heard Paul's voice in the distance. "Good girl." Did he actually hear it or imagine it? He waited. Nothing, but he sensed that something was out there beyond the pines. The depth of love he felt for his brother was so overwhelming he fell to his knees cupping the snow and prayed. "Paul, I accept whoever, whatever you are. Please, come to me. Just come to me."

He pushed open the heavy door. Trisha brandished a steak knife and was thrusting it at Catherine who held up an ottoman against her assault. Ron quickly brought her down on the floor. "Stop," his voice boomed. "My brother is dead for Christ's sake. I think," he added tentatively. Catherine heaved the ottoman at Trisha's head, missing it by inches.

"Your bitch of a wife tried to kill me."

He got up deliberately, hoisting Trisha by the collar, depositing her on the sofa like a rag doll. "Sit," he commanded. Unused to aggressive behavior from Ron, Catherine backed away frightened. "He's not in there," he said, calmly. "Where is he, Cat?"

"I told you, he's alive," Trisha said weakly.

Catherine sobbed as she made her way to the liquor cabinet. "I'm frightened, Ron, very frightened. Don't do anything to me." She lifted a bottle of rum and took a long pull of it.

"I'm not going to do anything to you—you know that."

"You think I did something to Paul. I can tell."

"You did," Trisha snuffled. "He was married to you."

Ron stood over her. "If you don't shut up, I'm going to sedate you." She looked at him quizzically. "Ron, I knew—"

"Shut up!" he thundered. "I need to think." She collapsed and whimpered into a pillow.

"He's...not there, Cat," he repeated.

"Oh, God." She dropped her face in her hands. "Are they going to arrest me?"

Ron opened his bag and inventoried the contents nervously. "He's not there," he said to himself. He whispered, "Where the fuck is he?"

An enforced silence overcame them. Just the sound of quiet whimpering and deep breathing as they tried to calm themselves. They could hear the Neilson grandfather clock ticking and groaning in the den. Ron thought perhaps he should call the chief and report what he'd found. He paced into to the dining room trying to make a decision. Suddenly, there was an enormous banging on the porch steps; a one-two percussive pounding like two sledge hammers in syncopation. Instantly, they were at the picture window. The sound increased, now a one-two, three, and four, a massive pronouncement on the wood porch that shook the floor boards under them. Then, as sudden as it had begun, it stopped. They couldn't see anything. The door creaked; it bowed in slowly, creaking. It made a splintering sound as the hinges slowly gave way.

Cautiously, Ron approached the door. "No," Catherine begged. "Please." Trisha was up, her eyes open and wild like amber night lights. Paul unhinged the latch and backed away. The door ripped from the hinges and fell into the room with a tremendous crash. The open space was filled with moving white and black shapes that began to recede. Millie reared up on her back legs, smashing the porch light above her as she turned, taking the five steps in one jump, showering them with snow. In the warm light spilling from the windows and the moonlight reflecting on snow, they saw the rider turn back and smile at them congenially, if not apologetically. It was Paul, dressed in his riding gear. White flouncy shirt, brown embroidered suede pants, black riding boots, and his signature studded cowboy hat he'd picked up at the rodeo in Lancaster. Millie was outfitted with her finest Skyhorse Compadre saddle. Paul touched her left ear and she turned full face to them and crossed her front legs, bowed, shook her head "no," then "yes." And then she smiled, her lips revealing a set of immaculate clean teeth Ron had treated two weeks before, all twenty-four of them.

"She's smiling. Look, she's smiling," Trisha yelled.

Ron was staring at his brother's face, transfixed. It was Paul's face, but the expression was off. It reminded him of the Indian gods, their faces serene, a teasing smile of ultimate calm, and the eyes, Paul's eyes, seemed to be looking at all of them and none of them at the same time. They were focused inward, Ron understood with a shock. Paul seemed only to experience himself as he was now, transformed. Then, Paul's gaze shifted; Ron found himself staring at his own image in Paul's right eye. It seemed to transmit out of Paul's gaze, and enlarge before Ron's face almost a foot away. Then it was gone. It occurred to Ron, much later, that somehow Millie's expression had been similar to Paul's. Something about her eyes.

Paul lifted his hat, slid off his Red Stone bolo tie and tossed it to Catherine. Millie practically leapt into the air from her position and wheeled away from them, quickly attaining speed. "Paul," Catherine shrieked. "Paul, come back."

Once in the field, Paul put Millie through a routine of poses and feats. He stood on her saddle and waved his hat, tossed it up and caught it. He pressed his arms into her withers and performed half of an arm stand. He rode her facing backwards. She reared and he smoothly slid over her crop to her tail head, then disappeared under her by her stifle. They could make out his hands gripping the stirrups, his body being dragged through the snow drifts. He appeared atop of her completely white, an angular snowman riding a wild horse toward the ridge. Millie slowed as they got there as if she needed time to rethink the stone fence, which went through a low lying area before it rose higher than any other point. It led to the road half a mile from the lake. She made a wide turn, galloping straight for the porch. She picked up speed, lifting her huge frame out of the snow with awesome power, Paul bouncing up and down. Ron sensed that this was the finale, Paul's curtain call. Millie came up fast and short, dousing them with another shower. The three of them just stared at Paul.

"Paul," Catherine started down the stairs; she stopped and pressed the string tie to her mouth. Again, Paul bowed in the saddle and tipped his hat. As Millie reared and turned, her massive hooves swung threateningly close to Catherine. Horse and rider sped away.

Ron felt something warm on his face. He touched the tears streaming from his eyes as he mouthed the words to himself, "Goodbye. Goodbye, Paul…my brother. I will always keep you here." He placed his palm over his heart.

Millie ran with demonic determination at the high stone wall; she wasn't calculating it this time. They disappeared for a moment as they descended into the shallow valley. Trisha grasped the railing and leaned over. "Where's he going? Ron? What's happening?" Millie emerged near the top of the hill, galloping at a pace that didn't seem possible under the conditions. They saw her muscular front legs lift until they were air born; they seemed to fly over the wall, momentarily taking their place in the constellations that curved brilliantly around them in the black sky. They hung there for a moment, a fantastic ornament, and a symbol of transformation. Paul let out an ecstatic whoop, and then they were gone. Trisha extended her arms and hollered, "Don't go! I want to see more tricks!" Catherine grabbed the back of her outfit and threw her violently over the railing head first, causing Trisha to disappear into a deep drift, her gold footies kicking frantically in the clear air.

They didn't come back that night, or the next morning, or the next day. There was some pressure exerted on Ron and Catherine to account for Paul's whereabouts, a question of habeas corpus. How could he have disappeared, and on a big, white horse, no less? No one from Shrewsbury reported an odd sighting. A missing persons report was filed, but within a month foul play was ruled out due to lack of evidence, though it was damn curious. Even so, Ron got occasional calls from Chief Montecalvo to ask if he'd seen Paul around. Ron answered carefully so as not to create more suspicion. The Chief had already rejected Ron and Catherine's version of the event, assuming it was an aberration resulting from being holed up in the house during the storm. He'd made no mention of Catherine's stash she left on the kitchen table when he'd made his initial investigation. Nor did he include one sentence of Trisha's testimony into the record.

Ron had an idea, an intuition that was too fantastic to articulate to the chief or any sane person he knew (of which there seemed to be few left). He suspected that Paul had ridden off that night destined to take his place among those fabled and plagued creatures like Big Foot, Pig Man, the Dover Demon, The Wolf Man, and others. Those curious individuals who move painfully through the gloom, misunderstood, feared, and hated. Or loved, as Ron did his brother, and still hoped for his return in whatever form he chose to manifest. Desperate one afternoon, he consulted Madame Giselle in Framingham. One of his clients told him that she had made it possible for him to communicate with Pepper, his Siamese cat, after she passed over. Before Ron explained why he was there, Giselle described Paul in detail, including his ironic mindset and his desperate search for his true identity. She told Ron that if he didn't give up, if he loved his brother as she knew he did, he would find something. He would have to open himself up (first his wallet for a hundred and twenty-five dollars) and be willing to enter into the other world. Step through the doorway at least.

Amazed and reassured after his meeting with Giselle, he stopped at Niko's Greek 'n' Eat Café on Stafford Street. He ordered Paul's favorite: Haddock Saganaki, Greek salad, and a side of Kalamata olives. Paul had brought him there a few times. He'd wanted him to meet Niko's wife, Pasht. Paul had been tutoring her, or at least explaining aspects of *The Odyssey* to her and the foundations of Greek tragedy. Pasht was from Fira, the capital of Santorini, and had come to Worcester to live with her aunt and enroll in Becker College to get a degree in Hospitality and Tourism. She met Niko, who managed the food services at the college, and they were married within three months. She was nineteen. From the beginning, Niko treasured her like a priceless Grecian urn, causing her to become claustrophobic.

Pasht had one desire: to return home to Greece. Her father still maintained a restaurant and inn on a terrace high above the ocean. With her degree from Becker she could help improve the business and allow her parents a well-deserved retirement. She was obsessed with the native language and kept it up by attending St. Spyridon and participating in the festival, dancing and singing. She spoke with the old ladies for hours, immersing herself in the language. She'd found a copy of A.T. Murray's translation of *The Odyssey* (1919) and was reading it. Paul was impressed with her fierce desire to learn and offered her additional resources, including access to the Homer multi-text project, and some of his personal notes. She began emailing him on a regular basis, ostensibly with questions about dialect, etc. He answered her queries in detail, suggesting other texts and useful web sites.

She wanted to take a course with him at Holy Cross, but Niko forbade it. Paul was oblivious to Niko's rage when Pasht would sit across from him in the booth to practice some new vocabulary. Paul had brought the English department to Niko's for a Christmas party. Though enraged, Niko didn't want it to interfere with business; he just simmered with resentment. In a moment of flirtatious scholarship she said to Paul, "I would like to take a skewer and stab it in his green eye." Paul thought the reference to Polyphemus was charming. But he was genuinely shocked when Ron pointed out that he was part of Pasht's plan to return to Fira—it was obvious. Paul was stunned, but wondered fleetingly how much it would cost to transport a horse from Boston to an Aegean Island. The last time Paul saw Pasht she was working the register. She wore sunglasses, but the bruise extended over her entire cheek. She didn't answer when he asked how her studies were going and she seemed to have some difficulty lifting her arm. He went to Niko, who was carving a raw piece of sirloin. "Bastard," he said. Niko didn't respond; he kept carving, then stabbed the knife into the beef all the way to the hilt, his back to Paul. Paul left and didn't return. He contacted a travel agent and purchased a first-class one-way ticket to Fira. One of the waitresses slipped it to her in an order pad.

Eventually, Chief Montecalvo put it all together, or thought he had. The Chief knew Niko professionally as he'd investigated an assault that took place behind the restaurant some years earlier. A technician from Cold One who serviced Niko's walk-in and freezers was found beaten unconscious behind the dumpster. Niko didn't know anything about it. But the Chief and everyone else new that the guy had given Pasht his cell number. Pasht admitted that he had, but only in case they needed an emergency repair. The guy refused to sign a complaint against Niko and the whole thing went away, sort of.

Later on, when Pasht disappeared without a trace, the Chief, in cooperation with the FBI, tracked her down with the help of INTERPOL. It took approximately ten minutes to confirm that she'd returned to Fira and was managing the family business. Niko referred to her as "the dead one." It was just a matter of time before he would take his favorite carving knife and sail for Greece. He was due for a little vacation anyway. The Chief went outside of the usual chain of command, bypassed the commissioner and contacted a childhood friend, Spiros, who'd grown up with him in the neighborhood. Spiros held a high leadership position in what was called the "Greek Outfit." Spiros visited Niko's place and complimented him excessively on his tzatziki, Stuffed Peppers, and Mushroom Orzo. He tipped the waitress fifty dollars. Then he wrote out a recipe while Niko watched appreciatively. It was for a Moussaka with melted feta and chickpeas. It called for the testicles of Niko, ground fine in a meat grinder. Spiros slid the piece of paper to him and said, "I'd cancel my travel plans, if I had any. You know?" Niko canceled them that day.

Chief Montecalvo was a thoughtful man and had done his homework. He was aware of Paul's "friendship" with Pasht. He'd played along with the white horse hoax, Paul becoming an urban legend, or whatever crap that was about. After Paul's departure he was certain where he'd find him. He'd no doubt that Pasht had gone ahead to set up the comfy nest for his arrival. He immediately contacted someone at INTERPOL and got the details. There was no such person as a distinguished American college professor on Santorini, much less a white shire horse who performed amazing tricks for carrots. It turned out that Pasht was engaged to an assistant curator at the Archaeological Museum (ceramic vessels and vases dating from the Geometric and Hellenistic Periods.) In the year since she arrived, she had successfully increased her parents' business to the point that they did retire and got to visit her mother's sister in Worcester—without drawing any attention to themselves (after all, who knows what Niko might do to get revenge against Pasht?). Profoundly disappointed, the chief had no other leads left to follow. Reluctantly, he gave some credence to the possibility that something out of the ordinary had happened that stormy night. After all, it was Worcester.

The spring and summer after Paul vanished were brilliant with light and vegetation, as if in harsh contrast to the darkness and loss Ron endured. He'd taken up Tai Chi and joined a group of wobbly spiritualists who tried to channel passed loved ones, though it went against the scientific grain of his profession. He looked everywhere for signs of Paul.

Good to his word, he looked after Catherine, answered every call for assistance, supported her through mourning and depression, and had dinner with her at least once a week. He sat through her tirades against Paul, how Paul's ultimate selfishness left her alone, a widow without even a corpse to bury. Catherine had grown a powerful strain of African marijuana in the greenhouse. When she drank on top of it she seemed to be hallucinating. "Do you see him?"

"Who?" Ron asked.

"Paul. He's standing in the corner there. Look, the bastard is smiling at you. Fucker! He's holding up his index finger like he's saying, 'Just a moment—just wait.' Goddamn fucker!" These outbursts were as intriguing as they were distressing to Ron. It seemed that only women could channel the shadowy transactions of the other world.

Exacerbating his grief, by mid-October, Trisha was going off again. She'd thrown all of her containers of medication into the duck pond, causing some hyperactivity among the Goldeneye and Mergansers, who swam sideways, knocking one another around like feathered bumper cars. It was October 18. Paul was assisting in the delivery of a colt that had a leg wrapped around its neck. The mare was uncomfortable and jittery. It required all of his skill. He noticed the Jeep lurching down the drive, but was too occupied to check on her.

Trisha drove into Worcester, and checked herself and Grady into the Crown Plaza. She ran up a hefty bill ordering splits of champagne and extravagant meals to her room. All the time Strauss Waltzes echoed down the hall at an exorbitant volume. At some point, she appeared on the mezzanine balcony embroiled in a disagreement with Grady—they'd had a falling out. Hotel guests watched in shock as she strangled the bear and threw his already lifeless body on top of a group of beverage industry executives who'd come to tour the Polar plant. A maid rushed to cover her with a bar towel as she was wearing a torn negligee made skin-tight from spilled champagne, suggesting that she and Grady had roughed it up a bit. This might have been tolerable if the episode had ended there, but it didn't. She managed to invade the staff locker room and emerge in a bellhop's uniform and slip out the kitchen exit without being detected. Trisha hailed a cab and descended upon the DCU Center on Foster Street.

It was half-time between the Worcester Sharks and the Providence Bruins, a highly charged and competitive match, already interrupted twice by two line brawls. She got a ticket and moved easily through the arena, being taken perhaps as an official in her bellhop uniform. She followed a referee through the gate, then moved seductively toward Finz, the Worcester mascot, letting her drum-shaped bellboy hat drop, exposing her long, golden-dyed tresses. Finz, who was used to spontaneous behavior initiated by wild fans, went right along with Trisha and swept her up in his fins. To the delight of the crowd of six thousand, they performed an impromptu ice tango. It was picked up by all the local news media covering the game. The footage was then instantaneously transmitted to the New York affiliate and broadcast throughout the Metropolitan area. Unfortunately, Ron learned of it from a client in his waiting room; it had already made it on to CNN within an hour, and was featured in the Post the next morning: Hot Girl Bellhop Gets Down with Worcester Shark. Ron watched his wife clinging to Finz as he spun her energetically around, leaning her backward for a sultry tango kiss at the end. The crowd went nuts.

Ron sighed and calmly returned to his exam room to treat a cockatoo that had caught its wing in a blender.

Fortunately, there were no trespassing or criminal charges stemming from the bill she'd run up at the Crown Plaza. Ron took care of that. Her doctor recommended an innovative program in New Hampshire that involved water therapy and tuning forks. Ron resisted at first because of the distance. She would feel alienated. But he relented because there was nothing else for her in the Boston area. She would be required to stay there for the entire treatment period—no signing herself out this time. She agreed, and would not return home until just about the same time as Paul had disappeared a year ago.

It was the last week of October and Ron adjusted uneasily to the lack of activity in the house with Trisha gone. He was accustomed to chaos, shepherding her through her moods and fits. Constantly keeping watch over her. Most of his conversations were with animals, reassuring them that he could help; he could make them okay, most of the time. He'd adopted an old dog named Leo. He belonged to a farmer who resented his vet bill for Leo's arthritis. He kept saying, "I ought to shoot that old dog." Leo followed Ron around the house, stayed in the office as he treated his patients, and sat on the porch, sighing contentedly at Ron's feet, aware of his reprieve and the kindness of his new master.

Ron could hardly hear the phone on the porch. He'd hung up on reporters who wanted to interview him about Trisha's appearance on CNN—the video had gone viral and he didn't appreciate the attention. Some movie producer wanted to buy the rights for a film script. Ron answered at least one query about buying his practice. He'd been researching small towns in Northern California and toyed with the idea of just disappearing into one of them. Disappearing like Paul, maybe more like hiding. He loved the ocean and had taken Trisha to their house in Truro every summer she was able to go, which he calculated had been damn few times because of her illness, the "fucking illness," as he referred to it.

But now, with fall moving in and then facing the first winter without Paul, he felt taken over by the change of season, dominated by an irresistible lethargy. He'd sit on the porch swing most evenings sipping a stout or a claret and observe the quickening of the geese. He got out the camping equipment and selected a down sleeping bag and his Coleman gas Big Hat Camp Lantern. He and Paul had enjoyed the welcoming light it gave off on their camping trips years earlier. Paul used to joke that lantern light kept the phantoms away. He made himself comfortable. He even brought out the Coleman stove and threw an occasional burger on for himself and Leo. There was just too much of Trisha's energy in the house to spend all of his time in there. There'd been no frost yet and he'd sleep soundly on the hammock or he'd watch the constellations tumble like wheels of light and shards of molten glass through the sky. He realized that he would have to reinvent his life. He didn't really have a wife he could depend on. Paul was gone. Catherine was becoming intolerable, bitter, broken, and addicted. My only friends, he realized…are animals.

One evening at dusk he sat on the porch swing, Leo lying at his feet. He marveled at the scene. The hay, turning leaves, tree bark, stone fence, sky—all bore colors that seemed plucked from the burnished strings of an ancient harp. He noticed something in the grazing field. At first he attributed it to the mist that rose after sunset and the cool autumnal air settling upon the ground. There appeared in the mist a form that was slightly more illuminated than the space around. He slipped on his boots and walked slowly toward the form, Leo at his heel, crunching the brittle grass beneath them. As he approached, the shape seemed to rotate and resembled a horse and rider. He stopped and gasped. Leo growled.

"Leo, quiet." He wasn't sure if he was actually seeing what he thought he was seeing, because he'd seen it in his mind's eye so often. He could be imagining it. When he got about ten feet from the object, the rider removed his hat and regarded him with unequivocal affection. His feet became fastened to the ground; Ron stared at him, and then finally nodded. The rider returned his nod.

"Paul, is that you?"

Millie answered with a deep curtsy that tilted the rider's face closer to Ron's. He cried as he studied Paul's features. "I've missed you…Paul. I need you." Paul nodded again. With difficulty Ron commanded himself to walk forward. He held his hand up to Millie's muzzle. Paul backed her away gently. "Let me touch you," Ron pleaded.

Millie stood motionless. He approached her side and placed his hand on her flank and felt something, not solid, but more like moving air, condensed as if the molecules were bound tight and charged. He looked up at Paul, who reached down. Ron took his hand and held it firm in his. There was room for him behind Paul. Millie could easily carry them both; she was a powerhouse. He pulled on his brother's hand as if to mount up, but Paul kept him in place, gazing at him with more tender regard and care than Ron had ever known. A warm wave was moving down from Paul's hand into Ron's and through his body down to his feet. Ron repeated the words that had been sent to his mind from Paul, "Not now. Not yet."

"Paul, let me go with you." But Paul had released his hand. He didn't try to follow them when Millie turned and walked slowly into the mist. Then he could hear her trotting away through the dried leaves. Ron watched until they were enveloped in the mist. "Paul," Ron called after them. "Paul…please."

He didn't know how long he stood there. Leo rubbed against his leg and whined. When he finally turned to start back to the house he couldn't see anything through the mist. It had grown so thick could not see the sky and had no idea which way to go. He could not even see Leo sitting by his foot. Again, he stood and listened. He thought he could still hear the leaves kicked up and the twigs snapping as Paul made his way. But to where, Ron wondered. "Good girl," he seemed to hear Paul say. Suddenly, he remembered something Catherine had said that night, "We talk about love when someone dies. Why is that?"

He'd answered her, "Because it's all you have…when you can have it." He stared in the direction Paul had gone and again felt something move through the core of his body—his soul, as he perceived it. It was like the shock of ice on his bare back, but immediately warmed his spine. It was, he understood, he hoped, the love he could have—the love he would carry with him. His feet turned involuntarily. He picked up Leo and walked directly through the dense fog. He walked and walked without doubt or deviation until he could see the arching lantern light on his porch.

Fireball Fitness

Jim liked to tell me which part of the building he had just come from. The various floors, conference rooms, and closets held for him a majesty I didn't understand. He explained to me once that his folks never took him anywhere. He'd been born in Peekskill and had lived there all his life. He'd been to Albany just once to visit his grandfather in the VA Hospital. "Max," he announced excitedly, "I've just come from the boiler room." He might have been returning from Bombay or Prague. "We've got a problem." He waited for me to speak. He liked it when I was alarmed and asked questions.

"What is it, Jim?"

"Well, Max, it's water. Pump room's flooded."

"One of the pipes?"

"No. Least I don't think so. Charlie says it could be worse." Jim nodded appreciatively at my distress. "Worse?" I was thinking of the pump, the compressor, P.M. Filter, and the vast network of tubes and pipes that barely serviced our thirty-year-old swimming pool.

"Let's go." I pinched a note on the clipboard and turned to meet Courtney's unpleasant gaze. She was our yoga teacher and part time receptionist. She had an annoying habit of taking visual inventory before she spoke: "It's the runoff valve for the steam room. It ought to be flushed every night, not twice a week." She said her words exactly one at a time, dropping them like ordinance.

"I flush it twice a day since it acted up," Jim defended.

"It's not in the notebook," said Courtney, handing it to me with meaning. She had made it no secret that she thought I was ineffective and marginally involved with my job. She expected to be promoted to club manager when I left, hopefully before. I'd retaliate by bringing her printouts from the Internet advertising for yoga instructors in Southeast Asia. She also didn't like the fact that I was overly respectful to "underlings" and that I never worked out. I did have an aversion to physical activity, but I was naturally thin, wore the club shirt, and collected my money at least until I could finish my last year of grad school.

"We're going down to the boiler room," Jim whispered, wide-eyed and solemn, suggesting a voyage down the Nile River Valley. I told Courtney to phone lapsed members and offer them our come-back special, which included six months of free warm towels. She said we lost members because the place wasn't clean enough. She glared at Jim and gave me some too.

Jim and I retreated. "That girl gives mean eye time," he said. On the first landing, he bent down to pick up a granola bar wrapper. A heavyset man jogged past, leaving a vapor trail of Gold Bond Powder. "He's going to have himself a heart attack," Jim observed. Jim did not approve of rigorous exercise. He was skinnier than me and addicted to pork rinds and Diet Dr. Pepper.

Three flights down, I borrowed Jim's flashlight and examined as much of the pool shell as I could see. It was a rusted, square structure like the bottom of a barge, no longer seaworthy. It creaked and moaned as our members sloshed above in the stupefying chlorinated water. It was suspended from the ceiling like it had been dropped from a C5 and was supported by crumbling cement pillars. It sloped gradually from three and half to eight feet deep. Underneath it was a labyrinth of narrow trenches that had been dug to lay PVC pipe through the wall of the newly renovated fitness center. Our members had complained about the one-flight commute to the hot tub and power showers, hence the renovation. Along the dim, shallow valley of dirt and around the pipes, legions of roaches marched. They foraged, reproduced, and survived.

Occasionally, a big one would find its way into an exercise room and surprise the women twisting on the mats. They'd scream and run. Courtney would have to take it on with the push broom or snap a damp towel with lethal precision, which she was good at. At the moment, the women's Aquacise class was in progress. We could hear arms and legs swishing through the water as the instructor shouted above a pulsating boom box. Jim took the light from me and shined it into the filter/containment cylinder. "Nothing," he muttered. Sometimes he found diamond rings, or earrings, one time a diaphragm. We constantly reminded them to remove their jewelry and lock it up before entering the pool, but they either forgot or disagreed with the policy.

We made our way to the back of the room, down five deep steps that left us on the landing above the pump room. I peered in at Charlie who was hunched over a set of meters, a cigarette dangling from his lips. I saw the water just above his ankles slapping at his knee-high, yellow, steel-toed fireman's boots. Jim told Charlie that he'd found me at the reception desk. Charlie didn't turn around, "It be dryer up there than it be down here."

"Sure is," Jim said, sniffing the air, "and it smells like someone forgot to flush."

"What is it?" I asked. "The shell looks all right. Can you tell where it's coming from?"

Charlie angled his head toward the chlorine tank, smoke streaming from his nostrils like a great Black demon. "Somewheres," he answered.

Jim and I waded into the pump room and took a look at the meters; they were normal. Our entrance created a series of small waves that lapped against the cinder block walls.

"Max?" Jim said, waiting for me to answer.

"Yes, Jim?"

"Charlie thinks it's a hairline in the shell. That's what he told me." Jim looked toward Charlie expectantly. Charlie's reluctance to speak was calculated. He didn't like answering to a white man. Finally he did, "I think it be that, didn't say it was."

I glanced at the stairs feeling some relief. They were wet with boot prints. If the pool shell were leaking there would be a steady stream of water pouring down the stairs. Charlie seemed to read my thoughts and pursued a developing theory. "If the shell cracked in the deep end, it be leaking in the trenches, in the ground, you see. The water leak under the foundation and in the pump room here, you see. Water find its own level. That a fact of science." He flicked his cigarette butt into the brew and tapped out another, set it in his mouth and lit up in one effortless motion.

"You know, Charlie," Jim began, pedantically, "the pool shell's guaranteed for life."

"Whose life? Pool's? Ours? Was you here in 1972 when they put it in?"

I felt a wave of anxiety. I knew that the pool held about 155,000 gallons of water. If the shell were cracked, it might eventually rupture. And if we happened to be in the pump room, like we were now, the explosion of water would kill us without a doubt.

"Well, it is guaranteed," Jim's voice trailed off.

"Maybe some of them fine peoples upstairs pay more dues and buy us a new pool," Charlie said, one side of his mouth turned down. I knew what Charlie meant by "fine" people. He meant the ones with the cell phones and expensive workout gear. People whose soiled towels Charlie and Jim picked up. And me too.

"I wouldn't count on that," Jim said, tapping the WOG meter.

"We have insurance," I said evenly. I didn't want to let Charlie get started on this subject. He could be intensely caustic about the club members, as we all could at times. But he knew more about our rotting infrastructure than anyone else. He was the expert on Fireball Fitness. He was also one of the sixteen original Peekskillians who'd witnessed and photographed the famous Peekskill meteorite with its amazing fireball. The one that slammed into the red Malibu coupe in 1992, hence the name Fireball Fitness, because the first owner had been an astronomy buff. Charlie was fiercely proud of this and loved to tell the story. He seemed to feel that it gave him discrete scientific credentials.

I decided that the pool shell was not cracked. I took a chance and tried to spark Charlie's imagination toward problem solving. "I don't smell any sewage, so it's not coming from the locker rooms. Could it be a holding tank?" I guessed.

Charlie cocked his head to the side; a smile split his face and revealed a silver tooth. "Don't have no holding tank, Max." Whenever Charlie referred to me by my name, it meant that the playing field had been leveled again. We were more than equal, a premise I never questioned. At the last Christmas party, Charlie and I were pretty drunk, sharing some inappropriate innuendo about Courtney. He put his arm around me and said, "You're a white boy, Max, but you're a good boy." His gesture seemed kind and paternal. I gave him a bear hug and he shoved me against the Snapple machine calling me a "faggot."

"See up there." He raised his cigarette indicating two corroded pipes with plastic clamps around them. "Them the waste pipes. Busted 'bout a year ago before you got here."

"I remember that," Jim said. "I was in the Tower Room setting up for a meeting. The toilet flushed—scared hell out of me. Every toilet in the building flushed at once."

"We had a shit shower?" Charlie laughed. He waddled through the water, cigarette ash floating down his arm. As he stirred up the water, I noticed some bubbles surfacing near the center of the pool.

"Charlie, did you check the drain?"

"Nothin' wrong with the drain." He was emphatic.

"What are those things?" I asked, glancing at a pod of mustard colored bubbles that had just surfaced.

"Them is bubbles. They fill up with air and float to the top," he said.

I decided that it was time for me to act like a manager even if I didn't feel like one. Simultaneously, it occurred to me that I was going to quit this job, leave it to Courtney, and good luck.

"Charlie, let's assume the problem isn't the pool shell. What else could it actually be?"

Jim answered for Charlie; "It's got to be the catch under the drain."

"What you talking 'bout?" Charlie snapped at Jim. "The catch let water out but stop it from coming in. That's what a catch do."

"Maybe the catch is broken, or something is stuck behind it," Jim suggested.

"What do you think stuck behind it? A fish? Mr. Lloyd Bridges from the Sea Hunt? Catch is one piece of solid aluminum—nothing there to break."

Jim pressed his case, "If the municipal sewer system backed up, the pressure could have broken the catch." Jim eyes shone with pleasure.

Charlie glared at him defiantly, shook his head, and blew an exasperated cloud of smoke. "You forgetting this building on a hill. Water flow down, not up, fact a science."

I reached for a broom handle, hoisted it up with its bristles dripping rusty soup. I began raking it over the drain hoping to clear away whatever might be obstructing it. Momentarily, I heard a gurgling sound; it was a good sound.

"Look at that," Jim said. He aimed his flashlight on a cockroach floating on a matchbook along the far wall. "You wonder how they survive. They're smart. That one made himself a raft."

Charlie flicked his cigarette butt in front of the roach. It hissed. "One a them things comes out from under the pool yesterday. Big! You could put a saddle on it." He tapped down a fresh cigarette on his thumbnail.

"There's more of them," Jim said, spotting several roaches clinging to a scrap of wood. The water must have been attracting them from under the pool shell into the pump room and a watery death. "It's instinct," Jim added. "They like water. That's how they got here in the first place, on merchant ships and with the settlers."

"Bullshit," Charlie mocked.

My broom work had made rough seas for the insects. One had been swept overboard and was roach-paddling after the wood scrap. I held the broom down with my foot and twisted the handle, but it was stuck. I looked around for something else I could use to pry open the drain.

"They did so," Jim insisted. "We didn't have roaches in this country until they came over on the boats."

Charlie let out a harsh laugh. "Them cockaroaches sit around, play shuffleboard, drink champagne, that what they do?"

"The roaches came over here just like the rats, hidden in the bottom of ships."

Charlie was shouting now: "The rat come from the beaver. We got our own rat, got our own damn cockaroach."

Jim looked at Charlie as if he were a pathetic figure. "Have you ever heard of the Bubonic Plague?"

Charlie's arms flailed the air as he slopped toward Jim, red ash glowing. "American cockaroach kick ass compare to the foreign roach. Foreign rat don't know his ass from his elbow. Neither do you." The two men were inches apart and angry. I couldn't imagine they were going to come to blows over this.

"Charlie, is there a hose down here we could use?" I asked, trying to change the subject.

"Tell him, Max," Jim said, "You went to college."

I looked at the two of them, imagined the tableau we made, a bewildered skinny white guy, a kind coffee-skinned man, and Charlie, a fierce black god—arguing about roaches and rats. My sneakers were soaked and I felt ridiculous. "I really don't know," I said apologetically.

They continued to face off. Jim said, with authority, "I read it in the *Enquirer*, that the roach first came to America with Christopher Columbus. And more came with the Pilgrims after that."

"Oh yeah, them Pilgrims. That what you got upstairs with their hundred dollar gym shoes, and we down here standin' in shit. Right, Max?" Charlie looked hard into my eyes.

I didn't answer. We were quiet, engulfed in a fog. Only the lapping water and hum of pool machinery spoke. Finally, I said, "Let's run a hose out that window to the curb and pump it out of here. Where's the auxiliary pump?"

Charlie stomped by me and put his hand on a rusted piece of metal that sat atop an old chemical drum. It looked like something from the Guggenheim. "This be it, busted, mostly for decoration."

I kicked water up, splashing the row of meters and piping.

"Doesn't anything work around here? We're just going to have to rent one."

"What we need is a plumber," Jim said. "Someone who knows what he's doing."

"Charlie's a plumber," I said without irony.

"I am and I ain't. I do plumbing. Never said I was a plumber. They don't wanna pay a regular plumber seventy-two dollar a hour."

Jim took the opportunity to take a shot at Charlie. "You're not a plumber, and you don't know a thing about the history of roaches."

"Leastways I ain't no friggin' pervert reading the *Enquirer*, folks raising from the dead, two-headed baby, five hundred pound dog...bullshit."

"How'd you know about the five hundred pound dog unless you read the *Enquirer*?

Charlie muttered, "Ah, heard it on the bus."

A sound like a small underwater detonation got our attention. A pod of bubbles broke forcefully upon the surface. A series of mustard-colored rings spread over the water. "Look, Charlie," I said, "maybe it is the drain. Maybe it is plugged up. Let's try a plunger on it."

He was silent for a few moments, mulling over my assault. "If you wanna."

Jim clapped his hands together. "Good. I'll get a plunger. There's one, I'm sure, in the utility closet by the men's locker room." His eyes twinkled as he slogged up the steps with a sense of purpose and adventure one might take to Nepal.

The light had begun to fade behind the cobwebs in the windows. Charlie and I waited, listening to the meters tick, the tentative, creaking sewage pipes, and the increasing regurgitation of the drain. In the fading light I saw Charlie disappear and reappear in the gloom and cigarette smoke, his nostrils streaming white columns. He spoke quietly, reflectively, the animus seeming to have run out of him.

"Ain't my fault nothin' works 'round here. I told these people we need a new compressor. That a World War II compressor over there. Oughta be in a museum. What they 'spect a man to do?"

I exhaled with Charlie, staring down at the water between us. I watched a couple of roaches floating along, their legs no longer twitching. "Charlie, I gave you a good write up. I always do. I'll tell you something else…" For some reason I wanted to tell him that I was quitting, that I would probably be gone by the end of the week. It wasn't the kind of place you had to give notice. There was constant turnover.

"Ain't no way Columbus bring the cockaroach to America. Way I figure it each country got their own roach, got their own rat. Just like they got their own flag, you see. German folks is in Germany. They not in Taiwan, 'cause that where the Taiwan folks is. And so is the German cockaroach and rat, and the Taiwan cockaroach and rat. What we need Columbus to bring them here for? We got our own."

"Yes," I said, "yes, Charlie," a blanket of weariness overtaking me. I just wanted to be dry, dry and far away. "What do you think of prying off the grate? We'd get better suction that way. Is there a crowbar down here?"

"There was a cockaroach Olympics, I mean the bad-ass, mean-boy roaches 'round the world. I bet the American roach win hands down. You know why? American cockaroach more 'daptable and connivin' than the other. Cuz of competition, you see. We the big competition country in the world."

"I disagree." Jim stood atop the stairs, cradling a large, green jug in his arms. "I would sooner bet on the Swiss roach because as a people the Swiss have always been peaceful and stayed out of wars. Of course," he added quickly, "you can't draw conclusions between people and roaches."

"Swiss cockaroach made out a chocolate. They melt when you spray 'em."

Unperturbed, Jim entered looking satisfied with himself. "Would you believe that in this entire building there isn't a single plunger. But I found this." Proudly he held aloft a jug of Liquid Plumber, a priceless artifact from an Egyptian tomb. "By the way Max, guess what?"

"What?"

"Well, I went by the front desk on my way back from the men's locker room and Courtney is having a time of it. Somebody wants a refund on his membership right now. And someone can't get their locker open, and we're out of towels. And she said something crappy about you. That the place was mismanaged because you don't give a damn."

"What?" I started. "Never mind, Jim. Do you think this stuff will work?" The happy thought of seeing Courtney no more suddenly coursed through me. Unemployed was prettier than Courtney. I was starting to feel uplifted despite the putrid smelling water.

"It says here," Jim read out of his pince-nez, "will tackle the toughest clogging, will open a full slop sink of backed up water. Keep away from children and animals. Pour in full strength. Let's see, also, this is the industrial formula and should be used with extreme caution."

"Give me that shit." Charlie wrenched the jug from Jim's arms. "I'm the plumber. You two go up on the steps case this shit eats through your shoes. Jim and I retreated to the landing and watched Charlie remove the protective seal with a pocketknife that had about a six-inch blade.

"Better put out the butt," Jim called down. Says it's flammable." Charlie spit his cigarette out, then jabbed the blade into the foil, dried it on his pants, and slid the knife into his back pocket. Holding the jug steady in two thick hands he lowered it, turning the spout downward. A gel-like, bright green, fluorescent fluid dribbled down into the water. Charlie squatted, immersing it several inches deep, squeezing the sides, forcing it down into the drain. When it was empty, he backed away slowly, cautiously, hoping, I assumed, that nothing would happen.

"Look over there," Jim said. He aimed his flashlight on the scrap, a wedge of Styrofoam, bobbing and busy with many roaches competing for a place on the boat. There were chunks of cardboard and pieces of plastic carrying other passengers as well, a flotilla of roaches navigating very uncertain waters. "See Charlie, they're natural sailors like I said."

"All you got there is some bugs clinging to a bit a wood. Don't prove your bullshit theory 'bout cockaroaches coming to America with Columbus."

Jim spoke calmly, philosophically, convinced he'd won the argument, "Yes, they came with Columbus. They even came with our ancestors on the slave ships. Everything comes from somewhere."

Charlie bared his teeth, then smiled, observing, "I bet you the Africa cockaroach a wicked thing. Maybe kick the American cockaroaches' ass."

A low, terrible sound like an injured sea creature filled the pump room, as bruise-colored bubbles and gas broke violently upon the surface. Charlie backed away, his face frozen with a look of betrayal. He glanced up at Jim and me; we stayed as mute as lawn ornaments. Again came the eruption, this time sending up a greasy, sick geyser about three feet high. It sizzled, dispersing a chemical smell. Jim edged back another stair. "Sounds like it's going to explode."

Another violent disturbance shook the cement foundation and Charlie, with quick and uncanny power leapt onto the landing, his steel-toed fireman's boot smashing my foot. A bolt of pain shot through my foot like electricity and then up my leg. I howled in pain and fell forward toward the brink, but the guys caught me, held me up between them. I was dizzy, like I might pass out. I could hear Charlie apologizing close to my ear over and over. Somehow it was soothing. Yet none of us could take our eyes off the water.

A whirlpool took shape and the water level dropped. It spun around faster and faster pulling everything into its vortex. "There they go," Jim said, focusing his light on the drain. There in the center of the whirlpool were roaches, hundreds of them, maybe a thousand. They must have found their way down from beneath the pool shell along a pipe or a crack in the wall and we're being inexorably pulled into the spiraling water. Amazed, sickened, but somehow uplifted, feeling something drain out the soles of my feet, one crushed, I allowed my full weight to be supported by the two men, an arm around each of their shoulders. We watched until the last shiny brown huddle of insects went roaring into the drain with an enormously loud sucking sound. I could hear myself breathing with the pain and feel the men lean in to hold me up. We looked back and forth from the water line on the wall to the glowing wet floor, a chemical mist hovering above it. We just stood there...looking.

The Future of France

After the dark time, Earl explained to Dr. McKenna what he thought happened to him. For some reason he'd craved a violent rebaptism, a catastrophic interruption of his daily routine. He was compelled to fracture his staid existence, abandon the tenets of good citizenship he'd previously adhered to. The event would mysteriously free him to get on with the rest of his life. Why, he didn't know. He was as helpless as the hundreds of rainbow trout, bass, and walleyes he'd hooked and reeled in over the years. Something deadly and enticing had reeled him in. There was nothing to do but wait for a sharp blow to the back of his head dispatching him into darkness.

Dr. McKenna loved a good theory and manufactured them to fit his patients' symptoms after the fact. He was a devotee of Carl Jung's theories, and was convinced that Earl was an introverted personality forced to play a painful extrovert's role in the community. By virtue of Earl's public service, operating a bustling hardware store, Earl was constantly in the spotlight. He sold feed, hunting rifles, ammunition, fishing rods, bait, gear, tents and other camping supplies. Even sand-wiches, coffee, and firewood to accommodate the summer and fall car loads of tourists who got off the Northway to breathe the bracing pine air and witness the spectacular autumn display. Dr. McKenna suspected that Earl's break might have something to do with unexpressed grief or trauma. Avoiding any formal intake on Earl's childhood, he mostly went with his gut. Luckily, most of his patients seemed to get better on their own.

Earl tolerated Dr. McKenna's theories as he tolerated and respected all those he met in the course of his life. He found a thin book at the library sale, the teachings of Lao-Tzu, and devoured it like a Reader's Digest article in the dentist's office, feeling very much in agreement with Lao's precepts. He was particularly attracted to what Lao-Tzu said to Confucius: that he "was wandering in the unborn." Earl connected with the idea, and further, "The name that can be named is not the constant name." To Earl it was as straightforward as changing the oil and plugs in the Jeep. But he knew to be protective in sharing insight. He only spoke of it to Dexter Grot, his oldest friend, fishing partner, and the most natural, intuitive man he knew, a man who understood most things at a level others just talked around. Dexter had his own inscrutable saying. Whatever happened in town or the world, Dexter always reacted with, "Sure, what else y'd 'spect?"

In good weather Dexter wore a t-shirt displaying a fish skeleton, imprinted with the words 'Women Want Me, Fish Fear Me'. A bumper sticker displayed the same slogan on his truck. He drove a Tundra and needed the hand grip and side board to hoist himself in and out. A Sonoma would have been easier for him to maneuver, but he loved a big ride. Dexter was diminutive, wiry, with taut muscles. He'd hop into an outboard without shifting its weight. He was very quick; he could catch a Jumping Mouse in his hands. His appetite for fish fry, barbeque, church pot roast, Slim Jims, boiled eggs, and Ballantine Ale was well documented, though he could fit in a toddler's high chair. Fishing with Earl was his Tao. They'd spent days on still lakes in complete silence, surrounded by sentinels of Striped Maple, Paper Birch, and Alder trees. Spring fishing brought out Merry Bells,

Trout Lilies and a host of other wildflowers. They were sustained and nourished, in peace. The friends agreed there were other places of beauty on earth, but none as beautiful as their mountain lakes. Earl and Dexter were fishing buddies since high school. The men were physical opposites and spiritual brothers.

Throughout high school Earl worked for his dad in the hardware store that he'd inherited, his siblings attracted to academic or military careers. Earl's dad Willard was a no nonsense, get-'r-done type of man who believed in the intrinsic value of the rural lifestyle—on which, when the topic came up, he lectured inexhaustibly. He distrusted city folks moving into town to enjoy country life, not his kind of country life. His disdain for them rose to his occasionally parking his truck the on the I-87 overpass, from which he'd point out license plates to Earl, particularly suspicious if they were from Jersey or Connecticut. "Yeah, boy, they want our way of life all right. But with all the spoiled ways they forget to leave behind." Willard's disdain for these suburbanites diminished somewhat when they appeared in the shop to buy batteries, screwdrivers, get keys duplicated, and ask for recommendations: plumbers, electricians, and septic tank services. This kept Willard's friends busy. He accommodated them, even untangled fishing line on over-expensive rods they didn't know how to use. That irked him the most. He kept a sign taped to the cash register: My Other Car is a Tractor.

Earl's mother, Deline, was as north as Willard was south. He'd met her on a hunting trip near Quebec. The hunting party wandered into what they thought was a rip snorting tavern that featured live girl singers. It did. There was a chorus of girls, in traditional costume, singing the old songs of the province with piano accompaniment and a conductor. They'd happened upon Provincial French Pride Week. The guys turned tail for the door, seeking a more typical watering hole. But Willard noticed a petite brunette in the back row, and as he was fond of saying, "The moose froze in the creek." After multiple forays to Quebec and interminable concerts and endless cultural immersion, he managed to get her eye, her attention, and miraculously the girl herself. Coaxing her down to Warrensburg as wife and life partner was another story. He persevered again. She was perhaps enamored of a true mountain man (Earl had inherited his dad's stature, six foot five inches, two hundred-forty pounds. Once Deline was ensconced in the three-story Victorian on Clinton Street, she felt that she'd been transported to a savage, uncultured backwater, Warrensburg. Somehow she and Willard negotiated the terrain and the decades ahead.

Deline insisted that Earl and his siblings learn to speak French. This was not an entirely unreasonable idea; about two hours from the border there were many French speakers going back and forth. It came in handy at the shop. She also conducted a History of France class in the garage which allowed for large maps and photographs of both Paris and Montreal. This included important campaigns and battles. She'd secured a large plastic bust of Napoleon from the thrift shop and had the kids spray-paint it psychedelic blue, white, and red, with sparkles. On special occasions if she'd had a bit too much champagne she insisted that the kids refer to her as "Your Grace." Of all the siblings, Earl was the natural linguist.

Earl's high school career centered on accomplishments that pleased Deline. He was President of the Conversational French Club, and won an award for translating several Robert Frost poems, though compromising meter and content, such as: "The woods are lovely, dark and drab." He played French horn in the marching band. He was also a member of the 4-H Club and the proud owner of a prize-winning hen, Marie Antoinette, a lovely chestnut creature with a brilliant red comb. He took her to the New York State Fair in Syracuse to compete. Regrettably, Marie escaped from her cage before

the judging commenced and wandered into the field where the tractor pull was underway. She managed to scurry around a massive rear
tire, but a half-ton sledge followed, spreading her over eight yards
of mud and gravel. Earl walked down the line, following a streak of
blood, picking up golden brown feathers. He couldn't find her head.
This tragedy might have been one of the seeds that contributed to his
trouble that October night many years later. Dr. McKenna's ad hoc
theory of unexpressed grief might have been partially correct after all.

Earl's best doctor and expert on all things Earl was Jolly. Married
to Earl for twenty-nine years, she knew him inside and out like the
Swiss Army Watches he sold at the shop; she sensed that one of his
gears was slipping out of sync before it happened. Determined to
keep her man safe and on track, she did some research and discovered
that a macrobiotic diet was reputed to do wonders for many ailments,
including the psychic kind. Jolly went into motion. On Thursdays
she drove the Cherokee by herself, finally getting a license after a
quarter century, to Albany for macrobiotic cooking classes with Sally
Kleiner.

Jolly was fascinated by Sally, her apparent freedom and rudderless
approach to life. So different from the new young married women
at the Methodist church. Sally lived in a brownstone across from
the Empire State Plaza in downtown Albany. From the bay window
there was a view of the tower that rose above the city, the Thruway,
the shipping port and surrounding countryside. Sally decorated her
walls with posters of Indian goddesses, naked women dancing, multi-
racial children holding hands. She wore loose fitting pants or dresses,
beaded t-shirts without a bra, sandals with rubber spikes that massaged her feet as she walked. Her husband, spoken of blithely, was off
studying something somewhere. His return was a vague prospect.

Jolly became accomplished preparing macrobiotic meals of pure
fresh ingredients. She believed in the restorative properties of the diet.

Sally showed the class videos of folks who'd recovered from terminal diseases from becoming macrobiotic. Depression, mid-life crisis, or whatever it was, would be a snap to fix. Earl would be his old self, joking with the grandchildren as he carved the turkey come Thanksgiving. Though he and Jolly would feast on vegan Tofurky and root vegetables.

Obedient and accustomed to regimen, Earl sat down to plates of millet with red lentils, sautéed tempeh, or cabbage with salted plums. Dessert might be baked apples with miso, tahini raisin sauce. Fortunately, the Rotary met once a week at Augie's Backcheck where hot wings, Swedish meatballs, trays of grilled fish abounded. Dexter would be on Earl like a fly. "Whudya eat tanight, Earl?"

Earl would stare at his old friend, vacant and troubled, "Something…not sure."

Dexter was incensed, "Goddam mackerelodic cookin.'" He turned to Augie, "She's killin' 'im with that stuff."

Augie would get a plate of wings and meatballs *stat*. Both Augie and Dexer held Earl in high esteem. Like almost everyone in town, they had experienced his generosity and kindness. Most folks have a long reach to be selfless and therefore admire people who genuinely are. Earl was that person, but he was not at present himself.

Augie liked to tell the story of how he'd come down from New Brunswick after being cut from the Moncton Wildcats. He was greatly disheartened. Earl was the first one he met, when he stopped in to buy a pair of boots. Augie had taken a job in the mill at Whitehall but wasn't keen on it. Earl suggested that he open a tavern, of which Augie knew nothing except having been thrown out of a few with his teammates. The Wildcats strove to live up to their name. After a year at the mill Augie returned and Earl walked him into Adirondack Trust Company and secured a loan from Gerhardt Sachs with just his word and a handshake.

Augie went through a spate of anxiety, but folks came forward to help, some of them coaxed by Earl. The following spring Augie's Backcheck opened to great success. It was a bastion of mahogany, brass rails, trophy fish and heads, and a large oil painting of a hockey player, in the extravagant Baroque style of Rubens, prominent in the front window. Augie maintained sixteen beer taps, eight Canadian and eight American, one of which was Ballantine to accommodate Dexter's preference. Mounted over the bar was Augie's stick. He could topple the roughest woodsman with a modified slap shot to the groin if necessary, a penalty he rarely invoked. As an unexpected bonus, the teams began stopping in on their way from the RPI field house going both ways, to Montreal and back. It was not just an economic boost but a sense of homecoming to be with the guys again. He was gifted with posters, banners, pucks, a few broken chairs and bottles from the more rowdy teams whose lapses he was disposed to forgive. When he had enough time to think about it, he realized that it'd been Earl who'd handed him his life back with a gold cup.

By mid-September Jolly contacted Sally for a special consult. Earl was withdrawn, strange, his sense of place altered. When they stopped the car he'd stare at the building or street as if he'd never seen it before. He mumbled disparaging phrases under his breath, cursing in French. The cursing upset her more than the French; Earl never cursed. She and Sally sat in bean bags gazing at the monolith of the Empire State Plaza. After consideration, Sally prescribed large doses of buckwheat, quinoa, and Tekka for a grounding influence. Bancha tea would work wonders as well. Jolly felt hopeless. She would have to tie Earl to a chair and force-feed him with a funnel. Her eyes blurring with tears, she stared out at the towering marble-sided structure starting to darken in late afternoon. Some of the floors were lit, others dark, in eerie contrast to the diving sun. "Do you think," Jolly asked, "that Governor Rockefeller would have built all that if he were a macrobiotic man?"

Sally didn't hesitate: "Absolutely not. He would have been into carpentry or stained glass."

In October, a few days before Earl snapped, Gerhardt Sachs took Earl to lunch to convince him to run for mayor. The entire board was behind it; Earl was a shoo-in. Gerhardt noticed that Earl was preoccupied, playing with his fork, occasionally stabbing his dinner roll. Twice he sent back his Coquilles St. Jacques, calling it a "disaster." After, they walked down High Street to Earl's store, which he seemed to have difficulty identifying. He cut away abruptly saying, "And if the peasants revolt, then what?" It wasn't so much what Earl said as his vocal quality that alarmed Gerhardt. Earl's dependable baritone had shot up to a nasal tenor.

Fall in the North Country, whispering Indian corn on the door, brisk nights, luminescent patches of hoarfrost silvering the pastures and fields. Great star nights, heavenly bodies converging to crown the town sky, a reward for adherence to rustic ideals, the John Deere dealership lit up like an airport. Woodsmoke wafting above houses. The nearing smell of winter. A low moon spills its light over tops of bald, hump-backed mountains. The mute, dark, ancient sculpture of the Adirondack Park. For all the dietary therapy and entreaties, there were still emergency conferences with Dr. McKenna, who now theorized that Earl needed a vacation and was too proud to admit it. God knows he'd earned it. Jolly sensed that Earl was about to blow. Her feeling was palpable, the way she knew with perfect accuracy each time, a violent storm was about to rage through.

If Jolly had seen Earl leave the house that night she would have subdued him with a frying pan if necessary. He sallied forth from the garage, having become appreciative of its expansiveness compared to the front door of the house. That, and he'd also become weary of door handles and knobs. The VFW Halloween party would begin at eight PM. Jolly was waiting for the pumpkin pies to finish baking. She'd already packed up the vegan cupcakes decorated with eagles and flags.

Post 818 had been recently renovated with a handicap ramp and a wheel chair lift for some of the Iraqi War veterans. They'd also installed two three-hundred- sixty degree bathrooms and a defibrillator. Some of the vets had served in WW II. There was one distinguished gentleman sitting at the bar, Gitch O'Donovan, a WW I veteran, a highly respected individual. The younger veterans bought him drinks and food and saluted him earnestly. On Veterans Day, he rode high in the firetruck through town, lifting a frail arm in greeting.

Earl plowed wall-eyed over the leaf-strewn lawn. He was greeted with cheers, hoots, and comments from a group of men assembled under a Swedish Elm: a Ghost Buster, a blood-spattered chainsaw maniac, Dracula, Mae West, and a dog of sorts. Mae West called out appreciatively: "Hey Tin Man, give me some oil." The guys laughed uproariously. Earl turned away with a haughty step; his disgust was mitigated because their drunken revelry was quite normal for the provinces—peasants on holiday. The dog, Vinnie Secor, scampered after Earl, snapping at his ankle. Vinnie had smudged his nose and wore a large rumpled suit with a tail sewn on the butt. He'd topped it off with a spiked collar. He further amused his cronies by trotting over to the bushes to raise his leg.

Earl stepped into the room with a flourish, taking in each corner with disdain. Dexter had turned out as a miniature Rip Van Winkle, complete with wooden shoes and buckles, size seven. He hurried over and put a plastic cup of dark beer in Earl's hand. "What'd ya eat tonight, Earl?" Earl's expression changed continually as if it were a kaleidoscope of flesh, distorted with rage, now grinning amorphously, then sharpened into a scowl.

"Thought so," Dexter whistled. "Goddam mackerelodic cookin.'" Earl started for the bar, his movements stiff, robotic, knocking Gus Farcus, who'd come as Charley Tuna, on his tail of sea-green foil. The long rectangular mirror was decorated with jack-o-lanterns and tombstones with orange and black crepe paper twisted around the borders. Earl caught sight of himself and locked in on the image, blinking confusedly. His face was mint-coin silver, including his eyebrows and ears. The paint, called Statue Gloss, he'd bought at Shea's Boutique in the mall, but at present he had no memory of making the purchase. It emphasized the bloodshot wires in his eyes; he had not slept well in many nights.

Gitch nodded to Earl, waiting for the usual handshake and warm greeting, which was not forthcoming tonight. He worked his tongue over his remaining teeth, savoring the blackberry brandy. Gitch didn't wear a costume, just the charcoal gray suit the guys gave him for his birthday, an American Flag on the lapel. He always wore his WW I campaign hat. His voice came out in hoarse tones, "What's yer gedup, Earl?" He continued to stare in the mirror, a sardonic expression, his eyes widening to an inexorable, frightening recognition. "Who ya s'posed ta be?"

"He's Jack Frost," someone called out. "No, he's the FTD flower guy, right Earl?"

"Earl?" Dexter touched his arm gently, then lurched back as Earl spun around, leaving a foamy ribbon of beer on Gitch's jacket. Throwing back his head, Earl drained the cup and hurled it at the mirror. "I am the Future of France," he declared. It got quiet for a moment, a few guys looking down into their cups. Earl repeated powerfully, "I am the Future of France!" His voice was a high tenor now and more strained than before.

"All right, Earl," Gus said.

"Vive la France," called out another.

Amid hoarse laughter and stomping, the light plastic cups ricocheted off the mirror, making a dull popping sound. Someone thrust another cup of beer in Earl's hand. He let it drop, slamming through the crowd to the gaping door, which framed an inflated orange moon rising. Earl strode outside, down the walkway, "Fools."

Dexter dabbed at Gitch with a napkin. "Sumthin's on his mind."

Gitch nodded solemnly, "'Spect there is."

Dexter paused to reflect, taking a sip of beer. Then he called Sheriff Cornell. "Earl's got it in his head he's the Future of France."

"Future of what?" Cornell asked.

"France. France, goddam it. Jus' walked outta here lookin' for a reason why."

"You don't say. Where'd he go?"

"Hopin' he went to Roy Roger's."

"How's that?" the sheriff asked.

"Counter-ak the poison. He's full of that goddam mackerolodic stuff she's been feedin' him."

"Jesus, I thought he'd lost weight." Cornell's tone was serious now. "Tell everyone to stay put. I'll take a ride down there." He hung up and called State Police Barracks L, just outside of town.

News of Earl's situation spread quickly. The rumors had been flying around for months; now they'd gone from yellow to red alert. The newspaper editor, a distrusted newcomer from Westchester, got wind of the story and took to the street to find Earl, formulating a headline for the morning edition: 'French Fried Man Fandangos Village.'

Gerhardt Sachs abruptly left the Planning Board meeting, rushing to Earl's house hoping to spare Jolly an upsetting phone call. The front door was flung open. Jolly had raced out, her dress powdered with clouds of flour and organic vegetable oil, the last few pies left to burn.

For the next hour and a half, Earl Kraft was an apparition. He was spotted, sighted, observed, and talked about as he carved his initials into the diaphanous stone of legend. Only two weeks ago, a trapper claimed he saw Bigfoot on Mount Marcy at Lake Tear of the Clouds. Now Warrensburg had its very own creature.

Earl marched down Broad Street chastising the motorists who swerved to avoid him. "You are very rude," he called out, his voice like that of a chanteuse. One over-confident driver decided to test the maneuverability of his brand new Subaru Turbo. Headlights bearing down on Earl, the car screeched within inches of his leg as Earl swung the scepter, smashing the tail light and denting the trunk. Momentarily elated by his coup, Earl had a sudden impulse for self-preservation and got off the road. He entered a field of dry, frost-covered weeds that snapped like pencils under his silver snowmobile boots, size eleven. His body rigid and stuttering, he stumbled up a ridge to a stand of pines, some burnt and twisted from a lightning storm. The orange moon had faded and now loomed like an immense frozen globe spreading spokes of light through tree limbs. Earl stopped to catch his breath. A barn owl hooted from somewhere; he raised his arm to shoulder level, waving a slow salute over his domain.

Augie got off the phone with Gerhardt and assured his crowd Earl was safe, just taking a little stroll. "You sure o' that?" someone said, staring at the face in the window. Earl stood completely still, looking frozen, his head cocked to one side in an attitude of thoughtful listening. Maybe he received a message from the savage wind that heaved along the street, turning his lips blue. Augie went outside to persuade him to come in for a hot toddy.

"What village is this?" Earl demanded.

Augie studied him for a moment then answered sadly, his throat tightening, "It's your home, Earl."

"Vicecount," Earl snapped, correcting him. "Are you the magistrate?"

"We have Shepherd's Pie, your favorite." Augie caught site of the State Police car prowling toward them, its light probing doorways.

Earl briefly acknowledged the faces pressed against the window and entrance way. "The peasants, are they loyal to the crown?"

"God almighty, Earl, come in and have a cognac. It's freezing out here."

Earl scooped Augie up in a terrific bear hug forcing the air from his lungs. "You will be rewarded." Augie's feet kicked helplessly a foot above the ground. He was about to slam the big man in the kidney when Earl set him down like a paperweight. Augie hitched back, his eyes locked on Earl's euphoric expression. "All is as it should be," Earl said, breaking into a lumbering trot. Troopers Van Doran and Le Boeuf gave chase in official grays, black stripes bending at the knees, the car left running on the street.

"He's not dangerous," Augie yelled after them.

Earl disappeared into an alley that led to the lumberyard, then doglegged to a section of Grace Cemetery, lapping Hilton's garage twice, confusing the troopers by his erratic course; they lost him. He wandered through a neighborhood, leering in windows, scaring the bejesus out of folks who expected little ghosts and goblins at their doors—not whatever Earl was. His throat dry, chest breaking with exertion, he found himself out on Route 9 again. A trucker spotted him limping into the Texaco station and radioed a south bounder on his CB. "It definitely be Halloween. Check out the silver dude with the wand when you pass the Texaco."

The transmission was monitored at the barracks L and Trooper Diaz was directed to proceed with caution to the Texaco. He'd been in the vicinity investigating a complaint that some local boys had dropped a load of cow manure in someone's hot tub. Jolly screeched into the gas station just behind Trooper Diaz, nearly missing the air pump. She'd been out looking for Earl and monitoring the CB. She started after him, but Diaz held her back. "Your husband's upset, Mrs. Kraft. Stay here." She struggled to get away from him as Earl wheeled around the other side of the station. Someone had left their keys in a camouflaged four-wheeler. The tires spit back gravel and leaves as Earl slid on to the highway, roaring toward town. Trooper Diaz sat Jolly in the car saying, "You need to stay with me."

The radio crackled with voices, orders from the barracks, something about use of force and protocol, and reports of a four-wheeler tearing up lawns, frightening children, and driving on the wrong side of the road. Diaz explained that he had the suspect's wife in the car and the language was mitigated. Then came a call about an abandoned camouflaged four-wheeler in the parking lot of Terwilliger's Miniature Golf and Batting Cages. The vehicle had flipped on impact with the chain blocking the entrance way. "Oh my God!" Jolly shouted.

Trooper Diaz made a quick U-turn and radioed, "Just passed it, going in." The dispatcher replied that the team was thirty minutes away. Diaz drove over the chain. The four-wheeler lay on its side, back wheels spinning. Jolly got out and looked under it; Earl was not there. They caught sight of him climbing the chain link fence into the park. Diaz tried to get Jolly back in the car. "He's my husband!" she screamed, breaking for the fence. Diaz ran after her. He located a gate next to where Earl climbed in. There was a sign that read: Closed for the Season. It was an eighteen-hole course with elaborate structures. The theme was iconic landmarks of the world like the Leaning Tower of Pisa, the Great Sphinx, the Berlin Wall, constructed of molded plastic and sheet metal. There was a replica of the Empire State Building with King Kong menacing atop.

Trooper Diaz made Jolly follow behind as they worked through a circuitous path. It took several minutes to locate Earl, who was pacing near a metallic pink replica of the Eiffel Tower about eighteen feet high, a large blue seventeen painted on the side; a pinwheel on top blurred in the wind. "Earl, you had me worried to death." Jolly said as she stepped forward. Diaz blocked her.

Earl made a stiff bow, squinting into the beam of Diaz' flashlight. "Madame?"

"Oh Earl, it's me." Jolly's heart pounded as Diaz took small careful steps toward Earl. He'd unbuttoned his holster. A surge of adrenalin prickled hot through her body. She heard her voice speaking to herself as never before. The tone was calm but resigned, *If he draws his gun I will stop him. I will tell Earl to run. If I can't I will get between them. If it is to end here with us on the ground I will hold Earl. It will end here.*

"Good evening, Mr. Kraft," Diaz said, his official voice demanding attention.

"Bonsoir," Earl replied making another bow, and again to Jolly, "Madame." Consumed with diverse thoughts and important matters, Earl turned away and walked behind the tower.

Diaz barked, "Stay put!" Earl emerged from the side, muttering to himself. Jolly noticed that Diaz had placed his feet wider apart. She'd seen that at the gun club; it steadied the marksman. Her hands tingling, she moved closer to the trooper. He called out to Earl. "You must be cold, Mr. Kraft. It's warm in the car." He trained the flashlight on Earl's scepter. It was made of a cleaning rod with a glass doorknob attached. He knew that Earl sold weapons. There was no reason to doubt that he had a handgun stowed in his skin-tight silver snowmobile suit, or the top of his boot. Scanning Earl with the light, they saw ripped patches of nylon stained with blood. It looked like the outfit took most of the damage. A bruise on Earl's forehead was oozing. The red mixed with the Statue Gloss sliding down his face in knotted lines. If Jolly hadn't known it was Earl it would have been horrifying.

"Why don't you let me drive you home, Mr. Kraft?"

Earl mumbled, "Admirably, triumphantly," repeating it like a mantra. Jolly was almost on top of Diaz. He pushed her back and stood equidistant from the two, both potential adversaries now.

Diaz regretted not waiting for backup before he'd gone in. It was not professional and if this didn't come out right it'd be on him. The face of his four year old daughter flashed in his mind. Desperate, he decided to play a hunch. "Monsieur Kraft," he said. "Monsieur Kraft," his voice bouncing off the various structures creating an echo effect. Earl came to attention. "It is imperative you come with us immediately." Diaz had migrated to the North Country from Boston after the baby was born. His pidgin French with a broad Boston accent with Spanish overtones was as out of place as a skyscraper in Warrensburg.

"But why?" Earl demanded.

Diaz covered his bet, "Monsieur, it is urgent. The magistrate must see you immediately."

Angering, Earl replied, "He knows my mind." He stepped forward. Diaz had a solid grip on his weapon.

"Not well enough," he shouted. "Don't move," he whispered to Jolly. She imagined them, she and Earl, lying dead on the green turf. How could their lives come to this?

"Something has come up?" Earl said.

"It has, Monsieur. He won't see anyone else. You must come."

Earl laughed grotesquely, "Fools. They are fools. And the king?"

"The king is…" Diaz was stumped. What should he say? "The king knows nothing of this."

"Fools, they are fools." Earl pounded the Eiffel Tower with his fist.

"Then you will come along, Monsieur?" His voice shaky, legs trembling. He heard the backup unit pull into the parking lot. In a few moments they would toss a net over him and shoot him with a tranquilizer gun. It would be over.

Earl stood motionless, weighing grave matters, the repercussions, the consequences that might be visited on the nation if he refused to go. He would see that fool of a magistrate and advise him. "Let us go quickly," he snapped, his voice going flat, exhaustion about to fell the tree of his euphoria. He bowed to Jolly and began walking, erect and formal, toward the swirling lights and squelching radios in the parking lot, Trooper Diaz following close behind.

Without fanfare, blaring sirens, or flashing lights, nothing to indicate the presence of a dignitary, Diaz drove Earl to the VA Hospital in Albany. Dr. McKenna was alerted and he made preparations for Earl's arrival. He would be treated with every courtesy and kindness.

The initial dose of Thorazine and a round of shock treatments did more to snap Earl back to his normal personality than did therapy sessions with McKenna, where Earl patiently listened to McKenna's theories about the Collective Unconscious. Earl managed to steer the conversation toward fishing. He and Dexter had planned a spring expedition up to Ogdensburg, which Dr. McKenna was plainly inviting himself to, causing Earl to tread lightly because it would cause Dexter to jump overboard. Dexter liked to say, "If yur fishin', fish. If yur talkin', talk, goddammit. Jus' don't do both." Earl realized how excited he was about the trip, fishing a quiet lake with his old friend. He felt that he was back in the sun.

Thirty-five days later, the day before Earl's discharge, Jolly sat in McKenna's office; she wanted to thank him for restoring Earl's mental health, for giving her back their lives. McKenna was obviously proud of Earl's recovery, but expressed concern about a possible relapse. Jolly said emphatically that there would be no relapse. McKenna went on to spin his ideas about what happened to Earl, events in his adolescence, an unusual relationship with his mother. Though he admitted he didn't know what had actually caused Earl's break. "Did you know about Earl's hen, Marie Antoinette?" he asked.

"Yes," she answered quietly, peaking at the wall clock. She wished now that she had just phoned him.

"It was a dearly loved pet," McKenna gassed on. "Which kept leading me back to the idea of unexpressed grief."

She bit her lip, "That was forty years ago." She stood, offering her hand.

"That long?" he said. She walked briskly down the hall looking forward to the cold air and promise of snow. McKenna called after her, "He's a hell of a guy." I know that, she thought.

She snapped her down vest against a blast of cold air. It was much colder now and the sky which was blue and cloudless on the way down this morning looked like an inverted gray bowl. There was chatter about snow on the country station. Cruising north on I-87, inside the warmth of the Cherokee Chief, she felt her spirit rise. She would bring Earl home tomorrow. A weather alert came over, promising at least six and half inches by morning. That's what all-wheel-drive is for, she said to herself. It was already five o'clock when she reached the Saratoga exit, reminding her of a conflict she wanted to resolve. Sally Kleiner said that if Earl was to be healed, Jolly needed healing as well. She needed to be with other women experiencing support and empowerment, feminine power. She urged Jolly to visit a certain coffee house in Saratoga where there was an ongoing women's group. Sally told her that men were overrated. She had promised Sally she would go and felt a wave of failure as she passed the exit. Just then a Willie Nelson song came on, her favorite singer. Humming along with it she promised herself she would get there.

She would meet the women and hear what they had to say. But that's for another day, she thought, I have things to do.

The sense of failure faded; she felt light-hearted and confident. She thought with certainty, Well, I am a woman. And I will get there. I have some things to say. A few miles outside of Warrensburg the snow began to fall, thick flakes of chenille. Thank you. She had survived this ordeal, regained a foothold in a world she loved. Tomorrow morning she would bring him home; he was himself again. She drove on into the white succulent flakes, the beautiful curtain of snow, her excitement growing. Now she just wanted to be home, to make preparations. Get her Bosch convection oven going. Earl got it for their anniversary. He liked to dip croissants in his coffee. She turned the radio up loud and told Willie Nelson that it was time to throw the comforter over the bed.

I-287 Investigations

I have two heroes and one iconic structure I esteem: Henry Hudson, Washington Irving, and the Tappan Zee Bridge. Henry's portrait hangs on my office wall, a copy from the New York Library Print Collection, and a nickel-plated bust of Irving sits on my desk, a lucky find from the Salvation Army Thrift Store in Peekskill. The bridge is a scant two hundred fifty yards from my unique window.

Like me, Hudson and Irving were private investigators, one of exploration and trade, the other of letters, and the human heart; Irving was the first to write America, to stamp the pioneer culture of this valley from a Dutch prospective. Their work, four hundred years later, creates a deep sense of place for me. I am installed here, a native of Port Chester, settled happily in Elmsford. My office is upon this ridge looking back at this wide expanse here on I-287, aka Westchester's Platinum Mile.

Some people just see a bridge, a convenient link at the widest point of the river, a conduit that connects Rockland and Westchester Counties at the hip. I see a church of commerce, a gateway to endeavors sacred and profane. Commuters, cross country haulers, and criminals of all stripes travel this royal road. It is not just a convenient view from my window, but it is where I witness truth in the form of metal, glass, rubber, and imperfect mortals who pilot the machines. Thankfully, it is also the source of my considerable income.

A handy pair of Nikon 12×32 Marine StabilEyes VR Binoculars with a Photo App, at $1,299.95 confirms this for me every day. The long distance eyes were a gift from a very happy client. I watched his wife giving head to a guy on the middle eastbound lane one Super Bowl Sunday morning. The guy had a real time counting out his change, who wouldn't? You'd have thought he'd have E-ZPass. Fortunately, she sat up for me and sipped her latte after she'd performed the deed. I know because I could read the trademark on her Starbucks cup with my StabilEyes. With a slight adjustment, I scanned her diamond necklace, Janet. Click, click, click. This cheated-on husband who'd hired me, was a top PepsiCo executive who had done the leg work for me. He'd provided all the information: the car model, license plate, approximate time of travel from the other guy's country home in Pawling, so I could ID him on the bridge that morning while sitting leisurely at my desk. I swiveled around to my panoramic window and watched. My client was ecstatic; I saved him his farm in Larchmont, a bone-crushing alimony payment, and a Ferrari 612 Scaglietti, approximately $313,000—she didn't want much. Not that she didn't get plenty anyway—they always do.

My desk chair, I might mention, is an Ergohuman Mesh High Back with a headrest, reduced from $1,210 to $637. I've slept on this baby without a twitch. She rotates like a greased bar stool. It's an absolute necessity for my work, and I've solved more cases from that chair than you can imagine. The idea that private investigators have to nose around dumpsters, alleyways, and morgues is an old one. I have my iPhone, laptop, and the Internet, for Christ's sake, and a cadre of snitches from here to Coney Island eager to please for a dime. I solved one high-profile case—sorry, no names—by Googling (Who killed so-and-so?). It told me. The killer had bragged about it on his blog: Iactuallydidshootthesheriff.com. I checked out a couple of facts, reread the coroner's report and called a certain friend at the 115th Precinct. They nailed the guy an hour later, and a nice check was in the mail.

Location, location, location! Another reason I love my office coordinates is that the folks who need my services can access me easily from either side of the river, and even from Jersey and Connecticut; I'm licensed in all three states. Did I mention that? This is the big one: I can ride my bike to work over the back roads from Elmsford. The suburbs to me are the Promised Land. Riding through the neighborhood, under a canopy of venerable maples and elms, past the old houses and the quirky municipal buildings with their statues and plaques, is rewarding as hell. The convenient shopping plazas, if you know where to look, have some of the best noodle and sushi joints in the county—a filling, delicious Shrimp Thai bowl for $8.95 including tax? Not a problem.

The entire area is percolating with history, my undergraduate major until I discovered the joy of snooping for dollars. Folklore, tales of the bizarre, and ghosts are the sediment of this valley. You can't be successful here without reckoning with certain entities both seen and unseen. When it's slow in the office, you can find me snaked into my chair rereading Washington Irving. His place is just down the road from here on Route 9, Sunnyside. I've biked down there and scoped it out thoroughly. The place practically glows at night. He's the man, the one who breathed life into Rip and Ichabod, and a host of others, and for my money, the Dean of American writers. In my line of work, I've dealt with some headless characters, which of course complicates identification unless you're an expert in toenail DNA.

I usually pull in at 10:15 AM, roll into the lobby and lock her up in the mailroom. I like the sound of my riding shoes as I click over the mock marble floor. I always slide my hand over the brushed aluminum-face directory board for good luck: Frank Sinclair, 287 Investigations, 3rd Floor.

"Mo'nin' Frank. You look like shit." Delbert greets me this way every single day of the calendar year. Delbert and I go back. I'd got him out of a jam once when I worked for an agency in the Bronx—the last one before I'd gone solo. He'd been in the wrong place at the wrong time, which was good enough for the uptown NYPD. Evidence to them was an encumbrance to shed with a stroke of a pen or the swing of the night stick. There was some heavy movement of crack on his block, a real infestation, and some guy wound up in a recycling bin in a way that made him fit perfectly.

Delbert was just walking his dog when the boys descended. They took him in and questioned him for two days. I showed up at the precinct with his alibi, pay stubs, priest, and a Purple Heart from Desert Storm. That did the trick, and cemented our friendship. I'd also helped get him the job in my building on 287 when his dried up at the VA satellite office. But we still maintain an edgy street-love dialogue from the Bronx. "Yo light was on when I lef las night. What the fuck you doin' up there, Frank?"

"I figure it out, Del. That's what I do. Keeps us on payroll. Any hits?"

"There's a lady," he rolled his eyes, "some lady, be back 'bout eleven, she say. Prob'ly went shoppin', not that she need it from the looks a her."

"Pretty?"

"She a big white angel, cake ongoin'."

Cake was a term the guys used at Riker's for a woman with a nice big ass.

I eschewed the elevator and took the stairs two at a time so Del could see me clear the first landing, then one at a time. Finally, I leaned against my door on the third floor and sucked air like a

Hoover. I can bike to Croton Falls and back, but stairs kill me for some reason.

I didn't feel like changing out of my riding gear just yet, so I hopped into my executive's chair, leaned back and fired up the Keurig custom brewer system, $99.99, down from $129.99 at Target. I get most everything from Target. What a business model. Keurig markets 250 choices of coffee, tea, etc., but I'm partial to the Van Houtte French Vanilla. I have a very fine porcelain cup I scored in Chinatown. If you squeezed it too hard, it would break in your hand. It greatly increases my anticipation when I spin around for my first look out of the anti-glare, panoramic window, created for yours truly by the Anderson Window Company. Not their typical product. I had a case that involved one of their senior partners, something to do with two young personal trainers, who happened to be brother and sister, beautiful Colombian kids. Allegedly, there were some unusual exercise routines and positions, recorded on a video-cam in the dude's office at the corporate headquarters. I got enough from him to help the kids bring the rest of the family in to the states. Did I mention, I love "illegal aliens." Their foods and cooking styles provide an endless culinary variety for me and the other hungry gringos in this country. And they're cheerful; they smile about life's hardships. I settled with Anderson for this deluxe window. They even installed it, which was a coup because they had to remove and replace some of the building's façade to fit it in. I call it my window on the world, my crystal ball.

The nights when I sleep in the Ergohuman chair, bathed in moonlight, I probably look like a Pietá floating behind the glass, if anyone bothered to look up here. No self-aggrandizement intended. I'm also convinced that when I'm asleep, and the planets are playing pool, I receive a few side pockets of insight. Many mornings I wake and jot down the fragments I retain from my dreams. They have often led to big breakthroughs in some very difficult cases.

At 10:45 AM traffic is moving freely on both sides of the span. It won't back up again until rush hour starting around four. The river this morning is a fine brown sparkling champagne, living up to its reputation: The Rhine of America. The trees are decked out in their late October best, giant torches of yellow and red running up the hill and along either shore of the river. I sense something and flick on the security camera to pan the lobby. Del is greeting a woman, bowing like a count, and giving her detailed directions to the elevator five feet away. She nods at him, confused and worried, like she's about to take her GRE's. Quickly, I open the bottom drawer and pull out the issue of Vogue. I don't subscribe to the magazine, but it's a holdover from a hair consultant who fled the building with an outstanding utility bill, $2,700. The woman on her way up in the elevator looks a hell of a lot like the model on the cover. Stunning, I think, stunning and trouble. I'd have to play this one real careful.

I stowed the magazine next to the Jack Daniels, Cousin Jack I call him, and took a moment to caress the smooth shape of the bottle. I use Jack like the Native Americans use peyote, "the sacred medicine," drinking small amounts at a time, which opens me up to insights, not necessarily the spiritual kind. Three slow shots of Jack erase the realms between the living and the dead. It's another technique I employ to solve mysteries without dragging my ass all over the metropolitan area. The whiskey allows me to run a couple of programs at a time through my head, increasing my deductive powers.

I spun back around and waited. I never get up to greet or shake hands with a client; I let them sweat a little work first; it puts the onus on them to start talking, which saves time. Rule number one and all rules after that is: everyone's a liar.

Sipping my coffee, I noticed that there was a truck stopped on the westbound lane having inadvertently dumped a load of pumpkins all over the place. I grabbed my StabilEyes and assessed the damage.

There were a couple of two-by-fours on the road that must have dropped off another truck. The guy probably hit them at about fifty-five, bouncing his vehicle around, snapping the hinge that held the gate closed, thereby losing his load. Pumpkins rolled like lopsided basketballs. Cars dodged them or smashed them, slowing everything down as a huge orange stain spread slowly across the lanes. The driver was standing on the side yelling into his cell phone. Had he turned another couple of inches more I could have ID'd the number he'd called. Happy Halloween; it would be in a few days, which usually meant a spike in my business of the more gruesome kind. Who was this phantom clacking her high heels on the flagstone floor behind me?

"Mr. Sinclair?"

"Door's open." The door was open; I'd forgotten to close it.

"Mr. Sinclair, can you help me?" She was panting like a Chihuahua in a motor boat.

"Who's me?" I asked.

"I'm Cynthia Bulwark."

"Call me Frank," I said, hinging back around to get a better look. Her eyes widened as if she'd expected something else; maybe it was my riding gear, which exaggerated the groin area. She was a piece of 'wark' all right. Looked like she'd been put together by a geological event: all curves, valleys, and summits. She had nice shaped kiss-me-quick lips, a pale, flawless complexion that would have winced at a bar of commercial soap. I detected a familiar essence; it was Crabtree & Evelyn Cucumber Cleansing Lotion, an English import. Layered into that fragrance was a perfume I'd never smelled before, one of those potent French concoctions designed to spark the dark side of the male sensibility. One whiff and you'd be licking it off of her ankle.

It sounded like they sent out every emergency vehicle in the county. I spun back around to take a peek. People scurried around, grabbed up pumpkins, and threw them into the back seats of their cars. It looked like a game show. The truck driver chased them around for payment. Finally, a state trooper, R. Siegel, (I love my Sta-bilEyes) locked him up in the cruiser. One guy went down in the mush and slid several feet into the bumper of a mail truck and hit his head, knocked himself out. "Always good to shop early," I said, turning back to Ms. Bulwark.

"Mr. Sinclair, I need your help," she reiterated, and then gave her blouse a tug, smoothing it out over sumptuous terrain. The prospector in me took notice. But I didn't care how good she looked or smelled; I distrusted her. I learned a long time ago to look at a client as a paycheck and nothing more. I happened to glance at my desk calendar of 365 Literary Quotations and said, "I'm sorry, Ms. Bulwark, I smell a rat in Denmark."

"It's your office, Mr. Sinclair. Do you ever have it cleaned?" I made a note to have the office cleaned. Then she asked me if I minded if she smoked. The ashtray contained the remnants of cigar ashes, the byproduct of a very nervous gentleman who'd begged me to relinquish some candid pics of him in a diaper. I did, for a finder's fee. I dumped the ashtray, pulled out a Wet One and wiped it clean, then slid it over to her deliberately as if I were placing a hockey puck into my opponent's corner.

She smoked those extra-long lady's cigarettes with a flower design encircling the filter. She offered me one. I don't smoke, but I nodded, opening the desk drawer. I accepted the cigarette with a pair of chop sticks and set it carefully on my legal pad. I'd have her prints ID'd with a personal history by rush hour. She reached into a dainty purse spattered with pearls and garnets and extracted a box of kitchen matches. It seemed pretty damn strange that a woman dressed in approximately $1,800 worth of designer clothing would use a kitchen match to light her cigarette. I confronted her: "Excuse me, Ms. Bulwark, don't you have a lighter?

"No, Mr. Sinclair, I don't. I do a lot of camping—the matches come in handy." She sucked in the smoke greedily. The liar alarm went off in my head. The only camping this gal did was at the spa. I studied her face, as she gazed absently at me. Maybe she wanted her portrait done. But I ain't that kind of an artist. I had to zero in on her. Who was this stylish, wild-scented woman, and what did she really want from me? You make a lot of enemies in this business, and I'd put some real thugs away for a long time. She might have been sent here to set me up. With her looks she could easily be some thug's squeeze, except for her nose, which I hadn't noticed before. She had a perfect button nose like a Raggedy Ann doll from which she exhaled trails of smoke with demonic authority. At one point she tilted her head back and exhaled across the desk, the corner of her mouth screwed up in a savvy smirk as if she'd done something clever.

It was her eyes that finally clued me in, pale moonstones, glacial beauties of polished control, which bespoke a chilling, sardonic intellect. Something told me that the ice woman had come. Luckily, she had the warmest eyebrows I've ever seen before. But the eyes told the story; sure, they were beautiful; you wanted to believe them, take them home to mom, the body straight to a motel. There was no doubt she was going to play me like a tin drum, and I wasn't up for a beating.

How had I overlooked her tic? Well, I had been studying other things, like the faint, floating outline of her nipples under her sheer blouse, moving in and out of focus with her breath. Every few seconds her tongue darted in and out of her mouth like a kitten lapping milk. Was she doing this on purpose? I sat there watching her tongue dart in and out of her mouth, in and out. Should I offer her a bowl of milk? I decided that it was a nervous tic, exacerbated by my interviewing technique. Either that or she thought her lipstick was pretty damn tasty. The evidence was mounting quickly, coming straight at me: Ms. Cynthia Bulwark, if that even was her real name, and I'd know that by four o'clock, was a pathological liar, a borderline personality, the type that sticks pins in caterpillars while they're laboring to become butterflies.

"I need your help, Mr. Sinclair."

"Call me Frank," I answered. It seemed like we'd been over this already. I decided that she needed a reality check. "You know, we all got to make a living, Ms. Bulwark. I'm not running an orphanage here."

She looked like she didn't understand what I meant. If I was going to sit here and watch her tongue darting in and out of her mouth, she'd have to pay me for it. I decided to give her a few moments to think about that, so I pushed off from the desk and spun around to check on pumpkin boy. They'd cleaned up the mess pretty good; the orange stain was already fading in the gray drizzle.

Traffic was back to normal. Something else caught my eye. Mid-span, I noticed a car stalled or stopped on the extreme eastbound lane. A woman got out and walked over to the railing. "Shit, a flyer," I said.

I grabbed the cell. I know most of the toll-takers, but hoped Rabia was on her shift. She usually worked 6:00 AM to noon. Duh, I swung the StabilEyes over and peered into her booth just as she was lifting her cell. "Rab, we got a flier, eastbound mid-span. And she's in the sweet spot." The woman must have Google Earthed it. She'd parked right at the highest point above the water, 138 feet. She meant business.

"I'm on it. She's on camera—they're coming." Rabia hung up.

I looked back. An SUV and a cab had stopped behind the woman's car. Two men ran toward the woman, a squat Hispanic guy from the cab and an old guy out of the SUV. The woman was on the railing, studying the suicide fencing to see how she could climb around it. She grabbed hold and managed to pull herself up with one arm and lift just above their heads—a real athlete. The men yelled to her and raised their arms up to reach her. She wasn't going to jump into them like a child. The Hispanic guy grabbed hold and climbed on to the wet metal, but slipped off and fell on to his back. He got up and said something to the old guy, who was on his cell, and motioned for him to be quiet. They went back and forth, gesturing and posturing, annoyed with one another. The old guy's face was red. The cab driver took a swing at him. The old guy got him in a head lock and they went back and forth, bouncing off the side of the SUV. The woman climbed up a bit further and must have realized that she wasn't going to get over it before the cops got there. She looked down at the men fighting, her face an image of frustration and disgust. The fighters stumbled between the cars, dangerously close to traffic that continued to press ahead. I noticed that she was dressed for the occasion in workout clothes and Onitsuka Tigers by Asics, $70 on Amazon. She shimmied down, surprisingly fast, agile as a monkey, and slid into her car; then she was off like a bat out of hell. The Good Samaritans didn't notice she was gone and continued beating one another to the best of their abilities.

"Jesus Christ," I mumbled. I looked at my cell; it was Rabia.

"We'll get her on this end, next stop Westchester Psychiatric."

"Rab, you should have seen her climb down. She must be a Zumba teacher."

"Not a dead one."

I listened to the sirens for a few moments, relieved—she was alive; maybe she'd be OK. "Frank...Friday at Malabar, nine."

She signed off before I could say anything. A familiar sweet and sour rush invaded my chest cavity. So, she wanted another go-round.

I thought we were done, and I'd already paid my dues. But why not, she was hotter than chickpea carrot curry. There was a lot to admire and like about her. Rab had given up a lucrative teaching position at Marymount, Professor of Indian Studies, to become a toll collector, consciously deciding to go proletariat. She was tired of the administration, the infighting, the endless restructuring meetings, and spoiled brats from Scarsdale who thought they deserved an A raised up from a gracious D+. She wanted time to write, already working on her second novel. She'd picked my brain a few times to add verisimilitude to her crime scenes. And she was also an intense, erotic lady with specific desires she wanted fulfilled, kind of like Krishna with an ice pick, none of which I found heinous or taxing. In return, I got read racy bedtime stories in Sanskrit.

"How much is your fee, Mr. Sinclair?" It took me a moment to reboot to the situation behind me. The close call on the bridge had drained my crankcase of emotions, and the fantasy of Rab and me back in collaboration filled the rest of the void. I heard her behind me fishing around in her purse, then the unmistakable whoosh of a 14-karat gold Cross pen as the tip is exposed to its purpose. Next, the sound of the pen point skating over the surface of a blank check in a ballet of financial security.

"I don't start the car for less than five thousand," I said, my back still to her.

"What kind of car do you have, Mr. Sinclair?"

I wasn't going to tell her that my car was in the shop getting the radiator replaced, and that I mainly got around on my bike, or public transportation. Now that the financial arrangements were settled, I spun around; it was time to get down to business. In the interim she'd constructed a nice little log cabin with the kitchen matches. She'd even managed to get the roof to peak evenly, reminiscent of Little House on the Prairie. How the hell had she managed to get the matches to stick together? Then I saw the tube of hand cream with the cap off. I thought I'd smelled another aroma drift into the mix. She stared at me looking rather girlish, a sprig of red hair bisecting her cocked eye. She was proud of herself, for Christ's sake. If she was waiting for a compliment she'd have to wait a long time. Arts and crafts are not my thing. Personally, I would have used some of the matches to make a border around the cabin; it looks neater that way.

I scanned the desk for the check but didn't see it. Had she put it inside the log cabin? I peered between the thin slats but there wasn't enough light or space to see inside. Where the hell was the check? I noticed something else; my calendar now displayed Wednesday instead of Tuesday. She'd swiped a page off of my calendar when I wasn't looking—the little thief. This momentarily derailed me, and before I could stop myself, I said, "Everywhere man is in chains."

"Do you mean like snow tires, Frank?"

I was getting pretty sick of her games, and I'd be damned if I'd ask her what happened to the calendar, though I did have a hunch. She was an addicted shopper; it would fit her profile, a woman constantly in need of things. She used the back of the calendar page to write out a shopping list. I wanted her to come clean about it, so I tried some psychology: "Sometimes, Ms. Bulwark, we need things." I assumed she would just show me her shopping list.

"I need your help, Mr. Sinclair," she said, giggling senselessly as she pulled the check out of her purse and slid it across the desk. "Your *reindeer*, Mr. Sinclair."

I was stunned, but kept my cool. I leaned forward and took it. "Call me Frank," I said for the umpteenth time. The woman had a memory like a strainer. And she had referred to my retainer as my "reindeer." Christ, among her other afflictions she suffered from aphasia, and that tic—her tongue was going like a jigsaw now. She was way out there on the spectrum. The check; it was pink and drawn on the Barclay Bank for $5,000. The handwriting was almost indecipherable. I grabbed a magnifying glass; this would be the moment of truth. She'd signed her name, and now I would see it. All would soon be over. It said, in a tight scroll, slightly faded green, and definitely not the black ink that was used to write the rest of the check: Gary Samanski, Esq. *Who the fuck is Gary Samanski?* I wondered. I set it back down and stared at her, waiting for an explanation.

She said, "May I use the restroom, Frank?"

I raised my chin indicating the doorway. I assumed she was headed for the nearest exit, which was fine with me. As she stepped off, there was some tectonic activity in her skirt. The half oval continents of her ass swung from side to side in a slow drop-jaw display of goddess walking. She turned back to me at the door and held her hands up, her index fingers pointing left and right. I raised my chin, tilting it to the left. Her heels scraped the floor, then picked up speed, and became rhythmic, moving faster, until I realized that she was skipping to the bathroom. I thought I might have heard her singing as well. She was skipping and singing down the hall to the bathroom. I changed the setting on the security camera just in time to see her pull the door shut. Maybe she really had to go bad.

I needed time to think, and not just about her "cake ongoing" as Del had so eloquently put it. Though it sure brought out the baker in me; I wouldn't mind frosting those honeys. I swiveled back to the window; the view always helped me focus. Everything seemed status quo for the first time today. I checked my watch; I'd spent an entire unproductive hour with Ms. Bulwark, my "client" who hadn't revealed a single detail about her situation, why she needed the services of a private investigator. What she really needed was a psychiatric evaluation, just like the poor gal on the bridge. She was a certifiable head case, and had thoroughly jerked me around with her deranged antics. I was in possession of a large sum of money, twice what I usually ask for, signed by Gary Samanski, Esq., whoever the hell that was. But still, I felt sorry for her and bad for myself that I wouldn't be able to keep the money.

I grabbed the StabilEyes, thought I'd check out Rab and see if she was reading. She always brought a book or two with her, but rarely had time with the volume of traffic. I'd read somewhere that you should always try to say at least five words to a toll booth attendant because it cut down the suicide rate. But Rab seemed to love the job. I tried to sight the title, so I could check it out in the New York Times for a review. Then I'd bring it up at dinner on Friday, slightly modifying the reviewer's opinion. If it was an older book, or a classic, I'd scan the plot on Spark Notes, which is always helpful. Rab said that my opinions about literature were like Winnie the Pooh when he goes, "think, think, think." She claimed that Washington Irving was a misogynist because of his portrayal of Katrina Van Tassel. That really pissed me off, but I kept my mouth shut or she'd ice me out of her fringe benefits. One thing is for sure, if I wrote curriculum for Westchester County schools every kid would read Washington Irving and reread him in high school.

Something white caught my eye. It was way upriver; I adjusted the range to maximum. It was a vessel with at least four sails, painted in an ornate design, and tilting starboard. Not the typical craft, which are barges, motorboats, and the Day Line that carries tourists up from New York Harbor to see the valley. I sensed something and pivoted around.

Ms. Bulwark was taking an inordinate amount of time in the bathroom. I hit the security camera on seven for my hallway. I could see the bathroom door way down on the end. But there was something on the floor that looked like a blanket, and it was moving. I zoomed in. Slowly and sensuously Ms. Bulwark lifted her torso up with her thin, sturdy arms, followed by her knees until she was on all fours, pushing back on her haunches, then lifting upward. She hung there in a stretch for a few moments. Inch by inch she began to pull herself up into a standing position, and raised her arms over her head. She smiled like a loon. I buzzed Del: "You will be escorting Ms. Bulwark out of the building shortly."

"I thought she be too much for you when I see her."

"Just get up here when I call, OK man?"

"I be there, Frank, always am." I switched back to the hallway. She worked her way along in a formal manner, stopped to greet well wishers in each doorway, except there was no one there. Then she stopped, drew herself up, took several long strides and performed three perfect cartwheels, revealing the tops of her snowy thighs. Everything in my business is about discretion, or this would be going viral on YouTube.

She walked in as she'd left, her flesh responding deliciously to the movement of her skeleton. She snuggled into her chair, took out another lady's cigarette, and studied me with a solicitous expression. Was she worried about me? I was way done worrying about her. She had to borrow a match from the log cabin to light up. "Mr. Sinclair…"

"Ms. Bulwark," I interrupted, "have you ever heard of someone named Gary Samanski, Esquire?"

"No, Mr. Sin…I mean Frank." I knew I was on to something because her tongue was darting in and out like a wood pecker on a tree. I had to close in now or lose the whole game. "He signed your check, Ms. Bulwark."

"May I see it, Frank?" She took it, scanned it briefly, and then held the match up to it. It burned as if it'd been soaked in lighter fluid. She let it drift into the ashtray, crumpled and black. I reached under the drawer and signaled Del. Something occurred to me. "Ms. Bulwark, how did you get here? She strained in her seat and said:

"Gary drove me."

"Gary Samanski, Esquire?" I asked. I didn't wait for an answer but tuned in to the parking lot. The camera displayed the usual vehicles: the accountant, the dentist, the plastic surgeon, the investment guy. There was also an exterminator's van: Hurley's Bug Out, featuring a cockroach lying dead on his back with sunglasses and a tall drink on his side. The caption said "We send them on permanent vacation." The guy was just heading in to the building. He wore a green body suit and carried a tank and had a belt full of cans and industry paraphernalia. He also sported a light-up bug antennae that twitched—nice touch. Way in the back of the lot, as if it didn't want to draw attention, was a long gray limo. An extra-large guy leaned against the door smoking. He was dressed in a black outfit with knee-length black boots, a dress coat with tails, and a top hat. Not quite your typical livery clothes; he reminded me of a ringmaster. I described him to Ms Bulwark and asked her if that might be him. She looked down, pressing her lips tight. I could see she was done talking. But I tried once more: "Ms. Bulwark, do you have any connections to a circus?" There'd been one in a parking lot in Somers last week, but I thought it was gone. She blew a stream of smoke out that must have plumed two feet in front of her. What a pair of nostrils. She could probably blow up a balloon with them. I just stared at her, and finally said, "Smoking isn't good for you, Ms. Bulwark."

"It's your office, Frank. Do you ever have it cleaned?"

"'Scuse me, Ms. Bulwark, I've come to escort you to your car." Delbert gently pressed his hand on her shoulder then stood by waiting, the perfect gentleman/attendant. I remember sitting up with him one night after his dog got run over. He cried like a baby. He's an armadillo on the outside, but his heart's made of pure 100% sweet butter. And I know he'd do anything for me. Ms. Bulwark stood and looked at me with a complete absence of emotion, much less cognition. Del slid his arm through hers and gallantly turned her toward the door where the ringmaster now stood, filling it in like a black monolith. He was as big and square and threatening as she was sculpted and gorgeous, and pathetic.

"Good morning, Mr. Samanski," I said. Del gave me his 'what the fuck' look. He dropped her arm, ready to engage if necessary, and he knew how to. The big guy nodded and sighed as if the door frame was crushing him.

"I apologize if she was any trouble," he said, kind of slumping in the doorway. He had a high, flutey voice for such a hulk of a man. Had this been a cartoon, a goofy bird character would have popped up on the screen and said, "Well, have you ever seen the likes of this?" I was feeling a kaleidoscope of emotions. The first one to surface was sarcasm:

"And who the hell is she, Katrina Van Tassell?"

The big, possibly aggressive guy started to tremble, then dropped his face in his hands and sobbed: "She's my daughter, my daughter."

The poor bastard sobbed like an outboard engine. I could see where she got her pulmonary gift from. Between huge sobs that almost vibrated the floor, he said, "She's Sheila Samanski…my daughter."

She whimpered, and then ran to her father, the ringmaster. He held her protectively in his arms and they both cried for a while. He spoke over her head, which only reached up to his sternum, "We don't want any trouble…I'm a lawyer, I know what difficulties…." He trailed off, then disengaged from her and moved toward us. Del struck an attack pose; I knew he had a seven-inch blade in his jacket and it'd be out in a second. It didn't matter how big the guy was, a blade would slide between his ribs effortlessly. I nodded "no" to him.

"Look, here, this is for your trouble. She didn't mean anything." In his mitt of a hand he held out a pink check; I knew whose signature was on it.

"Is this a typical outing for Sheila?" I asked.

The pain on his face was palpable; it had the force of pushing me back into my chair. He placed his hands on my desk and leaned forward. Del was right behind him, his hand opening the blade. Mr. Samanski whispered in a tortured voice, "I won't let them put her away. I take care of any problems. She's…harmless."

"What's with the circus motif?"

"She likes it. When she was a little girl she went to circus camp to become an acrobat. She likes to pretend." His eyes were pleading with me. "I can give you more." I looked at the check; it was way more and it hurt a little to slide it back across the desk.

"Why don't you take your girl home," I said. What followed seemed like a series of black and white stills, a slide show: the big man backing away from me with tears in his eyes, Del relaxing his shoulders, backing away, the weapon sheathed, the father-daughter retreat from the office into the hall, the whoosh of the elevator. And they were gone.

Del sat down on Ms. Samanski's chair. We looked at each other for a while, then my hand slide into the bottom drawer and took hold of Cousin Jack. I have a set of three Libby 9.5-ounce Double Old Fashioned shot glasses I'd gotten on eBay for just $20.40. Really sweet. I poured out the whiskey and opened my mini-fridge under the desk. I prefer those little one-inch ice cubes to the big ones. Five or six of them mixed with that amber liquid is high on my aesthetics list. Del has complained that the baby ice cubes were unmanly, but he didn't say anything this time.

He led the toast. "This one for Destiny." Destiny was the name of the German Shepherd he'd lost. It seemed as good a toast as any I could think of. "Loved that dog."

"I know, man." I sipped mine; he downed his and got up.

"Gotta git downstair. That asshole exterminator sprayin' everythin' like he's goddam Ole Faithful. He gonna bounce now." Del closed the door very gently, his way of reaffirming our long-term, close friendship.

I pivoted back to the window and took a sip; it warmed my tongue and traveled directly into my sinuses, opening them wide. Suddenly, the smell of the river came to me, the smell I'd loved for so long. I wondered where that boat would be by now and lifted my Sta-bilEyes. It was much closer, being pursued, flanked by a field of whiteheads. It had five full sales aloft now and ripped through the waves. The Dutch flags snapped in the wind; seachests were secured on deck. Above was a network of rigs reaching up to the crow's nest. The distinctive red and white checkered pattern ran around the railings above the great wooden hull. The crew was dressed in period sailors' uniforms.

I called Rab. "You see it? It's the Half Moon."

"Yeah, so what?"

"It's the Half Moon, Henry Hudson, remember?"

She was slightly exasperated. "I've heard of him, Frank. It sails up to Kingston and back every year. It's a museum; they take the kids on it. Frank, you hear me?"

"Yeah, I know, just thought you might like to take a look."

"Are you looking down here? I got a mile of friggin' traffic backed up—Hassidic funeral coming from Spring Valley to the city. She waited for me to say something else, which I didn't. "Friday at Malabar, at nine, right?" She wasn't quite as self assured as the first time she'd issued the invitation. This got my attention. "Remember, your favorite Indian place?"

"Did you say *naan* o'clock, baby? I'll be there."

"Ha ha, Frank. You're buying dinner." She clicked off. I was beginning to feel like myself again, post Cynthia Bulwark/Sheila Samanski. It's like that in my business, a lot of whackos. I had started to consider interviewing clients on Skype, but that wasn't feasible. You need to see the body language up close to know when they're lying, and they're always lying. Triumphantly, the Half Moon passed under the bridge, making its way toward the city. They'd nailed it; the replica was perfect, and it gave me some comfort to know that Henry's ship still explored this great valley.

Going on noon, traffic was sparse again, and flowed evenly on both sides of the span. It began to clear up and the sun allowed for a gold swath of light in the center of the river. It grabbed some of the autumn fire from the trees and lit up the commuter trains on the Tarrytown side. The main span and caissons turned brilliant silver. I panned the binoculars back and forth, from South Nyack to the eastern shore.

Counterpoint was the term that suddenly came to me, a balancing of disparate parts, dependent and independent at the same time. In my business everything is about attention to detail. Without "looking," I see inwardly the entire canvas at once, the roiling river, the luminous bridge, the scrubbed shores lifting up to the river towns of the valley. And the souls, human and other, their motives, aspirations, and dreams I can only intuit. I know it is animated by my perspective, indecipherable, yet palpable. It commands attention. It must be observed with the vigilance of a watcher, an investigator, which is what I am here in this concealed lighthouse on I-287.

Three Baskets

The bone I have to pick with God is the size of a redwood. I despise His intractable righteousness and harsh punishments meted out for the slightest infraction—like the untucked corner of a bed sheet. They say He created man in His own perfect image, which implies that the Creator is deeply flawed, or perhaps just confused. I don't buy the Garden of Eden myth. Eve could have done nothing else but be tempted by that naughty spark in her mind, as God created her to court, spark, and be tempted. Admittedly, man is a grubbing, dishonest creature, capable of modest acts of nobility when prompted by personal gain or if someone is watching closely. It is written that all misfortune is due to man's innate wickedness, factory-installed by guess *Who?* At the very least, there is a case to be made of faulty judgment. But who is to bring that case against Him? So why do we (not me) throw our hands up to the sky and kneel in the sand begging for His forgiveness when we're already guilty as charged!

In 3200 BCE I was a high official in Pharaoh's court, a card-carrying executive Egyptian, in particular the Chief Baker—and I'm not just talking hot cross buns. I was witness to one of greatest civilizations on Earth. I participated in rituals and observed the endless rites and services, and the unseemly parade of the Gods: Horus,

Osiris, Nut, Ogdoad and company, and a host of others, creating, destroying, and sucking the blood and treasure out of the people who worshiped them. I never believed in a single one of them in any of their forms, human or animal. Yes, there were atheists, a.k.a. "realists" five thousand years ago. Historians like to conveniently distill cultures into thin pabulum like: "The Mayans believed in such and such." Maybe some of them did. There have always been miscreants and questioners, e.g. The Age of Enlightenment, followed a few centuries later by NASA and the Church of Scientology, which was not such a great leap forward, though it excelled at its core value, retail.

I didn't believe that my boss, Double Falcon, had a divine birth. Why? I knew his mother, Nub; she was no goddess, rather an insatiable shrew, a colossal nag, and a virtuoso demander, attended by five handmaidens at all times. Falcon would order her locked out of the throne room, otherwise she'd work him over, play him like a sistrum, exact more spoils than the Romans, who eventually ripped the veil off the Nile Valley and annexed us into their corporation, and put us under their brand. They also enlightened us with advanced forms of horrific torture. I was long gone by then and didn't really care.

Due to some unique circumstances I will explain, I have the advantage of a very, very long view; I've witnessed and come to understand that it is the nature of civilizations to devour one another. It's like biology: the amoeba surrounds a tiny particle of food (a country) with its pseudopodia (armies) and engulfs (annexes) it and digests (rapes, pillages) it. The wastes are transported outside the cell (to the dump) through vacuoles. Likewise, the cell can be compared to a bank. Its elastic walls provide structure but allow materials to enter and exit the cell (deposits and withdrawals). Human activity, empires, civilizations are all about appetite, absorption, and banking. In other words, it still is and always will be about the economy. Forget their robes, crowns, horses, legions, and battles; it's the gruel in the pot, the market value of wheat that season, the coin in the box, the unpaid foot soldier in the field, the well-placed bribe, the helpless minorities used for fencing practice, the priest on the alter spinning out the ancient spiel. Their play book is always the same: God, Country, the promise of a magnificent after-life, frequent public executions as circus, the manipulation of cash, goods and services… that's what keeps the millstone turning.

I am a realist and I understood that Double Falcon like the Pharaoh before him was, by the nature of his elevated position, our appointed personal representative of all the Gods. Wazner, before Falcon, was an adept panhandler; he could sell you your own camel seven times in a week. He and Falcon both had a line of a thousand products / Gods, each demanding his/her/its own temple, rites, sacrifices, holidays, and representations in stone. The bottom line was that rule and civil order must be maintained. Divine order, Maat as it was called, would be upheld with homicidal, ironclad certainty. Those who questioned Maat received divine order in the form of one hundred strokes or worse. You'd pay Pharaoh his taxes and speak no word against him or be tied up in a sack and thrown in the river. If your infraction was serious enough you could be devoured alive by crocodiles. God(s') will.

Speaking of mortality, Double Falcon's mother, Nub, met an untimely but appropriate death, finally liberating him. It was her love of gold that did her in. Each time she got his ear and complained, she exacted baskets of gold earrings, bracelets, necklaces, anklets, and chains to wear around her waist. She displayed more gold than a Syosset housewife. One June evening the moon spread a rippling ivory carpet across the Nile for Isis, in her eternal search for Osiris, to walk upon. Nub's maids bathed her in the marble pool. She'd polished off most of a jar of pomegranate yrp with a bit of tree resin with her meal. The maids were unexpectedly drawn to the windows to witness a comet leaping through the sky. Nub dozed off and sank with the weight of the gold adorning her body. She loved her jewelry so much she never took it off.

The servants took her body to be prepared for funeral rites. The maids were partially skinned, placed on spikes, and burned alive. So much for Maat.

Some time after Nub's entombment, accompanied by the requisite sacrifice of her remaining servants to assist her in the afterlife, I began to fall out of favor with the Falcon. I'd prepared a special Konafah for him, not too sweet; I worked some marjoram into the crushed pistachios as counterpoint to the poppy seeds on top and baked it until the sides were convincingly crusted brown. The trick is to dissolve the marjoram in rose water, not too much, and flick a few drops on the pistachios, creating a subtle, thin, delicious glaze. This is exactly how he liked it. It titillated him to taste something, a basic pastry with an unidentifiable ingredient. I knew his tongue as well as his adolescent whims and grandiose visions. My hands, somewhat shaky from the previous night's revelries, spilled a few crumbs of the Konafah on his vestment while placing the delight in his hand. A tiny, petulant twitch in the corner of his mouth, as if a gnat had touched there, announced that I had failed him; he was after all God stuffing pastry into his face. He chewed daintily and allowed a grudging smile to replace the twitch, then nodded imperceptibly that the offering was accepted, and I was dismissed. There was no one at that time, no master of flour, salt, oil, and unique preparation in the entire valley, or Persia, who could place these gifts in his hand. We both knew it, but he was evil. Why? Because he could be evil and get away with it, a delicacy sweeter to him, in the end, than any morsel I could have placed in his mouth.

The situation was tentative; he kept his Falcon eyes on me and I noticed that one of the court guards began to follow me around, apologetically, but typical behavior in regimes that feature absolute power derived from God. The final schism was the Fattah delivery incident. As the holiday ended I began preparing the dish. First of all, if you're not willing to grow your own bush for the mastic, plant your own cardamom, garlic, onions, and assorted herbs, or know a farmer you'd trust with your life, you shouldn't even bother. And you had better be intimately acquainted with every grain of rice you wash through your hands as well, for each has its own vibration and personality. I will give a few hints; yours will never taste the same.

My quarters were located on the lower floor of the palace facing the east, where the full glorious sun, the only one of their gods I admired, lifted my plants, vines, and fruit trees up from the earth like magic. Why? Because I sent my slave to the river bank to carry pots of silt to my garden where the seeds intuitively jumped from my hand into the soil. With a high priest in attendance, the lamb was slaughtered, under my direction, bled, and choice pieces were cut out to boil in the herbs to a stew. My preparation of ghee is too long to detail here, but rest assured, the browned, nutty, roasted flavor was present along with the layering of supporting flavors. The pita was born in Pharaoh's fields. Crucial is the correct assembling of the dressing—the secret taste: ghee, cumin, tomato paste, garlic, salt until the mixture darkens. Then the final table spoon of vinegar. And...wait.

I will admit to more than a journeyman's pride in this particular Fattah, having tasted a teaspoonful before I brought it upstairs to his private rooms. He was seated not upon his throne, but his commode, struggling to relieve himself of some mulish human waste. His expression said it all; he peered through me with his Falcon's eyes as if I were prey. His nostrils expanded taking in the savory aroma suffusing the room—a more agreeable bouquet than his business. I bowed deeply, wished him a good Bairam, set the offering in its deep bowl upon a bench and retreated with the knowledge that I would never serve this Pharaoh again, twice damned for having witnessed his two human failures: born of woman, not divinity, and the need to evacuate his bowels. God does not take a dump.

A note about my slave, Qeb. He was part of a group of captured prisoners from Persia, olive-skinned, blue almond-shaped eyes, alert and careful. He could read, had memorized the poetry of Abu'l Hasan and Sa'di, possessed the heart of a poet, and managed to pick up some of our language as he and the other captives were driven into our land. Double Falcon, while we were still on good terms, gave Qeb to me as he was quick and might learn the craft of a baker. And indeed he produced wondrous dishes of his homeland that he presented to me. I began to train him in basic preparation, maintaining the secrets of spicing and combining to myself, until the time came to teach him. He saved me much valuable time. No slave was ever treated with more equanimity and acceptance than Qeb. In late afternoons, while the bread and sweetmeats would bake, and the delicate perfume of sauces filled my courtyard, we would play Senet. I had begun to acquaint him with some of our finer wines as part of his apprenticeship. I taught him how to produce small batches and ferment them properly from my grape vines, that way exercising more control over my menu. Late one afternoon the sun made gold the garden and trees, and songbirds graced the air. Qeb, as usual, worked his thirty pieces off the board before I'd removed ten. He was quicker, more of a strategist than I, but with a secret shame I'd sensed that he finally revealed to me. He was a homosexual and lived in fear that he would be found out and punished. It was normal in his country for men to take attractive young boys as partners and he was used to it. He was unsure of himself in Egypt and prayed to his Christian God for forgiveness—good luck with that. All he could think about was coupling with men. He assumed that I would use him for that purpose and I laughed, "You are here to learn the secret of what is born of flour and water. If you wish to pray, go to the river and bathe in the black silt." When the Nile flooded in season and left the gift of silt, assuring that wheat and all vegetation would flourish, confirming once again our survival, we called it "The Coming of the Gods."

I handed him some coins and told him of a district in the Coptic area where certain men gathered. His eyes widened. "But do not allow yourself to become a slave—you must practice discretion, the utmost discretion." He was amazed and cast his eyes on the ground. "But I am a slave." I answered what I'd always known and would know centuries hence, even when enslaved and abused myself, "There is only slavery of the mind. Don't allow your mind to become enslaved."

I was arrested the next day returning from Isis' Temple, which I visited regularly in a false display of devotion. I composed many recipes amid the cloud of incense and aroma of apricots and the voices of the women who assumed I'd come to honor the goddess. It was important to keep up appearances. Later on in Hell I witnessed a tormentor shoving a metal shaft into a tangle of shrieking souls with a look of consummate boredom about his green muzzle and sunken eyes. There is something tedious about nonstop evil. The king's guard marched me to the prison hesitantly, with apologies, and locked me in. Some of them praised a soup, a beef and olive dish, or some confection they'd had the chance to taste. None dared say a word against the Pharaoh, but their faces burned with shame.

On the third day of my imprisonment, refusing to cook for the other inmates—what was I to cook with, dust, cups of water, the few sycamore leaves that drifted through the rafters? (though there are applications)—the thick metal door, trimmed with ornately engraved copper, slid wide and who should be thrown in at my feet? Falcon's butler, the Chief Cup Bearer, Nephir, blubbering like an infant, almost incoherent. He was so unnerved he didn't recognize me at first, and ranted about having been dragged before Osiris and his heart weighed against Maat's Feather of Truth. The sins of his heart outweighed the feather and Osiris beat him with his flail—not a typical practice. Then Horus sent him to the devourer where he was tortured horribly, then rendered into nothing. He twisted and wet my garment with his tears until I slapped him and he recognized me. "Mecalef! Mecalef? What are you doing here?"

"You didn't know? I fell out of favor. Double Falcon had me arrested."

At the mention of Falcon, Nephir's eyes filled with terror: "The master of the vineyard—I checked with him...Sekem-Ka...the finest grade, *nfr, nfr, nfr*. I prayed to Hathor before I served him that he would accept the cup and look kindly upon me...and then—"

"And then, you spilled some on him."

He looked at me wildly, "But only a drop, just a drop. It fell upon his hand, on his signet ring, a perfect drop of garnet wine beside the diamond. You know the ring?" I nodded that I did. "He raised his hand up to me and I removed the drop with my lips, then dried his hand and bowed—what else was I to do?"

"Nothing," I whispered, "he's a bastard."

Nephir trembled at my words, "He is God—do not say that." He grasped my sleeve. "He is our master; do not say that."

God again, lending His power to meaningless, heinous acts committed in His name. Word got around quickly that two of the Falcon's chief courtiers were imprisoned, followed by trays of fresh fruit and Shami Bread, and beer, which we shared with the others who bowed before us, as they'd recently dined on crushed scarabs, another transgression against Maat, and their own strained urine. We bided our time, ate and drank, and waited for Falcon's heart to soften, as water softens a stone.

Meanwhile, a caravan, winding like a snake, made its way through a sand storm with more slaves to serve the kingdom, foremost among them proud Joseph, the handsome, multi-talented Jew who interpreted dreams. Joseph the Seer, personally sponsored by the Almighty God, the Hebrew God. Joseph with his Hollywood looks: the square jaw, wide set searing eyes that detected and incinerated iniquity upon contact, his high forehead filled with high-mindedness, his mouth set and determined to tell the truth without delay or concern for the consequences.

Initially, he'd been taken to serve in Potiphar's house. Potiphar was the Captain of the Guard, Falcon's bodyguard; he oversaw the prison and determined our day to day pleasures or miseries. He was slow-witted for a security officer and his main vices were sweets and wine. He had a teardrop-shaped body with a thin head, and was capable of introducing large quantities of thick sauces and breads into his wide mouth. With a handful of wheat, oats, honey, and some baker's tools, I could easily please him, lessening the burden upon us inmates.

Joseph's assignment in Potiphar's house was short lived. Potiphar's wife Rail (I prefer the Arabian name) no longer accepted him in her bed. He functioned poorly or not at all in that capacity and smelled of the dank prison, a stench that contradicted her desire for complete freedom in all aspects of her life—especially the sensual. Rail was a career whore and serviced the courtiers and the palace dogs as well. At times when the men were at prayer or on pilgrimage, she'd hop a stiff mummy during preparation. She had her surgeons embed jewels in the tongues of slave girls to serve her purpose. I'll leave it at that.

When Joseph arrived in her house she determined he would be her lover. The tall, sun-tanned, handsome Jew was to her more exotic and forbidding than any of the slaves she'd commanded to her bed. But Joseph, so bolstered up with righteousness, holiness, dedication to his God, and honor for his present master, Potiphar, wouldn't have any of it. He refused her repeatedly; a new experience for her that conceived a molten rage.

So what did God do? He, after the fact, decided that she'd disappear. He stripped her of her name and didn't allow her even a cursory mention in the Bible. Why? Because she was full of lust, an adulteress, a temptress to His good boy, Joseph. She does get a brief mention later on by Dante; her shade is spotted in the eighth circle of hell. Comforting. God wanted her to be erased from history. If He was so incensed by Rail's promiscuity, her attempts to seduce Joseph, He should have equipped her with a finer character. As I see it, God set her up, then took her down, way down, a repetition of Eve's scenario. And for the record, I was bedding the horny Rail, summoned to her high room a multitude of sultry evenings for diverse and wild lovemaking. Strong Joseph, modest and pure, was to become the second most powerful man in Egypt. He was innocent, but a threat to me, long since silenced.

Potiphar was well aware of Rail's promiscuity and doubted her version of the events. She'd accused Joseph of attempting to rape her, which had to be answered, so he was put in Pharaoh's jail along with us, but instead, Potiphar installed him as overseer because of overt honesty and shockingly advanced management skills. Potiphar looked upon him as a son. The old man gave the Jew the run of the place—an accused rapist, an egotistic Hebrew. Joseph had old Potiphar snowed, or should I say sanded, since we were surrounded by the Red Land. He set him above us as a master, two high-ranking members of Pharaoh's Court: Nephir, the Chief Cup Bearer and myself, Mecalef, the Chief Baker. I, an artisan whose delightful creations are still coveted several millenniums hence. Admittedly, he treated us with deference; he was even kind, but great trouble he foretold for me. This Joseph was an insult not to be borne.

You may have heard about the dream, maybe not. Either way,

never tell your dream to a humorless prophet, ordained by God to serve downers wherever he roams. I dreamed that I carried three baskets upon my head, the top one filled with all kinds of delectable breads for the Pharaoh. The birds ate the bread out of the basket. So, Joseph, being the depressive Jew he was, said, in effect: three baskets equals three days. Falcon will lift off your head, hang you, whatever, in three days' time. And the birds will eat your flesh. Nice scenario. Normally I'm not a believer in such hocus-pocus, but Joseph's reputation as a prophet was impossible to deny, and I couldn't take the chance. I began making other plans immediately.

Double Falcon, even as he intended to terminate me, demanded one last service. Potiphar lied through his missing teeth when he said that Falcon wanted me to prepare his birthday feast, after which I would be restored as his Chief Baker. There was no one else who possessed such advanced skills. He was right about that one. Therefore, I was released and permitted to prepare the feast in my own quarters, where all ingredients and my bowls and utensils were available. The pastries, tarts, meat pies, biscuits, cakes, and other delicacies would appear like manna for his birthday celebration.

Inexplicably, Falcon restored Nephir to his prior state of honor, and he once again put the cup in his hand, though very carefully. A note about Nephir's character: upon his release Joseph asked him to remind Falcon that Joseph still languished in prison. Nephir promptly forgot and Joseph rotted a while longer with no dreams to interpret save his own, until Falcon had his famous dream that was beyond the skill of his advisers. Only then did Nephir mention Joseph and he was brought up like a consultant, told the meaning of the dream with alacrity, and was summarily promoted to number two man, vice king of the valley. He oversaw the grain houses and was given leave to be as righteous as the Burning Bush.

I took pains to ensure that the guests would never taste such refined flavors again. Qeb worked frantically beside me crying into the mixtures and dough as his master was, by necessity, finally leaving him. I tutored him thoroughly that long day and night, shared with him my secrets. Knowing Falcon as I did, I was sure he would appoint Qeb Chief Baker, and he was ready. I explained to him the nature of the Pharaoh, and how he was to conduct himself in his presence and other high officials. I instructed him on how best to protect his secret and remain safe. He wept until I made him stand back from the bowls. At dawn I awakened Qeb and sent him to Potiphar with the message that the feast had been prepared. The glorious flavors would perhaps not be so satisfying to Falcon as, he would learn soon enough, his sentence could not be carried out.

I kept my head, though unknown to the world until now, and landed on my feet, solid in the fertile silt and lithe reeds of the Nile, to commence my personal Exodus through multiple hells, arriving centuries later in the virtual Land of Milk and Honey, and vintage cars, Southern California.

On my way out of town I stopped by Rail's high room for a steamy farewell. Now that Joseph was removed from her sphere of lascivious gravity, she was happy to see me again. I left some choice pastries with one of Potiphar's trusted servants and a note thanking him for "everything." Later on, I did regret this jibe as it was unkind, and I was subjected to additional torments and penalties in the underworld. Why? Because that's how it works. And it gets worse. Soon I'd learn that I was no longer struggling against God but with Fate.

Just before my final departure I was quite fearful. As I said, I stood determined in the silt, the reeds brushing my skin. The sky, an infinite velvet dome, broadcast more stars racing, swirling, and chattering with light than I'd ever seen. I thought I beheld in Mars an eye watching me, which I interpreted to be a good sign. Carefully, I filled my double locket of silver and glass with precious silt, pressed it in firmly, fastened the stopper, and made secure the sturdy gold chain around my neck. I licked the thick, sticky residue from my fingers and swallowed it consciously. Then I took a deep breath and walked into the holy river of death seeking new life. Why? Because I'd had a dream that I could do it this way, a dream so apocryphal and charmed, replete with portent and radiance that it compelled me to follow. Given the alternative Double Falcon had planned for me, there wasn't much choice. I could only hope that the dream was real and not a fool's fancy. And who do you think never heard about my dream?

At some point, I don't know how long, I came into an uncomfortable, hazy consciousness. I realized that nothing would be the same as it had been in life. How could it be? But nothing could have prepared me for it, a vague awakening into a nightmarish existence. My body or whatever my body had been was now shattered into countless pieces. I wasn't aware of having a body, but my cells were suspended in a foul fluid helplessly floating, attempting to gain recognition of each other. I couldn't perceive light or darkness nor could I determine from where perception would come. I was sinking steadily down, my stomach sickened, wherever it was, and an unrelenting harsh force pressed in all around me. I heard or thought I heard these words: Worse than God is Fate. Fate is a Fate worse than God. Fate says it is destined to be this way. So, while you are praying to God, Fate stabs you in the back. Why? Because it's your fate. In common with the myriad of quirky Egyptian Gods, Fate is not required to comment on or reveal its ultimate purpose. As long as you suffer, the wheels are turning in the right direction.

I don't know how long I sank for, but eventually found myself on a cold marble floor with a body that I couldn't see but which felt acute pain. I will call this place the Lobby of the Lepers, a curious locale, lots of marble and glass, waifs in tattered sheets, skin peeled and falling off in pale sheaths. I was forced to eat the lepers' excrement, contract their disease and die a terrible death, only to arise and partake of their diseased feces again for breakfast. There were seasonings and herbs I considered that might have mitigated the stench of these droppings, and I did attempt to search my immediate surroundings to see if anything grew or flourished. There was a continuous rushing sound and battering about my body. I was perhaps at the bottom of the river. I found nothing of sustenance but the victim's stools, poison I was sentenced to eat and die a terrible death from for what might have been days or months. Time was not decipherable, and apparently I was to endure the bane of all star-crossed wanderers, road food. There were moments I would have killed for a Bacon Avocado Burrito from Denny's in El Cajon.

Eventually, the lobby began to recede and fade. This happened throughout my journey. One location would lose color and slowly disappear as another took shape. Frightened that I carried the lepers' disease in my blood, I found myself in a wilderness, a thick forest of towering trees and shrubs, inhabited by flesh-eating beasts. It was clouded, but more light than I'd seen since walking into the river. I began foraging for something to eat as I was starved. Trapping or hunting one of the beasts would be futile as they were huge and ferocious. I searched for something I could pound into a grain and somehow bake. I was pulling up a familiar-looking weed when I spotted a group of Puffball Mushrooms. I examined the inside of one carefully to determine if it was not the Pigskin Poison Puffball or the Destroying Angel. If I could manage to make a small fire I'd have a feast. This possibility flooded my heart with hope and I began to convince myself that I would survive each ordeal in the under- and outer worlds because of my innate skills and knowledge, my ability to create sustenance where there seemed to be none.

I began to gather the Puffballs when a frightening growl and a rushing sound through the bushes caused me to raise my arms in fear. A man, or man-like creature, with matted wild hair, covered in an animal skin, hurled himself at me before I could prepare myself for the next torment. He locked his thick muscular arms around my knees and brought me to the ground, where I lay waiting for his fangs to rip into my flesh. He let out a great cry, "Enkidu! Enkidu! My brother."

I'd heard the name of Enkidu before but could not remember what it could mean. The wild man sobbed, "Enkidu, my brother."

Finally, I said quietly, as not to agitate him further, "My name is Mecalef." He became enraged; lifting me with one blunt hand, he kicked me. "I am Gil. Go, slave!" he commanded. I ran terrified before him, tripping on roots, skinning myself against trees until I was raw, being kicked each time I faltered. Finally, we came to the sea and Utnapishtim, the decrepit ferryman, steadying his boat in the waves. My captor threw me unceremoniously into the vessel where I split my forehead open on the gunwale. Gil shoved us off and jumped in. Sorrowfully, we moved across the sea. Utnapishtim viewed us with pity and said, "There is no permanence." His pronouncement filled me with terror as I suddenly realized what Persian king I was in the service of. I knew of his quest for eternal life. How could I tell him what I knew, that what I seemed to have or thought I had was what he struggled to achieve. I would die again before telling him my secret. The wild man fell on the boatman's feet and kissed them, pleading for the answer. When we reached the shore and Utnapishtim's home, his wife convinced him to tell us about the plant, a plant that grows under water and restores youth to men. My tormentor dragged me to the water's edge where we dove repeatedly, searching for this miracle plant. We surfaced with handfuls of vegetation. He held a stalk of Eelgrass; mine was Aldrovanda, the Waterwheel plant.

He looked upon me, wild and perplexed. "Who are you?"

Again, I answered, "Mecalef."

"What were you in Uruk?"

I thought carefully. "I am a baker, a preparer of food."

"You followed me here?"

"Yes, to serve you." I hesitated. "Now that you have the plant."

He held up the Eelgrass.

"No, it is the Waterwheel," I said.

He drew close and examined the plant in my hand. "Why is it this one?"

I showed him how it resembled a wheel with tentacles reaching out of each of the eight growths that formed the wheel, which turned forward toward age or backward toward youth.

He considered it, clenching his hands as if he prepared to strangle me. "Then you will serve me here. Prepare it for me to eat and regain my youth."

I trembled with the foreknowledge of what was to come. "Master, eat it now and have your wish."

"I will bathe first while you prepare the plant for me."

"Master," I begged. "Eat it now while it glistens alive in my hand. Before the serpent—"

"Prepare it now!" he roared. He then removed the animal skin and bathed himself in the water. Resigned, I set the plant down and took up a rock to crush it with. The water roiled and the serpent's head reared high, hissing and trashing, its red eyes focused to strike. It snatched the plant up, piercing my hands with arrowed scales, and then returned to the depths. I heard him tread through the leaves and branches behind me. "Where is it?" he demanded.

"Gone. The serpent—." How easily he snapped my neck, closing my eyes again into darkness.

My next awakening was facilitated by a sharp kick to the ribs and a curse in some Nordic dialect. I rose quickly from the pile of straw

spattered with dung and ran to kindle a fire. It was dawn and snow
swirled like razors through my ragged tunic. A gang of hairy men
in skins watched and grunted as I prepared the meat—elk, deer, and
beef. The great hall filled quickly with smoke, the mounted horns
and antlers fading in and out of view. I set the loaves near the ashes to
finish baking. At first they scorned the idea of bread, and struck me
with the loaves or threw them into the fire. But once they tasted the
crust and the warm baked buttercream inside, they wanted them for
every meal. What I accomplished with roasts in the servitude of these
violent giants has stayed with me. Turn the trussed joints slowly,
then faster, throwing handfuls of fenugreek, thyme, and mustard, like
magic dust, until they appeared refulgent, dripping rivulets of juice,
hissing music on the hearthstone. Then to the wide boards of the
table where ignorant savages tore them apart with their hands and
devoured everything, sometimes choking on bones, collapsing over
bowls of wine, gasping, then dead and en route to Valhalla without
evoking any concern or farewell from their tribesmen. For me, it was
cook, clean, get whipped, sleep in filth, kicked awake at dawn, start
fire, cook. What remained with me in each wretched form I was fated
to inhabit on my journey was the talent, the knowledge of grains,
oils, herbs, combined expertly, but with strokes of this preparation,
that use of fire, some hitherto unthought-of manipulation or gar-
nish just before serving. The conveyance—stone, wood, steel, porcelain—would produce subtle variations of flavor whether my guests ate
like phantoms, animals, or gentleman.

A woman, Skirlaug, followed me around the encampment and
helped with preparations in the hall. She'd come down from the
mountains where her family had frozen and starved to death. Most of
the men had raped her and her teeth had been knocked out. I made
what accommodation for her that I could, placing her in an empty
stall and giving her scraps from the tables after the men had drained

every bowl of wine. At times, depending on their conquest or thirst, which was always great, I had to run with containers of mead into the hall until dawn, and was beaten if I were too slow. Then I cleaned the tables, collecting the rest of what would barely sustain one person, and shared it with Skirlaug.

Fate determined that I would not have to burn to death this time out; something more grisly was planned. I awakened to see flames everywhere; the entire hall was engulfed like a furnace. One of the drunken men had rolled into the fireplace in his sleep, disturbing pots of sauces I'd prepared for the next day and a huge pot of wax to be used for candles. The wax spread across the stone floor and ignited the benches and tables. I roused Skirlaug hastily as the fire had not yet reached the stable, released what horses and cattle I could, a sizable herd, and we ran toward the main path away from the hall, with flames towering above the trees. I led Skirlaug through heavy woods, along a trail I'd discovered that would lead us out to a rutted road that would take us to the next town and relative safety. There were Christians there, supposedly, but I knew too well how that could turn out. They would mistake us for the heathens we'd just escaped and nail us to wooden posts—Maat Nordic style. We ran for our lives into an open field, iced over and treacherous, directly into a wolf pack, mainly adults four to five feet in height and weighing perhaps seventy-five pounds on average. Then I remembered what would inevitably follow: my fate. They had had a brutal winter with limited hunting success, competing with the men for elk, moose, and deer. The men also made it a sport to hunt the wolves, so we were fair game. They attacked us as a matter of course. I lamented that I'd led Skirlaug into this end and embraced her as we were savagely torn to pieces. Up until that moment I'd thought that only I was meant to suffer, having taken on this journey alone. It intensified my pain and I felt sorrow that I'd taken her with me, not that her prospects were too good in this locale anyway. My last thought was that wolves are not eaten as they are close to the top of the food chain and their bodies filled with vermin from previous kills left to rot. I noted how effective, economical, and quickly they performed their task.

I hoped that my progress through these various fatal regions would be linear, that it would become more civilized as I was dragged forward in time. But it was now time to pay for disdaining Maat, traveling even further back than where I'd come from. I was thrust into Creation itself, gaining consciousness amid a war of gods struggling to maintain Maat against the forces of disorder, at which time the order of the world was being dissolved, setting me adrift in the primordial chaos, where there are few scraps to eat.

My surroundings, if I can call them that—nothing was solid, including me—were a formless void, with continuous explosions all around, and the corpses of gods or ultra-beings hurled about like scraps of paper. It occurred to me that we were waiting for cosmogony to end and the world to begin to exist, which required a demiurge to create order. And there was one on-site but of course it was hungry. My shivering vapor was summoned from a shadow and commanded to produce a hot meal, not sustenance as we know it, but something for the demiurge to "take," perhaps more as an offering, a way to begin its task. This would not be easy; in the realm of Chaos the cupboard is always bare. Additionally, Isfet, the opposite of Maat, was in control of the ball, and we, those of us who were "we" and whatever else was there, were suffering terribly. I can only describe it as the anxiety of not being and perhaps never being allowed to be. Injustice and violence streamed through the chaos at the intensity and speed of *creation* light, surpassing the usual scientific number. Demiurge stood, metaphorically, with arms crossed and foot tapping, staring at me as did all creatures, dead and alive or in transition, and other things without names or with shapes yet to be determined. Many thousands of years later I would enjoy televised cooking shows like Iron Chef or Chopped. I can assure you that those nervous contestants were up against nothing more than making tasty coleslaw compared to the tall order I'd just been given. Each moment became more chaotic and terrifying than the next. The torture Isfet inflicted upon me made it almost impossible to think, so I didn't. I began to turn my conglomeration of parts, gasses, molecules, whatever it was I was, and kept turning faster and faster until I was spinning. In this spinning state I visualized the sauces, meats, vegetables, grains, pastries, procedures, and methods I had employed in the ancient world and in my recent internships. I knew that I could not create a single dish that would satisfy this immense requirement; I could only envision, or call upon the essence of what I was, the Chief Baker. This resulted in a bluish-green roundish oval-shaped item, suspended in what air there was and rotating slowly—a prototype. It was phosphorescent with darkened shapes resembling continents. I was quite nauseous after this spinning and amazed by the results. The chaos quieted for a moment. Demiurge was no longer visible, but suddenly the oval I'd created was gone. I assumed that my offering was accepted. Slowly, a horizon began to take form, with welcomed cumulus clouds, and the monsters of disorder receded. The world would exist again, it seemed. I stood back gazing upon this wonder with a sense of relief and pride that I, my entity, could have created an offering such as to satisfy Demiurge, convincing it to remake the world. I admit to being a bit full of myself at that triumphant moment. And before I could crown myself Chef of the Universe, thinking I had some small claim to that title, Fate roughly took me by the scruff of the neck and threw me into a stark cell, centuries hence, in the Southern United States, on Death Row awaiting execution. I was to experience the great American advance in technology by a civilized culture, which promised equal protection under the law—electrocution.

I'd been fast forwarded so violently that I didn't have time to consider that I was at last in the United States, though it was 1930, and perhaps closer to my final destination, which would end my suffering, I hoped. I oriented to the situation quickly: the Black man I was dying for, a janitor, had been convicted of looking at a white woman. I had no idea what Fate had planned for him, nor did I know that we entities could be switched out for one another depending on the price to be paid, or just simple, meaningless, dumbass whim. In the Deep South at that time the janitor's transgression was tantamount to violating her at a church picnic. This sentence was condoned and considered rational under Alabama law and the DA had assured the jury that it was approved by the reigning Christian God, a.k.a. the gentle, forgiving Christ. It was okay to execute—or if need be, lynch—these folks because they weren't white, just as the Native Americans were red, not white, and the White Europeans had no qualm about penning them up on reservations or massacring them or both. They were red—what the hell. I found this Americanized form of Maat to be sadly ironic. Before my execution early one morning, I was served for my last meal steak, eggs, grits, and four pieces of something they called white bread floating in sop, which the prison chef considered an act of gourmet kindness. I was perplexed and asked, as a last request, if I might see the chef. He squeezed himself into my cell all smiles and full of curiosity. He explained that the bread was Wonder Bread. It was soft-whirled and enriched. And it was sliced—the first sliced bread in the country. I had actually thought to slice bread eight hundred years earlier. He added that Alabama Corrections was proud to serve it to their inmates. I didn't bother pointing out how white the bread was compared to the population of inmates who ate it. He said it came from San Francisco and was perfect for sop. I'd already determined the main ingredients of that misguided sauce, also used to saturate corn bread or slather on to whatever parts of the pig they ate. Then he asked me if I wanted him to pray with me. I watched as the big man hunkered down on his knees in the corner of my cell and prayed to God to "forgive and accept this poor, misguided Negro—for he know not what he do." Evil is so often enacted with the kindest of intentions. But I couldn't get the sop out of my mind—there was something lacking. I reviewed the ingredients as they strapped me into the chair: cider vinegar, water, black pepper, salt, Worcestershire Sauce, paprika, and cayenne. The warden asked me if I had any last words and I said, "maple syrup," as I had just hit upon it. I'd only use, next time out on the cuisine trail, if called upon to replicate Southern cooking, half a teaspoon of Worcestershire enhanced by a full teaspoon of maple syrup, since their diet is all about sugar sweet. The juxtaposition of vinegar and syrup would greatly improve the sauce. And that would make all the difference—zzzzzzzzzzzzzzzz!

I suppose it was fair at some point, to balance the scale, that Joseph should take revenge on me before my netherworld captivity ended. I could not have imagined a stranger sojourn than gunning my way through the east village of lower Manhattan in 1913. The brief incarnation began with Joseph, me, and God, who else, in an overheated apartment in the Upper West Side, the Seventies to be precise. We were embroiled in a couples' therapy session. The psychiatrist was, of course, God, as many patients view someone of this Ph.D. stature. In this case there was simply a pad and a fountain pen on a swivel chair—as usual, God was nowhere to be found. Joseph complained bitterly to the pad that I had cheated him out of his prophecy and made a fool of him. The swivel chair vibrated a bit to show that God had acknowledged his complaint. I attempted to make the point that

God appreciated invention and that I had taken the initiative, that I had been creative and found a way out of my dilemma. I should get some credit for that. The cap popped off the fountain pen and it wrote on the pad, in a surly scrawl, *overruled*. Next, Joseph suggested that the sentence could still be carried out. I should be executed according to God's will. This caused a temporary break in the proceedings. Finally, God wrote: *It's been a while.* Clearly, this irritated Joseph and he began to pout. I pointed out that I'd been maimed and executed multiple times since I escaped Cairo. "You got what you want," I told Joseph. "And You, Sir," I addressed the pad, "where the hell is mercy, Sir?" The chair rolled forward threateningly and I withdrew my comment with sincere apologies to the court. It went back and forth like this, heating up until Joseph and I almost came to blows. We were red face to red face, and Joseph blurted out: "Under different circumstances you could have been my lover." We stared at each other in complete shock. Then he babbled, "I meant brother. You could have been my brother." He ran over to the pad: "I meant brother." Immediately, I seized upon this technicality and moved for God to dismiss the case based on Joseph's Freudian slip. He kept insisting that he meant to say brother, not "lover."

Then the pen wrote in a prickly script, "Order, I will have order." And so it went: Joseph, petulant and surly, hurling one charge after another at me until I did something that concluded the session with fatal consequences for me, per usual. I whispered in his ear: "OK, you have God on your side. You win. But I am more talented than you. You're just an old school grain salesman. Don't ever forget that."

Things got a bit hazy after this and I found myself in an overcrowded apartment in Queens, with six guys, unshaven thugs, cleaning revolvers and machine guns at a kitchen table with a lace tablecloth. I was standing over a huge skillet of blintzes and one of them yelled. "What, it takes a year to fry one of them things? Get it out here!" I scanned the items sizzling in the pan, determined they were golden brown, and quickly threw some cinnamon and sugar over them, guessing at their preferences—my travels having sensitized me to the various taste buds I served. In this case I determined a distinct Eastern European slant, possibly Romania. Fortunately, the sour cream was already on the table—I wouldn't have known as I was still adjusting to the culture and cuisine. One of the guys, a hairy specimen with a cigar clamped into his infant-sized mouth, held up his machine gun, sighted it, and said, "Pow, pow, pow, Mr. Pinchey. Au 'voir, you filthy bastard!" I placed the food on the table, nervously scanning the kitchen to see if there was something else I was expected to do. The men ate like the troglodytes had in the Norse country. Fortunately, there were no bones in the blintzes.

A short, stout man in a pin-striped suit got up from the table and clamped his hat on. "'Sgo," he ordered. Everyone was up, grabbing hats and weaponry. I followed them out as it seemed expected. The short guy stopped me. "Forgettin' somethin'?" I looked around and grabbed the remaining Tommy Gun off the table. I sneaked a look above the mail slot outside—Joseph Rosenzweig, Custom Tailoring—and realized where I was. I'd been inducted into Joseph "Joe the Greaser" Rosenzweig's gang. We were on our way to rub out Philip "Pinchey" Paul, who'd moved into Joe's territory and challenged him. Seated in the sedan was "Dopey" Benny Fein. Used to constantly providing sustenance, I'd wrapped up and brought the remaining blintzes and a side of sour cream. Taking a sniff, I was certain they could benefit from a drop or two of vanilla. Benny stuffed one whole into his pelican-like mouth, and then another.

"D'ere a bit different dan usual," he remarked. I waited nervously, and then he added with a stuffed smile, "but good. I like dem."

We caught up with Pinchey and his gang on Hester St., where he quickly bought it and so did I. They had me positioned on the running board of the car and I couldn't figure out how to slip the safety off to access the trigger. I took a full clip of twenty forty-five caliber bullets and was summarily dumped in the East River after the party. Joe went to Sing Sing. I floated along vagrant currents around the island, eventually winding up in the harbor, where it was determined, by You Know Who, that I'd be ensnared in some netting, then dragged off by the passenger ship "California" via the Panama Canal, on a thirteen-day luxury cruise, and finally released above San Diego like trash to float into shore. Conscious, but basically drowned for two weeks, my lungs full of excrement from the dumping grounds of the great cities we passed, I was glad to finally arrive at what I sensed would be home and freedom.

It had been thousands of years. I'd been dragged around the earth, chained and whipped, forced to endure unimaginable indignities and scenarios that would have reduced a less stable personality to a drooling, babbling, idiot. I was in reach of my destination, bobbing in the surf, feeling the warmth of the sun on the surface when I felt something pulling me back down, a dark and vicious undertow. I was drawn with such force and rapidity that I fell into the void—my default vacation land.

Apparently, there was one more dubious call to make before Fate would release me of my ancient debt. I was to meet and serve someone of commensurate evil and political wrangling and clandestine motives as Double Falcon: Dick Cheney. In this case, I was sentenced to inhabit the body of his cook, a gifted Mexican chef, in the White House staff kitchen. For Cheney's breakfast I prepared oatmeal, dusted with a swirl of nutmeg and clove and the tiniest pinch of dried mustard, so fine a powder it made you sneeze. Plus a touch of Brie with grits (a half drop of sesame oil—believe it?), and Virginia ham, next to which I fashioned a tart plum jam made out of a leftover dessert from which I shaved the mold casing, to enhance the ham and his biscuit. Had I not the expertise to painstakingly remove the mold, it might have been his last biscuit, and history would have been the better for it. After what I've seen, I'm a devoted pacifist; I'd actually die for that belief.

I'd also applied an additional touch, a not-generally-known glaze on the ham, that I struggled briefly to recreate with the limited ingredients available, something from the Old Kingdom called Slave's Blood, thick and delicious—perfect for the occasion. Standing at attention at the sideboard, stiff in my service whites, remembering that I was momentarily a Mexican, though it didn't matter, I watched him lean over in his wheelchair to lick the surface of the ham. He couldn't help himself. Then he spooned the plum preserves into his mouth. He shot me a wry, questioning smirk and a piercing glance, as if to confirm I was the usual Hispanic who prepared his morning meals. It was, I might add, 2009. This was to be his last breakfast in the White House as he and the dim, troublesome puppet he worked for would be heading back to Texas. A fleeting moment of condescension sparked through the synapses in my brain: They're all the same, I thought, just starving, spoiled children, easily, yet suspiciously delighted, forever casting a wary eye upon the cooks and servants who might one day slit their throats. And often that is the case, a conveniently overlooked truth that's played out since the dynasties. Otherwise there'd be no nervous, temporary spates of democracy, which lasts, with any luck, in most incarnations, about as long as unrefrigerated salmon.

Apparently shocked and overcome by the flavor and satisfaction I'd placed before him, he spun around again in his chair and applied close surveillance upon my person. Having attained a modicum of clairvoyance due to my horrendous and varied experiences, I knew he was going to try to hire me out and hustle me back to his Texas kitchen where his gastronomical pleasures would be well served.

Instead, he snagged the house Mexican, who conveniently was looking for a ticket home to Texas to rejoin his wife and kids and their extended family across the border (where they would happily return in a year's time after arriving back in Texas). I could see this as if it was a news video in my head, and I understood that my presence was a favor, a good deed to help out another professional. *Vaya Con Dios, Amigo.* Cheney went back to his plate, leaving it as if it had been power-washed. My work was finished. My purpose remains: illuminate the palate. That is what has preserved and kept me going through the centuries. I was just a guest chef for that morning and off in a tumultuous, thorn-ridden, confusing cloud by lunch time. I regarded the powerful man as I began to fade and go blank, Juan Carlos' consciousness overtaking mine. "Whoever I am," glancing at him for the last time, "even trapped in limbo, I break no law; I harm no man, woman, or animal."

That tumultuous, thorn-ridden cloud I mentioned stormed west, producing much vomiting and dizziness. The entertainment was a looped, edited version of my misadventures projected with deafening volume. I watched myself being killed over and over again, struggling with circumstances insurmountable and foreign to me. At the designated coordinates I was dumped back into the ocean in a painful belly flop. My arrival was less than auspicious. Fate had ultimately determined that I should be deposited like flotsam beneath the Oceanside Pier at the foot of that trendy beach town. I spent a good hour exhausting myself dodging pilings and mad surfers if I strayed out from the pier too far.

Finally, I was disgorged from the tepid saltwater upon the shore at high noon and was ridiculed by a group of diligent camp counselors, all tanned and blond, as I frightened children in a play-park making my way up to the pier's entrance. I waved lamely and tried to smile to show the children there was nothing to fear, but some of them burst into tears. A counselor approached me shaking a piece of drift wood. I cowered and moved as fast as I could.

Once at the pier's entrance, exhausted, gulping mouthfuls of air, I realized that I was only wearing a thin cloth wrap about my private parts, as if I'd escaped from a medieval painting of the Crucifixion. That did not discourage an avid salesperson who approached me and insisted that I tour a luxury condo just across the way, conveniently located near a *spectacular* eatery known as 333 Pacific. I scanned the upscale facade, cleverly named for the address, from which wafted the bouquet of noon-hour mussels steamed with, I thought, too generous an application of garlic, though served with a fine chardonnay; I did not have a problem with the parsley—I never do—which mixed well with the salt air and streams of fresh weed-smoke produced by skate-boarders. I was somewhat confused from my half-drowning ordeal, as the woman produced a coupon for a vodka cocktail at the afore-mentioned restaurant if I took the condo tour. I explained that I was new in town, having just arrived in the community, and would pre-fer to shop for clothing first before securing housing. She pressed the importance of the location of the condo, adjacent to the waterfront and pier activity, not to mention the Thursday night street fair that took place just above the railroad tracks. Her insistence taught me that folks in California are too smart to dismiss an unshaven vagrant in a diaper, because anyone could have money—think about Howard Hughes or Jim Morrison.

Two uniformed officers appeared on either side of me with a Ger-man Shepherd exposing its well-kept fangs ten inches from the vicin-ity of my groin, causing me to freeze in place. I did not wish to suffer Osiris' fate—his phallus eaten by a catfish, though later restored by Isis, and I suspected this could be more grisly and with a less success-ful outcome. It had been predetermined by Fate, I learned quickly, that I'd be introduced to, or rather thrust upon, an American culture in the throes of paranoia due to the 9/11 attack a decade earlier. I learned later that there were other homeless people in town who groaned, grunted, farted, and squeaked their shopping cart wheels through the neighborhoods and waterfront area, but they knew the local scene of well-kept yards and spiffy beach houses, and only came out at night. As I appeared decidedly Middle Eastern, my complexion and body darkened and scarred from torment and endless forced travel, the recipient of evil, planned and random, bearded, clothed in a swami diaper, I was the perfect candidate for enrollment in the Homeland Security lock-up program. This was confirmed when the officer asked me to produce a picture ID. I glanced down at my body instructively so he'd notice I hadn't any pockets, and said, with the thinnest of accents I could muster, "I'm so sorry, officer, I seem to have forgotten my wallet." They took me away with the saleswoman still waving the coupon. I could tour the condo after I'd posted bail, she assured me.

There was no bail for three weeks while I fattened up in the Oceanside Jail on refried beans, chicken fajitas, red rice, fresh avocado—much appreciated—and bottled water. It gave me time to review my journey and plan my next career move, which no doubt would be in the food industry. At least I was on the gold coast. The psychological profile administered by the county mental health department determined that I was a harmless, homeless, drug-compromised hippie who'd lost his way back to his group home. Why was I in the water? The psychologist hypothesized that I imagined I could swim to London to relive the budding roots of the British Invasion.

As my profile matched many others who wandered around the affluent beach town, I was released to a helpful ashram, which took in vagrants, further down the coast. I was subjected to meditation, gluten-free cookies, and preaching on the liberation gained from menial labor, i.e. house cleaning for our beloved guru. Accustomed to being a captive, it took me a while to realize I wasn't being held against my will. I strolled out one moonless night while the devotees argued peevishly over the ashram's distribution of chores and policies, and who was most devoted to the non-bathing guru, who stored their wallets and jewelry in his private safe. I wandered through the streets and answered the first sign I saw in a shop's window: Baker Wanted, Some Experience Required. I entered the shop happily, the bell tinkling behind me like the sound of Paradise. In short order I was promoted to Head Baker, requesting that I preferred to be addressed as Chief Baker, in charge off all three of their outlets, which increased profits at a surprising rate, according to the owner.

After my self-emancipation, having once again created means, which I have done repeatedly with the scantest of resources, I returned one evening out of nostalgia to the Oceanside Pier and snagged a coupon from the same condo saleswoman, who didn't recognize me cleaned up and looking prosperous. I promised to take the tour after I'd had a drink to calm my vertigo. I then paid a professional visit to 333 Pacific, not to conduct a formal review, just a courtesy call. I cannot resist an opinion. Corporate restaurants, which I will never work for, those specializing in steaks and seafood, hyper-creative appetizers, assorted, outrageous "bites" (I hate it when they call them bites) and artisan crafted cocktails swirling with fresh fruits and dashes of flavorings and invented concoctions *du jour*, (which might include some of the seasoning combinations I've created), as posted on Webtender.com, are to the consumer what Pleasure Island turned out to be for the little wooden puppet, Pinocchio. After you've dropped two-fifty or three hundred dollars and filled yourself with grass-fed beef or Oxford-graduated lobster with shaved chestnuts, you feel like an ass. Why? Because you're unfulfilled. You're not just eating the food, you're attempting to eat the ambience. You're incorporating the trappings of the room, its elegance, it's overt wealth, into yourself, somehow increasing your value. In essence, you're making a statement that: "I can afford this luxury while others cannot; therefore I am... I am what? I am out of three hundred dollars." The issue, once again, being one of place and self-worth, which, as I've stated, contributes to the world of mischief. I can make you a bowl of fresh lemon lentil soup with a poppy-seed roll with sweet butter, and a glass of very decent claret for $2.95 to $3.75, and you wouldn't feel like an ass afterward.

But enough cuisine-speak. Enough of my tribulations. And enough of God snoring in His heavenly cave, and Joseph a pile of dust beside Him. I've been the guest in His house of horrors and managed to avoid His final mercy and judgment for almost five thousand years, and I have done pretty well for myself. My card, if I may: Mecalef Imhotep Weingruber. I took my wife's maiden name as an added layer of protection, the elegant Sheila Rae Weingruber. Why Sheila? Because she is the embodiment, the Holy Grail, the repository of gourmet, exotic, skillet, culinary, and sensual arts. She is the missing piece of my soul if I have one. She understands food and life and the living of it more than anyone I've met in the many worlds I've traveled. Yes, my card: *Three Baskets Bakery, Encinitas, CA – Baked goods and sweet meats to satisfy the Pharaoh in you.* And why wouldn't they? They're my original recipes, I who was once honored to place them in the Pharaoh's hand until I fell out of favor. We are consistently voted the best bakery in San Diego County, eighteen years running. They come to pay homage: stars, presidents, the art crowd from Laguna Beach in their white raiment and sea-green debit cards, shopkeepers, dock workers. Even illegal aliens, my favorite kind of people and employees. I cannot make enough Eesh baladi (local bread) to satisfy them all. They eat of my cakes, tarts, meat pies, and biscuits, of the life-giving rock flour, the bounty of the

Nile, actually. A note about my meat pies: folks in my neighborhood, which is affluent, have a low regard for visible animal husbandry, though they would donate their kidneys for their pets. Speaking of which, I make dog- and cat-shaped breads—following the ancient tradition—that fly off the shelves. I am not opposed to the slaughter of animals, if done according to Halal practice. I have, by necessity, for a catering job, dispatched a chicken or two in the tool shed, quickly and humanely.

And how does all this happen, you wonder. Sealed in the glass and silver double locket, hung from my neck, resting upon my breastbone, is the secret of my longevity and continued success: dried silt, turned granular, the size of a grain of sand or clay, composed of quartz and feldspar, gathered in haste that December dawn I escaped the Black Land. A century's worth of grains, and just a particle of one is good for fifty years. One speck placed in the Encinitas soil, suffused in the marine layer, results in the fertile ground that blessed the lowlands—the Coming of the Gods. My domain extends to the coveted white sands next to the Self Realization Meditation Gardens. The red barley, wheat, beans, chick peas, flax, and fruit grow joyously, rocked by the vibration of the percussive waves and Ra's golden eye. The Killdeer, Rock Dove, Merlin, and Common Raven that snatch the fruit and seeds from my bounty grow in size and beauty, and their song renders pale the Sirens' garish tune. I emphasize that they feast upon the bounty of my garden, not my flesh as Double Falcon intended.

I look to the future because I can. I have just signed a contract with ETV (Extra Terrestrial Ventures) for five thousand square feet in the Mega Mall on Mars—*Coming Sooner Than You Think*. It'll combine a bakery, authentic Ancient Egyptian cooking, dancing, and culture classes, and an Atlantis Theme Park. The only mention of the gods will be reserved for copyrighted theme drinks: Iced Isis Rum Balls in US of A Coke, Taweret Tower of Power Swirled Gin with Local Spaceberry (I will grow them), Maahes Mojito with Freshly Orbited Mint and Crystal Stick, suffused in brine,etc.

The Atlantis Theme Park was an afterthought, a gift that dropped into my lap. Among the benefits of So Cal, besides the cotton-wear weather and fresh fruits and vegetables year round, are the folk-lorists, magicians, soothsayers, and freaks. One made his appearance in the shop looking for work one day. He'd been a soup maker, latte steamer guy at Naked Café in Solana Beach. Belt-length grayish-blond ponytail. He'd been fired for "thinking too much," or so he said. He gave me that vacant, all-knowing reefer stare and asked, "Are you like really Egyptian, man? I mean like Egyptian?" I assured him that I was actually Egyptian; then he wanted to see my palm, which I refused. "Then you know. Man, you know." I knew that I wasn't going to hire him, but nodded affably, wishing to harm no one. "Do you like read *The World's Only Reliable News?*" I told him I didn't. "Come on, man, you know."

"Know what?"

"Atlantis, Atlantis on Mars. They traded with Ancient Egypt, man. It's a fact."

I happened to know that it was patently false, never having encountered a Martian near the palace, but I didn't have an extended period of time to explain. There was bread rising in the sun room and pots of sauces, meats, and fruit crying out for their ultimate destiny. He buzzed on about an Egyptologist, Mr. Conrad Vetsch, who'd recently discovered a scroll proving that Atlantis was located on Mars. "Do you know how Tut actually bought it, man?" Actually, I did, but said I didn't. I'd heard fairly reliable rumors from a relative of his manicurist. His eyes widened at my ignorance and he spit out the answer belligerently, "In a space shuttle crash with an alien crew, man. That's how they offed the dude!" I directed him to the

San Diego Astronomy Association where he might find other like-minded folks who think too much. If that was closed, he could try the zoo because of the interesting landscape and stone formations designed to convince the inhabitants they were still in their home towns. I gave him a date-nut roll and a coffee for his pilgrimage, in which he dumped five packs of Sugar in the Raw, as expected. Before he set off he asked for money so he could take the Coaster downstate. I obliged.

After his departure I did a bit of fringe research, the Internet being perhaps the greatest modern improvement for keeping an eye on all the mischief in the world—other than the garlic press and the convection oven—and read about the top secret Martian probes the government was hiding, identifying remains of temples on the surface of Mars. Additional "evidence" pointed to the elaborate model of a glider found in King Tut's tomb, all of which I knew to be nonsense. Tut wasn't known to be a deep thinker. He was a morsel in the snapping jaws of time, gone by eighteen. But my sojourn through heaven and hell, having at times played the entertainer, though most often, with deadly results, having been the entertainment, has taught me one thing: people like an attraction. I determined that my King Tut Death Shuttle Ride would give folks a thrill without being terminal. They'd zoom through a laser-spiked pyramid with horrific mummies grabbing children's legs, dodge giant belching asteroids, zip through a cave of flesh-eating monsters eating each other's flesh, avoid jagged Martian cliffs, and land safely at the Double Falcon Souvenir Shack and Snack Bar, *where the buns are as good or better than the hotdogs.* The vast majority of humankind is looking for something to do, hence the gods, the laws, the dishonorable wars, the horrid punishments and executions. My only remaining fear, repeated deaths having inured me to the scary mask of mortality, is a man with nothing to do, who has advanced organizational skills, and who knows how to "make friends and influence people," to quote an American entrepreneur.

Sheila and I are treated royally as we enter the Sunnydale Egyptian American Society headquarters. They are hosting a celebration dinner honoring a longstanding Egyptian business that has been a supporter of arts and culture in the community. In this case it's Three Baskets Bakery in Encinitas. Sheila is resplendent in her jeweled nemes, from which her raven black hair spills sensuously, and a simple but elegantly designed kalasiris, supported by one strap to showcase her tanned shoulders. The intricate beading on her dress shimmers in the candlelight. I have pulled out all the stops in my leopard-skin cape. Traditionally, that would cover the Pharaoh's torso, but I've donned a gold silk t-shirt out of modesty, though I will mention that my chest and thigh musculature is pronounced despite the wear and tear it's seen. The lion's tail hanging from my belt is realistic looking, but synthetic. My shendyt features detailed pleating. The khol applied around my eyes helps create an authentic look, though there is no desert glare in Sunnydale. Completing my ensemble are decorative sandals, not the cheap papyrus ones I shuffled around in in Potiphar's jail. We are led to the head table, which is set upon a platform surrounded by Meadowfoam and Blazing Star in blue porcelain vases, plus firm bright pillows. The hostess bows to me and calls me the Pharaoh. Sometimes irony is sweeter than honey. We settle in before trays of olives, well-intentioned bread, figs, dates, grapes, sliced coconut, fish, and sparkling wine, which the young servers pour with joy and dignity. I am gratified and marvel how they admire my Egyptian queen, looking so much the goddess tonight: Sheila Rae Weingruber. Their questions are kept general and polite: When did I arrive in Encinitas? Was I actually born in the mother country? Are my parents still there? Where on earth did I attain my bread- and pastry-making skills? (That's a good one.) What are our plans for the future? (I think I've covered that.)

The feast, everything, was delicious. I was able to censor any critical opinions about preparation or consistency. It was a night to celebrate. I couldn't wait to get Sheila home to our great bed beneath the open skylight overlooking the moon-drenched sea. In the morning, I will drop the smallest bit of a shaved grain of dried silt into her Licorice Root Tea—she's a keeper.

It is just after four AM; a welcome fog covers the street, business parks, and shopping strips. I slip onto the property of Old Mission San Luis Rey de Francia, King of the Missions. I've parked a few blocks away to avoid detection. A side door has been left conveniently unlocked, and I make my way inside through the courtyard, past the gift shop, to the viewing area, which overlooks the private Retreat Gardens, the home of the great Pepper Tree (Schinus molle) also known as false pepper, but not to me, planted in 1830 by Friar Peyri. Like me, the molle del Peru is a long-lived tree, an evergreen that produces fruit year round, and is drought-tolerant.

The kindly Friar A. greets me in silence, a tall, bearded, stooped, worn-looking man of many skills and serious scholarship. Among other subjects he'd pursued at seminary was Egyptology. We have formed a productive relationship. In exchange for the pink-red berries, called pink peppercorns, the ones that fall from the tree and are gathered without the slightest harm to this living monument, I provide the Friar, in turn, with every bit of my memory, story, description, and nuance, about the ancient kingdom and my "travels" that brought me to this auspicious destination. I don't know if he accepts my story as truth, but he shows great interest and patience in hearing it, as well as having sworn eternal secrecy. Who'd believe it anyway?

I hand my friend a gift certificate to the bakery and we clamp hands tight in friendship. I carry the precious fruit and berries, supposedly poison, in a plastic bag and walk slowly to the car. Poison is a result of ignorance. I know how to prepare these gifts. A faint pink light spreads across the ocean, which I can smell if I stand still and close my eyes. The sea, of course is life. If you wish to worship, worship the sea. The fog has lifted, but further out, moving toward the shore, is the flat, gray plate of the marine layer, which signifies a good day of growing, and will by noon give way to brilliant sun, encouraging the diverse activities and endeavors along this coast—the land of the Paiute.

My friendship with Friar A. has allowed me to experiment with my menu. Three Baskets is perhaps the only bakery/café in the world that has successfully fused traditional Egyptian foods with Peruvian, Incan, and Mexican flavors, resulting in lines of hungry followers, and stunning reviews. They run out of superlatives trying to describe what blend of remarkable spices contribute to the overall flavor of each dish. I love watching them work their mouths, lick their lips, and wrack their brains attempting to isolate the ingredients, though it's truly about the whole, not the parts.

What is just as gratifying is my alliance with Sister Garcia Loma Dorantes. She maintains a small storefront infirmary/luncheonette in the Barrio, and is considered a local saint and a healer. In the 1970s, she was one of the organizers who courageously demonstrated and took over the area that was to become Chicano Park. I met her some years after I'd arrived and was giving away my baked goods for free on the street in the neighborhood. I was so happy just to be there and I gained clientele quickly. She appeared before me on the sidewalk in her trademark orange skirt and white gypsy blouse and gazed at me in perfect peace. I spread some of my Heka Foie Gras on a cracker and offered it to her. We Egyptians had a God for everything, including Gengen-Wer who looked after geese, hence my Heka Foie Gras. She removed her turquoise stone cross and swung it above my cart in a blessing. I instinctively kissed her hand and our friendship was sealed.

Once a week, Sheila and I drive down to San Diego, a true Mecca of coastal beauty, to Sister Garcia's storefront with the fruit and berries I have distilled and prepared carefully from the remaining molle into a medicine that is useful in treating wounds and infections due to its antibacterial properties. It can also be used as an antidepressant and relieves rheumatism and menstrual disorders. It even controls pests, which are everywhere in these warm climates. I am particularly proud of this accomplishment as it relieves some of the suffering your U.S. government inflicts on the good souls who risk their lives to come here to clean garbage cans for gringos and prune their trees—American Maat. In spirit, I feel more Mexican than Egyptian. Why? They're more fun, and they embrace life.

At some point we always wind up in the little kitchen, tasting from each pot. Sister G.L. Dorantes, as some call her, Sheila and I, and sometimes a family of four or five adults and children, are squeezed in there shoulder to shoulder breathing in the invigorating steaming essences. I have a "doctor's bag" of seasonings and spices and surprises I always bring along, some of this and that, including new combinations of seasonings to try out. I taste each item, then confer with the chefs. I might offer a pinch of something from my bag. At first they are nervous and uncertain of these strangers in their safe house. But that melts away with subsequent tastes and lively bilingual discussion.

The children set the table on the side porch and roll the shades down against the brilliant western sky. There is Tequila Lime Chicken, Queso Flamado, tamales, refried beans, stuffed peppers, skillet casserole, the all-important rice masterfully prepared—nothing but rice and water—and a heroic soup of black-eyed peas and chorizo. There are about fifteen of us now around the table and the mood is decidedly hopeful, no one is observing us or asking to see our papers or taking our fingerprints. I have the distinction of being the most undocumented alien at the table, practically from outer space, or will be when the Mega Mall on Mars opens. Sister takes Sheila's hand and we all join hands. She says, "There is much to be thankful for." She smiles tenderly at the children. She waits: "There will be opportunity for you and your families," she tells them. "Your lives will be blessed. I have seen the work that good people do." She looks at Sheila and then me, a look I almost cannot describe, but could only call mercy. "We all come from far away," she says quietly. "Some of us from very far away." We nod to each other, acknowledging the mercy and truth of fellow travelers. She prays in Spanish; heads are bowed. "Buen apetito!" With moist eyes, sturdy hearts, craving stomachs, and joy that exceeds the power of the peso, the euro, grain, silver, and the almighty dollar, we eat ravenously and in community. I lean over and kiss Sheila's soft, ageless cheek. Her gold hoop catches a glint of Ra as he sneaks through the striped shade and sits upon the reclining ocean. "You look younger every day," I whisper.

About the Author

Mark Morganstern is a native of Schenectady, New York. He studied at the Manhattan School of Music, played bass fiddle, and toured with jazz and classical ensembles before deciding that music was not his best choice of profession. An avid reader and writer, he switched majors, studied with Edna O'Brien, Maureen Howard, and Jonathan Wordsworth, and graduated from the City University of New York with an MA in English/Creative Writing. His fiction has appeared in *Prima Materia*, *The Crescent City Review*, *Piedmont Literary Review*, *New Southern Literary Messenger*, *Hunger Magazine*, *Expresso Tilt*, *Mothering Magazine*, and other journals, and was anthologized in *Tribute to Orpheus II*. He received an honorable mention for his story, "Tomorrow's Special," published in the *Chronogram* 11/06 Fiction Contest issue, selected by guest judge, Valerie Martin.

Mark subs at the local high school (everything from physics to gym, occasionally even English) and books concerts for The Rosendale Cafe, a vegetarian eatery he owns with his wife Susan and their children. He hopes to retain that position despite his kids' threats to fire him for writing fiction on the job.

Contact Mark at *markmorganstern@gmail.com.*

Made in the USA
Middletown, DE
03 January 2016